Red Chaser

A noir thriller of the 1950s, the Cold War
and the Brooklyn Dodgers

By
Jon Spoelstra
findjon@msn.com

Red Chaser

The novel **Red Chaser** tosses you right into the 1950s. You'll meet the kinkiest and most beautiful spy this side of the Iron Curtain. You'll meet Joe McCarthy. Best of all, you'll live the life of Jake McHenry.

Jake seems to have a near-perfect life. After all, he spent five years in Germany after World War II and came back laden with ill-gotten Nazi riches. Being young and rich ain't bad.

Back home in Brooklyn, Jake became a private detective for the simple reason that he needed a pretend job to hide the source of his riches. Mostly, however, he went to Brooklyn Dodgers games at Ebbets Field and drank beer.

Then Joe McCarthy entered the picture. A childhood buddy introduced Jake to Tailgunner Joe. They wanted Jake to steal a secret list of celebrity communists from the Ice Queen, a rich high-society leftist named Arabella Van Dyck. The Ice Queen also happened to be the most beautiful--and most depraved--woman that Jake had ever seen.

The break-in of the Ice Queen's brownstone in Manhattan was easy, but it unleashed a flurry of Russians, North Koreans, J. Edgar Hoover and mobsters in a wild chase for the list.

The backdrop to all this is the greatest pennant race in the history of Major League Baseball. The New York Giants chased the Brooklyn Dodgers all summer long for the National League pennant. That's the year that Bobby Thomson hit the "shot heard 'round the world." The pennant--and Jake's life--comes down to the last inning and the last pitch at the Polo Grounds in New York City on Wednesday, October 3, 1951.

Red Chaser

It's sometimes difficult to portray accurately historical incidents in a novel. Some facts—like the Giants winning the pennant in 1951—are absolute. Other facts, because of sometimes conflicting and contradictory source material, are not so rock solid. So, in this novel, fact, theory, conjecture and fiction are blended at the author's whim. Additionally, the historical characters and wholly fictional ones act and speak as the author dictates.

***

1.
Friday, September 14, 1951

I went to war poor. Nine years later, I came back rich.

Along the way, I became known as a Red Chaser. Now, I was going to meet the greatest Red Chaser of them all. Senator Joe McCarthy. Tailgunner Joe himself.

I was in Dowling's Oyster Bar, a small saloon in Brooklyn. It wasn't a fancy joint; it was a drinking place more akin to pubs in Ireland. Gray cigarette smoke filled the room as if it had been pumped in from a sputtering bus.

Coming in the front door, there were four booths that went down the wall toward the toilet; three booths were wedged against the front window. A long bar ran the length of the room, dominating it. Above the bar was a sign: *The food here is for the convenience of the drinkers.* Bill Dowling, the owner, didn't want people to think his joint was a restaurant, even though he had the best crab gumbo in the world.

This bar was just down the street from Ebbets Field, where the Brooklyn Dodgers play. Even though the Dodgers were playing a road game against the Pittsburgh Pirates, the bar was filled. The game blared over the large radios that Dowling had placed in each corner of the bar. It was hot in the middle of September of 1951. The drinkers didn't mind the heat: they had their beer and their Dodgers had a five and a half game lead in the National League pennant race. It couldn't get any better than that. Ebbets Field and saloons like Dowling's were where I spent most of my time during the summer. Baseball and beer, that's this rich man's life.

Tailgunner Joe came barreling through the open front door like a fullback from the New York Giants football team. There was a New York Giants baseball team, of course, but I don't talk about them much, if I can help it. Sure, I had seen McCarthy's picture in the papers and I'd seen him on the television in the bar, but this was the first time in real life. He was big and blocky—maybe a hair shorter than six-feet—an offensive guard size. His pants were wrinkled as if he'd slept in them. His wrinkled white business shirt was soaked through with sweat in spots and matched the color of clam chowder. His tie had been loosened to where it looked like a colorful lasso.

As he clomped toward me, my immediate thought was that he could take care of himself in any bar that he walked into. He looked like he was born to a bar—the only thing better than a good dirty joke would be a good fight. A beer bottle smashed across the face would be considered hilarious.

He walked right over to the booth where I was sitting, stuck his meaty right hand in front of my face, took my hand and shook it with a quick crunch. "You must be the Red Chaser," he said.

2. Friday, September 14, 1951

Before I could answer Senator McCarthy, he slid into the booth across from me. Quick too, he was. My long time friend, Nick Salzano, grabbed a chair and pulled it up to the booth. He was the matchmaker who had brought Tailgunner Joe and me together.

I had known Nick since we used to pop open fire hydrants, freeing gushers of water to cool us on those blistery summer days when we were kids. It was either the fire hydrant or grab a dime somewhere and go to an all-day Saturday matinee where the best feature was often the new air-cooled air. Heck, now we had cooled air in some bars.

Nick grew up to be a movie-star handsome guy—a tall, dark Italian movie star. He was an inch or so shorter than my six feet two, looked like he could go three rounds in the ring right now, hadn't seen any of his hair run off, and had a face that should have been on a male model.

The one flaw—and if he had been a male model he would have had to have it fixed—was his broken nose had never been set properly. Halfway up the bridge of his nose, there was the unmistakable bump of a long-ago broken nose. That was courtesy of me. We had not had a fight; it was basketball and his nose got in the way of one of my elbows. Nick had always been a ladies man, even when we were just twelve or thirteen. The broken nose added to his allure—a bit of testosterone plastered on his pretty face.

While Nick and I were like twins growing up, we weren't *identical* twins. One look at Nick and you knew he was Italian. One look at me and you knew I was Irish, even though I was half German, fair skin, some freckles. I didn't have carrot hair, but it was what some would call dirty blond.   With the blue eyes and almost blond hair, I would have been a guy that Hitler would have waved on to the procreate line.   Put Nick out in the sun for a while and he would bronze; put me in that same sun and I would blister.

We both went to college, which was something for our neighborhood.   Nick went to Columbia; I went to Brooklyn College.   Then I went off to the war and Nick went to law school.   I guess Uncle Sam must've figured he needed lawyers more than just another grunt.

In college, Nick married his high school sweetheart, Gina Provenzano.   Her father worked at the docks just like Nick's, but I think he was pretty high up in the mob.   He went by the name of Tony Pro, and I didn't think it was just a nickname that shortened his last name.   Gina had huge tits and Nick followed them around everywhere like a puppy dog.   Being a good Italian Catholic girl, she would let him fondle them on occasion, but if he wanted to get into the honeypot, as he had told me years ago, he'd have to make the big commitment.   So, he made that commitment; he married her.

Nick and Gina now had a couple of kids.   His wife Gina, he had told me recently, had added some ample padding around that big bosom.   Instead of the hourglass figure she had in high school, Nick said, she was looking more and more like a squash.   "I think she's grown a third tit and it's bigger than the first two," he had told me, laughing, "but it has no nipple and she claims it's her stomach."   He now worked for some law office in Washington, D.C., and I had to figure that marriage hadn't slowed him down with the ladies.   That would have been like swearing off air to him. I'd bet there wasn't a good-looking woman in DC within wooing distance that was safe from Nick.   I wasn't a natural ladies man like Nick even though I had matured into a rich, single guy.   Any girl was safe with me—I had to make a big effort just to get to know the ones I wanted to know.

It was just two weeks ago that Nick had unexpectedly sat down next to me at a Dodgers game at Ebbets Field and said, handing me a beer, "Hey, Pal, you want a beer?"

"Whoa! What the hell are you doing here?" I asked. I was surprised to see him. It had been about a year since we had tossed back a few beers together. His movie-star face had started to age a bit—light crow's webs were stretching around his eyes, and a small puff had sprouted under each eye. All work and all play would age even Nick.

It was after a couple of beers, a couple of Nathan's dogs, a homer by Duke Snider, a great play at the plate when Roy Campanella threw down a tag that would dent a tree that Nick said, "I got a guy I want you to meet."

"Sure," I said, "who?"

"Joe McCarthy."

"What? The guy on TV?" I asked. "The senator chasing down Commies?"

Nick nodded his head as he plopped the tail end of his second hot dog in his mouth. "The one and the same. I'm working for him now. Great guy. You'll love him."

"What's this all about, Nick? When'd you start working for him?"

"Whoa," Nick said, "he just wants to meet a guy like you. You'll find out why when you meet him."

Nick wouldn't tell me anything about this mysterious meeting. No matter how many beers I bought, I couldn't pry his tongue loose to tell me. So, here we were, two weeks later, me—Jakob Finbar McHenry—and Tailgunner Joe.

Nick ordered a round. The waitress—a stout Irish lass named Betty who could probably munch on glass like it was peanuts—brought a pitcher of Schaefer's and a Scotch and soda for Joe. While Nick was pouring from the pitcher, Joe clanked his glass down on the table top. It was empty. He raised his hand above his head—the sweat ring under his arm was the circumference of a basketball—and waved to Betty for another.

"This was only half full when you delivered it," Tailgunner Joe said, grinning, when Betty brought him a fresh one.

"Yeah, Sweetie, here's the other half," she said handing him the new drink. "Hey! Aren't you that guy on TV?"

"Rocky Marciano?" Joe asked, referring to the heavyweight champion of the world.

"Nah, you ain't him," she said, "but I'll figger it out."

Joe took a sip of his drink. Now it was indeed half empty.

"So, Jake—I can call you Jake, right—you were a Red Chaser during the war?" Joe asked. No chit chat here.

"We got that fancy name because of Wild Bill Donovan," I said. Wild Bill was the founder of the OSS during World War II. After the war, Truman changed its name to the Central Intelligence Agency. "Red Chaser sounded good, but we didn't really *chase* any Reds."

"What did you do then?" Joe asked. He knocked down the second half of his drink. Another one was on its way.

"Well, we chased down Waffen SS officers who had been in Eastern Europe for the last few years of the war. After the war, these SS guys were all over the place, trying to blend in as if they were rank-and-file soldiers or citizens or anything but SS. We had to track them down."

"What's that got to do with Reds?" Joe asked. His third tall Scotch and soda was placed in front of him. My buddy Nick just sat drinking his beer; he knew this was Joe's show.

"These Waffen SS guys had spy networks in Eastern Europe during the war. It took them *years* to build those networks. These Eastern Europe spies had two missions: to rat on where any Jews were being hidden and, more importantly, to keep detailed lists on who the Commie sympathizers were. The Nazis had some great spy networks in Eastern Europe. The SS knew every Commie in Czechoslovakia, Bulgaria, Hungary, Yugoslavia, places like those. Wild Bill wanted those networks. He wanted the guys who spied for the SS to spy for us—not spying on Jews, of course, but spying on Communists. That was Wild Bill's plan. He knew way early that it was the Russkies that would come out of that war as our enemy—and he wanted an experienced, built-in spy network."

"Brilliant," Joe said, "genius. *Built-in spy network.* So how many networks did you corral?"

"You know, I've never really talked about it. I think it's confidential, but since it's you, I guess I can tell. I personally picked up seventeen networks. I had to first find the Waffen SS guy, then turn him, then get all of his information about his spy network. I didn't go into the East to work the networks; Wild Bill had a different crew for that. That's why I say I really wasn't a Red Chaser. I guess you could say I was sorta a Red Spy Network *Finder*, but that didn't really sound so hot, and Wild Bill sure knew how to make things sound better."

8

Joe sipped his drink. This time it was just a sip. Almost ladylike.

"Interesting," he said and took another ladylike sip. I guess his drinking was slowed down when he was thinking. I'd say a minute went by with nobody talking, though it seemed like an hour, just sitting there, not drinking, not smoking, just sitting.

"What'ya do for a living now? Private cop, Nick tells me," Joe asked and answered in the same breath. "What type of cases?"

I don't seriously consider myself much of a private detective. When I came back from Europe as a rich man, I didn't want anybody to know that I was rich. Certainly not the OSS, definitely not the tax man, surely not my friends. But, I *was* rich. To follow my passion for baseball and beer, I had to at least *pretend* to have a job.

What better than a private detective? I could work my own hours, be out all hours of the night and nobody really knew who my clients were or who was paying me. I certainly didn't need an office in an office building. When my folks bought the house out on Long Island in Levittown—my Mom had always wanted a backyard with trees and grass and maybe even a little tomato patch—I bought their brownstone in Brooklyn. There's plenty of room for me to live in and, of course, to have an office. The office is where I kept track of the baseball box scores. I also kept a few files of my detecting work there.

"Divorces," I said.

"Pay much?"

"About a hundred a week for each case. Sometimes I've got three cases in a week and sometimes I don't have any."

"So you sneak around…" Joe said, holding up his big hand like it was a stop sign, "I don't mean to offend, Jake, it's just that you're *used* to sneaking around, being invisible, getting the goods on some guy."

"Or some woman." I said, "And I take no offense at your 'sneaking around' comment. Sure, when I'm working, I sneak around. I did that in Europe, too. The type of work I do isn't like a door-to-door Fuller Brush salesman. I *gotta* be sneaky. That's what I do."

Joe was back to sipping his Scotch, back to thinking.

He asked Nick to give him an envelope. Nick propped up his briefcase. It was one of those slim jobs. It might hold a sandwich, but never a thermos. Nick extracted a plain brown envelope, the sort you could buy at the post office. He pulled out a picture and laid it down on the table in front of me, right next to my beer. The picture was a head shot of a woman.

She was the most beautiful woman I had ever seen in my life. When I say that, I'm not exaggerating. Heck, I had the pictures of Betty Grable and all the rest over in Germany. Betty was beautiful, and there must have been a million GIs that wanted to jump in her panties, but she was beautiful in a fake movie star way. You know, everything was posed and perfect and staged.

The woman in the picture in front of me was *real*. This wasn't some glamour magazine picture with hours of makeup and queers fussing over her hair; this was a woman with little or no makeup staring into the camera in such a way that it was a miracle that the camera hadn't melted. Now this might have been a one-shot wonder in which the camera had just caught her perfectly and, if she twitched her head just a little, the picture would have lost its magic, but I don't think so. I got the feeling that you could take a warehouse full of Kodak film and snap pictures until your thumb fell off, and each picture of this woman would grab you and pull you into it.

I figured that she was all-day beautiful.

I imagine a professional fashion guy would say that she didn't have a perfect face. It was clearly asymmetrical. Maybe she didn't have the most beautiful nose you could find. Or the most stunning lips. Or the sultriest eyes or the best hair. But, there was no doubt about it, when it was all put together, this was a face that could knock you on your ass. And even though the picture was in black-and-white, I could just tell that her hair was flaming volcano-hot red.

I just stared at the picture. It was as if the noise was turned off in the bar.

Finally, after a part of a lifetime, Joe said, "The Ice Queen."

"The Ice Queen?" I found it strange that it was difficult to find my voice.

"Diamonds, Jake, diamonds," Joe said. "She's the heir to one of those Dutch diamond merchants in New York. She wears them on her ears, her neck, her ankles, and for all I know on her little toes."

I looked at the picture again. I couldn't tell if there were diamonds on her ears. Her hair cascaded down covering anything on her ears whether it be diamonds or pickles.

"What's her name?" I asked, "I mean, she doesn't go by the Ice Queen, does she?"

"Arabella Van Dyck," Nick said.

"I want you to do the same thing that you did with those SS bastards—I want you to get her Commie network." Joe said.

"She's a Commie?" I asked.

Joe nodded his head. "She's got red hair, red toe nails, a red heart and a deep dark-red soul. She's a Commie, all right. She's like the Queen Bee. Everything flows through her, she's got all the names that count; she knows everything. We've been told that the Ice Queen keeps a private list of celebrities that are Commies or lean so far left they walk around in a circle when they're trying to walk straight. These celebrities come from all different types of Commie front organizations. Arabella Van Dyck is so connected to so many Red organizations that she knows which celebrities are in which Commie organization. There's movie stars, there's TV people, there's newspaper columnists, there's magazine editors, all belonging to different groups, but the Ice Queen has put together her own personal master list. Hell, you said yourself that you're the Red *Finder*. This is right up your alley. I want you to find me a *lot* of Commies."

I had experience tracking down Nazis in all types of backwater towns in Eastern Europe, but the Ice Queen wasn't a Waffen SS and this wasn't blown-out Europe. "Why not the FBI? Isn't this what they do for you? Track down Reds? Isn't that what gets Hoover going every morning?"

"This isn't a Hoover thing," Joe said. "Sure, Hoover has slipped me plenty enough files over the year, but most of them—*all* of them, let me say—are intended to embarrass Harry Truman. I certainly got no problem with embarrassing Truman, but this list ain't state department folks. This list is celebrities and media types. If the FBI grabbed the Ice Queen, she's Hoover's, her information is Hoover's. He's always sidled up to media people like Walter Winchell. He's always parceled out the information to his media favorites like penny candy, one here, one there, but rest assured, he's always got headlines every time he handed out a little sweet. So, if that kinky bastard got the Ice Queen's information there's no guarantees he'd pass it along to *me*. He'd probably just use it as blackmail to get himself more ink. Nope, this is all off the books. This is my *private* venture. This is a big deal. You get me the Ice Queen's list and this will be a bigger blow to Communism than if you put a bullet between Joe Stalin's eyes."

"How do you expect that I'm going to get this list?" I asked.

"That's what I don't want to know," Tailgunner Joe said. "You can talk to Nick about all the details, but me, I don't know. I will tell you this, it's not likely that she's going to mimeograph the list and hand it over to you." He laughed hard—a good bar room laugh.

Steal it, that's what Joe meant, but he didn't want to say it nor did he really want to know if that's what I would do. All he wanted was the Ice Queen's list.

"Do we know where the list is *supposed* to be?" I asked.

"We've heard it's in a safe in her house—a brownstone on the Upper East Side," Nick said, speaking for just the second time since he sat down.

Joe asked Nick to give him another envelope. This envelope was the size of a normal business envelope. It wasn't glued shut; it had a rubber band around it.

"Expenses," Joe said. "There's two grand in there. That's to get you started. There's no end to it—you need more, call Nick, we got an unlimited supply for this job."

I didn't reach for the envelope.

"Get us the list, Jake," Joe said. "I've got a young tiger on the committee—name's Bobby Kennedy—and he's chawing at the bit to get at that list. He's an intense little sonofabitch—a real pisser. Hell, he's more intense than Richard Nixon, but Nixon looks like a criminal, my little guy looks like a fucking altar boy. But he's an assassin, a real assassin. His old man, Joe Kennedy—a former bootlegger no less—wants to get rid of Commies as much as I do. Along with my boys back in Wisconsin, he'll fund whatever we need. Go on, pick up that envelope. The Ice Queen is waiting for you."

Before I could answer, Joe was out of the booth as if he had just sat on a thumbtack. "Got another meeting to go to," he said. He turned to Betty and twirled his fist signaling another drink. With his new drink in hand, he had his roadie. He turned to me, tossed out that big hand and shook mine. "Nick's got all the details," he said. Then he looked me square in the eyes so hard that it seemed that a few volts of electricity jumped from his eyeballs to mine, "This is important to me, Jake. Really important. Don't let me down."

He turned and barreled out of the bar, roadie in hand. If a guy with a beer in his hand had been standing in his way, that guy would have been the seven bowling pin on a seven-ten split. I thought at the time that the Commies better head for the hills because that guy was going after any and all of them with a maniac's fervor.

After Joe was out of the bar, I said to myself: Yeah, I'm going to do it, I'll chase that Ice Queen, I'll get all the things that she knows. It wasn't for the money, it wasn't because I hated Commies, it was for one reason and one reason only. I wanted to see that picture materialize into a real person. Yep, I wanted the Ice Queen.

3

Monday, September 17, 1951

"When are you going to go in to get the list?" Nick had asked me Friday night at Dowling's Oyster Bar.

"In a week, probably," I had said.

Nick had shaken his head. "We don't want to wait. We want the Ice Queen's information now."

It seemed like every client wanted the goods right away. The cuckolded husband wanted evidence right away and didn't want to wait for me to get rock-solid evidence on his wife's next tryst with the tennis pro at the country club. I guess getting a list of Commies was no different.

"Well, usually I like to case the place," I had said. "I like to go into a house when I know nobody's there."

"Nobody'll be there," Nick had said. "I'm gonna give you a couple of shortcuts. The Ice Queen leaves her brownstone every Monday morning for most of the day. I guess that's her day to go down to Wall Street and visit her money and then go to Fifth Avenue and spend some of it. That's this coming *Monday*, pal. She lives alone in that big old brownstone, does not have a maid, doesn't have an alarm system, doesn't have a dog, doesn't even have a fucking cat. It's got locks. And a safe. You told me you could handle that, right?"

I nodded. "They taught me that stuff in OSS."

"The place will be just sitting there waiting for you. And, if you want to do some homework, study this." Nick reached into the briefcase and brought out a set of blueprints.

"That's her brownstone, right there," Nick had said, his finger stabbing at the blueprint. "Look at it over the weekend to get a feel where the rooms are, go in on Monday, snatch the list, and we'll have a few beers afterward. Easy as pie."

"Nick, you've got this job really scoped out," I said. I was amazed. "Why don't you guys do it? Why me?"

Nick stared at me. "Jake, for Christ's sake, we're the McCarthy Committee of Un-American Activities, we don't do such things. We don't have any B and E guys on our staff. Just lawyers. The FBI could do this, but then the list would end up in Hoover's mitts and not Joe's. So, I thought, we want the list, we know where it is, why not bring in an old buddy who knows how to do these things, who wouldn't mind making a pretty good hunk of change for a pretty easy B and E and do something patriotic in the process."

All those reasons made sense, but I wasn't feeling comfortable about it. I felt uncomfortable going in so quickly without being able to case the place to my own satisfaction. It's not as if I had a regular routine for breaking and entering. Heck, I'm the good guy, not a crook. There have been *occasions* where I've had to break-in to get some evidence in a divorce case, but no way could breaking and entering be considered as one of my usual activities. Still, with all the background stuff that Nick already had, it did seem to be easy as pie.

So, today was the easy as pie day. Monday, September 17, 1951.

The break-in would be a three-man job. The first man was me, of course. Then I needed a lookout in case the Ice Queen came back unexpectedly. That would be Rafael Ordonez.

Rafael was a Puerto Rican kid who lived in Red Hook, the neighborhood bordering Brooklyn Heights, where I lived. Many

Puerto Ricans tended to live close to where they worked, and many worked at the rope manufacturer in the Brooklyn Navy Yard in Red Hook. I had met him, however, not in Red Hook but at a Dodger game. I caught him trying to pick my pocket. I offered him alternative employment and I used him occasionally on jobs like this. This beat working in the rope factory.

Rafael had spent most of his young life dodging the police, so he was a world-class lookout. He was thin, a little bit shorter than me, and looked as innocent as a choir boy. The cops in Brooklyn knew that he would steal something in a blink of an eye, but here in Manhattan he was a portrait of honesty. He was even carrying a small shoulder satchel that made him look like a delivery boy.

The third man wasn't just critical—the safe cracker—but essential. I was accurate when I had told Nick that the OSS had taught me how to get into locked safes. Easy, just blow it open with dynamite. But, this job was *stealth*. My resident safecracker was a person nobody would ever suspect. It was my secret weapon from Japan. And she wasn't a man; she was a *she*.

Hiromi Kitahara could pick a lock almost faster than I could open it with a key. She could crack a safe faster than I could memorize the combination. These skills had been developed, oddly, after her family had left Hiroshima.

It's a long story, but her family had immigrated to the United States two years *before* Pearl Harbor. Hiromi's father came to help his younger brother in his business. Considering that Hiroshima was literally blown off the map just a few years later, the move to the United States should have been considered a gift from God. That gift, however, wasn't free. Just two years after Hiromi and her parents had arrived in the United States they had been tossed into an American prison in Tule Lake, California. Our government didn't call them prisons, of course; we called them Internment Camps. Welcome to the good old U.S. of A.

In the Internment Camp, Hiromi refined two skills: painting and locks. The locks was a family thing. Her father was a locksmith as was her uncle and her grandfather. While in Internment, Hiromi learned the family locksmith trade. She practiced on the locks on the doors. With the painting, I'm not talking about painting a wall or something, I'm talking about *art*. Hiromi's painting brought her a scholarship at Pratt Institute in Brooklyn after the war.

Halfway through her first year at Pratt, she found my house. Our family house in Brooklyn was massive; a classic three-story brownstone on Middagh Street in Brooklyn Heights.

We had been taking boarders since I left for the war. When my folks bought the house out on Long Island in Levittown—tomato patch and all—I bought their brownstone in Brooklyn. Hiromi became my third boarder on my third floor.

She was nothing close to the buck-toothed slit-eyed thick-eyeglassed Jap that the movies had stereotyped the Japanese to be in the 1940s. Her eyes were much rounder than a movie goer would expect. She had black hair that was so shiny that it seemed that it was wet. She didn't wear glasses. She was taller than the women I would see down in Chinatown—I would imagine she was about five-six or so. She had a smile that Pepsodent could use in a magazine ad. She was thin, of course, but instead of frail looking she looked athletic. I don't think she was beautiful in the sense that we Americans understand—not knock-down beautiful like the Ice Queen was or the big tits like Marilyn Monroe—but there was a certain radiance about her that made her pleasing to look at.

Like any college kid, Hiromi needed money. When I found out that she had this unusual skill with locks, I made her a part-time employee. Cash didn't exchange hands exactly. We worked on the barter system. For every lock she picked, she'd get a free month's rent. She just had one rule for me: she would not use her skill to *steal*. However, getting evidence about a wayward husband was, as she would say, hunky-dory. So, working part-time for me was a heck of a lot better than working in a Chinese laundry.

That was my team: a Puerto Rican, a Jap and me. And today our United Nations-like forces were going to invade the Ice Queen's castle. Easy as pie.

4

Monday, September 17, 1951

I found a parking spot on the Ice Queen's street, a few houses down from her brownstone. She lived in a large brownstone on 72nd Street, in between Second and Third Avenue in the Upper East Side. The street was lined with three-story brownstones. Nick had told me that the Ice Queen lived alone. No relatives, no live-in maid, no caretaker, no nothing.

Hiromi and I were in my parked Ford when the Ice Queen stepped out of her brownstone. Rafael was already positioned down the street.

I savored what I was seeing: the Ice Queen was tall, I'd say about five-eight or so; she had long and shapely legs that looked strong and feminine at the same time. She walked with a certain bounce that spilled off supreme confidence. Her hair was indeed flaming red. You could tell from a mile away that her hair was no dye job. It bounced and flowed as she walked, leaving a lightly luminous trail.

She was wearing a dark green suit that made her look like a million dollars, which being the Ice Queen, was probably worth at least that. You don't see too many women that have that presence; I would bet that most men who met her would be instantly intimidated. The files that Nick had given me said that she was thirty-one—the same age as me—but she had a bearing that practically made her timeless. And, somehow she had become a

Commie and was under the microscope of Tailgunner Joe McCarthy. What a waste.

From his position at the end of the block, Rafael could see the Ice Queen walking toward him. He would stand by a pay phone, giving the impression that he was waiting for instructions for his next delivery or pick up. He would stay near the phone after the Ice Queen caught a cab. If the Ice Queen came back earlier than he expected, he could see that from his position near the pay phone. He would then drop a nickel into the phone box and call the Ice Queen's home, allowing the phone to ring just once. He would then hang up and quickly redial the same number and allow it to ring twice. That one-two rings sequence would give us the warning that the Ice Queen had changed her patterns and was coming back to the brownstone earlier than expected.

After the Ice Queen started to walk toward Third Avenue, I pulled out of the parking spot and found a spot on the street behind the Ice Queen's. I liked to break into a house through the back door. Exits were better too at the back door.

Hiromi and I walked toward the Ice Queen's street and turned in to the alley. We ducked through the gate to the Ice Queen's backyard and walked up to the back door. A deadbolt lock stared us in the face.

"Easy to crack," Hiromi said as she nimbly worked her tools to pop open the lock.

"That goes for safes, Hiromi," I said, "Not for deadbolts."

"What you say for deadbolts then?" She whispered.

I said, "Pick." She looked quizzically at me not knowing if I had tried to make a joke. After about ten seconds of fiddling with the lock with her kit of bobby pins, she opened the door. She led me to the foyer at the front of the house as if she had been born there. Hiromi walked with a certain familiarity through the house; she had studied the blueprints better than I had.

The blueprints showed that the Ice Queen's safe was in a small office off of her bedroom on the second floor. Hiromi knew the path better that I did; she was a woman on a mission, all business-like, heading up the stairs moving as quietly as a ghost. I followed.

I walked up the stairs slower. There was art lining both walls of the staircase. It was marvelous art, including a Pablo Picasso. I touched the frame and jiggled it. It wasn't screwed into the wall. This would have been easy to swipe. It seemed strange to me to have works of art like Picasso and not have some type of protection against thievery. Maybe the Ice Queen had so much money that she didn't give a fuck.

"This way," Hiromi whispered with some urgency underscoring her words. She moved so quietly that she had already found the bedroom and had floated back to me admiring Picasso.

At the second level of the brownstone, there were six doors that branched off the hallway. Hiromi pointed to the first door on the right. It was open.

"Ice Queen's bedroom," Hiromi whispered.

She motioned for me to follow her. We walked into a very large room. On the far wall was the biggest bed that I had ever seen. It looked to be the size of three queen-sized beds. Above it was a huge mirror bolted into the ceiling.

"Funny times," Hiromi said, smiling, pointing at the ceiling. That was the first time she had ever said something to me that had a hint of a sexual connotation. It looked like she blushed, but it wasn't easy to tell with Orientals.

Hiromi skittered ahead while I gave the bed a closer inspection. I wondered where the Ice Queen had got sheets big enough to cover this monstrosity.

I walked to a large Hieronymus Bosch painting on the wall. With all of its demons, half-human animals and tortured souls, I found a Bosch to be a strange painting to have on your bedroom wall, but what the hell, I wasn't the Ice Queen. I jiggled it. Like the Picasso, the Bosch wasn't screwed to the wall and I could have lifted both. The Picasso might have worked in my house, but the Bosch I would have donated to Dowling's. Let those drunks there figure out what the hell Hell was all about.

Hiromi hissed a 'pssssst' at me. She moved around as quickly as a dragonfly over water; she had probably cased the whole upstairs while I was looking for myself in the Bosch painting.

She motioned me to follow her. She led me to a bathroom. Some bathroom! There was a large bathtub that could pass for a swimming pool in some neighborhoods. There was also a walk-in stall shower. This bathroom was bigger than most people's living room.

"Funny times here, too," Hiromi said, this time not blushing.

She then pivoted and led me across the bedroom to two open French doors leading to a small office. On the opposite side of the small office was another door, leading to who knows where.

"Safe," Hiromi said, pointing at another Picasso. It was located just left of the desk. This Picasso, like the one on the stairwell, wasn't a print. It was the real McCoy. Hiromi pulled the Picasso frame from the left side and it pivoted like a door. On the wall was the safe.

"Excuse me now, Jake, I must listen. You be quiet." Hiromi twisted the combination dial a few times and put her ear to the lock. I wandered back into the Ice Queen's bedroom.

I had never seen a bed so large. It had to have been custom made, along with the dust ruffles, the sheets, everything about it including the mirror above it. I leaned over and looked at myself in the mirror.

Before I could fantasize about the different movie sequences running in my head, I heard Hiromi say, "Okay."

It had been just a minute—two at the most—and Hiromi had cracked the safe. When I walked into the office, I just saw the open safe in the wall. "It's all yours," Hiromi said.

I carefully pulled out of the safe a large bundle of papers. They were held together with a rubber band. The papers were of various sizes with some longer with their ends sticking out of the pile. I put the papers down on the desk and began to sift through them looking for a list. Hiromi had the small camera ready to take photos of any of the pages.

Hiromi pointed at the safe. I looked in the deep recess. This was a very large safe. I peered in. Cash. I pulled out one bundle. It was all hundred-dollar bills. Probably about fifty of them. There were at least ten more bundles. I put the money back. We were there to get The List, not steal. No Picassos, no cash for us—we had *honor*.

I pulled the rubber band off of another pile of papers and started to shuffle through them. Halfway through the papers, I ran into something surprising. It wasn't the list; it was a bundle of folded papers that looked like they were written in Japanese.

"What do these say?" I asked Hiromi.

She looked at the papers. "I don't know," she said. "That is Korean." She said it with a very slight sneer; if she had been raised in Brooklyn she would have said, "I don't read that shit." I guessed that she didn't like Koreans. That stumped me; I'd ask her about it later.

"I don't read Korean. But, look at this," she said, pointing to a page full of diagrams. I stared at the diagrams. I couldn't figure out what the drawings represented. I did know they didn't represent a bike or a baseball diamond; it looked like they represented some type of bomb.

"Take a picture of this page," I said, handing it to her. I found five more pages of drawings to be photographed. She snapped off pictures as quickly as she turned the pages.

The phone rang and Hiromi and I both jolted up straight. It rang only once. We froze. After a three count, the phone rang again. This time it rang twice.

"Let's go," I said. I folded the Korean sheets of paper back into the bundle and put them back into the safe as we had found them. Hiromi closed the safe door and actually repositioned the dial to be at the same number that she had found it.

We walked quietly back through the massive bedroom. In the hallway, we heard the lock open and somebody walk across the hardwood vestibule. Rafael must have been asleep at the switch, I thought. There was no way the Ice Queen could have walked down from Third Avenue to her brownstone in the time between the phone call warning and the opening of the front door.

"This way," Hiromi whispered. We tiptoed through the master bedroom again, tiptoed through the office, and Hiromi opened the door on the far side. It led to another bathroom. This was a more conventional bathroom. Next to the bathtub was another door and Hiromi was through it like a practiced tour guide. It led to a smaller bedroom. Two beds, a large wardrobe dresser, a sitting area with two large chairs and a love seat. Across the way was another door. A closet.

Hiromi whispered, "We can hide in here until she leaves again."

"What if she doesn't leave?" I asked.

"We wait," Hiromi said, separating the hanging clothes with her hands as she burrowed in to the back of the large closet. There must have been a hundred dresses hanging in the closet and maybe two hundred pairs of shoes. We had burrowed to the back; for the Ice Queen to find us she would have to decline to wear the ninety-nine dresses in front of the last one that was hiding us.

We were in pitch darkness, and feeling like we were suspended in a vast void. Through the closet door, we heard the voices of a woman and at least two men. Both of the men were speaking with Asian accents.

Hiromi touched my face with her fingers and then positioned her mouth over my ear and whispered in the darkness, "Korean." The word didn't titillate me, but her whisper sure did.

We stood there in the back of the closet; my arm around her shoulders. We heard a tinkling sound—one of the men was taking a piss. He said something and both men laughed. He didn't flush. Then we heard nothing. It seemed like they had left the bathroom.

About ten minutes later, what we heard confused us. It came muted through the Ice Queen's office, the bathroom and finally to us in the closet. It was a woman's squeal, then a laugh, then a scream, then another squeal. I tiptoed toward the door of the closet. A moment later, I peered out. Nobody was there. I heard the woman's squeal again and then some Korean words that sounded very harsh.

I whispered back to Hiromi, "Stay here."

I tiptoed out of the closet, then through the bathroom, stopped for a moment and heard a squeal that turned into a scream. I tiptoed through the small office and held my breath. There were grunts. I peered around the door to look into the Ice Queen's bedroom.

There she was on that football field-sized bed. She was naked. The two Korean men were naked. Their cocks filled two of the major orifices of the Ice Queen, her mouth and her vagina. The Korean that was filling her mouth was standing on the bed and the Ice Queen was in a doggy position; the other Korean had entered her vagina from behind her. They were all looking at the ceiling as if they were watching a dirty movie.

I felt pressure on my arm. Hiromi had ducked under my armpit to see what I was seeing. I don't know if she zeroed in on the same thing that I saw, but I saw that the Ice Queen's flaming red hair was indeed natural and something glittered from her navel. It looked like a huge diamond. The Ice Queen, you betcha.

The Koreans faces were contorted. They looked strong, their muscles extending. It looked like they were on the brink of a rousing finish. They twisted the Ice Queen around. I saw a tattoo on the small of her back. It looked like a *snake*.

Hiromi pulled my arm and I followed her through the bathroom to the office.

"I found a backstairs," she whispered, "I think it comes down into the kitchen. It is locked. I think I'll have a few seconds to pick it. Should we try?"

"Yes," I whispered. "Let's get out of here. She might be here all day."

From the guest bedroom where we had been hiding in the closet, Hiromi opened the door to the hallway. It sounded like the Koreans and the Ice Queen were still going strong. We tiptoed down the hallway. At the end was another door and Hiromi knelt down, her lock picks in her hand, and manipulated the lock. She opened the door, stepped through it and down the stairs. I gently closed the door and followed her.

Within a minute we were out the back door and in the alley. The fresh air felt to us like the air must feel to a released prisoner. Both of our faces were sweaty; both of us had sweated through our shirts; both of us just wanted to get back to the car.

I had never seen an orgy before, a ménage de la whatever hadn't been one of my experiences in life. I'm sure that it hadn't been one of Hiromi's life experiences either. As a voyeur, it was shocking. It wasn't appealing. It seemed so violent. I had never seen a rape before either—even in all my post-war days in Berlin— but the orgy we had witnessed had to be a cousin to rape. That could be the Catholic upbringing in me censoring my feelings, but I knew that that type of sexual exercise wasn't going to be a part of my lifestyle.

I did, however, still feel the sensuality of Hiromi's whisper in my ear when we were in the closet. I still felt the touch of her hand on my face and on my neck. When I looked over to her as we walked down the alley, I noticed her sweaty shirt clinging to her and saw a different Hiromi than the one I'd known as a boarder.

Back at the car, Rafael was waiting for us, leaning against the fender. He started explaining right away. "She didn't come walking down the street," he said, "she was dropped off in front of her home in a black Cadillac. Two Oriental guys got out of the car with her. That's when I called. Are you okay?"

I mumbled that we were. We didn't say much on our drive back to Brooklyn. I think Rafael was feeling so guilty about the close call that he didn't ask any questions and he slumped in the back seat taking a quick siesta.

When I pulled the Ford onto the Brooklyn Bridge, Hiromi finally spoke. "Did you see the diamond on her stomach?" she asked.

I nodded. Then I asked a dumb question, "How does it stick? How does it stay there?"

"I think it was attached to her skin," Hiromi said, "like those African natives that we see in *National Geographic* that have different things sticking through their bodies. It's probably like an earring that is stuck through an earlobe, but this is her belly button instead."

I winced. The Ice Queen was really weird. She had a body that didn't need any adornments, so why in the world let something be jabbed through her belly button?

"Yakuza," Hiromi said.

"Yock what?"

"Ice Queen have tattoo, you see? Only gangsters in Japan have tattoos," Hiromi said. "Gangsters. Yakuza. Gangsters."

5

Monday, September 17, 1951

The phone was ringing when we walked in the back door to my house.

I walked to the living room to answer it.

"Hey, buddy, how'sitgoin?" Nick Salzano asked.

Wow. News travels fast.

"Can we talk over the phone?" I asked. Yes, I was getting paranoid. After all, I was on a secret mission for Tailgunner Joe against the Commies. Before my drinks with Tailgunner Joe and Nick, I was pretty naïve about Communism in America. I knew we were *fighting* Communism way back when I was working for the OSS. Wild Bill Donovan never let a day go by when he didn't remind us. But that was *Russian* Communism.

That Communism wasn't on American soil; it was on *European* land. After Tailgunner Joe had left Dowling's, Nick told me the full scope of Communism in America. It seemed that half the people I saw walking down the street could be Commies. In a span of two days, I went from thinking that Communism was for a handful of beatniks down in the Village and union rabble rousers to a wicked virus that had caught the right winds from Europe and seeped into almost every household in America. Heck, I was getting just as paranoid as Joe McCarthy and Nick.

"Not really," Nick said. "Just tell me if you got the list or not."

"I haven't got it yet," I answered. How did he know that I have already been in and out of the Ice Queen's brownstone? Was he in New York? Was he casing the Ice Queen's place?

"How did you know I've already been in her house?" I asked Nick point blank. "Are you in town?"

"Naw, I'm in Washington," Nick said. "You told me that you were going in first thing Monday morning. I figured it was a pretty easy deal. Joe's anxious about this and he wanted me to call. Heck, he wanted me to call a half-hour ago, but I knew that there was no way you could be back already. So, what happened?"

"We did go in first thing. She left just about the same time you said that she would. I got into the safe all right, but there was a lot of shit in there. I was going through it, but she came back just thirty minutes or so later. I just didn't have the time and had to hightail it out of there."

"Okay, but what'll I tell Joe? When are you going back in?"

"Do you know the Ice Queen's movements on any days this week?" I asked.

I heard rustling of paper coming from Nick's end of the phone. "I got nothing on Tuesday or Thursday," Nick said, referring to his notes, "must mean that there is no pattern. She usually leaves the house on Wednesday morning for a couple of hours. That might be the safest time to try again."

"Well, I'll go in Wednesday then."

"That'll work for me," Nick said. "I'll give you a call on Wednesday about noon or so. If you've got the list, I'll take the train up to New York and we'll have a few beers and laughs."

"Got it," I said.

"See you then," Nick said, "gotta go, Joe's calling."

Nick hung up the phone first. I held the handset for a second and then heard another click on the line. Was Tailgunner

Joe listening in? Was somebody else listening in? Or, was it my paranoia kicking in? My paranoia was a treasured tool for me in Europe. Most folks consider paranoia a mental disorder, and in its extreme I guess it is. But, if you're trying to track down former Nazi SS, you find out quickly that you can't trust anybody. At times, it seemed that the world I was in was full of liars. So, I looked at paranoia as giving me an edge. It got me back to Brooklyn and it got me rich.

It's not that my paranoia was left behind in Europe. God knows it was still around, but each day it seemed to seep further and further into the background. Now it was asking to be recognized. For reasons that I was having trouble in identifying, I didn't feel good about this job for Nick and Tailgunner Joe.

Still holding the phone in my hand I asked myself: Why in the world had I taken this job anyways?

Sure, the Ice Queen herself was mesmerizing.

And, being asked by Tailgunner Joe could be considered an honor, of sorts.

And, the money. Two grand in one week was about what a working stiff could make after a few months.

But, those were all bogus reasons. I sat down on the couch and examined each reason.

The Ice Queen was indeed beautiful. I wouldn't be the first guy to get snowed into making a bad decision because of a beautiful face; I wouldn't be the last. So, this reason was indeed stupid.

As for the honor of working for Tailgunner Joe—now that was really stupid. I wasn't even sure if I liked the guy. Or believed in what he was doing. I didn't believe in politics; I believed in living my life, going to Dodgers games, having a few beers and that's it. Being a private detective was a *pretend* job. I needed *something* to do that was unaccountable to anybody else. Being a private detective with a modicum of divorce cases was just that.

The last reason—money—was the dumbest reason of them all. I already had enough money to last a lifetime. That money wasn't exactly legal, but it was safe.

The phone rang, startling me. If it was Nick, I might just quit the job now.

I answered the phone.

"Jake, Ed Stebbings here." Ed was a hotshot lawyer from Manhattan whose skin I had saved once.

His wife's attorney had hired me to catch him in the act of doing the deed with some broad. I did catch him; it was some of my best photography. Really graphic stuff. With those photos, I had him crucified. It was as if I had him stretched out on the cross, the nails clenched in my teeth, the hammer gripped hard in my hand and one nail was poised on his open palm. All I had to do was pound and he was as nailed to the cross as anybody could be. He found out about my pictures and offered me a lot of money to lose the negatives. I didn't take the money. Nor did I hand over the prints and negatives to the wife's lawyer. Surprisingly, I had developed a conscience; by accident I found out that the wife wasn't any saint either. So, I withdrew the nails from my pursed lips, threw the hammer away and helped him up off the cross. He was the sole case where I had burned the photos and the negatives. Ed got divorced, but under more favorable terms.

"You forgot," Ed said.

"Forgot what?" I asked.

"*This Friday night!*" Ed practically yelled into the phone. "Friday night! I'm throwing my divorce anniversary party at the Stork Club. Remember? You promised you'd come. Without you I'm just a little piggy on my ex-wife's skewer."

"I did forget, I'm sorry," I said. "There's been a lot on my mind."

"Not the Dodgers, pal, there's no way they could fuck this up. You're coming Friday, aren't you?"

I thought about it. I'd never been to the Stork Club. A high profile joint like that wasn't exactly my style, but it did pique my interest.

"What time?" I asked.

"You can get there anytime, but the little celebration starts at nine. Everything's on me...dinner...booze...you got it all. I'll leave your name at the door to get you in."

"Sounds good to me," I said.

"And, Jake, scarf up some date, would ya'. If it's a Brooklyn broad would you tell her not to snap her gum when she walks in the joint," Ed said, laughing like a free man. I laughed with him.

"A date to a divorce party?" I asked. "Not exactly a romantic type of thing, Ed."

"Look, only you and me and a couple of the guys know it's really a divorce party. If any of the wives knew, they wouldn't come. Look, I'm not hoisting a piñata with a picture of my ex-wife on it where we'd beat it to smithereens; this is a *couples* thing, not some fucking stag party. It just so happens—pure coincidence, of course—that this party is on the anniversary of my divorce. *I'm* bringing a date—and wow is she *hot*—so, I'll see you there, right?"

It was then that I had a wild thought, a terrifically wild thought. If I would have thought about it through for a minute or two, I'm sure that this wild thought would have evaporated. Instead of pausing for even a few seconds, I said, "Okay, I'll bring a date."

The date I had in mind wasn't any of the women I knew down at Dowling's Oyster Bar. Hell, that wouldn't work; they'd be snapping their gum like alligators on a dog. I was thinking only of Hiromi.

"I might bring an Oriental," I said. "Any problem with that?"

I held my breath. I didn't have a problem renting one of my upstairs rooms to a Japanese person and I didn't have a problem

34

taking one to a fancy-dan restaurant. Hell, I had grown up in Brooklyn with almost every nationality on the face of the Earth. While that diversity brought a dose of prejudice to a lot of folks, it never touched me. I guess I could thank my folks for that. They never allowed the negative slurs of nationalities—like whop, dago, hebe, nigger, spic, chink, and so forth—to be uttered in the house. Letting fly with one of those epithets was tantamount to saying over dinner, "Pass the fucking butter." Blurting out either one would give me a swift cuff to the head and loss of allowance for at least a week. My time in Europe also blurred any hard lines brought on by nationality. It wasn't something I worked on, it just was.

"A chink, you say?" Ed said.

"Not a chink, Ed. A Japanese heiress," I said. I figured other folks who might not be that enlightened about race might feel a little bit better if that person was a princess.

"A *Jap*? A Jap heiress? What're you talking about?"

"A Japanese heiress," I said, smiling. "You've heard of all those princes over in Japan, right? They owned all the land; well her father was one of those princes who had stashed a mountain of yen in Swiss banks. So, any problems about me bringing a Japanese heiress as a date?"

"The Stork Club doesn't fancy having Negroes in the joint," Ed said, "but I would think an Oriental is okay. What the hell—we won the war didn't we?"

Ed then told me how the club had refused service to Josephine Baker, the famous Negro singer/stripper, who had become a legend in France. The Stork Club didn't flat-out refuse service; they just told her when she ordered a certain entrée that it was no longer available. When she tried to order a different entrée she found out that it wasn't available either. In fact, nothing on the menu was available to her, and when she realized that, she started shouting, eyeball to eyeball, at the wrong guy—Walter Winchell. Winchell was a full-blown regular at the Stork Club. I guess she blamed our fearless gossip king for not coming to her aid. Winchell always had the last word. He promptly labeled Josephine Baker a Commie in his column. Surely, Tailgunner Joe would have her on one of his lists.

So, that's how I decided to have my first date with Hiromi. I figured that us breaking into apartments didn't count as dates. I had taken her to a Dodgers game once, but that wasn't a *date*. That was just going to a baseball game.

6

Tuesday, September 18, 1951

I got up early and after a quick breakfast I went down into my basement to my built-in darkroom.

Over the past year or so, there have been some jim-dandy photos developed in that darkroom. No legit newspaper or magazine would have published any of those photos, of course, but they were graphic enough to win a divorce in a landslide.

I didn't have much to develop, just those photos of those Korean drawings that looked like it could be a bomb of some sorts. But, those drawings made me curious. I wanted to show them to somebody.

I didn't have to go far. With the photos in an envelope, I walked down the street in front of my house to the neighborhood candy store.

A tourist would think that it was a quaint candy store in Brooklyn. At Gonnella's Candy Store, a tourist could choose Mary Janes, Atomic Fireballs, Candy Buttons and Slo Pokes candy from a whole wall of penny candies. A tourist could also get a soda and a hamburger. To read while eating, a tourist could buy a newspaper or magazine.

If a local went into Gonnella's in the afternoons, he could wend his way to the back room and join a friendly, low-ante poker game. Or, he might buy an Irish Sweepstakes number along with his bag of Jelly Beans. If a local was more interested in the New York teams than the Irish Sweepstakes, he could place a bet on the Dodgers or the Yankees or Giants or Knicks or Rangers or the football Giants or even Notre Dame, which seemed like a local team even though it got somehow located in Indiana. The betting here was regular, frequent and often. Even the beat cops in the area would put down wagers in Gonnella's. The phone company hadn't made a mistake in installing nine phone lines for this small candy store, all but one of the lines being connected to phones in the basement. It was there, in the basement, that Dominic Gonnella made his money; candy was just a social service to the neighborhood.

I went to Gonnella's for another reason. Its owner, Dominic Gonnella, had two unusual traits: he was the best-read man that I had ever met, and he was like a human telegraph without any of the dots and dashes. *The New York Times, the Herald Tribune, The New York Sun, the Daily News, the Post, the Brooklyn Eagle* and the other papers may have served the city and its boroughs with information about wars and killings and politicians and weather, but Dominic knew things that weren't in the papers. And, if it was in the papers, Dominic had read it. Dominic was a fanatical magazine guy. He'd stay up nights reading *Time, Newsweek, Life, Colliers, Look*—you name the magazine, he would have read it. He collected *Time* magazines as if they were some heirloom. To preserve each precious *Time* magazine, he would carefully place it in its own envelope and stack them in a fireproof metal file cabinet. Before I got myself further into something I shouldn't get into, I needed Dominic's opinion.

I would show Dominic the pictures that Hiromi had taken of the Korean hieroglyphics on the drawings that looked like bombs. They sure looked like bombs to me. If they were, I felt this put a much different spin on my assignment for Tailgunner Joe. It's not that Dominic was our resident physicist, but he did know a lot of things and I valued his opinion.

As I walked over to Gonnella's, it started to sprinkle. If that sprinkle turned into rain, it wouldn't affect the Dodgers; they were at St. Louis to play the Cardinals.

Dominic was on the sidewalk in front of his store with his broom. Normally, he was sweeping off the dust; today he was sweeping off rain drops. You could eat off of his sidewalk. If you wanted to stereotype a candy store owner, Dominic was it. Short, balding, a big belly, mid-forties, a kindly grandpa's face. If you imagined a stereotype of a bookie, Dominic wasn't it. He was a candy store owner all the way.

"Jake, m'boy, how'r'yadoing?" Dominic asked as I walked up to him.

"Terrific," I said. Heck, I would say terrific if I was suffering from gangrene. If I went around and told people my troubles, eight out of ten people wouldn't care and the other two would be glad I had those troubles.

"Do you like Red Barber?" Dominic asked me about the Dodgers radio announcer.

What a strange thing to ask; that was like asking me if I liked Jesus Christ.

It's not that I grew up as a kid with the old Redhead. The Dodgers had started to broadcast their games in 1939 when I was in college. At that time, game broadcasts were a new thing for New York. WOR carried the Dodger games, and they stole the best radio announcer in baseball, Red Barber, from the Cincinnati Reds.

Back then, Barber's southern accent and funny expressions was like a foreigner talking to Brooklynites.

"Sometimes, I can't figger out what da hell dat bum's talking about?" Dominic said. "Barber says one time, 'The boys are tearing up the pea patch,' and I don't know what the hell that means. Then my nephew Ralphie—who I can hardly understand *his* English—did a translation saying it means 'a rally is in progress.' Why doesn't Barber speak English for Christsakes?"

Everybody in Brooklyn learned a form of Southern shorthand and in the process Red Barber became the most unlikely wizard in the Land of Brooklyn.

"I probably have listened to Red Barber more than any other person in my entire life," I said.

"Well, I like our young guy, Vin Scully," Dominic said. "I can understand what the hell he's talking about without having Ralphie doing a fucking translation."

"Here, hold this," I said to Dominic, handing him an envelope that held the photos I had taken at the Ice Queen's. I took the broom out of Dominic's hands and started to sweep away a raindrop here, a raindrop there. Some raindrops I swept before they hit the cement.

"You must want something," Dominic said. "Ever since you were a little kid, you'd help around the store when you wanted the candy. This time, I bet it's not candy you want."

"That's right," I said. Just as I was going to ask him to take a look at the pictures, a tall gangly guy yelled Dominic's name from across the street and then ran across to where we were standing in about two giant steps.

"Jackie, you know Jake?" Dominic asked the tall guy. I could see now that he was really a kid, but big, probably at least six-six, maybe taller. He couldn't be much more than nineteen or twenty.

"Jack Molinas," the kid said, pushing his hand out to me. I told him my name and let my hand disappear into his large hand. His fingers reached up to my wrist. Meat hooks, they were.

"Jake's been over fighting the friggin' Nazis," Dominic said to Molinas. "He don't know that he's just shook the hand of a star, a real star."

"I'm in a rush, Dominic, can I see you for just a minute?" Molinas said.

I took the hint and walked into the candy shop. I watched them through the window. Molinas was a good-looking guy, probably Jewish if he was a basketball star. It seemed like all the star basketball players were Jewish except for the lone Negro that was allowed for most city college teams. Molinas was true to his word—he had spent only a minute with Dominic, and he bounded back across the street and down the sidewalk. I rejoined Dominic.

"Columbia," Dominic told me. "Jackie was just a junior last year, averaged almost thirty points a game. Good kid. Bad bettor. He's down more than eighty large this summer."

"How much did you say?" I asked, astounded.

"Eighty thousand."

"How does a kid like that get that kind of money? Are his folks rich or something?"

"Nah, the old man runs a hot dog joint out on Coney Island during the summers. Jackie ain't rich. And, he hasn't paid any of his debts. Yet."

"You give him that much credit?" I asked. Dominic extended credit to everybody, but the credit would reach its ceiling at a hundred, maybe two hundred dollars. Eighty thousand, no way.

"Yet, I said," Dominic said, "*Yet*. What part of the word *yet* don't you understand?"

"Let me explain," Dominic said. "Don't *you* bet on any Columbia games next season without talking to *me* first. We'll get our money back in spades next winter during basketball season."

When Dominic used the collective pronoun 'we', he wasn't referring to him and me. He was referring to himself and some of the other bookies that formed a loose network. Each had his own bookmaking business, but in the end it was all tied together with the mob. If Dominic wanted to be an independent bookie, he couldn't. There was no such animal. That was why his information was so good. It wasn't just things that Dominic observed or heard; he had eyes and ears all over the city. Dominic and his buddies would have been a great network in Eastern Europe. The Commies wouldn't have had a chance.

"The kid got twenty grand a game last year for shaving points on certain games," Dominic said.

"Twenty grand! Things sure have changed while I was over in Europe," I said.

"Yeah, this is big business now. Everybody gambles, everybody needs the action. So, at the going rate, Jackie will be all square with me after four or five games this winter," Dominic said. "It's a damned good investment for me, that kid is. So, Jake, what do you need from me?"

"I need to ask you a question," I said.

"So, go ahead already, ask."

"Take a look at the pictures in that envelope," I said, pointing to the envelope he was holding for me.

Dominic pulled the eight-by-ten black-and-white photos out of the envelope.

"Let's go inside," he said, "I wouldn't want any raindrops on this stuff."

Inside we sat at a table in the back.

Dominic looked carefully at each picture.

"So, wha'cha got yourself into?" he asked.

"I dunno," I said. "What do those drawings look like?"

"I'm not sure," Dominic said, "but I don't think these have anything to do with a divorce, what you're usually involved with."

"I came across them by accident," I said, "on one of my jobs."

Dominic nodded. He knew that one of my jobs didn't mean I was working checkout at one of the local grocery stores.

He leafed through the pictures again, very slowly.

"Korean?" he asked.

"How could you tell?" All Oriental writing looked the same to me.

"The dry cleaners over on Atlantic Avenue, they're Korean, their writing looks like this," he said.

"The power of an observant mind," I said. Dominic smiled.

"Whad'ya think?" I asked.

"I don't think these are drawings of just any bomb," Dominic said. "It's too complicated. Also, I don't like the idea of the Korean writing. It's like they copied the drawings and then wrote notes in Korean on every page. That's not good, not good at all. You might have stumbled on something you shouldn't have. I'd get rid of these, Jake. Send them to somebody that knows."

"The cops?"

Dominic looked at me like I had just said I should send them to the Moon. "Nah, somebody in government. How about your former boss?"

"Wild Bill Donovan?"

Dominic shrugged. "I don't know, maybe him. But I wouldn't just hang on to these. In fact, I wish I hadn't seen 'em." He put the photos back into the envelope and handed it to me.

As I walked back to the house, I was thinking how much more fun it was to shadow a husband who had a wandering cock than it was to pilfer a list from the beautiful Commie.

7

Wednesday, September 19, 1951

At the third level of the Ice Queen's brownstone, Hiromi led me into what looked like a miniature ballroom. At the end of the room was a raised platform that looked like it could accommodate a small band. In the middle of the room was a large hardwood floor that certainly was used for dancing. Hiromi motioned me to the back of the room where there was a door. Inside was a small office with an adjacent small bathroom. It looked as though this room and bathroom could have once been a maid's quarters.

"There," Hiromi said pointing to a landscape portrait on the wall. "Behind that picture is where another safe is."

It pays to study the blueprints. While I was examining paintings and big beds, she was flitting around the brownstone like a possessed fly.

She walked to the painting and sure enough it was on a hinge. Behind the painting was a wall safe. It was as if she could smell safes.

We had started fifteen minutes earlier with the first safe, the one that we had cracked when the Ice Queen came home too early. The entry to the brownstone had been as easy as it was two days before. We followed the same pattern. Again Rafael was stationed down the street to give us a warning if the Ice Queen unpredictably returned. We were betting that lightning couldn't strike twice at the same time at the same place.

After entering from the rear door, we had walked up the front stairs and through the master bedroom. The oversize bed loomed to the side. Hiromi didn't even glance at it. Kinky didn't seem to be her style. I glanced at the bed more to make sure that there wasn't anybody on it, it was so large. Still embedded in my mind was the image of the Koreans and the Ice Queen. I wasn't for the kinky stuff either. I hadn't ever seen anything like it, and I don't feel that I had lived a sheltered life. I remember those French postcards over in Europe, a little larger than baseball cards, with photos of a man and a woman going at it. These French postcards were quite a hit with the GIs. The ones that I had seen, though, weren't a frantic ménage a trois. I'll leave the Ice Queen to her sex life; I just wanted to get her damn list and get out of there.

Hiromi cracked the first safe as easily as before. The same items were still there—the papers, the bomb drawings and the cash. No list, however. We put everything back and closed the safe and wandered up to the third floor where the blueprints told us that second safe was.

The ballroom was a dandy. If the Ice Queen ever ran out of money, she could start an exclusive nightclub up on her third floor. It was big enough, it had a dance floor, it had a restroom, it even had that back room where the booze could be stored.

"Quiet now," Hiromi said as she put her ear to the safe and started the slow turning of the dial listening for the cylinders to click into place. Her eyes were still, practically glazing over, as she forced her senses to focus on two things: the sound of the cylinders and the feel from her finger tips. I watched her and was awed by her concentration. I don't think that I could concentrate on *anything* as intensely as Hiromi did on that safe. While she was listening for cylinders to click in, I was thinking about the Dodgers. The Dodgers had lost to the St. Louis Cardinals the day before. Our record was still the best in the National League; we were four games ahead of the New York Giants with just twelve games to play. A shoo-in for sure.

In a minute, the safe was open. It was a larger safe, probably twice as big as the one downstairs and that one was big. Inside the safe there was a larger pile of papers than downstairs. On top of the pile was a large brown envelope. This had to be the list. In seconds we could get the hell out of here. I reached in and pulled out the envelope, opened its metal clasps and pulled out the contents. Inside was no list; instead, there were eight-by-ten black-and-white photographs.

"Oh-oh," I said, looking at the first one. It was the Ice Queen having sex with a middle-aged man. Only one guy this time. His face had been facing the camera and it was contorted in sex, ready to make that last plunge that he imagined would shoot the Ice Queen to the Moon.

Hiromi looked at the picture. Instead of turning away, she *studied* it. "I wonder where camera was?" she asked. Sometimes Hiromi skipped prepositions and verbs, but I always understood her. Sometimes I felt like she was talking in shorthand. There were quite a few people that I knew who could've taken lessons from Hiromi and used fewer words. "The picture not taken from bathroom where we were. Camera must been on other side of bed. How could that be? I didn't see any camera when she was with the Koreans. Was camera in wall?"

"Dunno," I said. It didn't make any difference to me that the Ice Queen took some homey snapshots. I just wanted her list of Reds.

The face of the man in the photo was vaguely familiar, but I couldn't place it. Actually, it wasn't so much of the face that was familiar, but the hair, or lack of. The man was bald on the top with long gray hair on the sides.

I looked at the next picture. This picture featured a different man with the Ice Queen. Same activity, different guy, and not surprisingly, the same contortion on the face. This guy didn't look good in the flesh. He would have looked far better with a three-piece suit on to cover his rolls of fat and the matted hair on his back. It looked like his hair was sweating. Clearly, the Ice Queen couldn't have been having sex with this guy for fun; he was instead the subject matter of a photo shoot.

I leafed through about ten more pictures. Each one featured the same activity but a different guy. About three or four of the guys seemed familiar somehow. One guy seemed *really* familiar, but I couldn't place him. He was probably in his late forties and had a big handlebar moustache that had been waxed so much that it was probably stiffer than than a pencil. I handed the photo to Hiromi and asked, "Do you recognize this guy?"

"Mr. Walrus?" Hiromi said, giggling. As usual, she held her hand over her mouth to hide the giggle; some Brooklyn girls I knew would just throw their head back and give a big old horselaugh. "No, I don't recognize him."

Still, I had seen his face someplace. I hadn't seen it contorted as it was in the picture, but the handlebar moustache was like a signature.

There were about thirty pictures in all. I leafed through some more. There were some different sexual permutations, but there was one thing that was consistent. In each photo, you could clearly see the face of the guy that was the Ice Queen's *cock du jour*. These weren't Frenchy postcards meant to titillate. These pictures were clearly pictures catching somebody in the saddle that shouldn't have been riding that horse. I knew this type of photo. I had tried to get them in my year as a private investigator. It wasn't easy. My photos were usually taken through a window from a fire escape. The quality of the Ice Queen's pictures was far superior to the quality of even my best shots. My pictures were grainy and blurry, these pictures were tack sharp. If I cared to, I could count the number of sweat beads on a guy's face. Great quality they should be—the Ice Queen performed on a well-lit *stage*.

"Oh-oh," I said again. The picture that I was looking at was of a guy that I did *clearly* recognize. No handlebar moustache was necessary to tease my memory. The face was enough. It was a square face, a block that looked like it was going to explode like a hand grenade. This guy had thin hair on top and a hairy body that covered the Ice Queen like a quilt. This guy was intense, he was strong and each of his thrusts must have felt like a punch. It was none other than my newest best friend, Tailgunner Joe.

Joe looked like a bull in a China shop when he was fully dressed; buck naked he looked like a huge gnarled fist with a pecker. This picture would not play well with the Bible Belt fans who were lapping up the congressional hearings of the McCarthy Committee on their new TVs.

I turned to the next picture. Another one of Tailgunner Joe. This photo was taken from the same angle. The only saving grace about this photo was that Joe's face wasn't fully pointed at the camera as in the other picture. This one showed his face from the nose up to the top of his head; the lower half of his face was buried in the Ice Queen's muff. Joe's ass stuck up behind him like a hairy mountain. Not very flattering, no, not very flattering at all.

Thoughts ran through my mind. Had the Ice Queen been blackmailing Tailgunner Joe? Did he know about these pictures? He must not have known about these—otherwise, why wouldn't he tell me to retrieve them and their negatives and forget about the silly Commie list. Or, was the list that Joe wanted *not* a list of Commies, but a list of *customers* of the Ice Queen?

"We should try to find the negatives," I told Hiromi, "but first let's take photos of these photos." I didn't want to just steal these photos. Without the negatives, stealing these photos would only alarm the Ice Queen and whatever organization she had behind her in this scam. I didn't want to do that.

The Ice Queen's operation was big business. This business had 'extortion' written all over it. Someplace lurking around it—or fully in it—had to be the mob. I didn't need that type of attention. I did, however, want a copy of the pictures. I didn't need the pictures because some wife wanted the goods on her strayed husband and was willing to pay me big bucks to nail his ass. I didn't know the reason I wanted the pictures, but I figured it was better to have copies than not.

Hiromi placed each photo down on the floor and I inched along taking a photo of each one. She stacked them in the same order that we had found them. We would place them back in the safe in the same manner.

Hiromi reached into the safe and pulled out another envelope. "What about these?"

I had to look at those too. Who knows who might pop up next in the Ice Queen's photo album? I opened the clasp and pulled the pictures out.

"Oh-oh," I said for the third time since looking at the pictures. The Ice Queen was not showing any part of her private anatomy. In fact, the Ice Queen wasn't in the picture at all. The people in these pictures had their clothes on. The first picture was of Hiromi and me walking across the Ice Queen's bedroom.

There was another shot of me leaning over the football field-sized bed to look at the mirror bolted to the ceiling. Nice profile, idiot. The last photo was of the two Korean guys boffing the Ice Queen. Way in the background peering out of a slightly opened door, there were two shadows of faces. The upper one, I might guess, was me. The lower one was Hiromi. Her eyes were as round as golf balls. The photographer must have been in place for when the Ice Queen brought the Koreans back. Lo and behold, Hiromi and I walk into the bedroom. We weren't part of the script, but the photog did what he does best—he took pictures. Imagine the Ice Queen's surprise when she reviewed the photos of the latest nominees to the Ice Queen Extortion Club, and she spotted two uninvited spectators.

I handed the photos to Hiromi. Lines creased on her forehead as she deciphered the photos. Her mouth formed an "o." The lines on her forehead then evaporated and I could tell that we were both struck with the same idea at the same time. We needed to take these pictures with us *and* find the negatives.

We trotted back to the Ice Queen's bedroom. "Over there," I said, pointing at the large painting above the head of the bed. "That's the angle from which the camera took the pictures."

"Do you think somebody is back there now?" Hiromi whispered.

"We're about to find out."

We stared at the painting. It was an oil painting of a jungle of flowers, lots of colors and lots of swirls. We were looking for a spot that would be smaller than a dime where a lens might look out. I hopped up on the bed to get a better look. Was I staring right into the lens of a camera right now? It was almost impossible to tell. In the shadow of a flower was a dark area that didn't quite match. That could be the spy hole.

I tried to lift the painting off the wall. It wouldn't budge. I looked at the corners. This painting wasn't just hanging by a nail; unlike the Picasso or the Bosch it was bolted to the wall.

"There's a hidey-hole behind this wall," I said to Hiromi. "We might be able to get to it from another room."

We left the Ice Queen's bedroom and turned left. The hallway ended about where the bedroom ended. There were no doors. We tapped around the wall to try to find a secret entrance. There was none.

"Let's try upstairs," Hiromi said. "Maybe they come down through a ladder?"

We were back in the third-story ballroom. Both of us had broken into a sweat, our clothes sticking to our skins. On the side of the ballroom that would have been directly over the Ice Queen's bedroom, we saw a closet door. I opened it, ready for anything to pop out, including a photographer. It was a large walk-in closet that also served as a darkroom. As a guy who knows about darkrooms, I knew that this one was well equipped. There was a Zeig photo enlarger that only the best fashion photographers would have. In the middle of the floor was a trap door. To open it, all I had to do was pull the ring up, which I did. I didn't peer down into the hole right away—who knows what was down there waiting for my mug to show itself? We listened. We didn't hear a thing, no breathing, no nothing.

Hiromi found the light switch for the darkroom, turned it on and the room was bathed in red. This wasn't Commie red, just photographic developing red. I looked down the hole in the floor. It was empty. A ladder was attached to one wall and I climbed down. I found a little panel in the wall that slid to the side; light was shining through a small hole. I peeked through the hole and, sure enough, it was a ringside seat located just above the Ice Queen's performance bed. The hole was covered with glass and it was big enough for the photographer to have maneuvered the lens to get shots at all four corners of that huge bed. Tacked on the wall from floor to ceiling were empty cardboard egg cartons. Those egg cartons would muffle the shutter snaps of a 35-millimeter camera, though seeing the faces of those guys caught between the Ice Queen's legs the egg cartons might not have been necessary. You probably could have rung a bell, and they would have thought it was heavenly chimes.

I climbed back up the ladder. Hiromi had been searching the darkroom for negatives.

"There are no negatives here," she said. "They must be hidden someplace else."

"Well, the photos of you and me aren't incriminating," I said.

"Incrimin…?" Hiromi asked. Except for missing a few prepositions every once in a while, Hiromi spoke good English with melodious accent, but her vocabulary sometimes ran into blanks.

"In the pictures, we aren't doing anything that's illegal. Sure, we got in here illegally, but nobody knows that from the pictures. We *could* have been guests and were just looking around this marvelous mansion. The other photos, however, could ruin people."

51

My concern wasn't about getting nailed for breaking and entering. The real concern was that we were now known to the Ice Queen. She didn't have our *names*, I didn't think, but she did have our faces. With an extortion racket she was running—most likely joined at the hip with the mob—it wasn't good to have them know our faces. Know the face, eventually know the names. If we had found the negatives, we could have taken them with the prints and perhaps slipped into anonymity.

"Let's go back to safe where pictures were," Hiromi said. "I think there was another door at the *back* of the safe. Maybe a safe within a safe. Maybe the negatives are in the back of the safe, not in the darkroom."

Back at the safe, she asked me to hold her up so that she could reach into the back portions of the safe. The safe was about five feet off the ground and she needed more height to reach in toward the very back of the safe.

She had her lock pick in her hand. I put my hands around her waist. Her waist was so narrow that the fingers of my right hand practically touched those of my left hand. How could anybody have a waist that small and still eat anything? It must be all that fish and rice she cooks up in the kitchen. Hiromi reached into the safe, her arm disappearing in it all the way to her shoulder.

"I feel something," she said. "Can you push me up a little more?"

I inched her up. She stretched further into the safe, grunted lightly, and reached further inside.

"More," she said, "a little higher." I inched her up some more. Was this going to be a case of Alice dropping through the rabbit hole? I held her in this position for almost five minutes. Even though she couldn't have weighed much more than a hundred pounds and her waist was next to nothing, it was still holding a hundred pounds without respite. I was sweating like a bastard. I could feel Hiromi's shirt under my hands get slippery wet as if it had been dipped in a pond.

"I got it," she said. "It is a safe inside a safe. This one opens with key. I had to 'crack' it."

I didn't want to correct her on American slang. I think 'cracking' only applied to combination locks on safes. The key safes were *picked*, not cracked. I would explain it to her some time later.

Her face was a sheen of sweat. "The inside safe is open," she said. "You can pull out the stuff. My arms aren't long enough."

I reached in. There were a bunch of business size envelopes. I pulled out a handful and opened the first one. It was an English passport. I looked at the picture inside. It was the Ice Queen but with a different name than Arabella Van Dyck. I opened another envelope. Another passport, this one from the Netherlands. The picture inside was the same as the passport from England, but the passport had yet another name. The last envelope had a passport from Korea. Still another name. Not too many white folks had a Korean passport—in this version she must have built up a character that was from a missionary family. This lady was ready for making an exit, she just didn't know to where. Or when.

"No negatives," I said.

Just as I had said the word 'negatives' the phone rang. We froze. The phone rang again, twice. Rafael was giving us the warning.

We carefully put the pictures and the passports back into the safe. She closed the safe door to a snap. She then turned the combination lock to the same number it had been on when she first started to crack it. We grabbed our stuff and ran toward the back stairs. The lock on the door that Hiromi had to pick two days before was still picked—the door opened. We flew down the stairs as if we were on a sled.

We didn't hear anything coming from the front door. We quietly opened the back door. Nobody was out there waiting for us.

We walked to the gate by the alley. Nobody was waiting there for us either.

We walked down the alley and over to the Ford. We were drenched in sweat. The day was warm—not warm enough to make us sweat like this—but the stress of breaking and entering ramped up those sweat glands like we were playing basketball in a sauna. To push those sweat glands further, the Ice Queen hadn't added this new cool conditioned air yet to her home.

Rafael was waiting for us when we got to the Ford. We were sweaty wrecks, he looked relaxed, cool and happy. Ah, the job of a lookout.

"She came from Third Avenue this time," Rafael said. "Nobody was with her and she just strolled down the street to her house. Why are you so sweaty?"

I laughed.

As we drove back to Brooklyn I didn't say much. I was thinking. This whole Ice Queen business turned out to be a lot more than just getting a list of Commies. The photos were strictly for extortion or blackmail, neither one was very nice. While the Ice Queen was the honeypot, I would bet dollars to donuts that the organization behind her was pretty slick. I'd bet some more dollars to donuts that there were some pretty nasty muscle boys that the Ice Queen could send out to smash faces for those deserving it. We *deserved* it—after all we broke into her lair—now it was my job to make us transparent.

The picture of somebody's dick in the wrong place was where I handed things off, usually to a lawyer that the wife had hired. That's what I was going to do this evening—hand it off. I was going to dump this back into my pal Nick's lap. I'd show him the photo of his boss, Tailgunner Joe, and tell Nick that in my opinion the only thing red about the Ice Queen was her pubic hair and Joe's dick.

8

Wednesday, September 19, 1951

I sat across the kitchen table from my boyhood pal—and now legman for Tailgunner Joe—Nick Salzano.

He had phoned me shortly after Hiromi and I had returned to my house. Without even listening to what I had to say, he told me he'd be at my house at five this afternoon.

I had most of the day to just hang around the house. The first thing I did was make photos of the compromising photos that the Ice Queen had had taken, including the ones of Tailgunner Joe. I already had photos of the bomb drawings.

Then I sat around the living room, waiting. I listened to the Dodgers game against the St. Louis Cardinals. Listening to the game wasn't fun for me. Even the Schaefer's beers that I nursed while listening didn't turn my mood. There was too much going on in my mind. I wondered if this mood was like those stressed out businessmen who would pop into the ballpark to capture a sliver of their youth only to find the gnarly adult inside themselves blocking out the fun.

Preacher Roe, our ace, won his twenty-first game against just two losses. The victory was even more memorable for Preacher; his neighbors from the Ozarks had gone to the game and presented him with a new Cadillac. Our record was 91-52, just three and a half games ahead of the Giants.

Hiromi painted the afternoon away upstairs in the vacant room that she used as a temporary studio now that the two other boarders had graduated and moved back to their home countries.

I'd bet that she was about as satisfied with her painting as I was with the Dodger game. The Ice Queen's tentacles had reached out and touched us even though those tentacles didn't sense what they had touched.

I had told Hiromi I didn't want her around the house when Nick Salzano came by at five o'clock. While the Ice Queen's tentacles brushed up against Hiromi, I didn't want the tentacles of Tailgunner Joe to slither up her backside. It would be better that Nick never met my boarder. I sent Hiromi with two quarters—like a child—to the movies with one of her girlfriends.

Hiromi loved horror and science-fiction movies. There was one playing at the Loew's and it would be a good way for her to avoid Nick and to shake off the Ice Queen's tentacles. She was probably the only person in the world who thoroughly enjoyed *Bela Lugosi Meets A Brooklyn Gorilla.* I had seen the movie one day when the Dodgers were rained out and I didn't want to drink away the afternoon. Bela looked pretty awful and was probably fast approaching the time when his drug addiction would fully take over. His role was the mad Doctor Zorka, who injected an American crooner with a serum that transformed him into an ape. Sitting there in the dark theatre, there were more laughing than screaming. Hiromi, however, would do just what the director wanted her to do—she would scream. She loved Bela, junkie or not.

The movie I sent her to was, I think, of higher quality. *The Lost Continent,* starring Cesar Romero, was about an atomic powered rocket that disappeared over the South Pacific. An expedition to recover it landed on an unexplored jungle island filled with bloodthirsty dinosaurs. Good stuff to make Hiromi forget about the Ice Queen and all those faces that were caught grunting while the camera shutters were wildly snapping.

Nick arrived a little after five. I opened up a Schaefer's beer for both of us and we slugged down the first half of the bottle just like the good old days.

"So, wat'cha got for me?" Nick asked, getting right to business without any small talk about the Dodgers.

I didn't have the list that Nick wanted, but I did have some disturbing stuff. "Three things," I said. There was actually ten things, but there were *three* groupings in case Nick kept count. I didn't know in which order I was going to show the seven snaps of the Korean bomb drawings, the two shots of Tailgunner Joe in full firing mode and the two Koreans playing pin cushion with the Ice Queen. The photos of those grunting faces I kept in the darkroom. I didn't exactly know why I did that; for the moment I blamed my paranoia.

"There were no lists that I could find," I said. "I broke into her house twice. There are two safes and I got into both."

"You cracked *two* safes?" Nick asked surprised.

I nodded. I did not implicate Hiromi in any way.

"No list? You couldn't find the list and you busted into two safes?" Nick said, with a little bit more edge to his voice than I had expected.

I shrugged.

"So, what are the three things that you think would interest me, if you don't have the list?" Nick asked.

From a large envelope, I pulled the seven photos of what I thought were sketches of a bomb and handed them to Nick.

"What's this?" Nick asked, "I can't read that shit. Is it Chinese?"

"I think it's Korean," I said, again not implicating Hiromi. "That looks like the drawings of a bomb to me."

"Who gives a shit about this?" Nick said.

"Well, we're at war with the Koreans, aren't we?"

"It's a *conflict*. Hell, officially it's labeled a *police action*. That's like cops going into the Bronx. *Police action,*" Nick said.

"It has never been declared a war. Hell, it's chinks going against chinks. Who gives a fuck what they do? We're there because of one fucking reason—the United Nations. There is no Hitler in Korea, there is no Mussolini in Korea—nobody even knows the name of their dictator. This is just a bunch of chinks who want to rule other chinks. These guys don't want to take over the world, they just want to take over their neighbor and they're the same chinks anyway. You're not hearing that the North Koreans want to take over Thailand or Japan or Hawaii or Rhode Island for Christ sakes. They just want the rest of Korea. If it wasn't for the United Nations, we woulda let them take it, and it wouldn't even have made an inch in the newspapers. End of story."

"Aren't the North Koreans Communists?"

"Different kind of Commies," Nick said. "The North Koreans are *chink* Commies. Nobody here in the U.S. of A will listen to them except other chinks, and who gives a fuck what they think? I'm with the McCarthy Committee, which says, get the fucking *Reds* outa this country—the *Russkie* types of Reds. We want guys like Orson Welles."

"Orson Welles?"

"Yeah, he's a Commie right down to his toenails. He was a speaker for *The First Conference on American-Soviet Co-operation* in 1944—you can't get much more Commie than that."

"Sounds innocent to me," I said.

"That's just the point—all their stuff *sounds* innocent, but when you scrape away the bullshit, it's Commies plotting to change our way of life. If you think Welles sounded innocent, how about Little Caesar himself—Edward G. Robinson? He was on the *faculty* on *School for Democracy*, another Commie front. We were hoping that guys like that would be on the Ice Queen's list, not some drawings of a bomb that was probably already printed in *The Daily Worker*."

"What are you going to do with these pictures of the bombs?" I asked.

"I don't know. I'll take them, I guess I'll pass them along, but if I pass them along to the State Department, I'd just be passing them along to some more Commies. You should give them to your old boss Wild Bill. He'd be more interested in this stuff than we would. What else you got?"

That was the second time somebody had recommended that I give the bomb drawings to Wild Bill Donovan. But there was a problem with the Wild Bill recommendation. "They retired Wild Bill," I said. "He's not in the CIA anymore. He's just a lawyer."

"So give them to one of your other spook friends," Nick said. "They love chasing their tails."

From the same large envelope, I pulled out a picture of Tailgunner Joe on top of the Ice Queen and handed it to Nick.

He stared at it for about ten seconds.

"Where'd you get this?" he asked. His eyes burrowed into mine. This was not the buddy-buddy look of years gone by.

"Same place as those Korean drawings—the Ice Queen's safe. I tried to find the negatives, but couldn't. I searched everyplace, including her darkroom."

"Who else has seen this?" Nick asked in a tone that sounded more like it was an interrogation question.

"I can't speak for the Ice Queen, but nobody but me has seen it," I lied.

I then pulled out of the envelope the other picture of Joe, this one with his face in the Ice Queen's crotch.

"That *dumb fuck!*" Nick said. "Jesus H. Christ on a stick!" Nick stood up and walked over to the counter in the kitchen. He opened up a cabinet, looked inside and slammed it shut. He looked in the next cabinet, and slammed it shut. "You got anything stronger than this beer?" he asked.

I got up and went to the lower cabinet and pulled out a bottle of Scotch. I got him a glass, and he poured an inch of Scotch into it. He drained it faster than I could have thrown it down the sink. He poured another.

"So, what's the matter?" I asked. "Joe isn't married, is he? No divorce action here."

"Jake, you got a one-track mind on fucking and divorce. Yeah, Joe's not married, but that's not the problem with that picture." Nick poured a couple more inches into the glass. "Joe's a great guy, really a great guy, but he has one problem—he drinks like a fish—and that's probably gonna kill him. He does stupid things when he's been drinking too much. This Ice Queen is important to us—she's got the list that could keep us busy into the next century. With Joe dipping his wick into her, my friend, he could compromise himself. You don't have to worry about the press with this shit—hell, everybody knows that their congressmen and senators are lushes and pussy chasers. But this could really hurt the McCarthy Committee. This could derail everything we're working on. Can you imagine if Hoover got a hold of this stuff? He'd *own* Joe, lock stock and barrel." And cock, I thought of saying, but Nick was pretty fired up already.

"I thought they were on the same side, Joe and Hoover?" I asked.

Nick rolled his eyes. "In public they are on the same side—they're both against Communism—but Hoover has only one side. *His*. He would love to put Joe on strings and make him his personal puppet. And if you haven't figured it out after meeting him, Joe ain't a puppet guy."

Nick drained the two inches of Scotch.

"You're really into this Commie crap, aren't you Nick? Christ, you're more of a fanatic than Joe," I said.

"Jake, if you could see the stuff I've seen, you'd really be into it too," Nick said. "You were fighting Nazis—it was easy to fight them, they had *Hitler* for Christsakes. A madman. We could *look* at Nazis and clearly identify them. They wore black leather coats, they wore swastikas, they looked like...well...Nazis. Well, our bad guys look like us. They are us. They're all over the State Department. They're making movies. They're in labor unions.

They're fucking everywhere. I tell you that they want to change our country as much as the Nazis did except these people are our own goddamned people. This is like a silent revolution; if we want to keep what we've got we've got to fight them just as hard as you fought the Nazis."

There was no soapbox needed for Nick; I heard him loud and clear. He and Tailgunner Joe would rid the United States of Commies, and probably sweep the Ice Queen in with all the rest of them.

"There's more," I said, "I got some more pictures."

"More! Ain't that enough? What else you got in that envelope, for Christsakes?"

I slipped the last picture out of the envelope. It was of the two Koreans and the Ice Queen.

"Great!" Nick said in mock revelry, "She fucks *chinks* too! Jesus, I wonder if Joe knew that when he got his dick polished? That would just kill him."

Nick got up again from the table and walked to the sink. He looked out of the window into my small backyard.

"What else is in those safes?" he asked.

"More pictures of the Ice Queen with different guys. I didn't know who they were," I said. I didn't tell him about the photos that I took of the Ice Queen's photos. "There was also about fifty thousand in cash in one of the safes and three passports for the Ice Queen to different countries in another safe."

"The passports real?"

"I couldn't tell. They were issued from the Netherlands, England and Korea. I don't even know what their passports look like. She did have, however, a different name in each passport. Same picture, different names."

"One from Russia?" Nick asked hopefully.

"Nope."

"If there was one from Russia it would be enough to nab her. We could just haul her off the street and confiscate everything in her house."

"But, the negatives might be someplace else," I said.

Nick looked out into the yard some more.

"You need to go back in," Nick said. "It's a big place she's got. Those negatives are probably hidden someplace in that house. You just gotta look closer. You gotta go back in."

"That's it for me, Nick," I said. "One, the Ice Queen knows I've been inside her house; two, the negatives are probably hidden someplace else; three and most importantly, the degree of danger has jumped off the charts. That's it for me, pal."

"What the fuck does that mean?"

"*My* job is done, Nick," I said. "I went in there to find the so-called list and couldn't find it. What I did find is on the table. That's the end of the job for me."

"Bull*shit.* The end of the job is when I say it's the end, not you," Nick said. He was starting to sound like my old drill sergeant.

I stood up. "Nick, I quit. I've done what you've wanted. This is a lot bigger than just going in and swiping some list of fake Commies," I said. I was tired of this Commie stuff. Even thinking about chasing guys like Orson Welles and Edward G. Robinson made me long for a drizzly night on a fire escape trying to get a snapshot of a husband boffing some bimbo. After Orson Welles and Edward G. Robinson, who's next—a doped out Bela Lugosi?

I didn't offer to give him his two grand back. I had worked for that. I had done what they wanted—got into the Ice Queen's lair. It was just my bad luck not to find a list but to find pictures of her fucking the daylights out of Nick's boss.

"You know that Joe is really connected with money," Nick said. "He's got rich guys all over this country giving him big chunks of money to get after those Commies. I could get you more. How about *ten grand* to go in and get the negatives *and* the list?"

"You'll have to get somebody else, Nick. I'm not going back in there again. I'm going back to my normal work—chasing husbands. That's my niche, that's what I do, this stuff you're asking isn't up my alley."

"The *great* Red Chaser," Nick said with sarcasm that was thick enough to grease the wheels of a train, "you're just a home wrecker, a *great* home wrecker. A guy goes and gets a little off the side and you're there snapping away, fucking up his life. This has national importance, this has international significance, this is *our nation* we're talking about, pal, and you want to go off and chase some poor schmuck who gets a blowjob every once in a while."

Nick grabbed the photos, stuffed them back into the envelope and walked to the back door. He stopped and turned, "You're a piece of shit, Jake. When I tell Joe about how you refused to help, he'll be pissed, he'll explode, he'll erupt. Don't be surprised if he doesn't sic J. Edgar's boys on you." He turned, walked through the back door and slammed it hard.

It's not that I just gone down to the store and bought a bottle of ethics and drank it and now my new ethics wouldn't allow me to continue my work with Tailgunner Joe. Hell, ethics had nothing to do with it. I just felt that I had stumbled on to something that was much bigger than the league I wanted to play in. I had to figure that the mob was involved in this up to their eyeballs. Joe McCarthy or no, messing with a mob operation was an invitation to take a swim in the East River wearing a cement life preserver.

That the Ice Queen was involved with the Koreans somehow, didn't bother me. I wasn't bothered because she was most likely consorting with our enemy. Nick was right; this enemy, the North Koreans, ain't the Nazis. And, whoever the leader of North Korea is, he ain't Adolf Hitler. Nobody gives a shit about this war. It's Harry Truman's war. It's the United Nations' war. Nobody gives a shit except those poor folks who have a son sent over there. There were no great sacrifices being made here on the home front as there were during the Big One. I could buy gas. I could buy butter. I could buy fancy clothes. There were no shortages. So, the Korean connection wasn't the thing that really bothered me. I was more concerned about the extortion racket that the Ice Queen had going.

She had Tailgunner Joe in her muff. And, the other guys in the pictures looked all like big shots. No truck drivers or sewer workers or train conductors or longshoremen there. She either owned those guys, or would own something of theirs pretty soon. That sounded like mob all the way.

All I wanted out of life was to do my made-up job, private detective, and go to Dodger games and drink beer and maybe take Hiromi to a horror movie every once in a while. I wasn't trying to save anybody, or trying to save this country for that matter—mainly because I didn't think it needed saving. I had all the money I would ever need thanks to World War II; I was just trying to live the American dream and occasionally pay to the tax man as little money as I could.

9

Wednesday, September 19, 1951

After Nick left, I grabbed a Schaefer's from the refrigerator and sat on the top step out front.

I hoped that the Ice Queen business was over. It was over for me with Tailgunner Joe and Nick, that was for sure. If I was lucky it would be over for the Ice Queen. Sure, she had black-and-white evidence that two burglars—one a Japanese woman and the other an Irish guy—had come into her house. But, *nothing* was missing. All that cash that was in the first safe, those fake passports, the Picassos, the Hieronymus Bosch, all that stuff was still there. For all the Ice Queen knew, we had never got into her safes. She had photos of Hiromi and me gaping at her Korean sex carnival, but she didn't know who we were. She didn't know our names; she didn't know where we lived. We didn't leave any calling cards. After realizing that a Jap and an Irish guy had broken into her house, I hoped the most extreme thing that she would do was add an alarm system.

This was the first time where I had used Hiromi where I thought there could be dangerous repercussions. Each time I had used her before it had been easy in-and-out stuff without any complications. It was something to put myself at risk; it was altogether another thing to put Hiromi at risk.

I recalled her face when I had sent her away to the movies. It was a face of stress, at least as much as I can recognize in an Oriental. She probably looked like that quite a few times during the Internment. Then I recalled her face the one time that I had taken her to a Dodgers game.

Hiromi's reaction of awe couldn't have been greater than if she had stepped into St. Peter's Basilica. We had just entered Ebbets Field, where the Brooklyn Dodgers called home.

"This is for *baseball*?" Hiromi had asked me as we entered the rotunda, her arm outstretched pointing to the ceiling.

I had nodded with a smile. Every time I walked through the main entrance of Ebbets Field, I felt good. The entrance made everybody feel good. After pushing through the turnstiles, there was a huge rotunda built of Italian marble. It was probably four stories high. It always reminded me of a grand European train station. Inside the rotunda, we just didn't walk on plain old cement—we walked on *tile*. Once inside the ballpark, we'd see grass as green as God could grow it. I'd had a stopover in Ireland during the war, and I thought that the grass there had to be the greenest it could possibly be—except for the grass at Ebbets Field in the spring of the year.

Walking to our seats, I wondered if Hiromi could love the smells of fresh-cut grass and cigars and Nathan's hot dogs and beer as much as I did. Probably not; you had to be born to it. If I was a businessman, I would try to figure out how to put that ballpark fragrance into a bottle. Heck, thousands would buy it, not as perfume that you'd dab on, but as something to sniff during the long winter months when it seemed that baseball season was still an ice age away.

Ebbets Field was a baseball stadium with an attitude. Yankee Stadium could hold about twice as many fans; some called our ballpark a bandbox. The rightfield wall, which abutted Bedford Avenue, ran like a wild stream with a sharp bend here and a crazy bend there, driving most visiting outfielders nuts. Above the wall was the Abe Stark sign: *Hit sign, win suit*. That sign had been as much of a fixture of Ebbets Field as the wall had been. Our rightfielder, Carl Furillo, played that wall like a magician— routinely fielding a quirky ricochet off the wall and turning a double into a single. Abe should have given Furillo a suit just for the way he played the wall.

What made Ebbets special were the fans. Men, women or kids, it didn't matter, they weren't just spectators—they were part of the show. Heck, sometimes it was more interesting watching the fans than watching the game. We had Hilda Chester to help cheer us on. Hilda had been going to Dodger games long before I was born. She'd sit in the centerfield bleachers with her cowbell and whack that thing until the Dodgers came home with more runs, then she'd whack it some more. When I was a kid, she used a frying pan and a ladle. The cow bell worked better. Hilda was getting a little long in the tooth, gray hair, gnarly hands that were swollen and blue, but this year, she would clang that bell to another Dodger pennant.

Then there was the guy that sat in section six, row three, seat thirteen. Hiromi noticed him before I saw him.

"What's he doing?" She asked.

He looked like a legit guy, an executive even. He sat behind a drainpipe that blocked part of his view. He did two things during a game: he smoked nonstop, lighting one cig off of another, and he'd bang that drainpipe with a rolled up newspaper. Both of those things he did all game long. It was as if he was beating on a tom-tom and the smoke would somehow summon the spirits to help get the Dodgers a win.

"I don't know," I said. How do you describe maniacs? "Maybe he thinks it helps the Dodgers win."

Hiromi giggled, holding her hand over her mouth. Very polite. I thought for sure she'd say, "Crazy Americans," but these Japanese have too much respect.

We had our own music, but there was no way I could explain it to Hiromi. Our music was created by a group of guys that called themselves the Sym-Phony. They were always in

Section 8. There were enough former GIs that knew what a section eight was—crazy—so they called the section the Loco Section. There were about six to ten guys in the Sym-Phony, depending on the game. They had a bass drum, cymbals, trumpet, sax, sometimes a trombone.

They'd play ditties, they'd make funny sounds with their instruments, they'd play *Take me out to the ballgame* one inning and then when an opposing pitcher would be taken out *Who's sorry now*. My favorite was always reserved for the umps, *Three Blind Mice*. There were four umps, of course, but the song still worked, and besides, who was counting?

If I wanted to let a player know how I felt about him, I'd just yell. He'd hear me. When an opposing star player would strike out, I could hear one line coming from a lot of different mouths around me: "Eacha heart out, ya bum." Sometimes it would just be our version of an abbreviation, "Ya bum ya."

I tried to get Hiromi to yell, "Ya bum ya." She tried it in a sing-song way. Then she sang, "Ya bum ya ya bum ya bum ya." A few folks looked her way clearly wondering what the fuck was *that*? I laughed; Hiromi laughed.

After I explained what 'Ya bum ya' meant, particularly the 'bum' part, she didn't yell it again. Yep, way too much respect, these Japanese have.

This was a great time to be a Dodger fan. When I was growing up in the 1930s, it was Yankee time. *They* had Babe Ruth. *They* had Lou Gehrig. The Dodgers just had finishes in the second division of the National League. We got a little better in the 1940s—winning the pennant in 1947 and 1949—but I was in Berlin and other shelled cities in Eastern Europe. It was tough to keep up on how the Dodgers were doing. In the 1950s, however, I knew that was going to be The Dodger Era.

Walter O'Malley was the owner of the Dodgers. Up until that season, Branch Rickey had been his partner and general manager. It wasn't a secret that Mr. O'Malley and Rickey didn't get along. O'Malley bought him out. Rickey's legacy was that he had gathered a bunch of stars that us fans knew would be Hall-of-Famers. Surely Duke Snider would make it to the Hall. Our three Negro players—Jackie Robinson, Roy Campanella and Don Newcombe—had the ability to make the Hall. By the time their careers were over there probably wouldn't be too much objection to letting Negroes into the Hall of Fame. Gil Hodges, Preacher Roe, Pee Wee Reese all might make the Hall. Rickey had brought them all in. These players were basically new to me—they had all arrived in the mid to late forties when I was over in Germany. I had a lot of catching up to do.

Dodgers baseball was what I loved. That was true for almost every man, woman and child in Brooklyn. I, however, had the unique opportunity where work wouldn't interfere with the Dodgers. Heck, everybody else in Brooklyn *had* to work, some had to work a second or even third job. Their enjoyment of the Dodgers was in snatches. Mine could be—and *should* be—full time. Now that the Ice Queen business was behind me, I wasn't going to lose my focus on what was most important to me, the Dodgers. I wouldn't even take any divorce cases until the season and the World Series was over. Heck, I should even go down to Vero Beach, Florida for spring training.

I walked back into the house to get another Schaefer's.

Yep, life was good. In fact, life was too good to screw up getting involved with politics. If I ever got involved with politics again I should whack myself on the side of my head.

10

Thursday, September 20, 1951

When I woke up, I realized I only had two things to do that day. Well, three, if I counted listening to the Dodgers game on the radio when they played the Cardinals in St. Louis.

The first thing involved, perhaps, the security of the United States. The second thing involved Hiromi.

The first thing was those bomb drawings. While the bomb drawings didn't bother Nick, they did indeed trouble me. The United States was at war with Korea, even if the government called it just a police action. I decided to take both Nick's and Dominic's advice: I would contact Wild Bill Donovan, whether he was retired from the CIA or not.

Wild Bill had retired to private law practice a little more than a year ago. He had retired right after he convinced President Harry Truman to sign the National Securities Act. That one signature by President Truman created a more formalized successor of the wartime Office of Strategic Services. It had created the permanent Central Intelligence Agency.

Actually, history will show that Wild Bill—and me—was out of a job shortly after the war. Sort of out of a job. Shortly after the war ended, I had heard rumors that Wild Bill's military and political rivals were concerned that Wild Bill was going to create a peacetime intelligence service from the foundation of the OSS. To us in the OSS, continuation made all the sense in the world. What, did all the world's bad guys go away after the war? To the politicos, however, they didn't want a Wild Bill to become a J.

Edgar Hoover of the spy world. If there was going to be a spy agency of some sorts, they would prefer to have somebody that they could control. With a nickname of Wild Bill, I guess these political idiots didn't think their chances were very good in controlling him.

So, six months after the war ended, President Harry Truman dismantled the OSS. When the OSS was shut down, we were in the midst of chasing down Nazi SS thugs. Our operation was quickly transferred—without missing a beat, or a paycheck for that matter—to the State and War Departments. Somewhere in that government labyrinth, we operated as so-called aides to the chief prosecutor of Nuremburg. *Nothing* changed for us in Germany when they officially closed down the OSS. We chased Nazis while Wild Bill took off his hat and waved us on. The politicos back home must have slept better thinking they had dismantled the spy bureaucracy. They thought wrong. A few years later Wild Bill convinced Truman that a permanent spy agency was necessary. Truman was convinced of two things: One, the United States needed a permanent spy agency and two, that Wild Bill wouldn't run it.

If the Korean drawings were fishy business, Wild Bill would know what to do with them. Even though he was retired from the government, he still had more sources in the intelligence services than any man alive.

I started off the letter writing, "Dear Major General Donovan." I then wrote three short paragraphs. In the first paragraph I told him that I ran across some documents that I thought he should see. In the second paragraph, I told him that I didn't get these documents in a manner that I would like to tell my mother. I had phrased it that way because I didn't really know who—if anybody—he would pass this along to. I sure didn't want to implicate myself in writing that this was a breaking and entering job. The last paragraph was that if he wanted more information to have somebody call to set up a meeting. However, he needed to tell me *who* was going to call. I sure as hell didn't want to implicate myself to a stranger. Wild Bill would love my paranoia. He would feel good that he had taught me good.

I called information to get his mailing address. I attached my handwritten letter to the seven photos of the Korean drawings and slipped them into a large envelope. I sealed it, placed enough stamps on it to get it to Mars and walked it to the post office. I would send it *Air Mail Special Delivery*. He might get it tomorrow or Monday at the latest.

I walked to the post office. I dropped my letter to Wild Bill into the *Special Delivery* mail slot, waited a few seconds and walked away.

Walking back from the post office, I saw Dominic sweeping the sidewalk in front of his candy store. I walked over to him, took the broom and started sweeping.

"I just sent those bomb drawings to Wild Bill," I said to Dominic. "Special delivery."

"That's good," he said. "That's the right thing to do. Who knows what that shit is all about anyways."

I took a couple of more quick sweeps at some imaginary dirt.

"I need to ask you a favor," I said. I had thought again about possible ramifications of my break-ins at the Ice Queen's brownstone. She knew what Hiromi and I looked like, but I felt that she didn't know our names. My paranoia said different. So, I thought I'd get some help in the neighborhood.

"So, go ahead already, ask."

"Can your boys sorta keep an eye on my house for the next couple of weeks?"

Dominic looked strangely at me. No longer was this the friendly little Italian guy who ran the candy store. Dominic was, of course, connected to the mob. He wasn't a godfather or anything like that, but with his bookie joint in the basement of the candy store, he was connected. His 'boys', however, weren't mob hit men. They were guys—mostly relatives—who helped run the bookie joint. But, because they were in an illegal business, they did have the consistent awareness of seeing potential trouble. I just wanted their awareness to extend down the street to my house.

"You got some problems with the wrong type of people?" he asked.

"No, it's not what you think, Dominic."

"You ain't a gambler—I can't even get you to bet on the Dodgers—so you boffing the wrong woman?" he asked.

"Nah, it's nothing like that. It's a case I'm working on, and some goons might come looking for me. It's a little complicated; I'll tell you about it later."

"Has it got something to do with those chink bomb drawings?" he asked.

I nodded. The bomb drawings were part of it, of course, but that wouldn't be something that the mob would be involved with. They were too *American* to sell their country down the river. I was more worried about the extortion photos. That could be mob all the way; they did that stuff good.

"I can watch out for myself," I said, "but you never know. That's why I'm asking if you could sorta have your boys keep their eye out, let me know if there's anything suspicious going on."

Dominic took his broom back from me. If a stranger had asked him what I had asked, Dominic would act as dumb as that broom stick, but to me, I was neighborhood.

"Well, you know this neighborhood is one of the safest in Brooklyn. You know the coloreds or the spics won't try anything here. They know better. This neighborhood is crime free, *crime free* Jake. This doesn't have anything with…ah…my people?"

"I don't think so, Dominic, but I don't really know," I said.

"Well, if it's my people, I'd find out probably before you," he said, "then you and I would have to talk. If it's somebody else, then we've got no problems. Rest easy, Jake, I'll tell the boys to keep their eyes out on your place. No shit is gonna happen in my neighborhood."

I thanked Dominic and walked back to the house. When I walked this neighborhood, I didn't have to check my back in this neighborhood. Dominic and his boys would have it covered. I learned in Europe that being paranoid was a good trait to have, particularly if somebody was after you.

11

Thursday, September 20, 1951

The second thing I needed to do today was a lot trickier than mailing those bomb drawings to Wild Bill Donovan. This thing involved Hiromi. I had made the commitment to take Hiromi on what could be considered our first date to the famous Stork Club and she didn't know it.

If that wasn't enough, I had said that she was a Japanese heiress. She, of course, wasn't. She was the daughter of a locksmith.

Now let's toss a fluttering knuckleball to this whole situation. Neither Hiromi or I had clothes suitable for toney Stork Club.

I decided to start with the clothes first because I just wasn't comfortable in flat out asking Hiromi for a date. This sounds silly, of course. I've traveled the world, I've made a fortune, I've had my way with women, but Hiromi was different. I felt awkward. So, I took the chicken's way out; I'd sneak up on asking her by going to the clothes first.

I knew I didn't have a suit that was decent enough to walk through the doors of the Stork Club. I wore my suits hard on fire escapes and roof tops. Hiromi was an art student for Christ's sake so she didn't have decent nightclubbing clothes, let alone clothes that a Japanese heiress would wear.

I went up to Hiromi's room on the third floor. I hadn't been up there since I first showed her the room.

At that time, she had the choice of two vacant rooms.

She liked the one that faced the street. I told her, "This room leads to the attic, so occasionally—maybe once a year—I gotta come through your room to get to the attic."

She looked around the room. "How do you get up into the attic?" She asked. "No door."

I laughed. "Let me show you," I said.

The door to my attic was a bookcase. This was one of my rare home modeling projects and it dovetailed with my slight case of paranoia. When I took over the house from my parents, I had the grand idea of substituting a floor-to-ceiling wood bookcase for the attic door. A carpenter friend helped me with the mechanics. He had bolted the reinforced hinges and attached the bookcase as if it were a door. I thought it was pretty nifty. Remember, I had a shitload of cash and jewels that were my personal souvenirs for serving Uncle Sam. While I was steadfastly putting that stash into safe-deposit boxes or investments, my attic served as my temporary personal vault. Now the attic was basically empty. However, I had liked the idea so much, I did some other tricky things like that bookcase door around my house.

I walked over to the floor-to-ceiling bookcase against the wall. There were probably thirty or so old books on its shelves, some of them were my college text books. I reached under the third shelf, grabbed a small handle and pulled the bookshelf to me. It pivoted on hinges and voila, there was a door with a stairway leading upward.

Hiromi's round eyes got rounder as the open doorway revealed itself. She held her hands over her mouth in surprise.

"Follow me," I said. I led her up the stairs to the musty attic, which was big in floor space, but not very tall. At the apex, it was probably about six feet high and then it angled down toward the floor. I took her for a quick look at the attic to prove that there weren't bats or strange animals up there.

"If I rent this room, could I use the attic?" Hiromi asked, "I'm an artist—or at least trying to be—and it would be a wonderful little studio for me."

"Well, it's insulated, but it could get pretty hot here during the summer and cold in the winter," I said.

"That's okay."

Hiromi bought a couple of large fans and opened the windows at both ends of the room and turned up those fans as high as they would go. For a starving artist it worked.

I knocked on the door, but she might be up in her attic studio.

She opened the door. She looked at me with her face practically contorting into a question mark.

"Okay, girl," I said, "we need to take you on a special trip to the city. Fun time."

Hiromi looked at me like a dog would who's heard a distant sound, her head tilting a little to the side.

"What do you mean?" she said.

"Let's go, I'll show you. This isn't business. It's pleasure, no breaking and entering at all. You don't need to bring your tools. In fact, this is a bit of a celebration."

"Celebration?"

I nodded. "We aren't going back to the Ice Queen's brownstone," I said. "I quit that job."

Hiromi reacted like I told her that we were going to Coney Island.

That seemed to clinch it for Hiromi: no more Ice Queen. We got into the Ford and drove over the Brooklyn Bridge to Manhattan. Every time I drove over the bridge, I remembered a story about how the Brooklyn Bridge was built. I told Hiromi the story. The bridge was built just twenty years after the Civil War. Hiromi knew all about American history. After all, she had studied it when she was a girl in Internment in California. Heck, she probably knew more about American history than I did. But, she didn't know about the Brooklyn Bridge.

The bridge was built for wagons and horses and people, long before cars and trucks. It was the first suspension bridge built in this country, and they didn't quite know how much weight it should hold. So, they built it to support ten times more weight than they thought would be needed if the bridge was covered with wagons and horses. Now it's covered with cars and trucks. The Brooklyn Bridge should be considered the eighth wonder of the world. The ninth would be the domed stadium that the owner of the Dodgers, Walter O'Malley, was rumored to want to build in Brooklyn. Yeah, Brooklyn was a wonderful place to live.

I drove over to the Plaza Hotel on Fifth and 60th and gave the car keys to the valet. While it had been sprinkling rain on the drive, the raindrops were now a little bigger, but I had an umbrella. Hiromi and I practically skipped down the street under the umbrella.

"Where are we going?" Hiromi asked.

"You'll see," I said. I pulled her into Bergdorf Goodman. I was going to tell her that the site of this fancy store was where one of the richest men in the world had lived—Cornelius Vanderbilt with his 17-room penthouse apartment—but I didn't think the extension of her American education needed to cover fat-cat Americans. Still, the wealth of Vanderbilt dripped through Bergdorf's to where you could practically smell the money. No sir, no Bloomingdale's or Macy's for Hiromi and me, Bergdorf's was just the right ticket for what I had in mind.

I'm sure that this was the first time Hiromi had been in Bergdorf's, or any store in that price range. We meandered through the store, took an escalator up and ended at the expensive evening wear department. Blouses here could be had for fifty bucks, which was more than most folks made in a week.

I had never bought some clothes for a woman before. I had bought flowers and some boxed candy, but never clothing of any kind, let alone the best that Bergdorf could show us.

"We need some dress-up clothes," I whispered to Hiromi.

"I don't understand," Hiromi said.

I said, "It's all part of the job. Trust me."

I'm not sure if Hiromi trusted me, but she did seem to humor me. And, I could tell that she was really curious about what this crazy American was up to.

While Hiromi was in the dressing room trying on an outfit, I caught the saleslady's attention. Hiromi and I sure didn't *look* like Bergdorf clientele. We weren't uptown; we were *Brooklyn*. I pulled a roll of bills out of my pocket—all hundreds from the stash that Tailgunner Joe had given me—and peeled off five bills and handed it to the saleslady. That would give us all the credibility we needed in the hoity-toity regions of Manhattan. "When we reach that amount, tell me and I'll give you some more," I said.

All of a sudden, we didn't look like we were from Brooklyn anymore. She probably figured me for a mob guy. But, our money was as good as high society money. Hiromi got the royal treatment, as if the Japanese had won the war.

After she had tried on a couple of outfits, Hiromi came over to me. She whispered, "These dress-up clothes are too expensive. We should go now."

I told her that the fancy clothes were needed for a job that I needed her help on and that it was all on expenses.

"Expenses?" She asked.

"That means that somebody else is going to pay for it. It's all part of a job that I've got." Mr. Petty and Mr. Cash were paying for the clothes, of course, but I had the cash, a lot of it, so I figured it wouldn't hurt to spend like a big-shot for once in my life.

"What's the job?" she asked. Then she said, smiling. "This clearly is not going to be a breaking and entering thing."

"Nope, no breaking or entering," I said. "It's dinner, in the city, at a very fancy place."

That question mark curled up on her face again.

"Is this…is this," she stammered, "is this a *date*?"

"It's dinner at a fancy place," I said, "that's what it is. It's a *job*." That's how I told her about our first date. She seemed to be embarrassed about her question, and she seemed to accept that dinner at a fancy place was a *job*. At least I think she did.

For the better part of two hours, Hiromi paraded different outfits in front of me. The emerald green was my favorite; the dark blue was hers. The green dress had straps exposing her shoulders and accentuating her tidy bosom. Strangely, before the escape from the Ice Queen's brownstone I had never really considered Hiromi as a *woman*. I knew she was female all right—I'm no dummy—but a real live somewhat sensuous woman hadn't translated in my brain until we were walking down the alley after hightailing it away from the Ice Queen. With the green dress with straps and a pair of high heel shoes that accentuated her calves, she had become an exotic looker.

We bought the green dress and the blue one. Both had an Oriental touch to them—a slight slit up the sides—and fit as if she had been born to them. We also bought some everyday clothes from an adjoining department, and when Hiromi was changing into that, the saleslady motioned me over to her.

"We've reached your amount and then some," she whispered.

"How much?"

"Seventy-five more."

I peeled off another hundred and palmed it to her. Now she had to figure I was with the mob. Almost six-hundred bucks! I had never spent that much on anything in my life except for my house. The Ford even cost less than that pile of dresses.

On the way out, we stopped at the beauty salon at Bergdorf. A New York haircut would be the final touch. I suspected that the salon had not had much experience with Orientals, but hair was hair, and style was style and, more importantly, cash was cash.

I met the beautician and palmed her a hundred-dollar bill. When the beautician looked at the C-note, it looked like she was going to faint; I don't think she had ever palmed a bill that big even at Bergdorf's. She also probably figured me as a mob guy. It was getting to be fun acting like a big shot.

While Hiromi was in the salon, I wandered out of Bergdorf's to a men's store across the street. My suits at home were used for work and they looked it. A little rip here, a little stain there. If I wore one of those suits when Hiromi was looking like a princess, I'd probably get a quick toss. I picked out a navy blue double-breasted suit and tried it on. It's amazing what a really good suit will do for a guy. I looked like Wall Street all the way. I checked the price tag—two hundred bucks. That was twice the monthly mortgage of a new house out in Levittown.

My suit's size was a perfect forty-four long. The only thing I needed were cuffs on the trousers. I said to the salesperson, "If you can have cuffs put on these trousers in the next fifteen minutes, you've got a sale."

He called out to somebody in the back room. A little Italian guy came out, marked where the cuffs should be and I took the trousers off in the dressing room and handed them to the tailor. "I'll be back in ten minutes."

In those ten minutes, the salesman was able to sell me two new shirts, cufflinks, two ties and a pair of shoes, totaling the two-hundred dollars I'd paid him for the suit. With all that fancy stuff, I could have passed for a *boss* down on Wall Street or even better, an *investor*.

I walked back to the salon with boxes of clothing in two bags. They had finished styling Hiromi's hair. I wondered if the beautician was as awed by Hiromi's hair as I was sitting there watching.

They had styled her hair short in the back, but with long sweeping sides and some bangs on her forehead. Stunning!

We were a little euphoric after our shopping expedition and it seemed that neither one of us wanted it to end. So, I drove over to Chinatown and parked the car. We strolled through the narrow streets and my entertainment was watching Hiromi examine little curios in the shops. I marveled how she could look at something as simple as a candle, examining its texture and shape as if it was a fine antique. I bought her a knick-knack every once in a while, and she thanked me like I had bought her another hundred-dollar dress. There were times we laughed, but I couldn't recall why; we were just having fun. We finally ended up in a small restaurant and feasted on noodles, chicken and Moutai, a Chinese liquor. The Moutai was distilled from fermented sorghum, the waiter told us. I nodded as if I knew what sorghum was.

We drove back across the Brooklyn Bridge with the trunk full of goodies and a back seat full of candles and fans and other knick-knacks. It was now raining hard.

On the radio, Red Barber told us that when the Dodgers beat the Cardinals yesterday Preacher Roe had a 'tired arm'. How could the Preacher man get a tired arm? He had said in the papers, "I got three pitches: my change; my change off my change; and my change off my change off my change." That meant that all he did was throw junk. Most of us fans figured that he had a fourth pitch, one that he didn't talk about. The outlawed spitball.

On my porch, I juggled the bundles and fished inside my pocket for the key. I retrieved it, contorting to unlock the door without dropping the packages and opened the door. Hiromi touched my elbow and turned me to her. She put both her hands on my shoulders, reached up and kissed me on my cheek. It was a short kiss, not more than a peck and far less than a smooch. She said, "Thank you." Then she giggled, pivoted and grabbed her packages and dashed up the steps laughing. I stood there dumbstruck. Her lips felt wonderful and her giggle lifted my heart. And then she screamed.

12

Thursday, September 20, 1951

Another scream followed her first by less than a breath.

I dropped the bundles and ran into the house. Over to the right side was my living room. It looked like a tornado had made its way through the keyhole and then grown like a monster and blasted its way around the living room.

Hiromi was at the top of the stairs. "My room…my room…" she gasped. "Somebody…somebody…destroyed my room!"

I bounded up the stairs right past her. She followed me to her third-floor room. The tornado had hit that room as fiercely as the living room.

"My paintings!" Hiromi screamed.

The bookcase hiding the doorway to the attic was still intact.

Hiromi pulled the bookcase open and sailed up the stairs. I followed, a little less gracefully.

Everything was intact. All of her paintings were there. The tornado hadn't struck up in the attic.

"I am so relieved," she said. I was relieved too. Replacing a painting that she had been working on for days or weeks even was a lot more difficult than reversing the destruction to my couches and chairs.

We checked the rest of the house. My office was now my concern. There was a lot of cash in there. My war fortune wasn't there, of course—that had long ago been put in investments, safe-deposit boxes or hidey holes—but the Tailgunner Joe money was just sitting in a drawer. My one hope was another bookcase. I had been so pleased with my bookcase door that led to the attic that I had decided to replicate it at the end of the hall on the second floor. At the end of the hall was the entrance to my office. It had at one time been my sister's bedroom. If I had looked down the hall when I was a kid, I would have seen a closed white door. Now when you looked down the hall, you'd see a floor-to-ceiling bookcase. Good books too, some Charles Dickens mixed with Mickey Spillane. I walked up to it and pushed inward. It led into my office, which, I was relieved to find just as I had left it, a little messy, but that mess was my handiwork, not done by some burglars.

I checked the desk drawer. My money was still there. That was good. But, the fact that my house had been tossed surely wasn't good, and I knew that this hadn't been the work of some local punks. A group of men looking for something specific did this tossing. Anything that didn't look like what they were looking for was tossed aside.

There was one last place to look—my darkroom in the basement. The door leading to that was also a bookcase, my last fake bookcase. However, if the idiots had followed their noses instead of their eyes, their noses would have led to behind the bookcase. The chemicals in the darkroom oozed fumes like directional arrows. If they had followed the fumes and done a little tapping here, a little tapping there, they would have figured out that there wasn't a cement wall behind the bookcase, but a room. King Solomon's mines might have been behind that bookcase, but my burglars were the crash-and-burn types.

For an hour, Hiromi and I tried to straighten up the house. The first thing I did was put some cardboard on the broken window in the back door where the crash-and-burn guys entered. Some things wouldn't straighten—like broken lamps—but we got the place to look like only a reasonable windstorm had blown through. The cushions on the couch in the living room had been slit open. The idiots could have unzipped the covers and *looked* inside, but no, they were in a hurry and they just slashed the cushion covers. We taped up the slits and placed the taped sides down. I would need a new couch, of course, but it passed the quick-glance test as being serviceable.

I left Hiromi to finish up while I walked over to the neighbors. Maybe they had seen something, maybe they had heard something. Nothing. This house was old-style construction—the type that were built with real quality, not those flimsy things that they throw up today. My mother didn't seem to mind flimsy out in Levittown; she was happier having a garden than being bothered by flimsy. I had common walls with my neighbors, but these houses were two distinct buildings sandwiched together. So, it was like having *double* walls. Loony bins should have this much insulation from sound.

I sat on the steps on my porch nursing a Schaefers.

I guessed that either Dominic hadn't been able to alert his boys yet, or they had been asleep at the switch. If it had been the mob who had tossed my place, Dominic would have known beforehand and talked to me, like he said he would. I'd go down and see him tomorrow and tell him about the break-in. He wouldn't be pleased about something like that happening in his neighborhood, but he would call around to make sure it was'nt any of his people.

Two things were obvious to me. It seemed obvious who had broken into my house. Sure, it could have been one of my divorce cases looking for all-telling photographs of somebody's dick being in someplace it shouldn't have been. There were lots of past candidates for that, but I had only two cases current. Both were in the negotiation stage now. This negotiation stage was all lawyers—the wife's lawyer showing the husband's lawyer naughty pictures of the husband and some bimbo. All dicks had been accounted for. I didn't think that one of those dickheads thought that by retrieving the negatives he could dodge the matrimonial gas chamber. Desperate dicks have been known to do desperate things, but deep down I didn't feel that this break-in was ordered by one of my divorce cases.

This had to be the Ice Queen. She had somehow identified Hiromi and me.

The second obvious thing was that while I may have dropped the Ice Queen case with Nick, it was pretty obvious to me that she was extending the game.

13

Friday, September 21, 1951

I couldn't just drive up to the Stork Club in my '48 Ford, so yesterday I had reserved a car and driver from Allesandro Bettino. Of course nobody but his mother called him Allesandro. Allesandro was Alexander in English; it was Allie or just plain Al in Brooklynese. Allie was another guy I went to high school with, and like me, he lived in Brooklyn. I first knew Allie when we started to play stickball in the streets. He was a little guy then, but he was quicker than most colored kids. He could dodge around the parked cars like a bird to catch a long stickball hit. He loved baseball almost as much as I did, and we'd catch a couple of Dodger games a month together.

While I was preparing with Wild Bill to chase Nazis over in Eastern Europe, Allie was in the 3rd Army with General Patton. He came home right after the war ended. In fact, Allie claims he was in that famous picture in *Life* magazine of a G.I. kissing a babe on D-Day. He pointed to a blob of ink on the page and said that was him. To me, that was good enough—he was in the picture, just not kissing the girl. After the war he started a chauffeured limousine business. It was going good for Allie; he's got three limos and six drivers. He told me his old man fronted the money, but I suspect it was some relative that was in the mob.

When I phoned Allie to reserve a car, he said, "About time, Jake. What's the occasion?"

"I'm going to the Stork Club on Friday night."

"Lotsa moola," Allie said. "She must really be something to get you to spend on something more than a Nathan's."

"It's not really a date, Allie, it's work, so how much is it gonna cost?"

"Cost! Cost!" Allie was practically shouting. "*I* would charge you? Are you crazy?"

"I got expenses..." I said.

"You'll need those expenses to pay for the champagne. If you want one of my cars, you can't pay. If you *really* want to pay, you gotta go rent from somebody else. Me, you don't pay, capiche?"

That was Brooklyn all the way. That is, that was Brooklyn for those who stayed in Brooklyn or, like me, had come back. It seemed to me that Washington, D.C. hadn't been a very good influence on Nick. Nick was no longer neighborhood.

The neighborhood was how I spent the day waiting for my first date with Hiromi. Sure, I had seen Dominic and he reacted like I expected. He would try to find out who the burglars were.

I listened to the Dodgers game on the radio. They were playing the Philadelphia Phillies at Ebbets Field. I could have gone to the game, but I hung around the neighborhood and fidgeted listening to the game. The Dodgers got beat on a grand-slam home run by Puddin Head Jones.

Hiromi hung around the house also. She spent most of the day tidying up her room. I saw her briefly in the kitchen in the late afternoon when she came down to brew some green tea.

I had looked at my watch. "We leave here at seven tonight," I said. "Wear one of those dresses we bought at Bergdorf's."

"We're still going?" She asked.

"We sure are," I said. "We'll have fun." If I would have been talking to Allie, I would've said something like this: What, the world stops because some chumps broke into my house?

"Seven tonight?"

I nodded.

Hiromi scampered upstairs.

I showered and shaved and slicked back my hair with Vitalis. I then put on that new dark blue double-breasted suit and looked into the mirror. Wow, I really looked legit, at least as legit as those Wall Street thieves looked.

I was sitting in the living room when I heard Hiromi step down the hardwood stairs.

She walked into the living room.

I've never felt like fainting before, but looking at Hiromi did make me lightheaded. She had chosen the cobalt blue dress that had Chinese overtones. The dress had a slit up the sides revealing a tantalizing peek at her long legs. Somehow she had gotten taller, her legs longer. She was wearing shoes with very high heels, and her hair was wound in a delicate swirl above her head. Her only jewelry was a pair of jade earrings. She wore white gloves that rose past her elbows. She walked over to me—I didn't think I could move my feet for a while—put out her two hands and clasped mine, then reached over and gave me a light kiss on the lips. She then bowed, lowering her eyes, and said, "Thank you." Very polite, these Japanese.

"You are very beautiful," I said, and it looked like Hiromi blushed, I think. It's a helluva lot more difficult to tell when a Japanese was blushing than an Irish.

"Thank you," she said again and lowered her eyes once more.

"Well, let's go, the carriage is waiting outside."

I took her hand and led her to the front door, and out to the waiting limo. The driver—Allie's cousin Carlo, which was Charles in English or Charlie in Brooklynese—opened the back door. Hiromi looked up at me questioning.

"I'll explain everything on the ride to the restaurant," I said. "You'll have fun." Hiromi still thought going to the Stork Club was part of some *job*.

Hiromi and I were not romantically involved, but we had developed a friendship, a kinship that I figured was more like brother-sister than anything else. She felt comfortable with me. I felt comfortable with her. She was also a coworker of sorts. I had never paid Hiromi for her expertise with locks; I just gave her a free month's rent every time she helped me out. Considering our two trips to the Ice Queen's brownstone, Hiromi had two more free months coming. So, I figured, why not take some of Tailgunner Joe's money and just do something outrageous with a friend and coworker? But, then, who was I kidding? I was kidding myself that's who. I *wanted* to be with Hiromi, not just breaking-in to someplace, but on…well, yes, a date. That was quite a revelation to me, and someday soon I'd probably fully admit it to myself and to Hiromi; maybe I'd admit it during dinner tonight.

On the ride to Manhattan, I told Hiromi how I had made up a story about the Japanese princess.

She stared at me when I told her. She said nothing. Finally she said, "Japanese princess?"

"Yeah," I said, "it was a joke."

She stared at me some more.

"Am I not right for you the way I am?" She asked me.

"You're perfect the way you are," I said. I didn't have to be a detective to figure out that I had said the wrong thing. I had said the wrong thing about the Japanese princess thing. Had I felt uncomfortable about taking just a plain Japanese woman to dinner and not some mysterious princess? I was freer of prejudice than anybody I knew, but it sure looked like some level of prejudice had bitten me on the ass.

A tear started to form at the corner of her eyes.

"No, Hiromi, no," I said softly. I grabbed a hankie from my pocket and blotted the tear. I then leaned over and kissed her cheek. I then kissed her lightly on the lips. "You are perfect the way you are," I said, "I was just being stupid when I was talking to my friend. Just me being stupid; you've seen that before; c'mon you've seen me do stupid a lot of times."

I held her and kissed her again. Suddenly she smiled. It was as if she had turned on a light bulb inside herself.

"I will be a Japanese princess," she said smiling. "Your princess. Jake's princess." Now she thought this was all great fun. She told me that she had always wanted to be a princess.

"I'm not going to introduce you as a Japanese princess," I said. "I'm going to introduce you as Hiromi Kitahara, my friend." That didn't sound right, but girlfriend sure didn't either.

Charlie maneuvered the big Cadillac limo to the curb in front of the Stork Club. There were about fifty or so onlookers, probably waiting for Joe DiMaggio or Frank Sinatra.

I stepped out of the limo first. I could have passed for a ballplayer—I had the age and looks of one—but I clearly wasn't Joe D or Duke Snider. Then Hiromi stepped out of the limo. It was as if the onlookers had caught their breaths all at the same time. Hiromi stood tall, and regally put out her right hand to me. I took it and guided her over the curb and onto the sidewalk under the green canopy. The gold chain awaited us.

I gave the doorman my name. He didn't look at any list, but said, "We welcome you to the Stork Club, Mr. McHenry. This way, please." He opened the heavy bronze door—it looked like it could rebuff a mortar shell.

The doorman unlatched the gold chain and ushered us through. We were in a small lobby with telephone booths and the hatcheck room off to the side. Since it was September, I wasn't wearing a hat and Hiromi wasn't wearing furs, and we walked past the hatcheck room. On the left was a large bar packed three deep. It was a big room by itself—I'd say about seventy feet long and about thirty feet wide; it was a lot bigger than Dowling's Oyster Bar. Above the bar, a long mirror ran the length of the room. It was easy to be seen in this room. The sound filled the room—popping champagne corks, the rattling of cocktail shakers, the loud male guffaw, the squawky and almost hysterical woman's laugh, the blur of a hundred voices. Hand in hand, Hiromi and I walked through the bar as if we owned it.

I heard a wolf whistle and turned. There was a solid boyish looking guy with a shit eating grin leaning against the bar. He was clearly drunk. And I clearly recognized him. Mickey Mantle of the Yankees. I looked to see if he was with DiMaggio himself. Nope, Mantle was with a skinny guy I recognized as Billy Martin. I knew Martin was from Oakland, California, but he looked like a punk; he looked like he came from Brooklyn.

Mickey was just a kid—nineteen I think—but the papers were trumpeting him as Joe D's successor. I had heard on the radio that batting leadoff a few games ago he jacked one in the rightfield upper deck. The radio guys were saying that if he had hit it more to centerfield it could have gone six-hundred feet. Mickey was one who slipped through Branch Rickey's Dodger scouting network. The other rookie, Willie Mays of the Giants, also must have slipped through Rickey's grasp. Both of them could hit with huge power and outrun the wind.

"My apologies, sir," Mickey slurred, "I didn't mean nuthin'." Nice country boy, that he was. He sure could hit the shit out of the ball; I wish we had him.

Continuing on, we came to a thick glass door and were met by the maitre d'.

Hiromi's palm was damp. So was mine, but it might have just been wet from her hand. Through the glass door, we saw a large L-shaped room. It had a huge mirror on one wall, gold silk draperies on another. Chairs were covered by yellow and gray satin. A large crystal chandelier that looked like it could challenge the ceiling's strength hung in the middle of the room. On the far wall was a bandstand. Looking into the room was like looking at the crowd behind the third base dugout at Ebbets Field—all the faces were melded into a large collage. The fine line details in this collage weren't shirt sleeves and beer like at Ebbets, but dark suits and low cut formal dresses and endless glasses of champagne. Hiromi squeezed my hand. I looked at her. She looked cool and calm—a strange glow of confidence—as if this was just another nice restaurant. Ah, these inscrutable Japanese. I could tell, however, that she was excited and would love to rehash this experience for days afterward.

"Mr. McHenry, I presume," the maitre d' said. My friend Ed Stebbings must really be a big-shot here. Ed had warned me about the Stork Club's version of tipping. "Now, Jake m'boy, don't be a cheap bastard with the tips."

I asked Ed how little did a cheap bastard tip.

He said, "Let me give you an idea. The headwaiter Victor Crotta has received some big tips. One night he got a ten thousand dollar tip from Fred Perry, the tennis star. But, that was only *half* of his best tip. That's right, another night he got a twenty grand tip." Before getting into Allie's limo, I put the hundred-dollar bill on the *outside* of my roll of bills. At least I would *look* like a big-shot when I took out my roll, unclasped the money clip, thumbed past the C-note and fished out a twenty and palmed it to the maitre d'. That was the most I had ever tipped anybody in my life.

Another man stepped in front of the maitre d'. He was wearing an expensive double-breasted suit, had thinning hair and looked like *he* owned the place. "Let me introduce myself," he said, "Mr. McHenry, I'm Sherman Billingsly." He *did* own the place. Ed Stebbings sure did things in style.

"And who is your lovely guest?" Billingsly asked.

"Miss Kitahara," I said.

Hiromi bowed her head, bent her knees slightly and looked down.

"Follow me, please," Billingsly said, smiling. I had heard that he had once been a bootlegger in Oklahoma. It looked like he had grown out of that racket well. We navigated through the room. I got the same feeling that I got outside when Hiromi stepped out of the limousine—that the crowd in this fancy-schmancy restaurant caught their breaths all at the same instant. Hiromi was a show stopper.

"I hear that you will be joining Mr. Stebbings for dinner in the Cub Room," Billingsly said to me, "and then go to the main room for some dancing." I nodded.

My lawyer pal had called the Cub Room the *Snub* Room. It's where the big-name movie stars or politicians or newspaper columnists like Walter Winchell were allowed to go. This was really Winchell's room to lord over. If Stebbings could get us in the Snub Room, he had a lot of juice.

Billingsly pulled out a chair for Hiromi and she seated herself at the table.

"Mr. Stebbings will be delayed," Billingsly said, "but he wanted you to get started. In fact, Mr. Stebbings is almost always late for dinner, so Mr. McHenry, please enjoy your dinner and Mr. Stebbings will surely join you for after dinner drinks."

We ordered drinks—champagne, what else? We ordered hors d'oeuvres from the menu—cherrystone clams and smoked Nova Scotia salmon.

After a few minutes, my lawyer friend pulled up a chair and joined us.

"Hi," he said to Hiromi, "I'm Ed Stebbings." Hiromi bowed her head slightly.

Ed turned to me and asked, "Has Sherman been treating you right?"

"Like we were royalty or rich or both," I said.

Ed laughed. "You've got everybody in this room buzzing. *'Who is that couple? Is she really the richest woman in Japan?'* Stuff like that. You're just lucky that Walter Winchell is out of town or you'd be the feature in his story, complete with pictures."

I laughed. It sounded as if Ed had taken my Japanese princess joke and pumped it up like a dirigible.

He asked Hiromi if she had been enjoying herself. She said, "Very much so, thank you." Very polite these Japanese.

"You two have fun, I've got to make my rounds. I'll catch up with you later, then we'll all go into the other room for dancing and drinking. Sound okay to you?"

I nodded.

"In the meantime, I'm sending over some of the house's best champagne. Don't leave a drop in that bottle. This stuff is usually reserved for somebody like Bogart or Kennedy...or the richest woman in Japan."

We ordered dinner; roasted Long Island Duckling for Hiromi and broiled lamb chops for me. Each cost about what most people would pay for gas in a month, about five bucks.

When the food arrived, we pretty much ate in silence, enjoying our meal.

Another bottle of champagne was delivered to our table, compliments of the owner, Sherman Billingsly. As I poured Hiromi another glass, the maitre d' brought over a telephone, snaking its long cord through the aisles between tables. This was the type of service that the captains of our country got.

"For you, sir," the maitre d' said.

I picked up the phone. It must be Ed wanting to tell me how hot he thought my Japanese princess was.

"Mr. McHenry," a woman's voice said.

"Yes?" I said. It wasn't a voice that I recognized.

"This is Arabella Van Dyck. Did you enjoy your fine meal?"

"Very much so."

"I was so surprised to see you and your stunning companion. You both look far different than you do in my little snapshots of you."

"You're here?"

"But, of course, darling, look across the room behind you."

I turned my head like the Charlie McCarthy dummy. Next to the mirrored wall sat the Ice Queen. She had a phone to her ear. She was wearing a red low-cut dress that hid the parts of her body that I had already seen. With the red dress and red hair, she was like a beacon in the room. I don't know how I could have missed her. She smiled and motioned me over, "Please join us at our table for a coffee or a brandy if you wish." Then she hung up the phone.

14

Friday, September 21, 1951

"Surprise, surprise," I said to Hiromi when I hung up the phone. "That was the Ice Queen."

"Really?" Hiromi asked.

"She's sitting at a table against the wall behind me. She wants us to join her for coffee."

Hiromi smiled slightly and her round eyes slid into slits. I wondered how Orientals could do that without making it look like they were squinting. Even sitting close to her, it was difficult for me to see that she was carefully scanning the room behind me. Her eyes widened just a bit as she saw the Ice Queen. Hiromi's inscrutableness was being tested.

"Are we going?" Hiromi asked, looking at me.

"I am, but just for a minute. You stay here."

"I go to the ladies room," she said. Then she whispered in my ear, "Tell me all about it when we get back to the table."

I walked over to the Ice Queen's table. She was alone, but there was a used napkin and empty brandy snifter next to her. Somebody had left so that the Ice Queen and I could have a nice little chat.

As I sat down a brandy snifter was delivered to me by the waiter.

"Cheers," the Ice Queen said, raising her glass. I played along and raised mine.

"So you have broken into my house?" the Ice Queen said. No subtlety there. "I don't think you took anything. Or, did you?"

I didn't say anything.

"Of course you didn't," she said, "or my people would have found it when they broke into *your* house last night. I hope they didn't make too much of a mess. Those boys tend to be so sloppy at times."

She laughed. It was not a pretty laugh. If I had to describe it, I would call it a Nazi laugh—laughing at something that wasn't funny, but something that would piss the other person off.

"Of course I knew who you were," she said.

I didn't say anything.

She felt she needed to explain. "When you were staked out at my house—that's what they call it isn't it, *stake* out—I spotted you when I came out my door on the first day. You see, Mr. McHenry, I have learned to be careful. J. Edgar might come in the Stork Club and be quite jovial, but he doesn't have a sense of humor, at least not for what I do and I always have to be on the lookout for his men. So, I spotted you and the Japanese thing sitting in your car. I memorized your license plate number. I called a friend from a diner. Before I had lunch that day, my friend had found out your name by calling our very cooperative police and giving them your license plate number."

I took a sip of brandy.

"Now that you know what I do, why don't you stop by when I'm there? Come by without your little Japanese friend," she said. I was amazed—she was coming on to me! She must not have known that Hiromi smoked her safes and that I had pictures of her pictures, I had pictures of her Korean bomb sketches.

"I won't have my little photographer," she said laughing. Well, I guessed wrong; she did know that we had gotten into the safes. "It would be just you and me and your Japanese friend, if you wish. You obviously know I don't have a problem with Orientals."

"Thank you for your offer, but no thanks," I said. There was probably not one guy in the Stork Club that wouldn't take her up on her offer. If she wanted pictures of every male in the club, she could get them. No guy would find it difficult in his mind's eye to erase that low-slung red dress and see her tits bounce out into his face. The Stork Club was probably the web that the Ice Queen snared many of her subjects.

"Oh, I hope it isn't because of my little exercise you saw me perform with those two Oriental gentlemen?"

"Not at all. It looked like you were having fun, filling what needed to be filled."

She laughed again like a Nazi.

Seeing the Ice Queen's photo collection was like meeting the most gorgeous woman in your mind, find out that she is loose and wants you, and then finding out that she has syphilis. The syphilis part tended to turn me off.

"Then since we can't get together, let me ask you just one question."

I took another sip of brandy.

"Who hired you?"

"That's confidential," I said.

"Was it one of my friends that I invite over occasionally?" she asked, referring, I thought, to those captains of industry that were caught riding her waves.

"I don't know who you invite over except for those Koreans..."

"Did I say they were Koreans?" she said. "They were Orientals..."

"I guessed that they were Koreans," I said, trying to cover up my slip of the tongue. "As you can see," turning my face toward Hiromi, "I can tell one Oriental from another, or as others might say, one chink from another. But, you shouldn't have to guess who hired me. It doesn't make any difference; I have resigned the account. I found nothing that would interest me."

"I would like to believe you, Mr. McHenry," the Ice Queen said, "that you found nothing that interests you."

Then she leaned toward me in confidence and I don't know what stopped her tits from popping out of her dress. She spoke in a low husky voice, "Since you resigned your client, perhaps you would let me hire your services."

"My services?"

"But, of course," she said, whispering close to my mouth. I could feel her breath on my ear. Up close like that, I could see that her skin wasn't as pure as it looked from just a couple of feet away. There were a few fine strands of a web crinkling from her eyes. However, she was an artist with the makeup. The guys she brought back to her brownstone wouldn't care about those wrinkles, nor did I, but it did show that the Ice Queen was a little less than perfect, just a small touch less.

If she did indeed want to hire me, and if I was still working for Tailgunner Joe, then this would be a terrific opportunity to get The List. But, I had resigned my job with Tailgunner Joe and I didn't need the money. What I needed was to stay away from that bitch.

"A woman always needs a private dick," she said with a slight sneer on her upper lip. Strangely, that slight sneer instantly reminded me of the first SS that I had murdered. The Ice Queen was such a beautiful woman; I remembered my reaction to first seeing her picture; it was amazing how she could turn that stark beauty into ugliness with just one quick look. "Isn't that what they call you types, *dicks*? Yes, I would like to hire your dick. I want your *dick*." She laughed again.

"Funny," I said, which she wasn't funny at all, "but, I don't hire out individual body parts. So my dick stays with me and I'm not for hire."

"I'll get your dick one way or the other," she said, her scowl was as nasty as any Nazi I had ever known.

I felt like laughing. My experience with the Ice Queen was over. I had seen evil over in Eastern Europe. I had *profited* from evil—somebody else's evil *and* my own—and my antennae was pretty good in picking up evil. The Ice Queen was one evil bitch. I was going to make a huge conscious effort to push her from my memory a little bit each day until there was nothing but a puff of nothing.

"Look it," I said. "I didn't take anything from your house, I'm off the job, you've struck back and ripped up my house, but it stops here and now. My apologies for any trouble I've caused you, but this is the end of it. Don't push it, lady."

I got up, dropped a twenty on the table for my brandy and walked away from the Ice Queen.

Hiromi was just sitting at the table waiting for me after she had gone to the ladies room.

"Want to hear some music?" I asked, "We can go in to the next room where the band is playing, find Ed and enjoy." She nodded her head.

I looked at the bill. Because of the free champagne from Sherman Billingsly and Ed Stebbings, the bill was less than what I dropped on the Ice Queen's table for the brandy. I knew Ed had offered to buy us dinner, but he wasn't nearby and I didn't want to seem like a freeloader. I paid it. The bill was more than what most folks would pay in rent for the week, but less than my cognac with the Ice Queen.

We left the Cub Room. I looked for Ed and couldn't find him so we sat down at a table away from the dance floor in the L-shaped room.

"Well?" Hiromi said, whispering in my ear, "What did the Ice Queen want?"

"She wanted me to be one of her next photo subjects," I said, chuckling. "She invited you too." Hiromi playfully slapped me on the arm.

I then told her that the Ice Queen had us pegged right from the beginning. She had admitted that she had my house ransacked. She also figured out that we had got into her safes. I told Hiromi that it was over with the Ice Queen, finished, kaput.

While I was talking to Hiromi I was scanning the room looking for Ed.

I didn't spot Ed, and it seemed as if Mickey Mantle and Billy Martin had moved on, but I did see somebody that really surprised me. Nick Salzano. Nick was as dressed up as smartly as I was. He was on the dance floor with a tall brunette, which wasn't his wife. He was holding her tightly as if he was at a senior prom.

The Stork Club was a place that the rich and famous went to be seen, but it was also a good place to hide. At this moment, I wanted to hide from Nick's eyes. I wanted to watch him, but I didn't want him to watch me. I repositioned myself so that the back of Hiromi's head covered Nick's line-of-sight to me.

Nick danced, completely oblivious of me. I wouldn't have minded dancing with Hiromi, but I needed to watch Nick more. Nick and his woman companion left the dance floor and sat at a table. I repositioned myself again.

"What are you doing?" Hiromi asked, seeing me swivel my chair a second time.

"There is somebody that I want to watch, but I don't want to be seen," I said. "I'm going to look you right in the eyes, but occasionally my eyes will drift past your head to watch him."

"Like a drunk?" Hiromi said, laughing.

"Yeah, like a drunk."

The waiter came by and we ordered two brandies. I kept my eye on Nick.

I made small talk with Hiromi. Sometimes I think it was just gibberish, but Hiromi nodded her head as if she actually understood what I was saying. Amazing linguists, these Japanese.

From the corner of my eye, I saw a red shape heading toward the dance floor. The Ice Queen with her red dress and flaming red hair had a short fat bald old guy in tow. I thought, this will be an interesting dance—the guy's mouth could rest on the Ice Queen's bosom. He most likely was another candidate for her photo gallery. Then she stopped and made a quick left turn toward Nick's table.

Nick saw her and stood up. He held his arms out wide. She kissed him on the lips—a little longer and a little too much on target to be appropriate—and folded herself into his arms. I guessed Nick had got over the prejudice of getting kissed by the lips that had sucked some Chink cocks. She then tilted her head back and said something. Because of the band, I couldn't hear what they were saying. And, I can't read lips. She then kissed him on the lips again—this time I could tell that tongues were active—then turned and pulled her little fat man on to the dance floor.

Ed Stebbings finally stopped by our table. As a big-time corporate lawyer in New York, I knew he worked impossible hours. I knew about his hours because I had to tail him for three weeks before I could get the goods on him. He played as if his life was on the line. He was an intense guy at work and play and not a bad guy to occasionally have on my side. He told me one time that he loved just three things: work, fucking and betting. Everything else was monotony.

He sat in the chair next to Hiromi, across from me, which provided me a little more camouflage from being seen by Nick or the Ice Queen. Ed tried making small talk with Hiromi, but she decided to play the I-don't-speak-your-language-very-well game. A few minutes later, the Ice Queen steered her little man off the floor and back to the Cub Room. I looked back at Nick and saw him walking out the door. It looked like he was calling it an early evening.

Hiromi's eyes were getting heavy. I didn't have to be a detective to figure out that it was time to get back to the pumpkin and head out before the clock chimed in reality.

I thanked Ed for the evening at the Stork Club; I thanked him for the champagne.

Ed said, "In case you're wondering, Jake, we're still not even. I still owe you, will probably owe you for the rest of my life. So let's get together for a Yankee game, or I'll even come out to see the Dodgers play."

We shook hands. Ed kissed Hiromi on the cheek, she bowed slightly, and we left.

On the ride back to Brooklyn, Hiromi snuggled her head against my shoulder and the car seat. Her hand crawled over my leg and found my hand. She clasped it lightly. Within moments, I knew she was asleep.

Even with Hiromi using me as a pillow, I rehashed the evening in my mind. I had met Arabella Van Dyck, the Ice Queen. That was unexpected, but if I would have thought about it, it was to be expected. After all, wasn't the Stork Club somewhere that the Ice Queen would call home? I did learn from her, however, that she had sent a couple of goons to break into my place. I guess I could consider that an eye-for-an-eye thing even though I didn't bust her place up. Now that I had quit the case, I hoped that she would quit. However, since she couldn't rent my dick, I supposed that she might send some goons after me to try to bust it a bit, and me along with it. I'd have to be on severe alert, but that wasn't new to me; there was always the threat that an irate husband would take my investigating personal and want to break me for having a hand in breaking up his marriage.

Lastly, I saw Nick Salzano. Seeing him at the Stork Club also shouldn't have been surprising. After all, he had told me that he was in New York on business all the time. Nick was always a ladies' man and where else should a stud like that, who was working for one of the most powerful men in the country, go for some female companionship? That Nick was married was never a problem for him.

Could I connect all these dots and see the picture? I didn't think so. The Ice Queen was an extortionist. Whom she was extorting, I didn't know. Nevertheless, I did know that those pictures weren't to paste in a fancy album and show to her grandchildren years down the road.

Nick was the wild card. He had never given me an indication that he knew the Ice Queen. In fact, he seemed genuinely shocked—and pissed—when he saw the photo of Tailgunner Joe boffing her. He seemed even more pissed when he saw the two Koreans doing their gymnastics with the Ice Queen. Prejudice could run deep in Brooklyn and Nick's surfaced pretty quickly when he saw that Korean photo. That prejudice disappeared equally as quick with that kiss he planted on the Ice Queen near the dance floor. He must've figured that she had washed her lips since she had been with the Koreans.

Nick and I had practically been twins when we were kids. He knew what I was thinking when I was thinking it; I knew what he was thinking when he was thinking it. Sure, over time we grew apart—me being in Europe, him being in Washington—but we still had the remnants of that twin thinking, I thought. The problem now was: I had no idea what he was thinking; I had no idea what he was doing; I had no idea what he was involved with. It was like saying about a guy you knew your whole life, who is that guy, anyway? We were strangers, that's who.

15

Saturday, September 22, 1951

After seeing the Ice Queen at the Stork Club, I knew that I would have to put myself, and Hiromi, on the type of alert that I learned in Germany. In other words, full-time paranoia. Sure, I would re-enlist Dominic. But, I had several other advantages.

One, I had been warned. I knew the Ice Queen's last words to me at the Stork Club wasn't the end of it. I felt that whatever was going to happen would happen in the next two weeks or so. This wasn't a Hatfields versus the McCoys that would last for generations.

Two, Dominic would be fired up. Dominic would most likely ramp up surveillance of my house just because the break-in occurred after I had asked him the favor of keeping an eye on my place.

Three, I would hire Rafael and a couple of his buddies to act as sentries. Sure, Dominic wouldn't like Puerto Ricans being involved, but I needed soldiers wherever I could get them.

Four, I would make my house into a fortress. I wouldn't have to do much. Built like a brick shithouse my dad used to say. Sure, the burglars came through the back door, but I would toughen that up with a steel door. I would put in an alarm system that could make the devil shit his drawers when the alarm went off.

Five, I had an arsenal of guns in the house. Most people I knew had a gun. I had lost count on how many I had. It was a habit—perhaps a bad one—that I had picked up in Berlin. In

Berlin, I was never more than two large steps away from *two* guns or more. It's not that Berlin after the war was like the Old West, but trust me, dealing with former Nazis—each one a little more desperate than the previous one—didn't make Berlin a walk in the park.

Right after breakfast I had made phone calls to get all my protection in place. Allie had a cousin who did industrial type steel doors and he'd be over this afternoon to do the measuring and then installing one in a day or two.

Dominic was horrified about the break-in, but he said he'd ratchet things up a bit. He didn't explain, but I figured the ratchet was a good thing.

Rafael and his boys would be available anytime. I particularly wanted to use them as escorts when Hiromi went out of the house and I wasn't available.

Finally, I was able to sit down at the kitchen table and enjoy a coffee.

I thought of Hiromi.

I had had plenty of relationships with women; the relationships usually *started* with sex then slid quickly into monotony. If I wanted to, I could create a list of Eastern European women that I had bedded when I was in Germany that had the looks to grace the pages of *Esquire* magazine, but after having sex I couldn't wait for one of us to leave. Sure, I could have dinner with any one of them, and even go to the theatre, but that was all preambles to the bedroom. In the neighborhood, I had gotten close to a couple of the girls, but, and this sounds awful, they were like pretzels—nice to have around when you're slurping up beer at the local tavern but would I want to wake up to a pretzel every morning? I wasn't like Nick or so many of my Brooklyn pals who quickly got married because it was the expected thing. In fact, I don't think I had ever really thought about marriage.

For quite a few years, I was married to the OSS in chasing down Nazis. Since then, if anything, I was married to the Dodgers and beer. The Dodgers and beer were far more predictable than any woman that I had known; the Dodgers didn't win every game of course, but Dodgers and beer were always entertaining. If the Dodgers won the pennant, it would be the ultimate orgasm to be retold for generations. I don't recall any old duffer in a bar talking about a piece of tail that he had had forty years ago. Sure, there wasn't any sex in Dodgers and beer, but they were making a bigger imprint on my soul than any woman had. If I wanted sex I could just go to the local tavern and spend some time wooing a woman that wanted to be wooed. She would wield sex like a flytrap hoping to get that certificate of marriage. So, I enjoyed Hiromi as we were, landlord and renter, partners in occasional break-ins, TV watching cohorts and now Stork Club diners. But, I knew I was just kidding myself again. I felt I was falling for this little Oriental.

I finished my coffee and went down to my basement darkroom, restless as hell. Copies of all the photos I had taken at the Ice Queen's were sitting there on my table. I chuckled at the photo of Hiromi and me peering through the crack in the door to see the Ice Queen and the Koreans go at it. I looked at the stack of photos of what I considered The Extortion Gallery, the guys that were caught humping the Ice Queen. Who were they? Damn, a couple of the faces *seemed* familiar, even with their faces distorted. I knew they weren't celebrities, but I also knew I had seen at least a couple of those faces somewhere.

I looked at the top picture on the pile. It was of some fifty-year-old guy that looked like he was having a coronary. He should be so lucky to die that way, I laughed.

Turning the top picture and placing it at the bottom of the stack, I then looked at the second picture. This guy looked like he was having a seizure. I wondered if I looked like that when having sex. One by one, I looked at each picture, stopping at each one for at least a few seconds. Still, no bell rang. A couple of these guys were just on the cusp of my memory; who were they?

The first picture now appeared on the top. I slid it into the photo enlarger. I cropped just the old guy's contorted face in the viewfinder. I wanted to see if I took the Ice Queen out of the photo would the identity of any of these guys snap to the forward of my brain.

With the photo in the enlarger, I snapped the picture. I then repeated this procedure with each Ice Queen victim. I had cropped the Ice Queen out of each picture. Then I placed twelve huffing-puffing cropped faces on each eight-by-ten print.

By cropping out everything but their faces, there was no evidence of what they were actually doing when they grimaced at the camera. They could be taking too big of a shit, they could be trying to pull a tractor out of some New Jersey swamp or if you wanted to think this way, they could be having sex. There was no evidence of the Ice Queen in these mug shots, not even one little sexy body part.

With a paper cutter, I cut the mug shots so after a few swipes I had a small stack of individual photos, each one the size of a baseball card.

I stared at the stack of cards. I thought: what the hell am I doing? I wasn't working the case. In fact, I had quit the Ice Queen case. These photos had nothing to do with Tailgunner Joe and his hunt for Commies anyways. I had no business whatsoever in trying to figure out whom these doomed fools were.

But, I did have some thoughts on self-preservation. If I identified some of these grimacing faces would it help me against the Ice Queen? Would that knowledge protect me and Hiromi? Well, the Ice Queen might figure that I *already* had that knowledge. She just might send her thugs to erase the knowledge that I didn't have. It seemed like my only alternative was to take the next step—try to figure out who her extortion victims were.

To do that I needed to visit a little old lady.

I put the stack of cards in my shirt pocket. I imagined that these faces belonged to captains of industry. After all, would the

Ice Queen go through all this trouble to extort some cab driver for a free ride or some newsstand guy for free newspapers?

Captains of industry were basically anonymous people to the rest of us folks. They weren't movie stars; they weren't baseball players. I didn't know what the president of the biggest bank in New York looked like; I wasn't even sure which the biggest bank was. There was one person that I knew who knew faces—famous or semi-famous. It was Roberta DiNardo at the Brooklyn Public Library.

Roberta had been at the library forever. I had always been a favorite of hers because I had borrowed more books from her library than anybody else. At least that's what she told me. Every time I would borrow a book—either when I was a kid or later on when I got back from Europe—she would like to talk about that book when I returned it. It wasn't too often that I could find a book that she had *not* read. So, after reading a book, Roberta and I would compare notes, sorta give each other a book review.

Roberta was the same way with newspapers. If something was written in the newspaper today, she had read it. In the newspaper, there were, of course, pictures. There were pictures of politicians, there were pictures of crooks, there were pictures of athletes and movie stars *and* there were pictures of captains of industry.

I walked over to the library unescorted. However, because Hiromi was in the house, I did have Rafael and two of his buddies come over and sit on my front steps. Before that I called Dominic and told him that Rafael was babysitting my house, just so some Italian goons didn't come along and give Rafael the boot. Protection is a complicated thing, you bet.

I felt Roberta was *always* at the library on Saturdays. That was a big day for kids at the library. She wanted to be the one to find them books, to unlock the secret joys of reading. And, she wanted to shoo away any bum that wanted to rest his head on a table. During the week when kids were in school she was a little more permissive about bums. But, when kids were around, the bums had to go. Today, many of those bums probably had wandered down to Ebbets Field trying to cadge a free ticket. If the Dodgers had been on the road, the bums would have still just hung around the ballyard on a Saturday.

When I walked in the library, Roberta was at her desk on the right side of the checkout counter. She gave me a big greeting, even though it was whispered. Her smile cascaded a thousand wrinkles.

I asked her if she could join me for a coffee. Since I got back from Europe, she and I would share coffee at least once a month. I think she felt like it was a date even though she was most likely fifteen years over retirement age and weighed all of ninety pounds, maybe. She was probably older than my grandmother. If I had wanted to, I could have taken Roberta to the Stork Club and passed her off as the missing Romanov from tsarist Russia. She would have been great until she spewed out the thickest Brooklyn accent that any of those fat cats at the Stork Club had ever heard. Hell, those refined fat cats probably would have thought she was speaking Russian.

Over a cup of coffee, I said, "Roberta, I need a favor."

"Shua," she said, which was Brooklynese for 'sure.' If I closed my eyes and just listened to her voice, I would hear Bugs Bunny. Bugs Bunny had a classic Brooklyn accent. If I wasn't so *shua*, I'd swear that Roberta did Bugs' voice in the movies. "Of course you needin' a favor, so what favor can a littl' old lady like me give yah, Jake? Is there some rare book that yah want me to find?"

"I need for you to identify somebody."

She looked at me quizzically.

"This is like a game," I said. "I'm going to give you a picture of a man, but it will not look like the man."

"What do you mean? Will he look like a frog or an elephant or something? Is he in disguise or what?"

This wasn't going so well. "You might think of it as a disguise," I said. "I think the photo is of a big-shot businessman. But, when you see pictures in the paper of those types of guys, it's usually a stiff posed mug shot that was used in the annual report or he's smiling at some gala function."

"Yeah?"

"With the pictures I have," I said, "each guy is in heavy exertion like he was pulling a sled full of cement blocks. Here's the first."

I handed her the first photo from my small stack. This seemed so silly.

Roberta looked at the heaving face. She laughed. "It looks like the Big Bad Wolf in Littl' Red Riding Hood. I'll huff and puff and blow your house down."

"Yep. Can you recognize the face, even though it's not the pose that you would see from this guy if he was in the newspaper?"

"I can't," Roberta said. "You got another one?"

I handed her the second picture.

"Another Big Bad Wolf," she said.

I had a stack of Big Bad Wolves. It was all anonymous Wolves until I showed her the picture of the guy with the big handlebar moustache.

"This face I don't know," she said, "but I have seen this moustache. Let me think…let me think."

We had a refill of our coffee. She slurped hers down pretty fast. "I have to get back to work," Roberta said. "I'm sorry I couldn't help yah with da pictures."

"Can I give you these?" I asked, sliding the pack across the table. "You might see some picture in the paper that connects you to one of these pictures."

"Shua," Roberta said. "These are just like those baseball trading cards you used to collect, except these mugs are not thinking baseball, I can tell you that."

She laughed and tucked the cards into her purse.

"Can I show them to my older sister?" Roberta asked. "She's been a spinster her whole life. She would get a kick out of seeing all these men blowing a gasket having sex." Then she laughed. It's difficult to understand how such a small woman could have such a big laugh. That laugh belonged to a bartender, not a librarian.

I laughed too.

"You can show those pictures to your sister," I said, knowing that Roberta didn't really have a sister. "But, Roberta, *nobody else*. Promise me you won't show them to nobody else."

She promised.

I didn't think that those photos were dangerous by themselves, but they did come from a dangerous place and dangerous acts. When handling something that was potentially dangerous, it was important to think that the pin was pulled and it wasn't a good idea to play catch with a live grenade.

"Give me a call if any of those pictures ring a bell," I said.

"Shua will honey. Someday, show me the rest of the picture, okay?"

16

Saturday, September 22, 1951

I walked Roberta back to the library. She giggled like a schoolgirl about the men's faces in the pictures.

As I was walking back down the street toward my house, I noticed a guy that didn't belong. I had noticed him when I walked with Roberta to get a coffee. Now I had seen him as I was walking home. To make it pitiful, he was trying not to be seen. Living in the Brooklyn Heights neighborhood was like living in a fishbowl—all the fishes in the bowl would notice when a new fish was put into the bowl. Sure, the neighborhood was changing quite a bit, but we met all the new fishes. This guy that was trying to tail me stuck out like a turtle. Doesn't look like a fish, doesn't swim like a fish, wasn't a fish. A turtle.

The good news was that this guy that was tailing me wasn't a monster, you know some gorilla whose knuckles bounced on the sidewalk as he walked. And, as far as I could tell he was alone. He was older—I'd say in his late forties or early fifties—short at about five-nine or so, thin, wearing a dark suit and a fedora that might pass the muster at the Salvation Army but not here in Brooklyn Heights.

I made a small detour on my way back to my house. I walked halfway down the block and then jumped into an alley. My jump into the alley was almost a sight gag—the type that a Milton Berle would pull on television. With exaggerated movement, I made it look like I was going to race down the alley like Jesse Owens in the Berlin Olympics. Acting one-oh-one is what it was.

Once I jumped into the alley, I just stood there, waiting. Moments later the guy peeled into the alley like he was an Indy race car. I grabbed him and threw him against the brick wall. He fell to the ground. I pounced on him, my ass sitting on his belly and grabbed him by his ears and pulled his head up off the ground a few inches.

"Who're you?" I asked, looking into his face and suddenly feeling stupid. This guy was harmless.

"Richard Wolfemeyer. I go by Richard—Richard—I don't go by Dick," the guy said, gasping. "I'm a private detective. I got credentials." I guess I could see why he emphasized Richard. He probably didn't think that 'Dick the private dick' sounded too professional.

"I'll look later. Why're you following me?"

"I'm getting paid."

I lowered his head to the cement ground, but still held his ears firm. "Feel that cement on your head?" Then I raised his head by his ears. "Now figure out how that cement's going to feel when I smash your head down. Whad'ya think? I'll just slam your head into that cement pillow and you'll go night-night. Maybe I'll do it two or three times. Then you go night-night for a long time. Or you tell me who's paying you. Which will it be? Cement pillow or talk?"

"I'll talk, Mr. McHenry, you don't have to bash my head. I'm an old guy. I'll tell you whatever you want to know."

I pulled him up to his feet. He dusted himself off.

"Can I show you my ID?" he asked. I nodded and watched him as he pulled out his wallet. I looked at it. Sure enough, he was who he said he was. I wrote down his name, address and phone number on a piece of paper and stuck it in my shirt pocket.

"Okay, Richard," I said, "you're following me because you're getting paid. Who's paying you?"

"A big gorgeous redhead," he said. "Flaming red hair, absolutely gorgeous."

"Arabella Van Dyck," I said.

"I don't know her name. She had called a couple of days ago and had me come to her house. Beautiful. Up on the East Side."

"I know it." I said. "So what'd she want you to do?"

"Just follow you, that's all. No rough stuff. She just wanted to know everyplace you went. *Everyplace.* Made me promise to take notes. Here, I'll show you." He reached into his shirt pocket and pulled out a small notebook, the type that cops carry. I read his notes: "library 10:52am; coffee shop with old broad 11:04am."

"I hope she's not paying you by the word," I said.

He didn't get it. I yanked the page out of his notebook and put it in my pocket.

"When did you start following me?"

"This morning," he said. "I was supposed to have started yesterday, but my car was broke down and I couldn't get it running until last night."

I felt like he was telling me the truth; he didn't seem to be the type that had a purring Cadillac.

What he told me was surprising. The Ice Queen had wanted me tailed *before* I ran into her at the Stork Club. Was the Stork Club an accidental meeting or did she somehow know that I was going to be there?

I tried to figure the Ice Queen's angle on using this old, dried-up dick. It didn't figure. She could have hired a real pro—one that wouldn't have been discovered so quickly. But, maybe she was trying to send me a message.

"So, what's the message?" I asked.

"What? Whad'ya talking about, message?"

"Ah, nothing," I said, realizing I had been thinking out loud.

"How much you getting paid?" I asked.

"Twenty bucks a day. Cash in advance for the first two days. She wanted me to tail you for the next five days. She wanted a report of where you've been, who you've seen every day."

"What if I would've gone out to Idlewild and got on an airplane and gone to Los Angeles. What would you have done then?"

"I guess I would have called her to check if she wanted to spend that type of dough to follow you. You aren't going to California, are you?"

"Doesn't matter. Look, Richard, you and I are in the same business," I said. I showed him my business card. "I don't want you following me because if you do then I'd have to smash your head against that cement. I don't want to do that; I figure you don't want me to do that. So, what if I give you a couple of twenties—make that five twenties—you call up the lady and tell her I took off for California."

"Seems fair," Richard said, "you being a private dick and all that. Professional courtesy you know."

I reached in to my pants pocket and fished out five twenties and slapped it in Richard's palm.

"By the way, I appreciate you not beating me up," Richard said. "Damn, I'm getting too old for this shit. How old do you think I am?"

"I don't know. I'm never good at guessing ages."

"Take a guess."

He did look older than my original assessment now that I was up close to him. He was probably pushing sixty. At least. Christ, this old duffer might be seventy. And, I was going to bash his head in?

I said, "Fifty-five." It's always safe to guess lower unless it was a teenager or a little kid.

Richard laughed. "Nobody gets close! I'm seventy-two. Still working my ass off. Someday I'm gonna write a book about our business and tell all."

"Well, just don't tell about meeting me or then I will beat the shit out of you."

He laughed again and put his hand out to shake. I shook it and we walked out of the alley together.

"By the way, Jake," he said, us now being on a first name basis, "you probably fucked that broad—is her pussy as red as the top of her head?"

"Richard, what type of question is that to ask, you being such a veteran private dick? What do you think?"

"I knew it! I could tell that red was real."

I watched Richard Wolfemeyer walk across the street and kept watching him until he got into an old beat-up piece of junk and drove away. It might have been a '39 Ford. I admired the old guy a bit, but felt sad for him and for me, a little bit, too. Life goes by so fast. I wondered when he was my age if he ever thought he'd be an old man like he is now. He should be at a baseball game with his grandkids. But, one year probably turned in to another without him noticing it—working for a few bucks here and a few bucks there—and then all of a sudden he was chasing a guy that could beat the shit out of him. I had my fortune and if I watched it carefully and went to enough Dodger games, maybe when I reached Richard's age, just maybe, I wouldn't be wondering what color the pussy hair was on some broad.

17

Sunday, September 23, 1951

Things were going to hell in a handbasket.

I don't mean the Ice Queen or anything like that. I'm talking about the Brooklyn Dodgers.

They did something really stupid Saturday night. In fact, I had taken Hiromi to that game and she saw it too. I also invited Allie and his wife. I guess you could consider this a double date. Even though I felt safe at Ebbets Field, I felt safer when Allie picked us up in his limo and then parked right across the street from the ballpark. Rafael was left stationed on my front steps; a buddy of his was on the rear steps.

The Dodgers honored their manager, Charlie Dressen, that night. Before the game, they gave him a large portrait of himself. Nice, I guess. But, in the portrait, it said, "National League Champions 1951."

The Dodgers, of course, had not won the pennant yet. In fact, after the game, we were only three games ahead of the New York Giants. Just two weeks ago, our lead was twice that.

"The Dodgers haven't won the pennant yet, have they?" Hiromi asked me at the game when she heard the inscription on the Charlie Dressen portrait.

"Nah, not yet," I said. I thought a pennant race must've been new to a person who had spent a few years in an Internment Camp, but she was a quick study on everything American.

"Is that a jinx then?" Hiromi asked.

"Whad'ya mean?" I asked. I thought, what do Japanese know about jinxes?

"You know, saying you won something, but you haven't won it?"

I thought about that. "Nah, that's not a jinx," I said. "There's no such thing as a jinx." While I said that, it was like whistling while walking in the dark through a graveyard. *Everybody* in Brooklyn believed in jinxes. I was only glad that Hiromi had asked me quietly in her soft sing-song voice. If others around us had heard her, some of them would have wanted to grab a priest and have her exorcised between innings.

Predictable of a jinx, we lost that game Saturday night. The four of us went to the game on Sunday. We came back and beat the Phillies on Sunday, so stuff that jinx. Preacher Roe won for us, upping his record to an amazing twenty-two wins against two losses.

Over the weekend, nothing unusual happened. It was as if there never had been an Ice Queen. Maybe the old detective did actually tell her that I left for Los Angeles. And then the phone rang.

Sunday evening phone calls were never good news. While the phone was ringing I flew through various options of who it could be. I was hoping it wasn't the Ice Queen. On the fifth ring, I answered the phone.

"Jake, this is Major General Bill Donovan," the voice on the phone said.

"Hello Boss," I said, as if I had just talked to him yesterday.

"I got your letter on Saturday," he said, not apologizing for calling on a Sunday evening or even pausing for any small talk, "and I want to talk to you about it personally, eyeball to eyeball."

123

"I'm at your service."

"I would like to meet with you right now, but I can't. It took me most of today to rearrange my schedule, but how about tomorrow afternoon, say, three o'clock? Can you come down to my office?"

"Yes," I said without hesitation, "I can take the train down tomorrow morning." When Wild Bill Donovan calls, it's not a question if I'm going to jump; it's only a question of how high. And, for Wild Bill, I'd jump higher than I thought possible. Besides, the Dodgers were going on the road and I couldn't see myself just pacing around the house listening to the games on radio and thinking about jinxes.

"Bring an overnight bag," Wild Bill said. "I want you and me to talk tomorrow afternoon, and then there's some fellows I want you to talk to the next day. They're out of town and can't meet until Tuesday. I'll put you up in a nice hotel. If you get down here early tomorrow, you can check in at the Mayflower Hotel. It's right around the corner from my office. We'll meet in my office. At least I know there are no listening devices there." Except his own, I thought, and chuckled to myself.

"See you at three tomorrow," Wild Bill said, and hung up the phone. No small talk there either.

When I hung up the phone there were two thoughts that sprung from some recess in my brain.

The first one was: Wild Bill was certainly putting urgency on this. That Special Delivery was delivered quicker than I had expected. Saturday delivery. I wondered if guys like Wild Bill got priority treatment with the post office.

The second thought was that I couldn't leave Hiromi alone in the house. Sure, I had Dominic's assurance that he and his boys would keep a better eye on the place. And, Rafael and his boys could camp out on the steps. But, I didn't feel comfortable about leaving Hiromi back in the fort.

The Ice Queen had showed no overt act to rough me up, but the Ice Queen knew who Hiromi and I were. She had pictures of us staring at her in her big gymnastics bed. And she had had that old detective Wolfemeyer keeping an eye on us. Who knows whom else she had watching? If they reported that I left alone, would that be an invitation to come in and do some serious questioning of Hiromi? No question in my mind; Hiromi would have to accompany me to Washington, D.C.

18

Monday, September 24, 1951

I had reserved another limo from Allie.

"Where to this time?" Allie said.

"I just need it to go to Grand Central Station Monday morning."

"Short trip," Allie said, "just like big shots."

"Yeah, yeah, so how much is this short trip gonna cost?"

"Cost! Cost!" Allie was practically shouting. "Where do you see that *I* would charge you? Where's it written?"

"You got a business, Allie," I said, "you got expenses."

"Okay, smart-guy, here's what I'll do. I *will* write it down, and you can read it tomorrow. It will say, *Jake starts paying for my limo after the one-hundredth trip.* That work for you or what?"

I laughed and told him that I owed him. He said, "I'm keeping track."

Nobody tailed us taking Allie's limo to the train station.

The train to Washington, D.C. was uneventful. I did catch, however, some people stealing glances at Hiromi. She was wearing a very sharp gray pinstripe suit that we had bought at Bergdorfs. It's not that folks saw too many Japanese—particularly welldressed ones—on the train to the nation's capital. Before the train arrived at the station, Hiromi went to the rest room, taking a small pouch of cosmetics. She emerged just a couple of minutes later. At that particular moment, it seemed as if everybody on the train looked up from what they were doing and stared at Hiromi. It was like when she stepped out of the limo at the Stork Club; it seemed every man sucked in his breath just a bit at the same time. Hiromi was absolutely stunning. She smiled at me and then marched down the aisle, sat next to me and squeezed my arm. She thought this was all great fun. So did I, even forgetting for the moment why we were on this train in the first place.

Two hours later, I was walking in the front door of Donovan, Leisure, Newton and Lombard. Just a few minutes earlier, I had checked Hiromi and myself in to the Mayflower, getting adjoining rooms. I had told her to stay put, watch some television until I got back, and not open the door for anybody.

I don't think Hiromi would miss me too much—she could turn up the radio in the room and swoon over Perry Como, Tony Bennett and Nat King Cole. Or, she could watch television. It was during the day so there wouldn't be *I Love Lucy* or *Milton Berle*, but there certainly would be something she would enjoy. Although I had never watched them I knew there were soap operas like *Love of Life* and *One Man's Family* on during the daytime.

The television in the room wasn't quite equal to the Admiral sixteen-inch television I had bought just a few months ago, but it worked. The Admiral cost me a fortune, 379 bucks, and not too many folks around the country would get a set like that, but it had a triple play. As a baseball fan, the triple play lingo caught my attention, but Admiral's triple play was the TV, an automatic phonograph player that could play 33s, 45s or 78s—I guess that was *another* triple play—and Dynamagic AM-FM radio, all with a built-in Roto-Scope antenna. It didn't get much better than that. While I was slow to adapt to this triple play, except for listening to Dodger games on the radio or the occasional Dodger game on television, Hiromi knew how to navigate it as if she had invented it. She was particularly adept with the TV. Hiromi knew every character on every show.

She'd scour newspapers and magazines for stories about television. Those readings lead her to hint about color TV. "Your government," she said, although the United States was also *her* government since she had become a citizen after the Internment Camp, "is making rules for color TV. Are you going to get one?" She asked that question with a little kid hopeful expression on her face that eventually could make me melt.

However, I had seen color TV in a couple of bars. The costs of color TV sets were crazy stupid. If the government could ever agree on what technology should be the standard, it would take a lifetime before most folks could ever think about buying one. Maybe if they traded in their late model car they could get a color TV in return.

Walking into the lobby of Donovan's law office was like walking into the fist of power. That power didn't emanate from the oil paintings of landscapes or the heavy furniture in the waiting room or the receptionist who was a spitting image of the old farm woman in Grant Wood's American Gothic that was on the wall behind her shoulder. I could *feel* this power. These were offices of power brokers that played skillfully and ruthlessly on both sides of the political fence. Wild Bill had started this law firm before World War II and used it as a retreat between gigs for various presidents.

The receptionist looked me in the eye when I told her that Major General Bill Donovan was expecting me. It seemed like she was debating with herself on whether to snatch the pitchfork from the American Gothic painting and drive it into my chest or pick up the phone and let Wild Bill's secretary know that his guest—as unlikely as he looked—had arrived.

A moment later, Wild Bill's secretary ushered me down the long hallway to the corner office. Wild Bill got up from his chair and like a man with a purpose marched across the room to me. He was in his early seventies now, but he looked like he could walk into a bar and challenge a longshoreman to an arm wrestling contest and win. He couldn't win, of course, but he could make a challenge that was creditable enough to make the longshoreman think a little about it. There wasn't much hair left on the top of his head, and the stuff on the sides was mostly white.

We shook hands, and he motioned for me to sit at a large dark leather chair that faced a couch.

"Coffee?" he asked.

"Black," I said. His secretary went to fetch it.

Even though he was as direct as a bullet, Wild Bill did have some social graces, so there was a little catching-up small-talk. I told him that I was a private investigator, but that didn't seem to surprise him.

I finished my coffee, and that last sip was like the signal to the end of the small-talk.

"What you sent me were rudimentary—and accurate—plans on how to build an atomic bomb translated into Korean," he said.

I raised my eyebrows. "An atomic bomb? Like Hiroshima?"

Wild Bill nodded. "Even though the Russians stole our plans practically as we developed them, we didn't think that they would just give that technology to the Koreans." When Wild Bill used 'we' it was as if he was still director of the OSS, now renamed the CIA. "Now it looks like *we* are giving the plans to the Koreans."

"Even worse than the plans," he continued, "was information on page six of the documents. This information was a Korean shorthand version of how to *acquire* plutonium—where, how, all that—including contact *names*. It's France connected. Fucking frogs. Without plutonium, the plans are as useless as bread without yeast. We're tracking that down right now as we speak." Again the 'we.' I didn't think he was referring to his law clerks chasing frogs.

"But that's just one source," Wild Bill said. "This could be like the little Dutch boy that sticks his finger in the dike to plug a hole and another hole pops up. We've got to start plugging holes now, today, in France, in Korea and most of all, here in the United States."

Wild Bill walked over to his desk and picked up the phone. He said, "More coffee please."

Within moments, I had some more coffee.

"Now, Jake, tell me how you came across this dangerous information," he said.

I have trusted Wild Bill with my life for several years over in Eastern Europe. I would continue to trust him with my life. However, there are some parts of the Ice Queen story that needed to be kept confidential. For instance, the Tailgunner Joe part. Tailgunner Joe hired me in confidence; I couldn't abuse that. If Wild Bill got some of his old cronies to bust into the Ice Queen's brownstone as I had, he would see soon enough the pictures of Tailgunner Joe and the Ice Queen. But, I wouldn't have broken a confidence; I wouldn't have fingered him. So I told Wild Bill about how an unnamed client paid me to retrieve a document that was purportedly hidden in the Ice Queen's house. I broke in, didn't find the information that I was looking for, but found the drawings of an Atomic bomb.

"You know how to pick locks?" Wild Bill asked.

"No. That's one thing you didn't teach me," I said, "but you did teach me how to *hire* somebody to do something that I couldn't do. I hired a person that could pick a lock that made me feel that no lock was safe." I didn't tell him that the person that I hired was a woman Japanese artist who I paid in months of free rent and was now watching TV in a room at the Mayflower Hotel.

Wild Bill chuckled. "That's it?" he asked.

"That's it," I said. "I saw the drawings for what I thought was a bomb and the language was something Oriental. I didn't know what to do with it. Do I take it to the cops? They'd be more baffled about it than me. And, then they would be asking me questions about how I got it. The drawings really looked fishy to me—and since we're in a war with Korea—I thought only of you to send it to. If it was nothing, you'd toss it; if it was something important then I knew that you knew the right people to give it to."

I had not told the whole story. Sure, I told him about the Ice Queen; I just had not told him *everything*.

"You did the right thing, Jake," Wild Bill said. "As I told you, I've already got some people working on it. They are not officially CIA—or at least this isn't a CIA official mission—but they are people that I can trust. There are a lot of new people in the CIA, and they are very political. I think the agency is more into assassinations and changing entire governments than they are in being the eyes and ears for the United States. From what I hear— and I hear pretty good even at my age—the following assassinations are all but done: Ali Razmara of Iran, Riad Al-Sulh and Abdullah of Jordan and Ali Knah Liaquat of Pakistan. The CIA is also experimenting in germ warfare—I know, I know, this sounds like the Nazis—and they're going to have a simulated germ warfare project going in Mechanicsburg, Pennsylvania."

"Germ warfare? In the United States?"

"That's what my sources tell me. Anyways, I've got some reliable people looking into this Korean thing, but we'll need some political clout." There he was using that 'we' stuff again. I hoped I wasn't part of that 'we.' My job was as messenger, end of story.

Wild Bill looked at his watch. "I've invited a man over to hear your story. Don't worry, you can trust him, I guarantee that. He'll be here in about five minutes. Let me give you a brief background. Ever heard of Dick Nixon?"

19

Monday, September 24, 1951

The man that Wild Bill had invited into our little reunion was a Congressman, a Congressman who had built a reputation on nabbing Commies.

Richard M. Nixon from California.

Nixon had a position on the House Un-American Committee, or HUAC as it was referred to by the press.

Wild Bill told me that Nixon had ridden the anti-Communism wave to win his first election just five years before. It seems that his congressional opponent Jerry Voorhis had been a five-term incumbent who had been endorsed by a political labor organization that was suspected of Communist affiliation. Using anti-Communist bashing with energy like a Southern preacher, Nixon beat the hell out of the guy and rode into Congress.

From there, the HUAC recruited him.

"Nixon was the one that nailed Alger Hiss," Wild Bill said. "Hiss was the type of guy that Nixon *wanted* to nail—Hiss was rich, a pointy head liberal from Harvard and had been an aide of FDR at Yalta. Everything that Nixon wasn't. From the start—and you and I were over in Germany at the time—the American public believed Hiss. Pretty persuasive guy. Hell, the guy was handsome, Ivy League credentials and could talk real convincingly. Nixon brought Hiss to the witness stand and nailed him to the cross. That's where he got the nickname Tricky Dick—from the liberals who will hate him long after he's dead and buried.

"You'll find that Nixon is a fighter. He hates Communism, but he also knows how to use it politically. He's not like Joe McCarthy. McCarthy is putting on a sideshow. There's no benefit to America—McCarthy's going after a lot of people that were just stupid for a time. Every one of them, however, gets headlines for Joe. Joe is like tungsten; he's bright when he's lit, but he'll flame out quick, just watch my words."

"I've known Nixon off and on since he was a young lawyer. In fact, let me tell you a funny story. Nixon had gone to Duke law school. He came up to Washington to find a job. *I* interviewed him here. This was before the war, of course, before you and I had our little projects in Eastern Europe. Well, I interview this young guy, Dick Nixon. You could tell that he was an intense SOB. He tells me that he was interested—at least eventually—in politics. I told him, 'Go home then, don't start in Washington. Go home, practice law, build some political base and then go for it.' Damned if he didn't take my advice. Against my own advice, I offered him a job, but no, he said he was going home, but that he would be back. Sure enough, he's back. And, this time, I think he'll eventually get on the Republican ticket. Who knows, he might one day be President of the United States. He's got the ambition, that's for sure. He also has the energy and most of all, he's got the political savvy. To blow this Korean thing out of the water, we'll need to take this public. The CIA would just finger fuck this thing all over the place; we need to take this public and Richard Nixon is the guy that could ride this horse all the way to the finish line."

As if on cue, the phone rang, Wild Bill picked it up and said, "He's here." Wild Bill walked to the door, opened it and Congressman Richard M. Nixon was standing there. He was taller than I had thought him to be—maybe six feet tall—but his five o'clock shadow was in Full Moon stage. That guy needed a shave at five o'clock more than I needed one at five in the morning. He looked tough in a tough street lawyer way. If he was after some poor stiff in the courtroom—like Alger Hiss—then you could kiss that stiff *good-bye*. His face lightened a bit—just a little bit—with a smile that was as forced as a hooker's.

Nixon stepped in to Wild Bill's office and awkwardly stuck out his hand like the Tin Man would in the Wizard of Oz. Wild Bill shook. He then introduced me and I shook hands with the Tin Man.

Wild Bill walked over to an armoire, opened the door and inside was the fixings for drinks. "It's about five o'clock and all this talk about Commies has made me thirsty for a real drink. What can I get you?"

I said I would have more coffee. Dick Nixon said water.

Wild Bill laughed, "Dick here is the best in the world at milking a drink. Hell, the ice melts before he takes his second sip. I've been with him when he's had the same beer sit in front of himself for hours."

"On second thought," Nixon said, "I'll have a cup of black coffee also. It's been a long day."

Coffee was on its way.

Nixon wasn't a small-talk guy. He asked about Wild Bill's wife, and said to the reply "That's nice." I got the feeling that if Wild Bill would have said that his wife was a heroin addict who was doing two-dollar tricks on the street Nixon would have nodded his head and said the same "That's nice." But, he looked tired, almost ready for bed-bye.

Finally, when we were all settled with our chosen drinks, Wild Bill said, "Dick's already seen the Korean drawings of the bomb, Jake. Tell Dick about how you got them."

I looked at Wild Bill; he nodded his head to signify that Nixon was okay. I told Nixon the same story as I told Wild Bill, almost word for word, leaving out the same stuff. As I talked, I could visibly see Nixon slowly become a little more alive. He'd stop me every once in awhile with a question and then listen intently as if I was giving him careful instructions on how to save his soul.

"Those fucking Korean Commies," he said when I took a breath. "Nobody in Congress is really taking them seriously. It's not our war, they say, this is the *United Nations* war. Just how fucking stupid is that? It's mostly our boys over there in that hellhole, it's our boys being shot up, it's our boys being killed. And, it looks like the Koreans have spies over here where our peace-seeking liberals just hand over top secrets to kill more of our boys."

Nixon said that all in one breath. He went from looking like he was about to drop into a coma to being fiercely agitated. I could feel his eyes pierce mine as if I was Alger Hiss. I felt like saying, "Slow down, pal, I'm just the messenger."

Wild Bill made an effort to slow down Nixon, "Dick, I just wanted you to hear this story. We know this is a very serious matter, but we don't have to burden Jake here with all of our problems."

This sounded like my exit line. Sure enough, Wild Bill got up and walked over to me. I got the cue and stood up.

"Jake, thank you making the trip down here," Wild Bill said. Nixon stayed seated. I guessed that they would stay and talk about their problems. Probably Commie problems. "You're checked in at the Mayflower, right?"

I nodded. I didn't tell him that Hiromi had also checked in to an adjoining room.

"Good, good," he said, "I'd like for you to come back here to my office about eleven tomorrow morning. I would like you to meet a couple of other fellas to tell your story. They *need* to hear it from you. Unfortunately, they couldn't get back in time for this meeting. I hope this won't inconvenience you at all."

"Yes, um, Jake," Nixon said, rising. "Thank you for the information." He had cooled down—he looked ready for bed-bye again. His five o'clock shadow had deepened even more and I wondered if he had to use a small axe to shave in the morning.

I walked out of Donovan, Leisure, Newton and Lombard and it wasn't even six o'clock. I felt like a little kid that had been excused from the dinner table just as the parents were talking about adult stuff. It wasn't a good feeling, but at the same time, I did *not* want to be involved in this Commie stuff. Still, the little kid feeling seeped into my brain making me feel a little uncomfortable.

20

Monday, September 24, 1951

As I walked to the hotel from the meeting with Wild Bill and Nixon, I figured I had two choices.

The first choice was to go get Hiromi and take the train back to Brooklyn tonight. I didn't feel like hanging around just to talk to some Feds. Wild Bill and now Nixon had heard everything I was going to say about the Ice Queen. The guys tomorrow weren't going to hear anything new. Tomorrow would just be the third performance of a bad play.

The second choice was to go back to the hotel—it was a fancy hotel at that—get something to eat with Hiromi, maybe see a movie and see the Fed types tomorrow.

There really wasn't much of a choice. I would have to keep the appointment tomorrow. If I just went home, I would be showing up Wild Bill. That I couldn't do. He had meant too much to me as a person, leader, even a bit of a father figure and perhaps a mentor. Although he didn't really take me aside like a college mentor and individually tutor me, he did collectively mentor me and the other guys. He did it such a way that it felt like a one-to-one relationship. Wild Bill had been great to me; I guessed that I could afford a few hours of wasted time.

I took the elevator up to my room. The door between my room and Hiromi's room was open. I looked in. She had fallen asleep watching TV. I sat down on the corner of the bed, making sure not to wake her, and just watched her. My God, she was beautiful. I thought of what a strange world this was—just six years before we had been fighting the Japanese and the only Japanese that I and most Americans on the East Coast had ever seen were those buck-teethed slant-eyed stereotypes we had seen in the propaganda war movies. I watched Hiromi softly breathing; to me she looked like an angel. I gently touched her arm. She opened her eyes, and she smiled. She stretched, pushing her arms upward, holding her smile. She then swept her arms around my neck and held on tight. I put my arms around her and held her tight.

"How did things go with your General?" she asked, her head on my shoulder.

"Fine," I said. "You know I have to meet some people tomorrow?"

I felt her head nod on my shoulder.

"So, tonight let's get something to eat, and maybe see a movie."

I felt her head nod on my shoulder again.

We could have gone to a baseball game. That night the local team, the Washington Senators, were playing a doubleheader against the St. Louis Browns. Who'd want to see that mess? The Senators were awful in seventh place; the Browns were worse in dead last. Neither team had a player that could play for the Dodgers. The Browns had one guy that I would have liked to have seen in a Dodger uniform. However, he only played one game and then was dumped. I would have loved to have seen him at bat against Sal Maglie of the Giants. Maglie's nickname was The Barber, mainly because his inside pitches were so close that they could shave the batter's chin. That one Brownie I'd like to see against Maglie was a guy that was only three-feet seven-inches tall and weighed only sixty-five pounds. Eddie Gaedel, the midget that the Browns owner Bill Veeck had sent to the plate on August 18. Gaedel walked, of course, on four pitches. His strike zone was only one and a half *inches*. Then they sent in Jim Delsing to run for him. With Maglie on the mound, the Dodgers would have to put a football helmet on the little guy otherwise The Barber would kill him. But, Gaedel couldn't join the Dodgers to drive Leo Durocher and Sal Maglie and the other Giants crazy. I think the commissioner had banned him for being too short. If Gaedel was banned, where did that leave the Yankee shortstop, Phil Rizzuto? Hell, he seemed like midget.

After we freshened up, we walked toward the White House and found an old joint that caught my attention. Its name was the Old Ebbitt Grill. It wasn't spelled the same way as Ebbets Field, but to me in a strange city, it was close enough. The sign outside said that the saloon had been around since 1856, so I had to figure that there were an equal amount of beers and lies in its history. Old Ebbitt Grill specialized in oysters, so Hiromi and I had a couple of plates and washed them down with a few beers.

I asked the waiter if there was a movie theatre within walking distance. He told me about the Bijou Theatre a couple of blocks away. He said that the Bijou didn't show the big Hollywood movies, just the B-movies and other movies that were a couple years old. I hoped that by chance the movie house would be showing *The Third Man*. That movie was starring Nick Salzano's Commie, Orson Welles. I was more interested in the locale—Vienna—because I had recruited two former Nazi spy networks in Vienna. But, if all the theatre had was a B-movie, then that's all that was necessary to suck up a couple of hours. I wasn't going there to do a movie review; I just wanted the movie to take up some time.

We saw the marquee from two blocks away; we saw the movie title from a block away: *Unnatural*. When I read the movie poster outside, I knew this would be a movie that Hiromi would love to see. Science fiction all the way, except there weren't any prehistoric monsters. I put down fifty cents for Hiromi and me, and we walked in.

About a third of the way through the movie, it was eerily reminding me of the Ice Queen. There was a mad scientist who had created a very beautiful woman via artificial insemination. Because her heritage was created artificially, she had no soul or sense of morality and delivered tragedy on a platter to everyone near her. That seemed to be the Ice Queen all the way. I hadn't uncovered any mad scientist with the Ice Queen, but maybe there was one lurking out there someplace.

Unnatural was less than two-hours long, so we stayed in the theatre to watch part of it again. It was uncanny about the correlation between the premise of a created monster and the Ice Queen. I wondered if one of the Ice Queen's parents was a test tube.

When we had finished a second box of popcorn, we got up and left the theatre. We were about three blocks from the hotel. We walked holding hands. As we walked back to the hotel, I saw a Hudson Commodore pull up to the curb about twenty feet in front of us. A driver got out, walked around the car and opened the back door that was curbside. Nobody got out. It looked like he was holding the door open for Hiromi and me.

I heard some footsteps behind me on my right and on my left. At the same time, a hand gripped my elbow that was toward the street. I heard Hiromi say, "Oh." I quickly turned to her. There was a big bastard holding her elbow. I looked at the guy holding my elbow. He was about my height and age. I had never seen him before. He didn't look like a mugger, but he didn't look like a hairdresser either. He was wearing a decent suit and could have been a Fed.

"This way, Mr. McHenry," he said smiling, with a very slight accent. "Mr. Jones would like to see you. He even sent his car." He pointed to the Hudson Commodore. His accent was familiar. Russian? I had heard that accent enough during my time in Berlin. I don't want to sound like I'm prejudiced or anything, but I never met a Russian in Berlin that I liked. Brutes, they were. Although I had never seen it, I had heard that the Russians raped every German woman under seventy in the Russian sector in

Berlin. Wild Bill filled us in on Stalin, of course. I think Wild Bill thought that Stalin was more evil than Hitler.

I had brought a gun with me, but I wasn't carrying it. I had left it in my suitcase at the hotel. Unlike my days in Berlin, I didn't naturally carry a gun with me everyplace I went. My paranoia should have stood up and told me to take the gun when Hiromi and I went out to dinner. Unfortunately, paranoia isn't always reliable.

The Russian's right hand was a vice grip on my left elbow; his left hand had been in his suit jacket like he was mimicking Napoleon. He brought his right hand out of his jacket with a gun gripped in it and stuck it in my ribs.

I heard Hiromi say "Oh" again.

There are a few times in my life when I've been able to think of a whole lot of things in just a sliver—the *smallest* sliver—of a second. This wasn't a part of my everyday thinking; most of the time my everyday thinking was a little sluggish. But, at this tiny sliver of time when the gun poked my ribs I was able to think so quickly that if my thoughts had been transferred into books it would have been larger than the entire collection of Shakespeare.

My first thought was that these guys were not the good guys.

My second thought was that we should not get into that car. My mother always had told me: *don't get into a car with strangers.* I assumed that this was one of those times that she was talking about.

The third thought was that the guy wouldn't shoot the gun. He was using it as a prop, an exclamation point. I had on occasion used a gun as a prop in Eastern Europe. It was effective. It caught a person's attention; they usually did what you wanted them to do without any fuss when a gun was stuck in their ribs. These guys that had attached themselves to our elbows wanted me to meet somebody. I assumed that meeting was to talk. Splaying me out on a DC sidewalk with a bullet hole creating a third eye wouldn't enhance the conversation. If I were wrong in my thinking, this thug would pull the trigger a few times, jump in the car and my last thought while living would be that I had guessed wrong. All that thinking was in the tiniest sliver of a second and then I reacted.

21

Monday, September 24, 1951

From my childhood training on the streets of Brooklyn and then applied to my bouts in the Golden Glove days, there were two things that I instinctively knew I had to use: quickness and explosion. No chit-chat, no conversation, no debates, no struggling, just *quickness* and *explosion*. I just hoped that Hiromi would dodge out of the way.

I did *quick* and *explosion* simultaneously in the same motion like a Flamenco dancer would do. I stomped the right foot of the guy on my left like I was trying to crack the cement beneath his foot. As I stomped I pulled my elbow free and fired it like a basketball player would to the guy's face, except faster and harder. The crunch probably could have been heard back at the Bijou. The guy went down like a sack of rocks. While I had used just a sliver of a second to think, I had used another sliver—this one a little bit larger—to drop the guy that had been clenching my elbow. It wasn't quick enough. The guy on my right—the one who had been squeezing Hiromi's elbow—was in a full swing when I turned to him. This guy looked like one of those Russian palookas in the Russian sector in Berlin—all brawn, no brains and a high tolerance for pain. I pulled my head back, but his full swing hit me on my left shoulder. He had sap in his hand and even though it wasn't a direct blow it felt like a cannonball had dropped on my shoulder from twenty stories above. I went down on my knees.

His foot was as quick as the sap, flying at my midsection like a missile. It connected full force. It penetrated my stomach so hard that his foot could have put a dent in my backbone. I went down on my ass. I couldn't breathe and I couldn't get up and I could barely see through all the light bursts in the back of my eyes. The big bastard tossed Hiromi across the sidewalk and she tumbled badly. He then hustled over to his pal who was flat out on the cement sidewalk. The guy I hit with my elbow was out cold, his face spewing a pool of blood as if he had turned on a faucet in his nose.

I forced myself to breathe. I was defenseless; if the thug wasn't attending to his pal, he could have finished me off right then and there. My eyes started to gain focus. Off to my right laying on the cement was the gun of the guy that I had given the elbow shiver to. I reached and grabbed it with my right hand. With that simple reach, a high-voltage shock of pain burst through my left shoulder. Who knows which broken bones were sticking out through my skin and shirt? However, if I didn't do something, my mother's greatest fear would come true—I'd be in a car with strangers. I didn't think they wanted me in that car to fondle me.

I grabbed the gun off of the sidewalk.

Like a three-legged dog I got to my feet—awkwardly. I stepped over to the bouncer, still attending to his pal, and slammed the butt of the gun as hard as I have ever slammed anything into his temple. Amazingly, his head started to turn toward me; he was trying to get his balance. Then he toppled to his left. I heard steps behind me. I turned with no pain. I must have been in total shock, just about ready to shutdown. It was the driver. He didn't look like a thug; he looked like a driver. He was smaller than the two thugs and wore one of those chauffeur caps. I pointed the gun at him. He stopped as if he had been shot. Yep, the gun can be a terrific prop. Most of the time, it gets folks to do what you want them to do with no fuss or muss. It doesn't work as well when used against a good

Catholic boy whose mother had always warned him not to get in a car with strangers.

"Get out of here," I said. The driver backpedaled. "Go, go, go." He went. I was still standing there, wobbly as the Scarecrow, as the driver yanked the Hudson into traffic and hightailed it out of there.

The bouncer somehow pushed himself up to one knee. I could tell he wasn't thinking great thoughts or probably any thoughts at all; he had arisen out of pure instinct. I gripped the barrel of the gun. I wound up with one clear intention—smashing his skull with such force that he would never rise up again.

I reached back, way back like I was going to throw a fastball, the gun barrel clenched tightly in my fist. I would let go of that gun barrel only when the butt would crash into the bouncer's temple. Hiromi grabbed my arm with both of her hands.

"Jake, noooooooooooo," she shouted. She was hanging on to my arm-wrestling her arms around my arm. I looked at her. I thought of shaking her off.

"*No, Jake, no,*" she screamed. "*Don't hit him again!*"

I wanted to hit him again. In fact, I wanted to *kill* him. The rage in me had taken over. I even felt like pushing Hiromi the hell away. I *felt* like it, but I didn't do it. I let her pull me away.

As she pulled me, the bouncer pushed himself up to a kneeling position. He clearly didn't know what world he was in. He then fell forward, pancaking his buddy to the sidewalk.

"Let's go, Jake, let's go," Hiromi said.

I'm not sure what I said, but I noticed that her knees were bloody from being tossed on the sidewalk. Blood was dribbling down her shins.

The two thugs were laid out on the sidewalk. I stared at them until my sense of sound—which must have been suspended during those seconds of action except for Hiromi's pleas—echoed voices in my ear. About thirty feet away, there were some evening walkers coming down the sidewalk. "Hey," a voice from down the street said, "what's going on?"

I turned, "Accident," I said, "these guys need an ambulance. Call one. Call one!" The Good Samaritan and his companions backed away. They had seen the gun in my hand. An ambulance might eventually come, but you can bet that the Good Samaritan would walk down a different street to his destination.

I tucked the gun into my belt and pulled out my shirt bottoms to cover it.

Hiromi and I walked back to the hotel. If any pedestrian had noticed my shuffling walk, it would have been a quick assumption that it was going to take a week to cure that hangover.

We staggered through the hotel lobby and to the elevators. Since the two guys hadn't landed any punches on my face and I wasn't bleeding on the outside, I think most people thought I was just another drunk from Capital Hill. There were enough drunks in business suits in this area not to draw any attention to me. I had one concern in the elevator: don't pass out.

Once in the room, I dropped down on the bed to catch my breath. Hiromi had rushed to the bathroom to get me some water.

My shoulder hurt like hell and my stomach pulsated. I thought that if that guy had kicked my balls as hard as he did my stomach and if I wanted kids later in my life that I would go straight to the adoption houses.

I asked Hiromi to hand me the phone by the side of the bed. I knew I should probably go to the hospital to find out if anything was broken or if there was internal bleeding. I could bleed to death and not know it until I was dead. Before I would even consider a hospital visit, I needed a temporary fix.

The fix I was thinking about could be provided by room service.

"I need two buckets full of ice," I said on the phone to the room service guy, "and a bottle of whiskey. If you bring this up to me in five minutes, I'll give you a twenty-dollar tip. If it's six minutes, you get ten dollars, seven minutes five dollars, eight minutes a buck."

Within four minutes I had my ice and whiskey and I fed the room service guy a twenty-dollar bill.

My shoulder and stomach were killing me, but the first thing I did was run cold water on a towel. I asked Hiromi to sit down on the toilet seat. Her nylons were ripped through. I pressed the towel onto her skinned knees. She stared at me. I looked at her and gave her a quirky smile. It wasn't until later that I remembered how she had stared at me when I cleaned her skinned knees. What could she have been thinking? In one moment, I was ready to murder a man—that's right murder—and in a moment after that I was gently nursing her cut knees. She probably was thinking: who is that maniac?

I then took another towel, laid it out flat and dumped a bunch of ice on it. I folded the edges. That one would be for my shoulder. I repeated the process; the second one was for my stomach. I then fished around inside my suitcase and found my little bottle of Bayer Aspirin. I downed twelve of those little tablets.

I carried my ice bags back into the room and gingerly propped myself up on the bed. Hiromi came out of the bathroom. She had taken off the ripped nylons and her business suit. She just wore a long slip and bra. She got onto the bed and lightly held the ice bags on my shoulder and stomach. With my ice bags in the two strategic spots, she leaned into my good side and held me. She was shivering.

While I had been preparing the ice, I had been thinking who could have sent those two thugs—who was Mr. Jones? There obviously wasn't a real Mr. Jones, but *somebody* had sent those guys. Who? It wouldn't have been one of my divorce cases; I didn't have any Russian divorce cases. If it was an angry ex-husband, I suppose he could have hired a couple of Russian thugs, but why wouldn't they just beat me up or kill me instead of trying to collect me and Hiromi and take us to Mr. So-called Jones? Naw, if it was one pissed off husband, he would have just had me beaten to a pulp.

If pissed off husbands didn't orchestrate it, I came to the name of who I knew it was, the Ice Queen. It was like the movie *Unnatural*, everybody that came close to that evil bitch suffered. My life before the Ice Queen had been like a sea of glass—smooth sailing, a slight trade wind, high clouds. But if I tapped the barometer now, the barometric pressure would be plunging like a Nor'easter was barreling down the East Coast right at us.

In my mind, I started to itemize the things that I knew about The Ice Queen:

One, she knew that Hiromi and I had been in her brownstone. She had pictures to prove it.

Two, she probably thought that I had gotten in to her safes. If I had gotten into her safes, I knew all about the Korean drawings of a bomb. I knew about the extortion pictures. If I knew those things, I could tell people what I knew. If I could tell the right people that could do something about it—perhaps like Wild Bill could—then she would have to do some serious dodging and weaving and probably have to run like hell.

Three, she was involved with something so important and so volatile that any loose end—like me and Hiromi—could ruin it all. If you're in the type of business that the Ice Queen was in, loose ends were bad for business.

Four, she had to remove the loose ends. The loose ends started with me and ended with Hiromi.

Five, I was hurting like hell.

Lastly, there was one thing that bothered me more than all the others and this scared me. It was the same feeling that haunted me in Europe. I had killed there, willingly. And, I didn't need to. These weren't just wartime killings; each one was a *murder*. I murdered willingly and I didn't lose a minute of sleep over my murders. Those murders led to, of course, me being rich, but I hadn't killed because of the money. At the time, I didn't know that there would be riches. I murdered because I *wanted* to. I didn't murder because of uncontrolled temper. Some of the murders were as planned, calculated and premeditated as they could get. In a court of law, I'd just be quickly passed to the electric chair.

This may sound strange, but the thing about the murders that troubled me the most was that I wasn't bothered by the murders. I thought that that was the way a psychopath would feel.

Over the past couple of years, the violence that had taken me over had disappeared. Baseball and beer, I guess, had become the right antidote. I started to think that it was the environment in Europe that made me a murderer, that the murders weren't the real me. And now tonight, the *desire* to kill had returned. It had returned in a flash like it had just been hovering, waiting, someplace close in a dark recess of my consciousness.

22

Monday, September 24, 1951

It wasn't until *after* the war that I killed a man.

When I enlisted, I had thought that killing was part of the deal. After all, in war doesn't one side try to kill the other? The side that kills the most usually wins. Killing a man in war is *duty*. The killings that I did after the war weren't duty. Those killings were murder.

The first guy that I killed clearly deserved it. I'm not even sure if a jury of my peers would convict me. In fact, each juror would probably have said, *Good job, I woulda done the same thing.* The jury might have even given me a standing ovation.

My first murder was a Waffen SS guy, but being SS wasn't the reason I killed him. There were a few Waffen SS guys that I did business with that seemed to be okay guys. I'm serious. These guys didn't run any concentration camps; these guys didn't stand a thousand Poles in front of a trench then slam bullets into them until they toppled into the pit. They were soldiers, real soldiers. It's strange, but I could see myself in their place. I'm not a bad guy, I don't think, even though I've killed and done a few nasty things. I was a mechanic of war just like they were. The particular specialty of the SS guys that I was dealing with was primarily spying. My particular specialty was taking over their spy network.

Long before V-J Day, Wild Bill Donovan's war wasn't with the Nazis. For twenty-four hours a day, he had us preparing our fight against Communism, Russian Communism. Heck, the Nazis were evil bullies who wanted to rule the world. We could stop that nonsense, and we did. The Reds were worse, I was told. They wanted take over our world one worker at a time. First it would be one European worker at a time. Then this Communism would somehow drift over to the United States like some plague caught up in the winds, and, one at a time, our workers would succumb to Communism. I didn't know too much about politics, but I was told that the Reds wanted to take over our world from the *inside* and that was like cancer. So, Wild Bill drew a line in the sand in Eastern Europe. He felt it started with a listening post. Eastern European SS networks had a practiced ear to the ground for at least a decade. Wild Bill Donovan wanted those ears to now listen for him. What he wanted to hear was about Communism.

Finding Waffen SS guys with Eastern Front experience was sometimes easier than it would seem. Some of these bastards had heard that we were looking for them. They'd heard that we wanted to work *with* them. If they cooperated, we would not only *not* arrest them; we'd give them a false cover and arrange for their exit to a South American country, most likely Argentina.

We'd even give them fifteen hundred dollars in American greenbacks to grease their trip. That seemed like a fortune to me. That type of money would go a long way in paying for a house in the United States. If the American public—particularly the Jews—ever found out that we were *paying* ex-SS killers, we'd probably have another revolution. But, that was the way it was. We had no experience with networks in the Eastern Front. The SS did. We were willing to pay good money—and freedom—to the right SS officers so that we could adopt their networks.

These SS officers didn't *own* their networks, like somebody could own a car or a house, but they had culled and gathered and managed those networks during the war. When the war ended, the SS officers lit out back to Germany, trying to blend in with the gray masses. However, they retained critical information about those networks—particularly the names and locations of the leaders. For us to start a network like that from scratch would take us *years*. Wild Bill told us we didn't have months, let alone years, in what has now been labeled as the Cold War.

So, if one of these bastards could deliver us a network that we could resuscitate, we had no problem about giving him money and a free pass out of the country.

The crazy thing is that we used the same system to get these SS guys out of the country that they used for themselves. This was an escape route that the Nazis themselves had set up. We had known about this escape route; we had collaborated with this escape route. It was funded by Nazis in South America with loot that they had stashed for years before the war ended. It was also funded by us, the United States of America. This escape organization was called Odessa. They called their escape route the ratline. After a while, we called it the same thing. The ratline.

Not every Nazi got this free ride, of course. The big names like Borman and Himmler and that bunch were off-limits to us. No free ride for them, at least not engineered by us. If and when these big-shot Nazis were caught, they were ticketed for the Nuremburg

Trials. We were looking for smaller fish, guys who wouldn't be star Nazis at Nuremburg. Besides, those big shots didn't control the local networks in the Eastern Front; it was the frontline Waffen SS guys that we wanted and the ones we ferreted out.

The Waffen SS Nazis didn't play the stupid innocent roles either. They knew what was going on with the concentration camps and all. It's not like those German citizens around Buchenwald who said they didn't know that the Nazis were burning bodies. What did they think that stink was—that the Nazis were burning tires or something? The Nazis I dealt with knew what was happening. In fairness to them, however, what were these SS officers to do? Protest? Their protest would have been the quicker ticket to the incinerator than being a Jew or a gypsy.

While there were some Waffen SS guys I could empathize with, there were plenty of others I felt were evil from the get-go. I suspect that the SS recruited quite a few psychopaths. If they were psychopaths when the entered, believe me they didn't get sane with years of service. When I got to these guys, they weren't in their full SS regalia—the power uniform of black, the black leather overcoats, the jodhpurs and knee-high black boots. By the time I got to them, they were dressed like privates who had hobbled home from the Eastern Front or bakers whose bakery and house had been bombed—but I could tell that they were SS. It was a certain arrogance that's difficult to explain, but it oozed through their rumpled disguise like an infected wound. Sometimes it was just a small sneer that I could tell would blossom into a snarl if the positions were reversed. These guys were bastards through and through. The problem was that I had to deal with a lot more of these guys than the mechanics of war.

I started dealing face to face with these Nazis about four years after I enlisted. I enlisted a few days after Pearl Harbor, December 7, 1941. I'd just got out of Brooklyn College the previous spring. I had a job as a trainee of Standard Oil of New Jersey, so going off to war seemed to be the best choice of beating boredom. Because I was a college graduate, the Army fast-forwarded me after basic training into Intelligence and air-mailed me along to England. By chance, I was snapped up by a new U.S. organization called the Office of Strategic Services led by Wild Bill Donovan. He was the founder of the outfit. So, I started with Wild Bill in the OSS as just a kid of twenty-two in 1941 and came home nine years later a much smarter, and much richer, guy at the tender age of just thirty-one. When other guys were just taking their first little steps upward in a career as civilians, I had already amassed riches. I was a real walking-talking success story, but because of the killing and stealing, I never thought I'd be the subject of any Horatio Alger story in *Colliers* magazine.

Wild Bill had grabbed me because I had one attribute that he had his bird dogs sniffing through all the Armed Forces for: I could speak German fluently. Toss in my college education and my record as a Golden Gloves boxer, and I was prime meat for Wild Bill.

I came by my fluency in German naturally. My mother was born in Germany. She married, of all things, an Irish guy. That's how a mick like me, Jakob Finbar McHenry, ended up half Kraut, half Irish.

My mother, however, didn't teach me the language. It was my grandmother. I was brought up in a neighborhood in Brooklyn that spoke a lot of languages, but rarely German. Grandma lived in Yorkville on the Upper East Side of Manhattan where German was the language of the day. If a tourist went to the Upper East Side, closed his eyes, he'd think he was in Berlin just by the sounds and smells. The folks on the Upper East Side spoke German, there was German music floating out of the apartments, and it seemed every other restaurant was German. Before the war, there were swastikas all over the place. They had their own German newspaper. They even had their own brand of Brown Shirts, which in Brooklyn we'd call a gang, but in Yorkville they were Hitler Youth. Once the war started, the folks in Yorkville didn't shitcan their swastikas, but just brought them inside and hung them there over their mantle.

In Brooklyn, we lived just the way that Adolf Hitler thought would be the ruin of the civilized world—races and religions all mingled together. There were divisions, of course. The Italians went to Lafayette High School, the Negroes went to Jefferson, and the middle-class Jews went to Midwood. Me? I went to high school with the Italians. Nick and I attended Lafayette together.

It didn't really make much difference what nationality anybody was when were kids; what mattered was stickball or stoopball or Catch A Fly or You're Up. Stoopball was my favorite because that really required skill. To win at that game, it was necessary to throw with pinpoint accuracy and be able to run like the wind. Since almost every house had a six or seven-step stoop, the designated thrower would fire the ball at the stoop. Depending on where the ball hit on the stoop, it would either rocket back as a line drive or take some crazy bounce. If it was caught on the fly, the thrower was out. If it hit the ground once, the thrower was credited with a single, twice a double and so forth. So, getting the crazy bounce took real control. If the ball bounced off of a car and was caught before it hit the ground it was an out. We learned to play the cars like Furillo played rightfield at Ebbets. We shoulda got Abe Stark suits on some of those catches.

So, mainly because I spoke German, I wasn't with the mob of soldiers in Times Square in New York when V-J Day came along on August 14, 1945. I eventually did see the *Life* magazine that had that famous picture of the soldier kissing the girl. I wondered at the time, did he know her or was this the prelude to one soldier's getting lucky on a lucky day? My limo friend Allie says it was him, of course. All I know is that I was in Berlin at the time of V-J Day. We celebrated, I guess, if you'd call a beer and a cigarette a celebration. Berlin was a landscape of rubble at the time. Many Germans looked just a couple of steps away from falling down and dying right in front of you. However, that's where I made my fortune.

That I was doing something patriotic while I made this fortune made it so much the better.

It was one of those guys—Franz Scheffler—who sent me, accidentally, on my way to riches. Franz was one true bastard. He did have blood all over his hands. He could have been ticketed for Nuremburg as easy as not. He also had a highly effective network in what was once Estonia.

"You are so lucky to have won," Scheffler had told me during one meeting. His English was remarkably good. There weren't too many times that he substituted a *v* for a *w*. His record keeping was better than remarkably good. It was almost perfect. One thing about the Germans, they kept great records on everything. They could have been great baseball fans with their record keeping and all.

Scheffler had given me the detailed records of his spy network a few weeks before. Another one of Wild Bill's guys went into the field to verify the network. That was the dangerous job. Thank God, I only had to do the deal with these Nazis. If the network was still viable, Scheffler had his free pass. Eventually, his network was deemed one of the better run networks that we had ever come across. Free pass for Scheffler, no matter how much blood stained his hands.

"Yeah, sure," I responded to Scheffler's stupid remark about luck. What, did I want to get into a debate with a Nazi?

"You vill see," he said, this time slipping a *v* in, "the Jews will rebound, they *vill* gather strength, they *vill* ruin your country. You, you have losts the war, not us."

"Yeah, sure," I said.

"You vill want to come to South America where it is safe. You vill see, you vill see, maybe if you live long enough."

A day later, Scheffler told me something more damaging.

"You know, Yank, I killed over a thousand Jews, too many for me to count," Scheffler said, throwing that sentence at me in a conversational tone like he was commenting on the weather or something.

I looked at him. He knew I couldn't or wouldn't do anything. He was immune from the law. We—the United States— had made a deal with him. It's not that we were so honorable about our deals. The only reason we would honor our deal was because we wanted more Scheffler types to hand over their networks to us. If we nailed Scheffler for what he had done during the war—like killing a thousand Jews—we might never get another network handed to us. He knew it and I knew it.

"Have you ever fucked a Jew?" Scheffler asked.

"Shut up," I said. "Shut the fuck up."

"I would fuck the good-looking ones—the ones that still had meat on their bones—before I killed them," Scheffler said. "I liked the twelve- year-old girls best."

I stood up, walked away, and looked out the window. Doing a deal with murderers like Scheffler was what I did for a living. The ones who were killers, puffed up with their arrogance in their evilness, were part and parcel of the job. If he had been on the Nuremburg list there would have been an easy answer—slap the cuffs on him and let him stand trial at Nuremburg and then watch him hang. But, while Scheffler was evil, he wasn't the big league evil that made the Nuremburg list. So, we did deals with his likes, babysat them for a while and then turned them loose on South America. Some of those South American countries should have sued the shit out of us for who we had sent them.

"I started to like killing Jews," Scheffler said, "I grew to really *like* it, better than sex, but I found I could do both, fuck and then kill. Sometimes I fucked and killed at the *same time*. Wonderful! The Jewess' vagina squeezes you so hard when you slit her throat and the blood is like beer. Rest assured I won't stop killing Jews; the first thing I do when I get to South America is to fuck and kill a Jew."

I jumped over to him and pushed him off his chair on to the floor. I grabbed both ears and banged his head on the floor, again and again. He was unconscious, bleeding on the floor. It was then, however, when I had a moment of real clarity. It was at that time that I started to think I had to kill the bastard, but that I couldn't kill him there. I sure didn't want to trade my life for his. I would kill him and nobody would be the wiser.

23

Monday, September 24, 1951

With Scheffler lying on the floor, I caught my breath. I went back to my chair. Scheffler was out cold on the floor with blood from the back of his head oozing onto the wood floor. In a moment, I'd patch him up.

I didn't bash his head because of any Jew that I knew back in Brooklyn, and I knew plenty of them. Nor did I bash him because of Jews in general. Those I didn't know. After Germany waived the white flag, Wild Bill took us all—I heard under General Eisenhower's orders—to Treblinka. It was like a school field trip except I was in the Army, and we went to a concentration camp. Wild Bill wanted us to *see* and *hear* and *smell* the evil of the Nazis. There's not a man alive who saw that that doesn't have scar tissue someplace in his mind that I know will pop up over the years. It was for those Jews that I saw in Treblinka that I bashed Scheffler's head.

Scheffler recovered quickly from my beating. We never discussed Jews again. Several days later, I got the word that Scheffler's network was as he said it was, and it was now ours. It was time for us to fulfill our part of the bargain.

We didn't just hand him his fake credentials and the cash and wish him good luck. We had to escort him to his rendezvous. Scheffler wasn't in custody during the time we checked out his network; he roamed the streets like any other former German soldier. But, we had one thing that he wanted—freedom. He wouldn't have to sneak out of Germany hiding from us—we would pay him and provide an escort.

When I got the word that his network could be converted to ours, I tracked down Scheffler. I told him about the rendezvous, which was set up by another section in Wild Bill's group. It was set for two days later at nine at night. For those two days, Scheffler didn't bait me mainly because we didn't see each other. He was preparing to leave; I was working to commandeer another network.

The rendezvous point was a farmhouse five miles outside of town. That was the starting point for the *ratline*. I picked up Scheffler on the south end of town in my jeep. He was carrying just a small duffel bag. We drove through the countryside in the dark. It was a clear night with a full moon. If a dog had stepped in front of my jeep, I would have seen it. A couple of miles before the *ratline* farmhouse, I took a sharp left onto a rutted dirt road.

"Where are we going—this is not the way," Scheffler said.

"Calm down," I said, "there's been a change in the rendezvous. You think we can keep on using that farmhouse as if it's a train station?"

We bounced several hundred yards down the dirt road. I stopped under a tree.

"Here," I said, "we wait here. Get your stuff, we wait."

Scheffler got out of the jeep. He couldn't see that I had my .45 in my right hand at my side.

"Over by the tree," I said. Scheffler took some steps in that direction. I pounced from behind him, thrust out my .45 to the back of his head and pulled the trigger. It was that easy and that quick. My heart was beating like a bongo drum.

I walked quickly to the back of the jeep. I grabbed an old bed sheet that I had stored in the trunk and laid it down on the ground next to Scheffler. I rolled Scheffler in the sheet, twisted the ends and dragged him behind the tree.

I had scouted this place out the day before. That's when I dug Scheffler's grave. So, was this murder premeditated? You better believe it was. I had been thinking and planning it for about a week. Knowing that I was going to kill Scheffler was the one thing that had stopped me from bashing his head to putty just the week before.

When I dumped Scheffler's body into the hole, I tried not to think of those Jews that he boasted of killing. I failed. I thought of those Jews, I thought of the South American women he had promised to rape before he killed them, I had a Technicolor nightmare going on live in my brain.

I went to the base of the tree where his small duffel bag had dropped. My first inclination was to bury it with him. But, I was curious to see what had seemed valuable to such a sick fuck—he had held it to his chest with crossed arms throughout the drive. I picked up the duffel. It was far heavier than I had thought. I unzipped it. Wrapped in a cloth was a gold bar. It glistened in the moonlight. There were some other objects that were wrapped tightly. Scheffler was a veritable Santa Claus—all those nicely wrapped packages for himself. Instead of unwrapping all of his gifts on the ground, I put them back into the duffel, carried it back to the jeep, and drove away.

I drove back down the rutted road and turned left and drove to the ratline farmhouse. I would complete the assignment, even if Scheffler didn't.

The ratline farmhouse was never manned. It didn't have any Nazis waiting for the animals to be delivered. The procedure was simple: we would drop a Nazi off, drive away and sometime during the night the Nazi would be picked up for the first leg of his trip to South America. I needed to go to the farmhouse; I wanted it to at least *look* like I had completed my mission.

I saw the farmhouse silhouetted off to the right and pulled into the drive. Typically, no lights were on. I was to check to see if it was secure—it always was—and then leave Scheffler in the farmhouse. His ratline contact would be along sometime after that.

I kicked open the front door and shined my flashlight in. A quick check inside showed that the house had not been occupied recently. I walked into the house and stepped toward the kitchen. I lit the candle on the table. I had pocketed a couple of cigarette butts that Scheffler had discarded and dropped them on the floor. I then ground them a little with my foot.

There would be repercussions about Scheffler not being at the farmhouse when they came to fetch him for the ratline. However, I could easily lie that I had done everything I was supposed to do. Scheffler clearly got the shits and ran early. *Where's Scheffler,* somebody would ask? Who the fuck knows? *Did you give him his new identity and cash?* Sure did, I would say, right after I checked the farmhouse.

Sure enough, two days later there were questions. And, sure enough, they bought my lies. But, I realized then that I had made mistakes. I would not make those mistakes again.

One mistake that I did not make was Scheffler's small duffel bag. On the way back from killing Scheffler, I stopped at another copse of trees. I had not dug a hole beforehand, so I dug a shallow trench where I buried the duffel, gold bar and all. I waited a couple of days after the inquiries to retrieve the bag. Late one afternoon, I dug it up. Behind the trees, I sat down and opened the duffel. The gold bar was there, still as shiny as if it had been spit-shined. Scheffler must have been polishing it to get it to glow like that. I unwrapped the three other bundles.

The first bundle had a stack of American greenbacks that was about three inches in height. All twenties. There was about ten thousand dollars there. Another bundle—bigger than the first—had three stacks of American smackeroos. There was thirty thousand dollars in these stacks. The cash pretty much took my breath away—nobody in my family, or nobody that I knew—had ever *seen* forty thousand dollars in *cash.* Heck, I'd bet that my father had never seen forty thou in *checks in his lifetime,* let alone cash. Some of my high school friends had gravitated to the

Mafia—remember, I went to a high school that was predominantly Italian—and I bet that *they* had never seen that much cash. While the cash took my breath away, it was the last bundle that practically made my heart stop. There was a tiara—I think that's what they're called—one of those things that women wear in their hair when they go to some formal deal. This tiara had by my count twenty-five diamonds. Five of those were bigger than any wedding ring I had ever seen. Obviously, the Nazis had stolen it from somebody rich, and Scheffler had lifted it to ease his settlement in South America. I had no way of figuring how valuable the thing was, but if I had to guess, I would say that it was worth at least as much as the cash.

Three months later, I did a deal with another Nazi just as evil as Scheffler. This guy's name was Krieger. I made up my mind early on that Krieger, like Scheffler, would never reach South America, dead or alive. He would be planted in German soil. Anonymously. This time, however, I had him meet me a week before he would be exiting. At that private meeting, I told him investigations from Nuremburg were heating up and his exit plans had to be moved up, that he was to meet me the *next* night. I would pick him up at a deserted area south of town.

I drove Krieger to my killing place, put a bullet in the back of his head and buried him. Krieger had a duffel bag that was a little larger than Scheffler's. I then drove to my hidey hole, half a mile or so from the secret graveyard that I had started. Without looking at the contents, I buried it right next to Scheffler's. I would look at it in daylight, not at night where I couldn't see somebody sneaking up on me.

There was more jewelry in Krieger's duffel. That stuff seemed to be the same super-high quality. It was impossible for me to guess how much it was worth. But, because there was three times as much, I figured it would be worth at least three times what Scheffler's was worth. I wouldn't know until I got it back to the

States, where I could then get rid of it through my old high school contacts.

The cash was easy to figure, of course. Krieger had almost sixty thousand dollars! All in American greenbacks.

On the real rendezvous night a week later, Krieger, of course, didn't show at the meeting place. I waited dutifully for two hours. When he didn't show, I went back and reported the no show. There wasn't much questioning—there wasn't even an investigation—because we had what *we* wanted, a spy network in Eastern Europe. One missing Nazi bastard didn't really bother us.

About six months later, I killed my last Nazi. If I had to rate his evilness, I'd put him a notch ahead of Scheffler, but a little less than Krieger. He not only had blood on his hands, but I think he probably swam in it. I took his duffel bag, too. It didn't contain as much jewelry as Krieger's, but there was more cash. When I added all the cash up, it was more than two hundred thousand dollars. I wondered at the time if Rockefeller had that much cash.

What I didn't know was how much the jewelry was worth. If my pure guesses were even close to reality, then the jewelry could be worth more than double the cash.

That's how I got rich during the war. Getting my loot back to the good old U.S. of A wasn't that difficult. I *mailed* it back. Working for Wild Bill, we had special privileges. One of those privileges was the Army mail. It was almost like the diplomatic pouch. I think I could have mailed back a bazooka, and nobody would have questioned it. I sent one package each month to myself at my parents address. I had, of course, tipped off my parents and told them not to open them. Each package was small—definitely not bazooka size—a pile of cash in one, a tiara in another, a pile of cash in the next one and so forth. The first time that I mailed a load of cash, I was real jittery. The last time that I was that nervous was when I first went to confession as a kid and didn't know if the priest was going to have me say the rosary or just pass me on straight to hell. There was a risk in mailing each package, but I thought at the time that even Rockefeller must have taken a few risks to get his fortune.

The packages were stacked in my bedroom in Brooklyn when I got home in 1950. The money wasn't earning interest, of course, but every dollar and every piece of jewelry was there.

While getting rich, I murdered three Nazis who would have raped and killed in South America. So what if I was the sole judge and jury? These guys didn't deserve to live—not only because of their past sins—but they clearly were going to repeat as much of their evil as they could. I didn't kill them for their riches. Hell, my first murder—Scheffler—I didn't know he had any money except the fifteen hundred in cash I was going to give him. I would have killed any of the three for nothing. Killing them, I figured, was just my undeclared extension of the war.

While I never wanted to test that jury idea of mine—that a jury wouldn't convict me for murder—I never wanted to publicly admit what I had done.

I never lost a minute of sleep over these murders. While the murders themselves didn't cause me to lose any sleep, the *thought* that I didn't lose sleep bothered me a little bit from time to time. After all, wasn't that a description of a psychopath—the wild ass person who kills a bunch of people and sleeps like a baby? Did I have some thread running through me that was psychopathic? That, I guess, I would find out sooner or later as I traveled through life.

24

Tuesday, September 25, 1951

The morning sun blasted into my hotel room like it was trumpeting the end of the world. I felt that the end of the world had come and gone. I found myself sprawled out on the bed, the towels soggy from the ice that had melted hours before. My shoulder and stomach were stiff and painful. My head felt worse; an empty whiskey bottle was between my legs. I had to take a piss that could swamp the toilet.

I just laid there breathing not knowing which part of my body to move first. My bladder, however, wouldn't wait much longer for me to decide so I put my left foot on the floor, then my right, then sat up, breathed a few more breaths, slowly stood up and shuffled over to the bathroom and took a piss. That piss happened to be the only activity of the morning that hadn't been painful.

The remaining aspirin in the bottle I popped into my mouth, chewed them and washed down the remnants with a short gulp of water. My watch said it was ten in the morning.

I edged back into the room and realized for the first time that Hiromi wasn't there.

The door to her adjoining room was open. I stepped as quickly as I could to that open door. Hiromi was sitting in a chair reading.

She looked up, smiling. "Good morning," she said about as cheerful as a person could get under any circumstances. She was fully dressed and looked like a young woman ready to go to work on Capital Hill.

"'Morning," I mumbled.

"I steamed the wrinkles out of your suit," she said, pointing to my suit hanging on a hanger on the back of her chair. I looked down at myself. At least I was semi-decent; I was in my underwear.

"Are you ready to go home?" she asked.

I thought about it for about two seconds. "Give me a few minutes to shower and shave," I said.

I didn't feel any better after showering and shaving, but I didn't look like a monster. Those different compartments of my brain that were in a runaway thinking mode somehow turned off some of the pain in my body, and I dressed quickly. After dressing, I called Wild Bill over at the offices of Donovan, Leisure, Newton and Lombard. He had at least deserved the courtesy of knowing that I wasn't going to show. He wasn't in the office at that time. I left a message with his secretary that something had come up, and that I had to go back to Brooklyn immediately. I left my phone number, even though he had it. If somebody wanted me to tell my Korean story for the third time, it was going to have to be in Brooklyn, not Washington, D.C.

The gun that I had taken from the two Russians was on the dresser. I stuck it inside my pants in the small of my back because I wasn't sure if I would meet another pair of goons for their morning treatment. I left my own gun in my suitcase.

The first set of goons might be in the hospital. One of them had at least a broken nose; the other I had hit hard enough on his temple with the butt of the gun to kill him. If Hiromi hadn't stopped me from belting him the second time, his chances of being dead would be greater than being slightly alive.

Outside the Mayflower, the sun was bright and Hiromi and I didn't spot any goons. And, there were no cops trying to track down an alleged mugger that had killed a guy by smashing in his temple.

I sat quietly on the entire train trip back home. Sure, I had some coffee and a bagel, but that was mainly medicinal, not to salve any hunger pangs. The train at that time of the day wasn't crowded. The only thoughts I had on the train were about how I was going to protect Hiromi and myself.

A few hours later, we walked up to the front porch of my house. One of Rafael's buddies was sitting on the stoop reading a newspaper.

I asked him if there had been any problems. He told me that the Italian guy down the street didn't like him.

I slipped him a twenty, and he walked the opposite way of Dominic's candy store.

I unlocked the front door and pushed it open. The door pushed back mail that the mailman had dropped through the slot in the door.

There was a slight squeak on the door hinges, but that squeak had been there since I was a kid. My old man had oiled it and later I had oiled it, but the squeak was a determined little bastard. The squeak had become as much of the house as I was.

I walked into the foyer. The house never had sounded so quiet. Usually, when I came into the house, I heard music coming from Hiromi's radio, but she had, of course, turned off her radio before we had left. There were no sounds in the house including my breathing—I found myself holding my breath to listen.

I walked through the house and didn't find anything that looked out of place. Then I sat Hiromi down at the kitchen table and brewed some green tea. I was going to tell Hiromi about the facts of life.

"We're caught up in something that is too big for us," I said. Hiromi stared at me; I guess she was waiting for me to say something that wasn't so obvious.

"Well, now that I've told General Donovan about the Ice Queen, I think he'll get his guys to do something about it. I think they'll shut down the Ice Queen."

"Shut down?" Hiromi asked.

"Arrest," I said, "put in jail." Hiromi understood that. "In the meantime, we should make ourselves scarce."

Hiromi gave me that questioning look that I had seen before. She hadn't understood the context of scarce.

"Do you need to visit your parents?" I asked. "You've clearly earned a free airline trip to San Francisco. Or, perhaps we should take a little vacation—Florida, the Tennessee mountains would be good this time of year, California?"

"Oh, you mean *run away*. No! I don't need to see my parents. And, after the Internment, I vowed to never run away from anything for the rest of my life." Her face was as firm as a pit bull.

"You see, my father taught me to have courage. Yes, I was frightened last night. I wasn't *prepared* for them. It was all a surprise. But, to run away when you *know* what the problems are is fear."

I'm not sure if I could distinguish the difference between frightened and fear, but I didn't want to interrupt.

"Fear is like putting yourself in prison," Hiromi explained. "Fear doesn't have barb-wired fences like we had in the Internment, but the walls are stronger if I allow them to be. Fear would keep me from doing things when I want to do them, fear would stop me from being the person I want to be. But, now that I know there are men after us, we can be prepared, we can act."

I thought this was pretty strong talk for a slight woman, but she was a feisty woman—someone who traveled in a land that had done her and her family wrong. As she talked, I could feel that she wanted to face fear instead of fear pulling the strings on her life. I wondered if that was the Samurai way.

"You mean fight back?" I asked.

"If that is what it takes, yes, fight back."

"Hiromi, how much do you weigh?"

"I don't know, one hundred fifteen or so," she said.

I doubted that. While she was tall for a Japanese woman, she didn't have the robust curves of an American woman. Heck, an Italian woman's breasts could weigh as much as Hiromi's leg. She could probably run a lot faster than an Italian or Irish woman, but she wasn't going to win any fight with a bruiser.

"So, a man my size—let's say about two hundred pounds—comes at you with a knife. You at one fifteen are going to fight back?"

"I know judo?" she said, drawing it in to a question as she sometimes did. "My father taught me judo in Internment."

I shook my head from side to side, "Not enough."

"Then with guns," Hiromi said. "Then I am bigger."

Yes, she was one feisty little woman. When she had done jobs for me, she had never shown any fear, just confidence in her lock picking skills. She had the nerves of a pickpocket. She didn't flinch from the danger even when we were attacked in Washington, D.C.; I think that on some of this stuff she had more balls than me.

"Well, we should at least get out of the house for a few days…"

"No! We just get prepared. I am not afraid if I am prepared."

Preparation meant weapons. I would have to show her how we were going to arm ourselves to the teeth.

"Okay, let me show you some secrets," I said to Hiromi.

I took her by the hand and led her to the living room. There was a bookcase on both sides of the fireplace. Unlike the three bookcases in my house that were actually doors, these weren't doors; they were legit bookcases that held books. James Jones best selling novel, *From Here to Eternity*, sat on one of the shelves. Jones' story of the war was a lot different than mine, and mine would never be made into a book; if it did end up as a book I'd end up reading it in jail. It's a lot more interesting of a book to have some soldier screwing some broad on the beach than plugging a Nazi in the back of the head and taking his stash.

I pulled the book from the shelf so that the back of the bookcase could be clearly seen.

"Push the back of the bookcase," I told Hiromi.

She looked at me with a question mark on her face.

"Go ahead," I said, "with your hand, push at the back of the bookcase."

She did.

With her fingers pushing, the panel pivoted upward on hidden hinges. The opening looked like a milk chute. The wood panel was a close fit. The bums that searched my house couldn't have seen that there was a small compartment behind that bookcase. Of course, they also didn't know that I had a fetish for hiding guns and money and jewelry.

"Reach down," I told Hiromi.

She reached down, felt around and brought out weapon number one: a Colt 45. The panel was spring loaded so that when Hiromi took out the gun the panel would spring back into place.

I told her to put it back, and she did. "Okay, follow me. This will be like an Easter Egg hunt."

I was explaining the intricacies of an Easter Egg Hunt as we walked into the kitchen for weapon number two. We went through the house until I had showed Hiromi the five secret places that I had stashed weapons. I showed her how to operate each weapon. No target practice was necessary. If Hiromi needed to use one of these weapons, it would all be close range.

We went up to her attic studio and had retrieved a sawed-off shotgun from a small closet at one end. "This one," I said, "you keep up here." I leaned it against the wall as if it was an umbrella. "If men come in the house, you run like a little mouse and get up here. That shotgun will stop *anybody* from getting upstairs." I laid down a small box of shells. I showed her how to load and reload the shotgun. The one thing about a shotgun—a pure amateur was like an expert marksman when they shot from just a few feet away.

If anybody came after Hiromi up those stairs, she would just point the sawed-off shotgun, squeeze the trigger and that guy would be blown to smithereens. She would have a reload to blast the next goon to the sixth level of hell.

"If you happen to be in the house alone up here painting," I said, laying down some ground rules, "keep the bookcase closed and keep that shotgun right near your canvas."

"Jake-san, you have so many guns?" Hiromi said. That was the first time that she had used the courtesy of a suffix. I don't know what that meant, but I thought it meant respect. "Why so many guns?"

I shrugged my shoulders. I didn't know. Maybe it was just a bad habit of mine that I picked up in Eastern Europe when I had guns hidden at arms reach all over the place. I had three guns hidden in my jeep; I had three guns in my room in Berlin including one under the bed on the floor, and one under the mattress; I had one hidden in the bathroom; I carried two with me at all times. If I chose to add them all up, I could make John Dillinger, Pretty Boy Floyd and J. Edgar Hoover all back down.

I never really thought about this acquired fixation with guns. I just kept adding to the collection during my time in Europe. The guns may have been a manifestation of my ill-gotten riches. After all, I had *killed* to get the riches. If *I* had killed and ended up rich, couldn't somebody else kill to get those riches?

I never really spent time thinking about why I had so many guns. I didn't have such a fixation before I went to Germany. I guess it was like guys that picked up the smoking habit in the Army. They never thought about it; they just smoked. Afterward, if they wanted to quit smoking, they found out how difficult it was. My habit was a lot different; I never smoked, but I hid guns like a drunk would hide bottles of booze. There was a big difference: The alcoholic had use for those bottles of booze; I didn't really *need* that many guns. In fact, up until now, I never really had a need for any of them. But, there they were, secreted away in all these neat little hidey-holes in my house.

We had enough weapons to turn back a siege, as unlikely as a flat-out siege was. Outside the house, however, we were vulnerable. We couldn't walk around Brooklyn like G.I. Joe. This wasn't the old Wild West. The best solution would be for Wild Bill or his cronies to pick up the Ice Queen for being a spy.

To hurry that along, I phoned Wild Bill's office. I felt that I should fill him in on the beating I took after I had visited him. I didn't want Federal protection; I just wanted the Ice Queen bitch to be picked up and locked away.

I got through to Wild Bill right away. I told him the whole story about last night—except for the feeling that I might have killed one of those thugs—and about the break-in at my house. I didn't mention Hiromi.

There was silence on Wild Bill's end of the phone. Then he said, "Yes, Jake, it does sound like you are in danger, that the Ice Queen is panicking a bit. Is there someplace you could go for a couple of weeks."

Good idea! I couldn't tell Wild Bill that I had suggested the same thing to this feisty little Japanese woman—who was a boarder and chief safecracker of mine—and she basically drew a line in the sand and wouldn't run. I couldn't describe how I armed us to the teeth to defend my doorstep from the Ice Queen's version of Normandy Beach.

"Are you going to pick her up, the Ice Queen?" I asked.

"We've got a bead on her all right," Wild Bill said, "but we can't pick her up just based on the information you gave us—which of course was acquired illegally. We're *working* on it."

I knew that was bullshit. Wild Bill and whoever he was working with could snatch her off the street right now. They could search her house, and if the evidence was gone, they could manufacture new evidence. That was not a new tactic. Knock down doors first; ask questions later. That wasn't a new tactic either. All's fair in love and war, and we were at war with the Koreans. We didn't have to ask, "Mother, may I?" I suspected that the slow-down was far more political than it was practical. J. Edgar Hoover probably figured into the equation somewhere and maybe that was the missing formula for action.

The 'working on it' answer wasn't very comforting to me. While Hiromi drew that line in the sand, there were bullies out there that would kick that sand in our face. In my house, I felt that we could defend ourselves. It would take an all-out assault by a small army to take us. However, we weren't going to *stay* inside for the duration.

We would need reinforcements. Where better to get reinforcements than Brooklyn? I would have to go to the mob.

25

Tuesday, September 25, 1951

Before I talked to Dominic, I needed to talk to Rafael.

Rafael wasn't such a tough guy himself—he was quick, he could run like the wind, he was a great lookout, he was responsible, he was smart—but he personally couldn't provide strong-arm protection. However, among other things, he was a *leader*, a leader of a new Puerto Rican gang a few blocks over. His *gang* could provide protection, particularly for Hiromi when she left the house when I wasn't around.

I phoned the number that I used to reach Rafael.

A girl—sounded like a teenager—answered the phone. It didn't sound like the same teenager as when I had called before. I don't know if those teenagers were sisters or nieces or just his latest lady. I asked for Rafael.

She said, "Who's asking?" These Puerto Ricans learn the Brooklyn way pretty quick.

"Jake McHenry," I said.

She said, "He ain't here." I felt like asking why she asked my name if he wasn't there. Maybe it was just Puerto Rican curiosity.

"Tell him Jake called. I've got a job for him."

"Okay," she said, and hung up. She left a lot to be desired as an answering service.

With the phone still in my hand I dialed Dominic's number. Dominic always had *somebody* answer the phone that rang at the candy store because he just never knew when a gambler would get the notion about a surefire winner. Additionally, if Dominic wasn't outside sweeping his sidewalk, he'd be in the back of the store reading magazines. If I held a reading contest between Dominic and Roberta the librarian, they would each win different categories. Roberta would win in the book category. Dominic would win in magazines. It's not that Roberta didn't read magazines because she did. It was just that Dominic was a maniac as far as reading magazines went. If Dominic wasn't sweeping his sidewalk, he was reading a magazine. It was that simple.

Dominic's phone was answered on the second ring by some guy.

"Who's this?" I asked hoping it was one of the guys from the neighborhood.

"Who the fuck is asking?" It was Jimmy.

"Jimmy, this is Jake McHenry."

"Hey, Jake, why didn't you say so? What the fuck was the little quiz?"

"I need to talk to Dominic," I said.

"He's out back."

"Yeah, I figured. But, get him for me."

"This is an emergency?" Jimmy asked. "Usually you just walk over. You in jail or something?"

"Naw, naw, but I gotta talk to Dominic right now."

"I'll get him," Jimmy said.

Within a minute, Dominic was on the phone.

"Dominic, I'm home from Washington, D.C. Got beat up pretty good there. Now Hiromi and I are home…"

"I'll be right over," Dominic said.

Dominic wasn't built for running, but he got over here so quickly that I swear he would have had to move his feet as if he was running. Hiromi greeted him with a big hug. She had always liked Dominic. She called him "The Candy Man" and he would always give her free candy. Dominic didn't cotton to many folks that weren't white, but he did to this young Japanese woman.

Hiromi would trust Dominic; she wouldn't trust Jimmy or Ralphie or any of his other boys. Heck, I wouldn't trust Jimmy or Ralphie either.

We walked back to the kitchen. I told him about visiting General Donovan and the beating afterward.

"Well, for what it's worth," Dominic said, "it ain't any of my people looking for you," he said. No small talk from Dominic on this day.

"I didn't think it was," I said, although I didn't really know. The mob sure liked to get involved with extortion and extortion was clearly one of the nasty things that the Ice Queen had on her plate.

"For the next few days, I've got the alley covered," Dominic said. "Anything suspicious in the alley and my boys'll be over here lickety brindle. And, if Hiromi's gotta go to the store or sumthin, I'll personally escort her. "

I thanked him.

"What about those Puerto Ricans?" Dominic asked. Puerto Ricans weren't his favorite type of people.

"Well, as you've seen, some of Rafael's boys are watching our place too," I said. "Not in the alley, though. Front steps." Rafael's boys liked sitting around, particularly since they were getting paid. I just didn't want Dominic's guys shooting Rafael and his guys.

Dominic shrugged, hugged Hiromi and then walked back to his store. He didn't look offended. He was probably just muttering something about the Irish bringing in Puerto Ricans to ruin the neighborhood.

I picked up the mail that was still on the floor by the front door and shuffled through it.

There was one personal letter. It was from Roberta DiNardo, the librarian. The letter had no postage. She must have dropped it off. I opened the envelope and unfolded the letter. It was same type of scrap paper that I had seen her use as a bookmark for years.

The handwriting was strong and legible, and she wrote as she would talk.

"So, you don't answer your phone or what?" she wrote, and as I read I could hear her Bugs Bunny voice. "I tried calling you all-day yesterday. Those pictures were bothering me. I searched all the newspapers. I found out who the guy is with the big moustache. You'd never believe it. When I found out who he was, I found two more. Better stop by and buy me a coffee."

I had completely forgot that I had Roberta doing homework for me. I now remembered how I had cropped the mug shots of the Ice Queen's boudoir and printed them out to the size of baseball cards. I thought my original idea was to get a line on those extortion victims, which would somehow provide me protection from the Ice Queen if I happened to need it. You know, something like 'my lawyer has all the evidence and if I'm killed or if I disappear he's going to hand deliver the whole kit-and-caboodle to the FBI.'

That, of course, was a *defensive* move. Then I thought of what some famous football coach or some Army general had said: the best defense is a good offense. Well, I certainly wasn't going to storm the Ice Queen's brownstone. That wasn't my nature. However, if I did find out who those grimacing guys were I might have some leverage. Maybe a whole lot of leverage. That left one thing for me to do—find out who those guys were. There was no better time than now.

26

Wednesday, September 26, 1951

Hiromi understood American football.

While being in Internment, the Japanese had formed football teams. This was a major sporting event at the Internment Camp. I had heard that Japanese in Japan loved baseball; they had even carved out baseball diamonds in the rubble of Tokyo after the war. The Japanese of the Internment Camps loved their baseball, but being in America, they also loved their football so they created football teams. She was a bigger fan of the New York Giants—the *football* team and *not* the hated baseball team in Manhattan—than she was of the glorious Dodgers of Brooklyn. I would have to speak to her about that someday.

She understood what the offense on a football team was trying to do; she understood that the defense tried to stop the offense. Well, we were going to put the principles of offense and defense to our own personal test today. Hiromi was going to be the Defensive Coach; I was the Offensive Coach. We were going to activate both when I went to see Roberta this afternoon.

I didn't want Hiromi to accompany me. There was no need to expose both of us to whatever might be outside. This was where the defense came in. Hiromi had to defend our house. I would go to see Roberta and perhaps the information she had for me would create some offense. I didn't think that these were big risk steps, either with myself going to the library or Hiromi waiting in the attic with a sawed-off shotgun. Anyways, I phoned Dominic to let him know that I was going to be gone for a while. Hiromi would be at home alone, and I couldn't find Rafael to guard the front.

"That figures," Dominic said. "I'll personally come over and sit on the front steps."

Hiromi was painting upstairs in the attic. I explained to her what I was going to do and what she had to do. She had to close the bookcase door to the attic; she had to keep on painting a masterpiece; she had to keep the shotgun right next to her easel. She agreed to all of those things, but I could clearly tell that she would have preferred to go to the library with me and see Roberta.

I walked to the library. The gun that I had taken from the thug in Washington was tucked in the small of my back under the waistband of the pants. That was another gun added to my collection. My shirt was loose, covering the gun.

Ten minutes later I waltzed into the library. Roberta's desk on the right side of the checkout desk was not occupied. She didn't sit there often; she was usually working with kids at a table or putting books back in the stacks. She was probably on a safari through the periodicals, checking pictures against the mug shots I had given her. She wouldn't sleep well until she found the identities of every one of the Ice Queen's gallery of rogues.

I didn't see her at any of the tables where the kids were so I headed for the periodicals. No Roberta there. Heck, she could be anywhere in this library—even the basement which was off-limits for borrowers and browsers—so I stopped at the checkout desk.

The woman there, Mary O'Halloran, was a few years junior to Roberta; she was probably only ten years past retirement. Good help was tough to find, but the library was able to hang on to these old folks until they couldn't stamp a book anymore. These old folks worked as volunteers and were paid from a donations fund about as much as if they were an officially paid employee.

"Hey, Mary," I said, greeting the old Irish lady that was stamping books. I would bet that there was a certain art form to that stamping—that these old ladies could tell when a rookie stamped a book. "You seen Roberta?"

"No," Mary said, "she didn't come in today. I've called a few times, but no answer. I'm worried."

"Was she catching a cold or something?" I asked.

"No, but she was talking about going over to Staten Island to visit her son."

Roberta might be in a lot of places, but she was *not* in Staten Island. Roberta talked all the time about going over to Staten Island to see her son, and she never went. It was only about once every six months or so that her son, with family en tow, would come and visit her in Brooklyn. Roberta always told me that he had developed into an 'uppity up,' which I found strange—I didn't think it was possible to be uppity living in Staten Island.

"I'll stop by her apartment and see if she's okay," I said.

Mary was clearly relieved. "Oh, Jake, thank you. I'm just so worried, with the break-in we had here last night and all."

It was like somebody had shaken my worry beads. "Break-in?"

"Yes, somebody broke a window in the back and went through our desks. You know, Jake, Brooklyn is changing so much. What's this world coming to—breaking into a library! My son wants me to move out to Levittown with him and his family. Your folks live out there now don't they?"

I didn't want to get in a conversation with Mary. That could last until next month if I let it.

"Yeah, they love it," I said. "Safe, fresh air, my mom's even got a little garden. Roberta lives over on 45th doesn't she?"

"Yes," she said and she gave me her address. I knew the building, but I wasn't sure of the address.

"I'll give you a call after I talk to Roberta."

"Oh thank you, Jake, you're such a sweetheart. It's just a shame that you're a little too young for my daughter." I think she was referring to the daughter that was about the size of a tugboat. I was delighted that age had put her off-limits to me.

I didn't feel good about Roberta not showing up for work and the break-in, which I felt couldn't have been coincidental.

My first thoughts were about that dirty old bastard Richard Wolfemeyer, the slimy ancient detective that I thought I had bought off. I coulda and shoulda beat the shit out of him even if he was over seventy. I *know* what he did; he played his sympathy card with me, which I bought for a hundred bucks, then reported right back to the Ice Queen at the end of the day who I had been seeing. Wolfemeyer would have said something like this: *He had a cuppa coffee with an old hag librarian. He handed her something that she was looking at.*

"Librarian?" the Ice Queen would have asked. She would have thought: libraries mean books and newspapers and magazines and, most importantly, *research*. A trained librarian doing research can cut through a lot of bullshit to find the right answers. The Ice Queen probably wondered, what *research* was Jake McHenry having done? Her next thought would certainly have been: it might be the prudent thing to send some of *her* 'researchers' out to ask the old librarian what type of research was she doing for that nasty thief McHenry. They could be very persuasive, of course, with muscle and threats.

The Irish part of me wanted to get in my car right now, drive over to Manhattan, find that bastard Richard Wolfemeyer and beat the shit out of him right on some sidewalk. However, the first responsibility was to get to Roberta.

Roberta couldn't have dodged the Ice Queen's thugs.

The gorillas, however, would have a difficult time in intimidating Roberta. There were occasionally high school kids that had tried that, and had found out that it was better to intimidate a two hundred and thirty pound Irish beat cop. At least they could reason with the cop, or if that failed, pay him off. Roberta had a voice that could singe off the first layer of skin. Sure, the Ice

Queen's boys would have been beefy, and probably sadistic bastards, and they would probably threaten her, but those are the types of people that Roberta grew up with. They might have even slapped her, but I figured it wouldn't have been a haymaker. They would want information from Roberta, not kill her. Or would they have snatched her and taken her to see the mythical Mr. Jones, who would happen not to be a Mr., but a redheaded babe named Arabella Van Dyck. I doubted that. Their Mr. Jones ploy with me was to get me in the car and take me to some isolated area where they could use very physical means to extract information out of me. If they had gotten in Roberta's apartment, it was isolated enough to put up a good threat.

While Roberta was a tough old dame—and a stubborn one at that—I hoped that she wouldn't try to be a hero, and withhold what she was researching for me. She should have given up my stuff along with a glass of warm milk and chocolate chip cookies. Heck, it wasn't really a research project; it was like a *game*, just a bunch of photos to see if we could match a name with the face. Roberta and I weren't the FBI, we weren't the cops, we were just trying to match a few faces with names. A silly game of curiosity killed the cat. But, one of us was clearly a schmuck—and that was me all the way. I had allowed myself to be conned by an ancient detective and thus wasn't able to protect a source.

I jogged back to my house to get my Ford. And Hiromi. We were now going to test our defense outside the house.

I had the feeling that I was going to need Hiromi's special lock picking talent. Roberta might have barricaded herself in her apartment and wouldn't respond to the doorbell. Or what if they had roughed her up a little and she couldn't get to the door? Maybe a broken arm or leg? Breaking her arm wouldn't have taken much more than a strong grip.

Hiromi could get us in right away.

As I neared my house, I spotted Dominic sitting on the steps. He was reading *Time* magazine so intently I probably could have stepped right past him and gone into the house. I did a professional cough, however, and yelled hello. He jumped a bit and then smiled. I told him that I was going to be with Hiromi so he didn't have to hang around. He walked back to his store, reading *Time* every step of the way.

As soon as I entered my house, I was calling Hiromi's name. I didn't want any false alarms where she would mistake me for a goon, take that sawed-off shotgun and blow me six ways to Sunday. When I opened the bookcase door to her, I hollered up the stairs.

"What are you screaming about?" Hiromi asked. "I could hear you from a mile away." It was amazing how she was picking up this American slang, but my shouting worked—the shotgun remained like a sentinel up against the wall.

I explained to her that we were going on a field trip. That needed a little more clarification, but not as much as the Easter Egg Hunt. She was delighted to get out of the house and be involved in a mission of *offense.* I told her that football adage about the best defense was a good offense. She liked that. She had understood that phrase better than talking about an Easter Egg Hunt.

There was a parking spot right in front of Roberta's apartment house. It was a three-story brick apartment building that had a lot of clones in Brooklyn. Hiromi and I quickly walked up the stairs to the front entrance. We opened the front door and walked into the vestibule. We saw a row of mailboxes on one side of the lobby. Roberta DiNardo, 3G. I tried the buzzer. We waited. I tried the buzzer again. I was hoping to hear her voice crackle through the speaker, "So, what's the hurry, who's there anyways?" But, there was no answer. I nodded to Hiromi. No matter what language different people may speak, the high sign is universal. I turned to look out the front door in case somebody was coming. "We can go in," Hiromi said before I could even focus outside. I turned around—Hiromi was holding the door open.

I took the stairs two at a time; Hiromi floated up the stairs like an apparition. We were in front of 3G.

What we were doing was pretty stupid. If I was smart about this, I should have called the cops. They'd, of course, question me as to why I thought that Roberta was in danger. "Okay, let me see if I have this straight," a Brooklyn cop would have said, "you gave this retired librarian pictures of guys fucking some Commie queen and she was supposed to identify who those guys were. That's what you're trying to tell me?"

I could have had Mary call the cops and a Brooklyn cop could have said, "You say this woman is in her eighties. She missed a day of work, but she technically doesn't work at the library anyways. And, because she missed *one* day of work—Christ my partner misses that much each month—you think something bad happened to her?"

It was smarter to call the cops. It was stupid to bust in. If Roberta was still alive, then that stupidity would be forgotten. However, if she was dead, I was drawing a line from Roberta to me.

"Go ahead," I said, "open it." There was no sense in knocking and waiting. There was *one* precaution I was going to take before entering. I would holler inside. That holler could alert somebody inside, but I was confident that the Ice Queen's boys wouldn't still be there. If the holler alerted Roberta and she put down her gun, then it was a good holler. I didn't know if she had any weapons, but why walk into a bullet when a holler would do?

Hiromi pushed open the door and I hollered Roberta's name. No answer.

The apartment didn't smell right.

We walked into the small living room. It had been trashed like the Ice Queen tornado that had hit my house. I didn't get the feeling that this time the Ice Queen was sending a message; these guys had turned everything upside down trying to find something.

I walked ahead of Hiromi. My gun was in my hand. The bathroom was straight ahead. It was small—I would have had a difficult time in getting my body positioned to sit on the toilet—and it had been hit by the same tornado. The medicine cabinet had been ripped from the wall and tossed in the small bathtub.

From the entrance to her bedroom, I could see Roberta's bare feet sticking out from under the bed. The bed had been flipped with the box spring showing. My nose first told me that she was not alive. I lifted up the box spring and set it against the wall. I put my gun in my pocket and pulled out a handkerchief to hold to my face.

I walked over to her. She was wearing an old gray housedress that she had probably put on every day after work. There was a crook in her neck where the break probably was. With a big guy, breaking her neck could be done with one hand like holding a number two pencil and pressing it with a thumb. Crack, it would have been that easy.

I couldn't speak. I just stared at Roberta. She had been with me and my books since I had learned to read.

Hiromi put her hand on my elbow. She tugged lightly to get me to back out of the room.

How could this be? A little harmless woman—a volunteer librarian no less—was killed by thugs? This wasn't even a street mugging where the bad guys would grab an old lady's purse and maybe knock her over. This was stalking, this was like tracking an old defenseless animal and then killing it.

To my regret, it looked like Roberta died a hero—at least in her mind. She didn't give those guys anything. If she had, would they have tossed her apartment as viciously as they had? And, it looked like they killed her before they tossed her bedroom. Otherwise, why was she *under* the overturned bed?

If I was to reconstruct what happened, the killers probably showed fake police badges or cooked up some easy ruse to get in. Even if Roberta wouldn't have bought the ruse, they could easily have kicked the door in. Once inside, they talked, probably threatened, she probably said something nasty being as spunky as she was. One of them probably grabbed her arm and squeezed his meat hooks to cause pain. Someplace along the way they felt they couldn't get anything out of Roberta so one of them just snapped her neck. Then they tossed the apartment. I would think that they didn't find what they were looking for even though they didn't know what they were looking for. Knitting needles and low-heeled shoes probably didn't make them say, "Hey, we've got it!" That's when they decided to hit the library. Easy to do—it's not a bank. Maybe they found the pictures there, maybe not. Roberta could have put them in the stacks someplace where they might be found years from now by a wandering researcher who hadn't even been born yet.

There was rage boiling up in me like it was being stoked by the fires of hell. This was my Irish heritage *and* my German heritage boiling over. If I were a prudent man, I would go home and try to cool down. But, when you're about to blow a gasket, it's not part of the mindset to be prudent.

The stakes of the Ice Queen had been raised to intolerable levels. Murder was intolerable—except for murder of fleeing Nazis which somehow seemed tolerable—murder of little old librarians was more serious than intolerable. That was serious payback time. Payback never returned a lost life, but somehow I thought payback helped a lost soul—in this case, my soul. I wasn't sure what I was going to do, but I knew I had to start the action right now. I couldn't just wait for Wild Bill Donovan and Richard Nixon to ride in with the Seventh Calvary and save the day.

27

Wednesday, September 26, 1951

I stormed out of Roberta's apartment. Hiromi scrambled after me. She grabbed my arm as we reached the Ford.

"Where are you going?" Hiromi asked, her voice cracking in panic. She reached around and grabbed my other arm. She had a death grip on both. She must have seen the rage in my face; the same rage that was capable of killing two Russians in Washington, D.C. "Are you going to the Ice Queen?"

Hiromi must have thought that I was going to go storm the Ice Queen's brownstone. I would have liked to, but even in my rage, I knew that wasn't the right strategy. I needed proof that the Ice Queen had been responsible for the murder of Roberta. That proof pointed me in one direction. That one direction was to moth-eaten ancient detective Richard Wolfemeyer. I needed to find out if he indeed was the link to Roberta and the Ice Queen.

I thought of taking Hiromi home first. Then I decided against that. I might need her to get into Wolfemeyer's apartment. I would stop at home, however, to pick up some weapons.

Driving back home the car radio was on and amazingly, considering the rage boiling inside me, I listened to some snippets of Red Barber on the Dodgers radio broadcast.

The Dodgers had lost two games to the Boston Braves yesterday. Ralph Branca lost the first game, his fourth loss in a row. His arm must be close to falling off. It seemed impossible, but the Dodgers had only a one game lead over the New York Giants. That was impossible! We had a sixteen game lead over them just about a month ago. Listening to Red Barber made me think of Roberta; she was probably getting really fidgety about the Dodgers lead up in the ultimate ballyard in the sky. Knowing Roberta, she'd probably try to see The Man—in this case God—and see if He could intervene on the Dodgers behalf.

Listening to Red Barber cooled some of my rage. The rage was still there, all right, but I had to be careful.

Once inside my house, I stopped in my office. I picked up the piece of paper that I had written Wolfemeyer's address on. I also called the police. I told them that they could find Roberta DiNardo dead at her apartment and I gave them the address. They asked my name. I didn't give it and hung up. They would probably investigate the murder and Mary O'Halloran would certainly tell them that I was going to check up on Roberta. If the cops wanted to find me, they would find me.

Thinking of Mary reminded me to call her. I didn't want to be the one to be the bearer of such awful news, but I would be better than her hearing it on the grapevine or by some cop.

I dialed the library and asked for Mary.

She answered with a whisper.

"Mary, this is Jake. I've got bad news..."

I heard her intake of breath on the phone. There was no good way of saying this. When somebody dies, there is always sorrow. That even happens when *bad* people die. When Wild Bill heard that Hitler was dead, he was disappointed and *pissed,* even *sad.* Wild Bill had wanted Hitler alive so that he could be tried and executed. So when somebody good—really good—like Roberta dies, there is no way to break the news except to break it. Could I try to break it gently to her and say, "All those people that have a wonderful friend named Roberta who is alive take one step forward," and then say, "ah, Mary, not so fast." Nope, there was no gentle way.

"Roberta is dead," I said. "She was murdered, it looks like a burglary."

I could hear Mary breathing on the other end of the phone. I hoped that the news wouldn't kill her.

"Was it awful, Jake, did she suffer?"

"I don't think so," I said, "I think it happened so fast she didn't even see it coming."

"Oh gracious," Mary said. She said nothing; I could hear her breathing.

I held the phone tightly during the quiet. I wanted to run down that sleazy ancient detective Richard Wolfemeyer, but that could wait a few minutes.

"Well, I guess I should call her son," Mary said, "and gather her things here. She's got a sweater on her chair—land sakes alive, that sweater's been in this library for years."

I knew the sweater. She would wear it in the winter. But, it's year-around home was the library.

"Oh! And Jake, I just remembered, she left a book for you."

I couldn't remember which book she wanted me to see.

"I was cleaning up after you left and there was a stack of books on her desk. While the burglars rifled through our desks, it didn't look like they even touched that stack of books. I was going to put them back in the stacks, when I saw one book had a slip of paper hanging out of it. We usually take those things out before putting them back on the shelves. The slip of paper was actually a small envelope with your name on it."

It could be only one thing: the identification of the guy with the handlebar moustache.

I told Mary that I would stop by later. The ID of the handlebar moustache was on my back burner right now. Richard Wolfemeyer was glowing hot on the front burner.

I took two guns with me. I put both under the driver's seat in the car. I didn't hand Hiromi any guns. I didn't want her to become the Bonnie with Clyde.

I took the Brooklyn Bridge to Manhattan and drove to Greenwich Village. Greenwich Village was a changing area that had some real dumpy apartment buildings. This was the spawning ground for coffee houses and liberals and a group of trash that called themselves beatniks. They all loved those run down places because they were cheap.

A bunch of actors lived in the area—cheap rent while they were chasing their dreams to become a star. I had read where one guy did make it big on Broadway, but chose to stay in Greenwich Village. It was Marlon Brando who starred in the Broadway play, *Streetcar Named Desire*. I hadn't seen it, but I was told his acting was like he had been brought up in Brooklyn. He should live in Brooklyn instead of with these beatniks and Commies.

Wolfemeyer lived on Perry Street. I parked in front of a fire hydrant and locked the car. While the Greenwich Village was supposed to be liberal, they could also be liberal at swiping things.

Hiromi and I walked up the steps to the stoop of Wolfemeyer's apartment. I had cooled down some, but I wasn't any less focused. What were my chances that Wolfemeyer would be in his apartment, I wondered, and then thought about if he wasn't. I would wait. Sooner or later the old buzzard would come home.

Looking at the row of mailboxes, I saw that Wolfemeyer had the basement apartment. In someplaces, they were starting to call these 'garden apartments,' but damned if I could tell where the garden was. Basement I know where, garden was make believe.

The door to his basement apartment looked like it wasn't closed tightly. I tried the knob. It turned. I looked back at Hiromi and shrugged. She didn't need to pick this lock.

I withdrew the gun from the small of my back and pushed open the door. The smell was not a good smell. And, it wasn't the smell of the apartment being the dump that it was. If I had to compare the smell to something, the only thing I would think of was some bad oysters left to rot in the kitchen, but this smell wasn't any bad oysters. I had just smelled a similar aroma at Roberta's apartment.

Wolfemeycr's apartment had not been tossed. He was slumped over the dinette table with his head resting in a plate of crusty spaghetti. Part of that spaghetti had been his last supper. There was a bullet hole in his left temple. His blood was all over the table, running together with the spaghetti sauce to where it was mostly dried and had a battalion of nasty flies flitting around in a frenzy. I didn't need to look closer. Richard Wolfemeyer was dead. He had probably been shot last night having his last supper. A gun lay on the floor.

I looked back at Hiromi. Her face was stone. I guess she had seen some awful things in her life and an old dead guy would not tip her over.

Even though my intentions were to beat the shit out of the old man, which I probably wouldn't have done—although I might have pushed him around a bit—I felt that a little bit of my soul had been scarred seeing his face congeal with the spaghetti. He wasn't a *bad* guy, an evil guy; he was just an old guy trying to live just another day.

I stepped away from the body and gave a quick look around the room. There were no pictures of a son or daughter or grandkids or former wife or a dog or even a cat. By the look of the place, he had lived there for quite a while, maybe years, but the only items that gave a hint of the old man's character was a stack of books by his bed. The bed was one of those Murphy beds, where it could be folded up into the wall to make more living space during the day. It looked like it had been permanently lowered from the wall. I picked up the top book. Mickey Spillane, *I the Jury*. Mickey was a Brooklyn guy. Heck, Nick and I used to go to Mickey's old man's bar to hoist a few before we ended up on different sides of the globe during the war. The second book in the stack was another Mickey Spillane, *Vengeance is Mine.* I'd heard that someplace along the line Mickey had got religion—Jehovah's Witness of all things—but this crusty old detective Richard Wolfemeyer probably dreamed of being Mike Hammer every night. There wouldn't be anymore sweet dreams for Wolfemeyer, or nightmares for that matter.

Even though he was an inconsequential little bastard that probably would only be missed by his landlord, and that would have been for just a week or so before some beatnik rented the place, I felt bad about the old man's end.

This whole Ice Queen thing had escalated far more than it ever should have.   Roberta DiNardo was dead; Richard Wolfemeyer was dead. Both were murdered because, I think, I had broken into the Ice Queen's brownstone. So she hired that ancient detective to shadow me and then wondered why I had met with a librarian. For all the Ice Queen knew, Roberta could have been an old aunt of mine. Didn't matter, she could also do research—that's what people in libraries do. Research was the scary word that made the Ice Queen panic. It had to be those damn drawings of the bomb that panicked the Ice Queen. She would be afraid of Joe McCarthy or Richard Nixon or J. Edgar Hoover who would make a public spectacle of her. A public spectacle could ruin her, and probably ruin her extortion racket in the process. The extortion racket had to be hugely lucrative, but those bomb drawings could blow up that extortion business like it was Hiroshima.

It was easy to read my Irish instincts. I'd just pick the right time and then kill the Ice Queen. It was that simple. It would be no more difficult for me to kill the Ice Queen than it was to kill that Nazi Franz Scheffler.   However, I couldn't just storm the Ice Queen's castle.

As I thought about it, I made a concerted effort to think things through. Yes, I would kill the Ice Queen. That wasn't debatable. Timing was debatable. As much as I wanted to do something right away, my chances of success were probably better if I picked the right time and place. Right now Hiromi and I were outnumbered; our opposition was far rougher than we were.

It seemed like we weren't going to get any immediate help from the Feds. Hiromi and I should be like the three-card Monte con players in Manhattan. When cops came walking up the street—the three-card Monte guys would pick up their three cards, pick up the money that was on their makeshift cardboard table and run like hell down the nearest alley to safety. They'd set up another three-card Monte game a little while later just a few blocks away. That was a good strategy for Hiromi and me. Just fold up and run like hell *today*. And, then kill the Ice Queen bitch in a few days.

28

Wednesday, September 26, 1951

Driving back to Brooklyn I was thinking of just one thing: where Hiromi and I should run. Hiromi wanted to draw a line in the sand and not run. That seemed to be the right thing at the time. I beefed up the protection on the house and showed Hiromi where the guns were. But, that was before Roberta and Wolfemeyer were murdered. I learned in Eastern Europe that it was smarter to retreat when facing a shoot-out. Then come back later and kill the bastards.

I didn't want any part of a shoot-out with the Ice Queen and her goons. She seemed to be in full panic mode right now. I didn't like dealing with people like that. You know, desperate people do desperate things.

Running wasn't heroic, but it seemed like the best option. Running wouldn't replace *revenge*; it would just postpone it for a while. There was resolve in my mind: the Ice Queen would die by my hand. It would just have to wait until she wouldn't expect it.

Predicting where she would send her killers to strike next would be pretty easy. My house. Hiromi and I would likely be the next targets. Had Richard Wolfemeyer reported that I was talking to Dominic Gonnella, the candy store man? I made a mental note to warn Dominic. He would laugh, but knowing Dominic he would have some of his boys like Ralphie keeping an eye out.

I found a parking spot right in front of my house. On the drive back from Manhattan I was thinking of California. We could catch a flight first thing tomorrow morning. I had thought about Florida, but it was too hot this time of the year. I had thought about Chicago—it was more like New York and it had two major league baseball teams. It would be fun to go to Wrigley Field and watch the Dodgers play the Cubs. But, the Dodgers had played there last weekend. This weekend the Dodgers were on the road playing the Philadelphia Phillies. These were going to be *huge* games. With the Dodgers just one game ahead of the Giants, we'd have to win both games against the Phillies. In the end, I thought California was about as far away from the Ice Queen as we could get; I could get the scores out there somewhere.

There were no major league baseball teams in California, but they did have some Triple-A minor league baseball teams that were pretty good. Joe DiMaggio had got his start playing for the San Francisco Seals. In San Francisco, Hiromi could visit her parents. I didn't think it would be appropriate for me to accompany Hiromi to visit her parents, but I could rent a car, drop her off for a few days and just immerse myself in San Francisco Seals baseball. Maybe I would head down to LA where the Hollywood Stars played. Wrigley Field in Los Angeles was a homer haven so it might be fun to hang out there. Maybe I'd even take the boat over to Catalina Island. The Chicago Cubs had had spring training over there a few times during World War II. It would be interesting to visit Catalina Island's version of Wrigley Field, even though there weren't any games there anymore. I'm sure, however, I could find a place with plenty enough beer.

The men sitting on my stoop were cops of some sort. It was getting dark outside, but these two guys didn't need a neon sign on them that blinked 'cops' on and off to give it away.

They stood up when we got out of the car.

I walked up to them. I don't know why it happens, but it seems that cops pair up in Mutt and Jeff fashion—a big guy and a little guy. This was the case with the cops on my stoop.

"Jake McHenry?" The Mutt cop asked.

"Yep," I said. I felt like saying something nasty. But, smart-ass comments with Mutt and Jeff guys never work. It would just lead them to do slapstick stuff like knocking me on my ass.

The little guy opened his wallet to show me his credentials. They weren't cops; they were CIA.

"Bill Donovan said you should read this first," Mutt cop said holding up an envelope. It had my name scrawled on it. Just from that writing, I could tell that it was from Wild Bill.

"Can my boarder go into the house?" I asked, nodding toward Hiromi. "She's got nothing to do with this." The less anybody knew about Hiromi the better.

"Yeah, sure," the little guy said.

I unlocked the front door, stepped in and turned off the alarm that had just been installed the day before. Hiromi scampered through the door. I stepped back outside closing the door.

"We're the two guys that you were going to meet yesterday when you jumped back to New York," Mutt said. "I'm Chet Morgan, my partner is John Gonski." Morgan was compact, not an ounce of fat on him. He looked like he could have played halfback in college and still be in good enough shape to fight for an extra yard to get a first down. He had dark hair, cut short and a refined face that said Ivy League.

The tall agent didn't look like one of those Ivy League guys that the CIA liked to recruit. He must have been a cop in his earlier life. He was bulky, probably had a bunch of scars on his body from his cop days and looked like he had graduated from Hard Luck U.

"Good-looking Jap broad," the tall agent, Gonski, said, turning his head toward the front door. Yep, he had been a cop. I could have taken offense a couple of ways, but I just looked at the stiff that said it. I could have taken offense on the Jap reference. That reference was the same sentiment as nigger or whop or dago or Polack or chink. But, if I took offense every time somebody uttered one of those nationality shortcuts, that's all I would be doing every minute of the day all-day long—taking offense. No baseball, no beer, just taking offense to slurs all my waking hours.

The 'broad' part didn't fit, of course, Hiromi at all. Broads were babes that we found hanging around bars, not a dedicated artist that happened to be a woman. But, just looking at that Polack Gonski, I knew the dumb bastard couldn't distinguish a woman from a broad.

I opened the sealed envelope. It was in Wild Bill's handwriting. It introduced the two guys. It said it was okay to cooperate with them. Wild Bill wrote that I could trust my life to them. That's all I needed. I would cooperate as much as I did with Wild Bill. But, like I had done with Wild Bill, I still felt a reluctance to tell *everything* I knew. And, there's no way I'd trust my life with them.

It's a funny thing about paranoia. Once you breathe some life into paranoia, it sorta feeds on itself, making itself grow. I had started to develop paranoia naturally over in Germany. After all, I had to ask myself continually one question on each operation I was involved with. That one question was, "What could go wrong?" If something went wrong, it could mean that I would end up dead. So, I went over details and permutations of details more than any baseball fan would go over player stats. I became distrustful. I didn't take *anything* for granted.

When I saw Wild Bill, I had decided that I would only talk about the bomb drawings. That decision seemed *natural* to me. I would stick with that decision. After all, what did the Ice Queen's extortion racket mean to the Feds? If I tipped them on that then I was throwing Tailgunner Joe under the bus. If these guys found out on their own, so be it. Somewhere in me, there was this code that I had to protect a client, even a client that I had quit. The Feds were interested in the bomb and the Ice Queen. So, I'd give them that information. Then, Hiromi and I were going to vamoose out of town for a while.

"You guys are a little out of your territory, aren't you?" I asked. If I had expected anybody, I would have expected the FBI. The CIA's charter restricted them from any action on American soil.

"We're on a busman's holiday," the tall guy said. "We just want to hear your story then we'll get out of your hair." I'd bet that he wanted to add 'fucking' as an adjective to the story, but he was being refined.

"Sure," I said, "since you guys are on holiday, you want a beer or something?" Always the affable host, that's me.

They looked at each other, then the little guy said, "Maybe some water." The little guy *did* look Ivy League, but maybe he had been on the rowing team—I assumed that's where the fanatics went to compete.

"C'mon in," I said, pointing them to the living room. I went to the kitchen to get the water.

I came back into the living room with three bottles of Schaefer beer in my hand and handed one to each guy.

"Busman's water," I said. They thanked me then looked at each other. Almost in unison we each hoisted the bottle to take a swig.

"There was a mugging last night near the hotel you stayed in DC," Mutt, or Chet Morgan, the Ivy League rower said. "You had left a message for Bill that you had got mugged, so we put two and two together and figured you were a part of it. The guy that ended up in the hospital was a VIP of sorts. Major concussion, the guy had. He's a Russian national—a guy named Ivan Bogachov— he's attached to the Russian undersecretary at the United Nations. If the ambulance wouldn't have come so quickly, we figure that his pals would have carried him away. Bad luck for them. The docs figure that somebody hit him as hard as you could hit somebody with a baseball bat, but there weren't any splinters so they figure it was something hard, like the butt of a gun. The reason that I'm telling you all this is because Wild Bill doesn't believe in coincidences. He doesn't think that it was a random mugging, not with those Russian guys involved. He also said that you could be a tough guy. He said you were Golden Gloves and you could knock out a silo and then his crew taught you how to *really* fight."

"Wild Bill's right about the coincidence," I said. The silo didn't need any seconding. I told them the whole story of the mugging starting from leaving the theatre and seeing the *Unnatural*. "My feeling's the same as Wild Bill—this wasn't any coincidence. I figure that those guys were sent by the Ice Queen. My house was also broken into a few nights ago."

Mutt and Jeff nodded.

"Did they get what they wanted?" Morgan asked.

"No, on two counts. They didn't get me, and I gave you guys what I had —the drawings of the bomb."

"The Russian national, by the way," Morgan said, "we didn't know he was on U.S. soil. We have him placed either in Berlin or Moscow. He's KGB of course. We think he's one of their assassins. However, he's *legal* in this country as long as he's attached to their embassy or the United Nations. Even though he may be legal, he doesn't have a history that we like."

"So what do you want me to tell you—she runs with a rough crowd," I said. "So when do you pick her up, get that bitch off the streets?"

We had finished our beers so I went to the kitchen to get a reload.

"In a week, maybe two or three," Morgan said. "We figure that anything incriminating in her house is long gone. So, we've tapped her phone, we're intercepting her mail, we're tailing her everyplace…"

"We've got her so covered that when she walks under a street light," the big one, Gonski said, trying to be funny, "she sees ten shadows instead of one."

"But, then she knows you're there," I said, poking fun at Gonski's analogy, "she'll see nine other shadows."

"That's right," Morgan said. "We're squeezing her hard to see if we can get her to panic."

I took a slug of beer. "How're you doing all this—like I said earlier, you're a little off your territory aren't you."

"We're off the books," Morgan said. "Wild Bill said you're one of us so we're leveling with you. We got twelve agents here working the Ice Queen—all off the books. This is FBI stuff, but you know Hoover. Hoover's the most powerful guy in the country—and the scariest—but he believes in just three things: One, there is no organized crime. Two, all Commies are Russian and three, how can he get good publicity. The Ice Queen might be getting cooperation from the Russians, but she is working the Korean side of the street. Shit, Hoover doesn't believe that Koreans pose any threat. We're at war with the bastards, and with what I read in the reports, we ain't winning that war. We—the CIA—are responsible for our national safety from the outside. That's why we're in Berlin, that's why we're all over the globe. But, what about in the good ol' U. S. of A? Hoover's asleep at the switch. So, we're looking at this off the books stuff as—like I said earlier—a busman's holiday. It's our job to nail The Ice Queen. When we get some more stuff, we'll yank her off the street and nobody will ever have known she had ever lived. No Hiss trial for this one."

"I think she's in a panic run right now," I said. "She could do something desperate, she could do something stupid." I told them about the murder of Roberta and Wolfemeyer. I didn't talk about the pictures—just about how the Ice Queen had hired Wolfemeyer to follow me and report who I had been in contact with. She then dispatched, I felt, some torpedoes to take out Roberta and Wolfemeyer.

Morgan took notes like a cop would in a small spiral bound notebook that would fit in his shirt pocket. He looked up and said to me, "So, you're thinking of going after her, Jake?"

This guy Morgan was a no-bullshit guy.

I nodded my head.

"You gonna kill her?"

I nodded my head again.

"Wild Bill would probably expect you to do that," Morgan said. "Hell, I would probably do it and I know Gonski here would already have done it. But, I gotta ask you to step back. You go charging up San Juan Hill like Teddy Roosevelt and whatdya got? We might have a dead Ice Queen, but I don't think we've got a dead Korean network. We want to roll up the whole thing, Ice Queen and all."

I went to get three more Schaefer's. It gave me a chance to think a little.

"I'll make you a deal," Morgan said. "You leave the Ice Queen alone—let us handle everything—and when we've got her corralled someplace safe from Hoover and the law, I'll bring you in. If we decide to pull the trigger on her in our own wild west court, I'll let you be the one that pulls the trigger."

"You got that type of clout?" I asked Morgan.

"I am the clout," he said, "because Wild Bill has given it to me. He's not associated with the CIA anymore, of course, but we've got our own version of the CIA within the CIA. Sorta like a shadow CIA. We operate in the shadows of the CIA. *Our* CIA isn't bossed around by politicians; we're not accountable to a director, who doesn't know anything, but is appointed by the president. We might be considered hard liners in protecting our nation, but that's what it takes. The diplomats can do what they want to do; we do what we feel is necessary to protect us. In our version of the CIA, I'm the director, I am the guy, I am the clout."

That was good enough for me. Let these guys do the latter-day shootout at OK Corral. If they kidnapped the Ice Queen and sentenced her to death in their vigilante court of law, I didn't even have to pull the trigger. Revenge for killing Roberta, and the old detective Wolfemeyer, didn't have to have me pulling the trigger. I just needed the *balance*—you take Roberta's life, you lose yours. It couldn't be considered a fair trade, but it was a balance of sorts.

"So, what if Arabella Van Dyck sends some more of her boys after me again?" I asked.

"It seems like you take pretty good care of yourself," Morgan said. That wasn't very encouraging. He wasn't offering any protection. I guess the shadow CIA within the CIA didn't offer such a service.

Even if I had to admit it to myself, I was pretty lucky in Washington that the two goons didn't know what to expect from me. They thought that the gun was enough intimidation to get me into the car. They thought wrong that time; I doubted if they would think wrong the next time. If the Ice Queen spurted full-blown panic, who knew how desperate her goons would be?

"How much time do you guys need?" I asked

"A week," Morgan said, "no more than two. We aren't going to sit on this. Let me tell you, I'm pretty close to sounding the charge. We want to do this legal, but we aren't going to wait around for evidence forever. We're at *war*. In a week's time the Ice Queen will be just a distant memory. Does that work for you? A week? Layoff her for a week?"

"A week," I said, "that works." It might sound silly, but the week didn't bother me that much. My house was fortified with plenty of firepower. Dominic was watching the neighborhood. Hiromi and I could hole up in the house for a week. Hell, the Dodgers were going to be on the road this weekend, so Hiromi and I might as well just camp out in the house and listen to the games on the radio.

Morgan handed me his business card. "If you want to, call me or Wild Bill to see how our little exercise has progressed. We won't be able to give you the straight poop over the phone, of course, but you'll get the idea whether it's safe for you to walk down Flatbush Avenue without worrying about getting mugged."

Morgan and Gonski stood up. The coffee table was littered with empty beer bottles. Gonski did a pretty good job of suppressing a belch. Manners that guy has.

I liked Chet Morgan. He seemed to be the type of guy that Wild Bill would trust. I didn't, however, particularly like the concept of a CIA within the CIA, a shadow CIA. I guess that having a secret cell inside a secret organization is inevitable—after all, the OSS kept operating long after the government closed us down—but being on the outside as a citizen wasn't as comfortable as when I was on the inside. I could trust their mission now, but where would it lead in the future?

29

Thursday, September 27, 1951

I slept like I was dead.

I was exhausted from the trip to see Wild Bill. Not only had I taken a beating, but I had given a beating and both took a huge amount of energy. Finding Roberta—and the ancient Wolfemeyer—dead sure wasn't an elixir. Then toss in the shadow CIA guys. All within a span of about twenty-four hours. The last thing that I remembered from the day was that the Dodgers won at the Boston Braves, but the Giants had won also. That meant that just one game separated the two teams.

The next morning, I had coffee, read the papers and decided to lie down on the couch for just a few moments to rest my eyes and all those aches. I woke up seven hours later.

I stumbled into the kitchen to start the coffee routine all over again. Hiromi was sitting at the table nursing a cup of green tea. She looked as fresh as if she had just spent a few days at a health spa; I felt like I had been dragged down the street by a truck.

The radio was on.

"The Dodgers are tied," Hiromi said.

I made some coffee, poured a shot or two of bourbon into it, and sat down at the kitchen table.

The Dodgers lost to the Boston Braves. Preacher Roe had lost just his third game of the season. He'd won twenty-two.

Red Barber told us about a typical crazy Dodger play that might end up in the record books forever. The Dodgers had brought up a rookie from their St. Paul farm club. A basketball player named Bill Sharman. He hadn't played a Big League game yet. Along with everybody else on the Dodgers bench, he got tossed from the game in the eighth inning. It was unlikely Sharman will get into a game during this pennant race. With rookies called up in September, you never know if they'll ever get into a game. If he doesn't get into a game in the future, he'd be the only player in the history of baseball to get tossed from a Major League game without ever playing in one. That sounded like something that should have been on a tombstone of a Brooklyn Dodger.

The same umpire that tossed all of those Dodgers also called Phillies Bob Addis safe at the plate in the ninth, which lost the game for the Dodgers. The Giants weren't playing, so the Dodgers were just one-half game ahead of them.

After the game, I checked the doors and windows and guns and decided that for all the good I had done that day that I probably should have just stayed in bed. So, after popping four aspirins and downing them with a small glass of warm rum, I was going to act like a hibernating bear; I crawled back into bed

The next morning, I felt better. There were still some aches, but at least I didn't feel like I was eighty years old.

I sat there at the kitchen table staring at the small backyard. It looked like a wonderful day out there.

I started to think that it wouldn't be a bad idea to start an art gallery. The more I had thought of the idea, the better I liked it. Hiromi the artist, me the manager. I was a thousand-percent sure that we could at least break even. Dominic might want to charge somebody else a lot of rent for that vacant space next to his store, but he would practically give it away to Hiromi. Hiromi had the talent; it was now time to showcase it.

The second part of the gallery idea really appealed to me— getting out of the private detecting business. I needed a cover so that I could spend some of my riches and go to Dodger games and drink beer. The gallery was a day job. But, it wasn't like running a grocery store where people were coming in and out all day and I would have to worry about deliveries and rotting fruit. With a gallery, people would wander in only occasionally. If there was a Dodgers day game and I felt like going, I don't think folks would feel deprived if they saw a sign on the door that said, *Gone to a Dodger game, come back tomorrow.* And, the Dodgers were playing a lot more night games now anyway. The night games posed a real conflict when I was detecting. Except for the nooners, most of the juicy stuff—the stuff that could make a wandering husband crumble in front of his wife's lawyer's eyes—happened at night. I was finding these conflicts—a Dodger night game or juicy photos—more and more of a problem. The solution was simple: become the owner of an art gallery. It was a legit business, a legit front, it gave me freedom during the day *and* at night, and it would provide Hiromi the platform that I felt was just the first step in showing the world her talent. Brilliant, I thought. Sometimes I thought I was a genius.

I made some coffee; I decided that I would first talk to Dominic about the art gallery. He'd laugh. Not at the Hiromi part. He'd laugh about me being the manager.

I opened up the sports page. My eyes glazed over the story about the loss last night. I started to think that maybe Hiromi and I should take the train down to Philly to see the Dodgers. Those games were going to be huge. Surely the Ice Queen wouldn't expect us to train it to Philly.

The phone rang.

I picked up the phone and said hello.

"Jake, I need to see you," the voice said. I wouldn't have to ask who that voice belonged to—it was the Ice Queen. It was not a voice that I was expecting; it was not a voice that I wanted to hear. What was she calling for—did she want to know if Hiromi and I could come out and play?

"What do you want?" I asked.

"I need to *see* you, Jake," she said, her voice a plea more than a demand.

I didn't say anything. She did want me to come out and play.

"Jake, I've got to see you, I've got to *give* you something," she said. Her voice wasn't haughty, it was sniveling. "I've *got* to see you."

I didn't say anything. I thought the Ice Queen was going to be out of my life in a week or so. Chet Morgan had told me to butt out, that he was going to roll up the Ice Queen and her network. He also gave me first dibs in killing her.

"I can't talk over the phone," she said. "I *can't* talk over the phone. I need to *give* you something. Meet me."

"Where?"

"Meet me in a public place. That's the only place safe. Jack Dempsey's? On Broadway between 49th and 50th? Do you know it? It's public. It's safe."

I had thought that the Ice Queen had panicked a couple of nights ago in sending some goons after Hiromi and me. She definitely had panicked when she had Roberta and Wolfemeyer killed. Her voice now had notes of stress and panic embedded in each word she spoke.

"What time?" I asked, surprising even myself. Why would I meet with such a wacko? Just wait, let Chet Morgan get around to doing what he said he was going to do, that's what I should do.

"*Today*, Friday," she said in a gush. "One o'clock. I'll get a booth that is private."

"Okay, I'll be there."

"Thank you, Jake, thank you," she said as if I was Harry Truman and had given her a Presidential pardon.

30

Friday, September 28, 1951

I put down the phone.

My eyes gravitated to the kitchen window. It was still bright and sunny outside. I felt I could tell by the birds in the backyard that Hiromi had awakened them with a cheerful song. She was up in her attic studio and I heard the slight echo through the heating vent Rosemary Clooney singing *Come On-a My House.* Everything seemed fine in Brooklyn, U.S.A.

I sat down at the kitchen table over a cup of coffee and glanced at the sports page.

I put down the paper and dialed the number that Chet Morgan had given me. Morgan wasn't there. I had left my name and number. I felt I should tell Morgan that the Ice Queen wanted to meet me for lunch. He would probably shit bricks about me even thinking of meeting her, but Morgan hadn't taken care of the Ice Queen business. I was in this mess, no matter how much I wanted to be out.

With the phone in my hand, I dialed Dominic's number. Ralphie took the call, told me that Dominic was out for just a few minutes, but that he'd tell him to call me as soon as he came in.

I picked up the sports page again. The American League team across town, the New York Yankees, could clinch their pennant tonight if they won one game of the doubleheader against the Boston Red Sox. So, three teams from New York were vying for two pennants. No matter which way this bologna was sliced, the World Series would be a New York series. God forbid if the teams don't have to travel over the Brooklyn Bridge to win the series. If the teams didn't have to use the Brooklyn Bridge, the fans cheering at those games would be jerks and pricks. Everybody in Brooklyn would attest to that.

I decided to have another cup of coffee. I even read the front page of the *Daily News*.

There was a story about another Korean surprise attack on our troops. The story wasn't big headline stuff; it was below the fold on the front page. It sounded like the reporter was bored. He must have felt that he was writing the same old-same old. Surprise attack here, surprise attack there, how boring the reporter must have thought that was. Except, it was *our* guys who were getting surprised. It was *our* guys that were getting killed. Obviously, that reporter hadn't been in the surprise party. He had probably gathered his information from sources at headquarters where, so far, it was safe; there hadn't been any surprises there.

I called Morgan's number again. Nobody answered this time. What good was his number if he wasn't ever near the phone?

Dominic called and he agreed to sit on my stoop while I went to Dempsey's.

Before I left, I went up to Hiromi's studio. I told her that I had to go out, but that Dominic would be downstairs. I told her to keep the shotgun right next to her easel and to keep shut the door to the attic.

Before I left the house, I strapped on a snub nose revolver. That type of gun wouldn't be good in a firefight. However, at short range—let's say the distance of a restaurant's table—it was as deadly as it needed to be.

Jack Dempsey's was in the ground floor of the Brill Building on Broadway. It was just about a block from Madison Square Garden. The Garden was where all the big fights were, so Dempsey's got a lot of sports fans. When the New York Knickerbockers moved to the Garden, Dempsey's got even more from the sporting crowd. The Knicks had played their first three years of existence at the 69th Regiment Armory on Lexington and 25th.

Dempsey's also drew from the music business. The Brill Building was a ten-story building that was in the center of Tin-Pan Alley—the pop music industry. The offices in the building were full with songwriters, arrangers, sheet-music publishers, agents, big-band bookers, record companies. If a company wanted to be in music, it would have to be in the Brill Building. So, nothing was more public than Dempsey's. I doubted that the Ice Queen would do something stupid there.

The Manassa Mauler was Jack Dempsey's nickname from his heavyweight championship days. He was usually there to greet his guests. I'd been to Dempsey's a few times over the years and I got the same greeting that a celeb would get, "Hiya, Pal." I didn't know if he couldn't remember names or the 'Hiya Pal' had become his signature greeting, sorta like Babe Ruth calling everybody 'kid'. I got my "Hiya, Pal" as I walked in about fifteen minutes before one.

Dempsey was in his fifties now, but he was still a brute of a man. Each fist was about the size of a waffle iron. If he cocked one and let it fly, the power was probably still as devastating as when he knocked out Jess Willard over thirty years ago. Willard was so busted up from the fight that it became part of boxing lore that Dempsey had loaded his gloves with a small hunk of steel. Now, Dempsey was the perfect host. He would sign autographs—never just scribbling his name, but always writing an inscription with 'good luck' or 'keep punching.' I've got one of those someplace at home on a menu. Dempsey's must go through thousands of menus a year just for his autographs. Dempsey would pose for pictures or just hold court whether it was with celebrities or folks in from Clinton, Iowa.

Dempsey's had, of course, a boxing motif. There was a giant painting of the Manassa Mauler that greeted people as they walked in. Inside, there was a sea of tables in the room. Along the sides were booths that were more private. That's where I saw the Ice Queen. I was fifteen minutes early because I wanted to case the place. She got there earlier. I looked around. I didn't see the Russians. What the hell, I thought, this was Dempsey's. Nothing could happen here.

I slid into the booth across from her. There was an empty martini glass in front of her.

"Do you want one?" she asked, pointing to her martini glass. "I've got another one on its way. They're famous for them. The bartender, Al Vadelfi was a former boxer you know."

She was just rambling, skipping any greeting and just rolling on about martinis. A waiter brought the refill to her table.

"I'll have one of those too," I said. I really wasn't a martini guy—you don't learn the pleasures of a martini by going to Dodger games. Wild Bill, however, had introduced me to martinis on occasions that we had considered special over in Berlin. Meeting the Ice Queen didn't qualify as a special occasion, but I had a martini anyway.

We sat there waiting for my martini. She went from rambling to stone cold. The only interruption in her coldness was a quick slurp on her martini. She looked awful. If a person could age ten years in a week, the Ice Queen had done it. Her red hair didn't have the flame and sheen that it had just a week ago. There were dark bags under her eyes. It almost looked like she had smeared charcoal under her eyes like Charlie Conerly, the quarterback of the New York Giants football team, would do to dampen the glare of the sun. Charlie Conerly was, of course, looking downfield to throw a touchdown pass; the Ice Queen was just looking to stay out of the clutches of the FBI or some other government agency.

The skin on her face had some blotches that her makeup couldn't completely cover. There was a whole bunch of sleepless nights and days of intense worrying on that skin. When I had first seen her in person when she stepped out of her brownstone, I felt that I would have given up half of my fortune for one night in the sack with her. Now, I wouldn't take half of her fortune for the same deed. I didn't need the money.

My martini arrived. I took a sip. It was a lot better than the concoction that Wild Bill would make in Eastern Europe. I took another sip. The Ice Queen looked at the menu.

"What would you like for lunch?" she asked, as if we were on a date or something.

"I'm not here to eat," I said. "I'm here to *meet*. You said you had to meet with me, well, here I am."

"Let's be civilized," she said with a crinkle of a smile. She raised her hand to catch the eye of a waiter. He was over in a flash.

"I'll have Long Island duckling bigarade with candied sweets and applesauce and salad," she said to the waiter. I looked at the menu. Two dollars and fifty cents for that lunch.

She then ordered for me. "He'll have your luncheon sirloin steak, medium rare, with mushrooms and a salad with French dressing." I couldn't disagree with her choice for me. That steak was three bucks and at Dempsey's, which was famous for its large portions, it could be half a cow.

She sipped her martini. A little bit of color was coming back to her face. It was amazing what a short-term cosmetic that martinis could be. The ultimate cosmetic would be if I powered down about four or five martinis. With that many martinis under *my* belt, her eye bags and blotchy skin would magically smooth out in my view.

"Since you broke into my house," she said, leaving the land of the civilized, "my life has been turned upside down. I think you're the reason. I want to return to my life."

"I admit," I said, "but I stole nothing. The only thing that stuck in my mind was when I saw you with your two Korean playmates. So, lady, go live your life. Just stay out of mine."

I had the very same impulse as when I clobbered that Nazi Scheffler. I felt like reaching across the table and belting the Ice Queen.

"Since you broke into my house," she said, starting from the beginning again, "I've been followed by—I assume—the FBI, my phones have been tapped and everyplace I go I've got a parade of men following me, sometimes discretely, sometimes not, but they aren't so discreet that I don't know that they are there. I want that to stop."

"Look, lady, you're talking to the wrong guy. I'm a private detective, I'm not a G-man. Go talk to J. Edgar Hoover."

When I said Hoover's name, it was as if I had poked her with an electric cattle prod.

"*Don't ever say that name to me again,*" she said with equal parts of venom and ice blended together. This was the Ice Queen that I knew at the Stork Club. "That man is a monster—he's the most dangerous man in the United States. Not just dangerous to *me*, but to *you* too, to every citizen, to even President Truman."

"As far as I know, Hoover—pardon my use of his name—hasn't had little librarians killed or ancient detectives killed or nice citizens like me beat up."

"What are you talking about, killing librarians, for God's sake?"

I told her about how I had rousted Richard Wolfemeyer and he told me who had hired him. I told her about me getting beat up. I told her about Roberta getting killed, although I didn't tell her about the pictures. Damn, I had forgotten to pick up that envelope from Mary at the library. I should have done it yesterday when I had just been lying around the house. I felt as if I should write myself a note and pin it on my tie to help me to remember to pick up that envelope from Mary, but that wouldn't be appropriate right in front of the Ice Queen.

"I admit I hired Wolfemeyer," the Ice Queen said. "I met with him once, gave him an advance and then I never saw him

214

again. No reports, nothing. He just scrammed with my money."
She said it with such a straight face that my first impulse was to
believe her. In fact, if I was on a jury and this had been her
testimony, I would have believed her. Innocent, I would have said.

"I don't know anything about any librarians," she said. "I
don't condone any violence, that's not my style." Yes, she was
convincing, but she was the most convincing liar I had ever met.

Our salads were delivered. The Ice Queen ordered another
round of martinis. It looked like she was going to test my notion
that enough martinis made a cosmetic that Revlon would kill for.

"I know who hired you to break into my house," she said,
swallowing some lettuce.

I didn't say anything; I munched on my salad.

"It was Nick Salzano," she said, "for Joe McCarthy."

I forked another mound of salad into my mouth.

"Both of them tried to fuck it out of me, you know. I
wouldn't let Nick between my legs just because he wanted it too
much. Joe fucked like a water buffalo." I had a hard time
visualizing the water buffalo part, but I guessed that the Ice Queen
knew what she was talking about.

"What did they try to fuck out of you?" I asked. This was,
of course, no way to talk to a lady, but I wasn't talking to a lady, I
was talking to the Ice Queen.

"They think I have a list, a list of Commies who are about
ready to bring down the United States government."

"Is there such a list?" I asked.

"I've got it right here," the Ice Queen said, bringing a large
envelope up from the floor. "It's a list of Communists, but Joe
completely overestimates their power. They're *talkers*, they're
thinkers, they have no power to take over *any* government. But, I
do have the list."

"So, give it to them," I said.

"No, I want to give it to you. You are to be my personal fucking messenger boy. I want to use a private dick to deliver what their dicks couldn't get."

The lady really sure knew how to talk. But, I would have the list and be out of this thing. That was worth the grief sitting with her at Dempsey's.

The Ice Queen didn't know what was in store for her with the shadow CIA, but it looked like I was getting my life back. Eventually, probably pretty soon, I would take her life away from her because of Roberta.

31

Friday, September 28, 1951

"I want it to be known that you *stole* the list from me," the Ice Queen said.

"That's possible," I said. I could lie on how I got the list, that wouldn't be a problem. After all, Tailgunner Joe *expected* me to steal it. Nobody expected the Ice Queen to just *hand* me the list. It wouldn't make any difference to Tailgunner Joe. He just wanted the list.

"Why me as the courier for your list?" I asked.

"You started it all by breaking into my house; you can finish it by giving them that list." That sounded simple enough. It also seemed simple that if the Ice Queen handed me the list that my troubles with her ended.

I could ask myself why was she throwing her Red friends under the bus? Where, in God's sake, was her loyalty? Tailgunner Joe would hound those folks to the ends of the Earth. But, did it matter? She had panicked. Right now, she'd throw her mother under the bus.

"If I did indeed steal the list, you think that will help you with your Red friends that are on the list? I mean, won't McCarthy and his committee be on them like dogs on a bone? Won't these Red friends blame you?"

"Look it, this is just a *list*. A list compiled by one woman, me. It's not illegal to be on my list. There aren't any secret government documents. If my Communist friends point their fingers at me, I can tell them that I didn't go over to McCarthy's side, that I didn't just *hand* over the list. The dirty bastard had somebody break into my house and pick my safe. And, besides, I'm finished with all the oratory and bullshit about Communism. Finis. Caput. Ended. I'm finished with all that crap."

She took a large gulp of her martini. She was putting on a great performance. I was buying the performance, but I couldn't quite buy the fact that she was throwing her friends in Tailgunner's claws.

"There are some strings attached to me giving you the list," she said.

"Strings?"

"There are several, but first I have to tell you a little story."

"A story?"

She nodded. "It's a story about a little girl that was born to tremendous riches."

"You?"

"No, my mother," the Ice Queen said. "This little girl—my mother—was brought up in England. She saw rich people there and many, many poor people. She asked her father why those people were poor and her father said, 'They deserve to be poor, they a*llow* themselves to be poor.' As she got older, she saw what her father meant except she saw that people like her father made sure that the poor remained poor."

"She then came to America, met a very rich man who also came from a rich family in Holland. What she saw in America wasn't much different from England. America was supposed to be the Land of the Free and equality and pursuit of happiness and all that bullshit, but it was just like England: the rich made sure that the poor kept poor. The poor in America were but farm animals. The poor had a job to do just like horses or cows, but a cow or a horse is never allowed to be anything but a cow or a horse—same thing with the poor. They're never allowed to be anything but poor. J.P. Morgan, the Carnegies, and the Rockefellers all set up foundations to *pretend* to help the poor, but that was a salve to heal *their* consciences. They were robber barons. To keep their riches, they had to keep the poor poor."

The main entrée was delivered. The Ice Queen was still working on her salad. She was doing all the talking; I was doing the eating so I put the steak in front of me and carved out a slice.

"My rich mother saw that things were not different in the United States, but there was a chance. What if the government could vote in people that would give everybody the same deal?"

"Communism," I said.

"Communism has become such a nasty word in America, but think of the *concept*. Why should the masses be so poor and a few hold all the riches? It doesn't make any sense. Does the laborer work any less hard than a rich man? Of course not. This became crystal clear to my mother during the go-go days in the 1920s. Men of little talent could make a fortune—a king's fortune no less—on a few trades of stock. The system—capitalism—is *all* based on greed. There is no greater good with capitalism. Only good for a *handful*. Therefore, my mother started to get involved to learn a better way. And, then the stock market crashed. Yes, some of the greedy rich were ruined, but the laborers, the farmers, the rank-and-file factory workers were set back where they could never recover."

I ate another big hunk of steak. Even though we were talking about the desperate poor and the filthy rich, I didn't have any problems in chewing a Jack Dempsey steak that a bum would kill for.

"Go on," I said, "I'm listening. I'm not sure how this connects to the list you have, but I think you'll get me there."

"You'll understand," she said. "This rich mother had a beautiful daughter after the Great Depression. She vowed that that daughter would learn the ways to make a better world. The daughter grew up very rich. With her mother, she attended many meetings about making the United States a better place. This daughter got involved with any and all organizations that wanted to improve the United States. She met a lot of people, she knows a lot of people. She probably knows more political activists than Joe McCarthy would ever think could possibly exist. Even for him. You could call the movement Communism, you could call it socialism, you could call it many things, but it would be better for all Americans..."

"Except those very rich," I said.

"Even for the very rich it would be better. Right now the rich are prisoners in their own mansions. That's not natural—the hoarding, the greed, the selfishness..."

"Look, I appreciate the little story," I said interrupting the Ice Queen, "but that has nothing to do with me. I could argue the point about personal initiative. I could argue the point that the great experiment of Marxism isn't working that terrifically well in Russia. I could argue that it seems that anybody that is in a union would qualify as a Commie. After all, don't unions preach same pay for all the members? I could argue a lot of things, but I don't want to argue anything. If you want me to give the list to Joe McCarthy, I'll give him the list. I'll do that but *I've* got one condition."

"Which is?"

"Get out of my life," I said.

"I promise you that I will do that. Now my last conditions."

"Shoot."

"I want it clearly understood that I have *nothing* to do with Koreans," the Ice Queen said, "*you* have to convince them of that."

"Hell, I'll tell them anything. I'll tell them you've got nothing to do with Korea. I'll say that, but I don't think they'll believe me. They know you have plans for the Atomic Bomb and it's got all types of notes in Korean."

"I didn't know anything about that," the Ice Queen said with the same believable conviction that she used on me earlier when she denied knowing anything about the violence directed at me. If I was on another jury, I would have told the other jurors *not guilty*. But, she was lying. I had to take that as an article of faith that she was lying. She was involved with underground politics like Communism. With an animal like Tailgunner Joe or Richard Nixon breathing down her neck, she would develop lying into an art form. Hell, the Ice Queen lied so convincingly that she probably couldn't tell herself when she was lying or telling the truth.

She hadn't touched her Long Island duckling; I was almost finished with my steak. For a brief moment, I wondered if it would be bad manners to ask her if she was going to eat her lunch. If not, could I peck away at it?

While she was telling me this story about a rich little girl from England, she had ordered still another round of martinis. Mine sat there untouched.

"That was an accident that I even had those drawings," she said. "You saw my two Korean companions...."

"Companions?"

"Hey, there is no law about fucking!" she said through gritted teeth, the words slithering out like they were snakes. "The Koreans asked me to keep the drawings in a safe place. I put them in the safe. I even forgot that they were there. I'll give you their names. I'll give you their addresses. I had nothing—let me repeat—I had *nothing* to do with those plans. Give McCarthy the names of the Koreans. Let him sweat those two bastards. Then he'll know I had nothing to do with those bomb drawings." She reached into her purse and retrieved a small piece of paper. She handed it to me. It had the names and addresses of two guys with Korean names.

Fuck 'em, dump 'em and fuck 'em, I thought. It looked like the Ice Queen was ready to throw everybody under the bus. Her list of Commies, the two Korean lover boys, *everybody*. She was frightened, terribly frightened about being linked with Korea. Even though the Korean War wasn't an official war, I'm sure she was thinking about one word: *treason*. That would be the same offense that the Rosenbergs were charged with. They got to sizzle in the chair. I doubted whether the Ice Queen was going through a change in philosophy. It was sheer, stark raving *fear* that motivated her to throw every Commie that she knew under the bus. She was past the wobbling stage. She was out of control. She knew she couldn't be identified with those bomb plans. She knew that there could be a small plot of land right next to the Rosenbergs waiting for her if those bomb plans were pinned on her like pin the tail on the donkey.

"I've got something else you can give to your Joe McCarthy," the Ice Queen said. She fished into her purse and pulled out an envelope. She tossed it on my remnants of my steak. I picked it up. Inside were the two photos of the Ice Queen and Joe McCarthy. Also included were the negatives.

"What about your lover boys, the other guys, not the Koreans, not Joe, the older guys?" I asked.

"They've got nothing to do with it," she said with as much ice as she could muster in her voice. "As you are well aware of, I am sexually...ah...permissive."

I raised my eyebrows.

"Okay, big boy, let me spell it out for you in case you haven't figured it out: I like to fuck."

I looked around our table. Fortunately, during our conversation she had lowered her voice to little more than a whisper. If she had raised her voice a few notches, she would have the attention of everybody in the restaurant. For now, only my ears heard her words. I had never heard a woman talk so explicitly about sex with the possible exception of hookers. In fact, I hadn't heard women use the word fuck. I had thought that word was a man's word to use as an adjective, noun, adverb, whatever.

"I would like to fuck you right on this table right now," she said, smiling. I think she meant it. It wasn't just the martinis talking. "But Jack Dempsey might think it a little crude for his luncheon crowd. I like to fuck. There's no crime in that. I also like to take pictures of me fucking. There's no crime in that if I don't sell them on the street someplace."

I didn't mention the extortion angle. I just wanted to get the list and get the hell out of there.

"When I'm not fucking, I like to look at pictures of me fucking. Is it sick? Who knows? Who cares? But, I'll guarantee you that not one of those gentlemen in the pictures consider it sick. If I had Jack Dempsey bring over a phone to this table, I could call any one of those guys right now and say 'meet me in the alley because I want to fuck in five minutes' they would be there in the alley in four minutes."

"Who are those guys, anyway?"

"Nobody you would know. I'm a nonpolitical fuck." She continued to speak in an even voice that floated underneath the din of a crowded room of drinkers and eaters. "I fuck Republicans, I fuck Democrats, I fuck radicals, I fuck nonpolitical types, I fuck white guys, I fuck colored guys and as you know, I fuck Orientals. One thing I've learned over the years is that a hard dick has no race and it has no politics."

She took a hefty slug of the martini. She seemed almost out of breath. I guessed that she was telling me the truth that she would like to fuck me right then on the table smothering her Long Island duckling with her churning ass.

I couldn't help but think of the juxtaposition of the Ice Queen and Hiromi. Here was one that was born rich. The Ice Queen had all the advantages. She chased ideological dreams of Communism. Her greatest skill was fucking. Here was the other who was born to poor immigrant parents. During her teenage years in this new and strange land, she had been tossed in an Internment Camp. Her greatest skill was bringing joy and thought through her paintings. How could this be? Only in America.

She held up the envelope that contained The List. "Two conditions," she said. "One, you have to convince them that I had nothing to do with the Koreans except fuck them and hold some papers for them. You have to make that very clear. The second condition is that you don't mention—that you don't even breathe a word—about my photo collection of fucking. That's something personal. That's our secret. McCarthy doesn't need to know. Besides, I've taken the liberty of destroying those pictures and the negatives. There is no evidence. Do we have a deal?"

"I can't make a deal," I said. "But, they do know about the bomb. With Joe McCarthy, my feeling is that you can dodge that Korean bullet by providing The List. About the fucking and the pictures, I won't say anything."

Nick had told me that Tailgunner Joe didn't care about Korea. He was after the type of Communism that was Russian. The shadow CIA was something else, but I hadn't even mentioned them to the Ice Queen. I had the feeling that whatever I would say to Chet Morgan about her conditions wouldn't be worth a plugged nickel.

She looked relieved. She tilted the martini glass back, but it was empty. "Thank you," she said and handed me the envelope.

I called for the check.

I got up, put my napkin down on the table.

"You don't want some cheesecake, sweetheart?" the Ice Queen asked me smiling. She actually looked appealing. What a chameleon! Was she actually coming on to me?

"What do you mean?" I asked.

"Cheesecake, Jake," the Ice Queen said. "Dempsey's has cheesecake that rivals Lindy's."

"No thanks."

The waiter came by with the check. I dropped down a twenty and a ten. That would have covered the lunches and all those martinis and had enough leftover for a pretty hefty tip. I started to walk away.

"Oh, Jake, one more thing," the Ice Queen said. "There's a surprise for you on the list. See if you can find it."

"What are you talking about?" I asked.

"A surprise, Jake, a *real surprise*," the Ice Queen said, smiling. She was clearly drunk. "Don't take the fun out of it; *find the surprise!*"

"I probably won't even look at the list. I'm gonna hand it over to Joe and Nick as is."

"You'll be sorry," the Ice Queen said, "yes, you will be very, very sorry indeed."

32

Friday, September 28, 1951

It didn't take me too long to make the phone call to Nick Salzano.

I stopped at the first phone booth I came to. I had the Ice Queen's list, but it was like a second baseman on a double play. Get the ball, pivot and get rid of it. I didn't want to hold on to the list very long.

I pulled out my little address book, found Nick's Washington, D.C. number and dialed the operator. I told her what number I was calling. She told me to deposit thirty-five cents. The cost of this one call would buy a decent breakfast back in Brooklyn.

A woman that *sounded* sexy picked up the phone after three rings. What a day—going from the Ice Queen who wanted to screw me on a table at Jack Dempsey's and talked saltier than a sailor to a secretary that sounded like she could give you a hard-on just by listening to her talk on the phone. That voice might belong to a woman who was as big as a train station, but I doubted that. Nick would only have babes around the office.

I gave her my name and asked for Nick.

"Is he expecting your call?" she breathed. "You see, he's in a very important meeting right now behind closed doors."

The way she said it *sounded* really important. I thought: Let's test how important.

"I wouldn't want to interrupt his meeting," I said, "but, can you just hand him a message? I'll just wait on the phone to see if there is an answer. Oh, and by the way, what is your name?"

She told me her name was Melanie. Yes, she could unobtrusively slide into the meeting. If she was going to slide unobtrusively, then I figured she wasn't as big as a train station or even a small house. In fact, she was probably damned good looking. Big ugly women don't *slide* very easily.

"Just write, 'I've got the Queen's List.' I know this sounds a little silly, Melanie, but Nick will understand. So, please write 'I've got the Queen's List.' Capitalize the Q and the L. Then write, 'do you want it?' That's it."

"That's it?"

"Yep, Melanie, that's it. Just show it to him. You don't even have to wait for an answer. I think he'll tell me himself."

Melanie put the phone down on her desk. I heard her heels click away on the hard floor. I wondered if the cost of this phone call would escalate from a breakfast to a steak dinner. I wondered if I should buy some stock in the telephone company. At least I'd get some of my long-distance charges returned to me in the form of a stock dividend.

"You've got it?" Nick bellowed into the phone.

"I got it."

"No shit? You got it?"

"Nick, I got it already. Want me to mail it to you?" I said, trying to see if he had a sense of humor today. When we were kids, he used to laugh all the time.

"Are you out of your mind, Jake? Jesus Christ, *mail* it to me?" Nick shouted. I guess he had lost his sense of humor somewhere back in the 1940s in Brooklyn.

"Joe's in New York right now. He's got to give a speech over at the Waldorf, but he can sneak out afterward. I think I can still reach him. Hold on, let me try to reach him on another phone." I heard Nick's phone clunk on the desk. I could practically hear the long-distance charges ratcheting up.

"I got a hold of Joe," Nick said. "He can meet you tonight. I'm gonna take the train up and meet him and then we'll get together. Why don't we meet at Dowling's Oyster Bar at nine. Joe liked that place."

That was fine with me.

"And, Jake, go home," Nick said, "don't go into some saloon with that list. Don't go to the Dodger game..."

"The Dodgers are at Philly, don't you know? It's a huge game," I said.

"Well, just go home, and stay there until we meet at the bar. Jesus Christ, this is a huge breakthrough," Nick said. He didn't mention the Dodgers.

With The List on the front passenger seat next to me in my Ford, I drove over the Brooklyn Bridge and was home within minutes of the phone call.

I stopped and said hello to Dominic. He walked back to his store. I then checked with Hiromi. She was still busy painting.

I sat down in my office and opened up the envelope. I had not even looked at the list when the Ice Queen had given it to me. What if the envelope was just filled with blank pieces of paper? Great practical joker, that Ice Queen. Har-de-har-har. Was that the surprise that the Ice Queen said was in store for me? Nothing but blank sheets of paper?

I pulled out the pieces of paper. It wasn't a practical joke as far as I could tell. There were names all right. There were about twenty-five or so names on each page. There were fifteen pages of names. I did the math in my head: there were almost four hundred names on her list.

The Ice Queen had drawn vertical lines down the sheets of paper. On the first column on the left was the person's name. The second column had the person's address and phone number. I guess that this would make it easier to hand the subpoenas to these Reds. The next column was the name of the organization. The column after that was the leader of that organization. The last column had some notations of how they were connected to Communism. A lot of this was initials and abbreviations. I didn't know what those meant. I bet Tailgunner Joe had a staff that was very familiar with those abbreviations. They could read them as if it was a third-grade book.

I scanned down the list of names for names that I would recognize. I didn't think that I would find any people that I personally knew. For instance, our neighborhood bookmaker, Dominic Gonnella, could never be considered a Red.

Edward R. Murrow caught my attention. I watched him on television all the time. I could never imagine him to be a supporter of Tailgunner Joe, but I also couldn't picture him all the way on the other side.

I saw other news media types on the list. This would cause a problem for Tailgunner Joe. It was one thing for Tailgunner Joe to go after movie writers and movie directors. Could they make a movie to defend themselves? Of course not. Movies cost hundreds of thousands of dollars to make. No studio would allow some faceless writer or director to make a movie to try to prove his innocence. Besides, the writers and directors were indeed nameless faceless guys. They could clearly become prime targets of Tailgunner Joe. If you're going to pick a fight, pick a fight with people that can't fight back. That seemed to be McCarthy's way.

Edward R. Murrow, however, could fight back. If I trusted the numbers I read in the paper about how many people were buying new televisions—it was in the millions—then there were millions that invite Edward R. Murrow into their living rooms every night. Nailing Murrow would certainly be a coup for Tailgunner Joe, but Edward R. Murrow could fight back like a banshee. I'm not sure that it was a good idea for Tailgunner Joe to pick a fight with him.

Was Edward R. Murrow the surprise that the Ice Queen said that I would find? Seeing his name might have been a surprise, but big deal. Who cared?

I looked further down the list.

Marlon Brando. Well, here was another name that Tailgunner Joe just might want to pass on.

Brando had probably attended some Communist-type meetings. Hell, he was an *actor,* for Christsakes. What do actors know anyway? Brando had been a struggling actor until *Street Car Named Desire.* It would be impossible to name one struggling actor that wouldn't be sympathetic to some all-for-one and one-for-all type of bullshit. They were *struggling,* for Christsakes. We would see what they thought about sharing their money once they became a star. I don't think they would be giving up their big mansions in Beverly Hills so that struggling actors could get food and rent money. Nor would they give up the fast cars. Never happen. That would be like telling Joe DiMaggio that he had to share his salary with that new rookie, Mickey Mantle. Joe D's many things, but he ain't gonna share his paycheck with some rookie.

There were a few more news media types on the list. Jesus, if this list was legit, there were way too many Reds preparing our news for us. We all know that there were two sides to any story. After seeing the names on the Ice Queen's list, it looked like there was *one* side per story. That one side was the one that the Red sympathizers felt comfortable with. Maybe there was something to Tailgunner Joe's mission. Maybe he wasn't just a blowhard that was trying to grab national attention for himself. That national attention might be the ticket he wanted to get to run for President. But, Tailgunner Joe might be on to something *real.* Was it real enough to catapult him to the biggest office in the land? Tailgunner Joe as President—that was a little tough for me to imagine.

On the ninth page, I got my surprise.

The twenty-second name on the list was a name that shouldn't have been there. How could it be there? This was the Ice Queen's practical joke—it had to be.

I stared at that name and then I stared at the name above it and the name below it.

I knew that I had to get this name off the list.

To Tailgunner Joe, it didn't make any difference if the people on the list were Commies or not. He'd be coming after all of them. They were going to go through the gauntlet of federal investigation. Hearsay and innuendo was rock-solid evidence to the McCarthy Committee. Some of the people on the list like Edward R. Murrow could fight back. Others couldn't. Tailgunner Joe would nail those people.

I looked at the stack of sheets. I couldn't erase any of the individual names. They were all written in ink. Even if I were able to erase that one name, the empty line would stick out like a missing arm.

The pages weren't numbered and the names weren't in alphabetical order. My solution was to remove the ninth sheet altogether. Everybody on the ninth sheet would get a free pass away from Tailgunner Joe. Everybody else would be subject to hell.

I was alone in my kitchen, but I felt that the world's eyes were on me. If I took that ninth sheet of names out of the stack, I felt I should do it secretly. A dark closet or in the corner of the basement would do. My paranoia was overactive anyway; it really spiked by just thinking about Tailgunner Joe and his power to destroy. The hell with it. I took the ninth sheet of names, folded it, and put it in my pocket. I'd find out later, I'm sure, if Tailgunner Joe had eyes in my kitchen.

I was getting antsy waiting for nine o'clock to roll in for my meeting with Tailgunner Joe. I decided I should make a copy of the Ice Queen's list. I brought my Minox camera out of the drawer, set up the pages of the list on my desk and snapped off two shots per page. I don't know what I would do with my copies of the list, but it was better to be cautious about these things.

When I eyeballed the list through the lens of the camera, I started to question the veracity of the list. I had started to think these thoughts when I first looked at the list, but then zeroed in on some of the names that I recognized like Edward R. Murrow and Marlon Brando. This list seemed artificial; it seemed manufactured. I'm not saying that these people didn't attend some Communist meetings that they shouldn't have in the past. Some of the notes on the list said that some of the meetings stretched way back to The Great Depression. As I understood the Great Depression, people would go to meetings just to do *something*. Heck, democracy wasn't working during the Great Depression. Why not take a look at Communism, this all-for-one and one-for-all that would shrink down the robber barons.

It didn't look to me that there were any Alger Hiss's or Rosenbergs on this list, but what did I know? Tailgunner Joe's crew would sure have fun burrowing into the mothballs of these people's past. Someplace, somewhere, they'd find something that would be their version of a grand slam homer.

There was a loud knock at the front door. I didn't think it would be any goons. First of all, I had made my peace with the Ice Queen, at least I thought I had. I was now her approved messenger boy. Secondly, goons wouldn't knock. Still, cautious as I was, and as paranoid as I could get, I put the Colt 45 in my hand and walked to the door.

On the stoop were Chet Morgan and John Gonski, my favorite shadow CIA guys. Morgan was standing there with his arms folded across his chest; Gonski was about to knock again. I put the Colt 45 in a drawer in the chest in the vestibule and opened the door.

"Mind if we come in?" Morgan said. It really wasn't a question. It was more of a statement.

I opened the door and stepped aside. We walked into the living room.

"Welcome back," Morgan said. "I got your message. I called but no answer. We've been tailing the Ice Queen while you were gone. And then today I get the biggest surprise."

"Tell me about it," I said.

"No, Jake, you tell me about it," Morgan said. "You agree to lay low for a while, which we agreed was a great idea. I even promised you the Ice Queen on a platter, when we were finished with her. Then after sitting in your house for a day, who do you have lunch with? One of our guys that's been tailing the Ice Queen follows her to Dempsey's. He goes inside, grabs a seat at the bar and waits to see who shows up. Lo and behold, who shows up but none other than our boy, Jake McHenry."

"You're right," I said, "I tried calling you."

"So, tell me about it now."

I did. I told him about the Ice Queen calling me this morning, I told him about most of the lunch. I told him how my client had been Joe McCarthy, but he had guessed that already. I told him about the list.

"That whack-job McCarthy," Morgan said, not trying to soften his disgust. "Here we are fighting in a fucking war and he's playing Beat the Band. So, what's this list look like?"

I got the list and showed it to Morgan.

He spent a few minutes running down the names.

"Commies? Edward R. Murrow…"

"I always suspected that guy," Gonski said, his first words he had said so far.

"Brando, Marlon Brando?" Morgan questioned.

"Wait until they make that movie about Commies," Gonski said.

"What movie? How do *you* know about movies?"

"My wife, she tells me. She loves movies. She loves Brando. She saw it in Winchell's column—they're gonna make a movie about unions on the waterfront here in New York—I think the Brooklyn docks. It's directed by that guy that McCarthy's after. Kasam, Kassan, K-something or the other."

"Yeah, well we'll let McCarthy worry about the movies," Morgan said. "You take pictures of these?" Morgan asked me pointing to the list.

I nodded my head.

"I don't know what I'll need it for but make me a copy, okay?"

"Yeah, sure."

"You got your own darkroom here?" He asked.

I nodded.

"I'll send one of my guys by tomorrow to pick up the copy."

"Fine with me," I said. I'm a cooperative guy.

"So, what else did you find out during your little lunch?" Morgan asked.

"She's really scared about those Korean bomb plans, really scared," I said. "I think that's why she's throwing all those people on the list under the bus."

"Yeah, if I was her, I'd be scared too." Morgan said. "That's treason, you know."

"If you can prove it," I said. "She told me that it was an accident that those plans were even in the house. You see, she's got a slight personal problem—she likes to fuck."

"So what's the problem with that?"

"She told me she likes to fuck everything. All the time. According to her, she hooked up with two Korean guys, invited them over to her house, fucked 'em both. They asked if they could store some papers in her safe. She claims that those drawings were there for only a week and that they're not there anymore."

"The Koreans or the drawings?" Gonski asked, thinking he was making a joke. Morgan gave him a hard look.

"Here are the names and addresses of those two Koreans," I said, tossing the sheet of paper that the Ice Queen had given me on the table. "Check 'em out."

Morgan picked up the piece of paper. "We'll do that. We'll do that." He looked closer at the names. "All these Korean names look alike to me."

Morgan put the piece of paper in his shirt pocket.

"Well, she hasn't been inviting anybody to her house in the past couple of days," Morgan said. "No Koreans, no nothing. So, if she's been fucking anybody, it hasn't been on our watch. Maybe she got religion."

"Yeah, the religion she got was the word 'treason,'" I said. "Look, Chet, I had lunch with her. She's starting to look like a piece of shit. She drinks like there is no tomorrow. If you ever wanted to see somebody that's losing it, look at her."

The two shadow CIA got up. They had the information they needed. However, I didn't.

"Did you investigate the murders of Roberta DiNardo and Richard Wolfemeyer?" I asked.

"Oh, yeah, I forgot to tell you," Morgan said. "The cops think that some punks busted in the old lady's apartment thinking that she had jewels or cash or something. The cops figure that she was there, that the punks pushed her around, but she's so frail that her neck was broken by accident. The other one—the old detective guy—they think suicide. Here's an old guy, no money, no family, probably got a body full of sick, and decides to end it right there. End of investigation."

"What do you think?" I asked. I had figured the cops to label these murders the way they did. These people were not prominent citizens. They were old and alone and lived on the outskirts of our society. The cops would complete their file—it was easy, it was logical, it wouldn't need any follow-up—and on to the next cases.

"I don't know," Morgan said. "We didn't investigate it. We just got the cops reports. It coulda been that the Ice Queen had sent some thugs like those that went after you in DC, but it coulda been just what the cops said it was. We haven't spent much time on it. Nor, have we seen any Russian mob guys hanging around the Icc Queen."

"When are you going to bring her in?" I asked.

"What are you asking?" Morgan said, "We don't have anything on that bitch except what you've told us. And you tell us that she no longer has the drawings. You tell us she likes to fuck chinks. I'm gonna haul her ass away and tell Wild Bill that we're going to sweat it out of her that she likes to fuck chinks? Look, Jake, we'll watch her—we think you gave us really valid stuff—but she's gotta make a mistake. Just one fucking mistake is all I'm asking."

It looked to me like the Ice Queen was burrowing way underground, so far down that she might be never found. If that was the case, then it was good for Hiromi and me. Sure, I probably would have to postpone avenging Roberta, but maybe—just maybe—the cops were right on that one. The murders *could* be coincidental. There were neighborhoods in Brooklyn that we're turning bad. There were so many folks moving out to Long Island or Staten Island or retiring to Miami Beach. Waves of immigrants replaced them. So maybe the murders were coincidental. *Maybe.* Probably not.

On the stoop, Morgan shook my hand and said, "I'll send a guy by tomorrow to pick up the copy of the list. Ten in the morning good for you?"

"Yeah, I'll have it ready then."

"Jake, call me," Morgan said, "if you decide to have lunch with the Ice Queen again. Call me if you hear anything new."

I said I would. I did the first time and nobody answered the phone.

I looked at my watch. I still had a couple of hours for Round Two of my meetings with the Feds, this time with Tailgunner Joe. I was ready to slam the door on the whole Ice Queen deal.

33

Friday, September 28, 1951

Billy Dowling didn't take any reservations at his bar, Dowling's Oyster Bar. He wanted to discourage folks that just wanted to go out to dinner. He was in business to serve the serious drinkers. This was the right place to meet Tailgunner Joe. We would need a booth, of course.

I called over to Dowling's and talked to Billy. I had downed enough beers in Dowling's over the years that he instantly made an amendment to his Drinkers Bill of Rights—the part that forbade reservations. "Yeah, I'll hold that booth for ya," Billy said. "I'll just stand in front of it for a while."

Billy was a huge man, but his hugeness wasn't the type of huge that would get him on a football field. He had the largest beer belly anybody in Brooklyn had ever seen. It looked like he fed it every night, which I guess he did when you own a bar and you drink free.

I could have taken Tailgunner Joe to the upstairs room at Dowling's. That was where couples could have a quiet dinner. I guess that was the room for the *eaters*. To get upstairs, you'd come in the side door by the backstairs. If I was taking my mother to dinner, I could go through the side door and avoid all the hooting drinkers at the bar. That was a genteel touch. It was like a separate restaurant upstairs—separate kitchen, separate staff and separate cash register. The Tax Boys thought there was only one cash register in Dowling's, the one downstairs behind the bar. All the food and drink that Billy sold upstairs was free from the clutches of our tax men at work. The upstairs—while more private—wasn't Tailgunner Joe's type of place. He was a *bar* guy, an *Irish* bar guy and Dowling's Oyster Bar was it.

I had stopped at the library on my way to Dowling's. The library stayed open until eight o'clock on Friday nights. I had finally remembered to pick up the envelope that Roberta had left for me before she was murdered.

Mary O'Halloran was at the checkout desk. We greeted each other, and then I asked her about the envelope that Roberta had left for me.

From the look of her face, it looked like her memory was failing her more than mine had.

"Yes, yes, I remember," she said. "But, you never picked it up, did you?"

"No, Mary, I forgot, plus I was gone some. I just remembered it as I walked past the library."

"Oh, what did I do with that?" She asked herself. "Did I mail it to you?"

"I don't think so," I said, straining my memory to match the strain of hers.

"Let me look," she said, and walked over to her desk. She opened the top drawer, then the second one and then the last one. Nothing.

"Oh! I know where I put it," she said like a little girl that just remembered where she had hid a dime for the movies. "It's in the Overdues," she said, referring to the cards of books that were past the deadline for return.

We walked over to the checkout desk and she reached into a drawer, plucked out the envelope and handed it to me. It was the right envelope; on the front was scrawled my name in Roberta's handwriting. It was sealed and taped shut. It felt like photos were stacked like a collection of baseball cards inside. After having lunch with the Ice Queen and then meeting with Chet Morgan, I didn't have a real urgency anymore on who those scrunched faces belonged to. I put the envelope in my back pocket; I would look tomorrow at the pictures that Roberta had identified.

As I had walked from the library to Dowling's, I could hear the Dodger announcer, Red Barber, every step of the way. The game seemed to be blaring from every radio in Brooklyn. Red's voice flowed out of open windows, out of shops, it was like God was speaking. Red had a new sidekick this season, a rookie announcer. He was a guy named Vin Scully and damned if he too didn't have red hair. This red stuff was starting to get a little bit too much.

Walking to Dowling's, I heard that we scored in the first inning. Jackie Robinson knocked in Pee Wee Reese with a single to center. Then in the second, we scored again.

I walked through the front door of Dowling's Oyster Bar and sure enough, Billy was standing in front of the last booth by the window. If a patron needed privacy in Dowling's, that was the one place. If the bar had customers four deep, which was most nights around six or seven during the week, then the drunks tended to overflow onto the four booths that ran along the wall. The drunks didn't actually join the people that occupied the booths; the drunks just *hovered*. This being a Friday night, the place was packed. With the Dodgers playing at Philly, Dowling's was standing room only. We had a half-game lead over the New York Giants. If we lost this game, God forbid, there would be a flat-footed tie with the Giants for first.

I walked over to the corner booth. Billy Dowling stood there like a Redwood tree stump.

"Dodgers up, two nothing," Billy said and then stepped aside so I could get into the booth. "Allie Reynolds threw a no-hitter against the Red Sox. That was the game the Yankees needed to win the American League pennant."

"Yeah, I heard," I said. Walking to Dowling's, one of our Reds—either Red Barber or redheaded Vin Scully—told me.

In Dowling's, the radios blared from the four corners of the bar. Too bad it wasn't on television.

I sat down in the empty booth and ordered a Schaefer's. Schaefer's wasn't the best beer, particularly compared to German beer, but I was loyal. Schaefer's had the big sign in centerfield at Ebbets Field. I supported the companies that supported the Dodgers, good fan that I was.

Nick joined me in the booth before I could finish my first Schaefer's.

"Hey, how're you doing?" he asked sliding into the booth. He looked at his watch. "I just got in from the train. Joe should be here in a few minutes."

I ordered him a beer from Betty, the tough Irish waitress that had been at Dowling's so many years that she might have thought she had been born there.

"So, pal, where is it?" Nick said after draining half of his beer.

I handed him the envelope.

"This is *it*? Really?" Nick was like a little kid.

"That's it."

Nick pulled the list out of the envelope and quickly scanned a couple of pages. "Jesus," he said, "there's some dynamite stuff here." He then put the pages back into the envelope. "Joe will love this, just love it." He handed the envelope back to me. "You give it to Joe," he said.

I flipped Nick the smaller envelope that the Ice Queen had given me, the pictures of Joe and the Ice Queen.

Nick opened. "Jesus," he said, "the prints *and the negatives*. Wow, buddy, you sure hit a grand slam."

"These, however, Joe don't see," Nick said, sticking the prints and negatives into his jacket pocket. "I never told him about the photos. He would want to kill her—but he would also be embarrassed—so sometimes we have to protect him from himself. He made an obvious mistake by fucking the Ice Queen, but now that we have the negatives, we don't have to throw it in his face. I'll just keep these and destroy them later. Him boffing the Ice Queen never happened."

That was okay by me. If I ever needed a copy, I had one hidden away in my house.

The front door to Dowling's banged open. Tailgunner Joe had arrived like a cyclone. He saw Nick and me sitting in the booth and like a large animal bounded over to us. A little guy with a set of rabbit teeth followed him. It looked like he had come with Tailgunner Joe, but he wasn't invited to the booth; he stood at the three-deep bar. He looked like a college boy that had probably been nominated to chauffer Tailgunner Joe around. The rabbit-tooth guy ordered a Coca Cola.

Joe sat down in the booth with a thud. "How'y're doing?" he asked me.

I told him fine.

Betty appeared like an apparition. "Rocky Marciano, right?" she said.

"Yeah, yeah, Rocky, that's me," Joe said laughing.

"Your usual? Scotch and water?"

Tailgunner Joe laughed. "My *usual*? My *usual*? I've been to this bar only one time in my life and you *remember* my usual?"

"I'd never forget Rocky Marciano," she said smiling. It seemed that Betty had taken a particular liking to Tailgunner Joe. I sure didn't need to see photos of what could happen there.

"So, what's your name? *The usual*?" Joe said, laughing as if he was a comedian at some nightclub.

"Betty, big boy, Betty," she said and then turned to get Tailgunner Joe's usual.

"Nice joint," Tailgunner Joe said. "Hey, my usual, now don't that take the cake?"

Betty delivered Joe's scotch in a tall glass with water. Then she set a second one down in front of him. By the color, I could tell there wasn't much water in those glasses. "This time," she said, "you get both halves at the same time."

Tailgunner Joe roared as if he had just heard the best dirty joke in his life. Yep, Tailgunner Joe was meant for Dowling's Oyster Bar all right.

Tailgunner Joe knocked down in one gulp one-half of one of his halves.

"You got the list I hear," Tailgunner Joe said.

I nodded. I handed him the envelope.

He snapped open the flap and pulled out the sheets of paper. He scanned the list with an intensity that I could feel across the table.

"Hey, Bobby," he yelled over at that young guy drinking a Coke near the bar. "C'mon over here for a minute."

The young guy slid into the booth.

"Bobby Kennedy meet Jake McHenry," Tailgunner Joe said. We shook hands over the table. I remembered the name. Tailgunner Joe had mentioned him during our first meeting—something about this young punk Kennedy being more intense than Richard Nixon. Now that I had met Nixon and all of his intenseness, it was difficult for me to fathom that this little buck-toothed college kid was more intense than Nixon. Nixon could stare down a rock. There must have been another Bobby Kennedy.

"Bobby, look at this list," Tailgunner Joe said, handing the list to the college student.

Bobby Kennedy looked at the list, his face aging as I watched. That was some show of intensity and the young guy wasn't putting on an act.

"Edward R. Murrow," Kennedy said, "we've suspected him all along. He considers himself a centrist liberal, which is spelled c-o-m-m-i-e." Kennedy took a swig of his Coke.

"Look it here, she's given us a road map on how to nail his ass—Mr. Edward R. Murrow of the *esteemed* CBS show *See It Now*," Kennedy said, putting sarcastic emphasis on esteemed. "*Mr.* Murrow was on the advisory committee for a summer school at Moscow University. We can track that down pretty good. How does Paley allow a guy like that to be on his network?"

"Okay, Bobby, settle down," Tailgunner Joe said. It was interesting to see that Tailgunner Joe was trying to provide some brakes on the young guy. "Murrow is a walking, talking, farting Red, but he's also on CBS. We're gonna need more than being on some advisory committee to some Moscow University summer school. Now, go back to the bar and finish your Coke."

I could tell that the young guy wanted to stay at the booth and talk about Communists. But, by tonight he would have the list and he could work until Kingdom Come to nail all of the Reds that the Ice Queen had fingered.

The bar erupted. If we had tried talking to each other, we wouldn't have heard a word. Roy Campanella had hit a home run in upper deck in left field. It was now three-nothing in the fifth.

When the bar quieted down to a livable din, I said, "The Ice Queen had a condition on giving up the list."

"Wait, wait just a fucking minute," Joe said, "you said she just gave you the list? Just *gave* it to you? What's going on?"

"She had me tailed, Joe, she knew who I was. She's scared to death about treason, that what happened to the Rosenbergs could happen to her. So, she's cooperating. She wants out. By giving me the list, she had a condition…"

"A condition!" Tailgunner Joe belched. "*A condition? We don't give conditions to Reds!*"

"Joe, let me explain," I said. "She gave me the list to give to you. But, she wants people to think I stole it. After all, she's fingered about every Commie that she knows and you're gonna go after every single one of them."

"You bet your ass I am," Tailgunner Joe said. "I'm gonna unleash that little cocksucker over there on every fucking name."

"Yeah, so she just doesn't want the Red world to know she gave up the names. You blow her out of the water with all of her Red pals right now, you can't go back to the source. You might need more information down the road. This is a *list*, and there is some detail here, but she could provide you more. She couldn't if you blow her out of the water. *She's cooperating*, Joe. *She's your inside accomplice.*"

Tailgunner sat looking at his glass of scotch. He was in his thinking mode again. His boisterousness had been shackled and he drank his drink as a fine lady would.

"How'd you do that?" Tailgunner Joe asked. "You fuck her?"

Before I could answer, he held up his hand. "No, don't tell me. Don't tell me."

After about two minutes of thinking, Tailgunner Joe said, "Yeah, Jake, yeah, it makes sense. I'll just say that we got this list on some raid of some Red meeting place."

Then as if a light bulb turned on in his head, he said, "Aw hell, I just won't ever say we've got a list. I used the list idea for that speech down in Wheeling, West Virginia. It worked good for its purpose. I don't have to mention a list anymore. We'll just start picking off these Reds one by one."

"There's one other condition," I said.

"Oh, boy, what's that?" Tailgunner Joe asked.

"She doesn't want anything mentioned about the Koreans," I said.

"What fucking Koreans? What the fuck are you talking about, Jake?"

I looked over at Nick. Nick said, "Let me tell 'im."

"Whad'ya mean by 'let me tell 'im'?" Tailgunner said, practically shouting. Even if he shouted, it wouldn't have made much of a ripple in Dowling's. Somebody was always shouting about something. A bad play by the Dodgers or a Dodger homer could practically bring down the ceiling.

"Settle down, Joe," Nick said. Nick looked at me like a young father whose three-year-old was staging a tantrum. "You got the picture, the one with the Koreans?" he asked.

I knew what picture he was asking about. I had brought it with just the vaguest feeling that I would need it when we were talking about the Korean connection.

I took the picture out of my sports jacket pocket and handed it to Tailgunner Joe.

Tailgunner Joe stared at the picture. "So," he said, "she fucks chinks. What's this about Koreans? These two dickheads are Korean? So what?"

Then he looked at the picture a little bit closer. I couldn't tell if he made the connection that the picture he was looking at had been taken by a hidden camera in the Ice Queen's bedroom and that same hidden camera could have taken *his* picture. He was in his thinking mode, having gone from volcanic to glacier.

"Those two Koreans," I said, "asked the Ice Queen to put in her safe some confidential papers...."

"So? Big deal," Tailgunner Joe said.

"The papers were drawings of an atomic bomb," I said.

That put Tailgunner Joe back into his thinking mode. He picked up his glass of scotch and tilted it back into his mouth. Nothing came out. He turned and called, "Betty, get me two halves!"

Betty delivered the tall glasses of scotch and water and Tailgunner Joe knocked one back like it had been a shot glass.

"So tell me about those two fucking Koreans," Tailgunner Joe said.

"That's one of the conditions," I said. "She doesn't want that drawing of the bomb to put her behind bars. She'll give up the two Koreans if you want to go after them."

"Koreans, who the fuck cares about Koreans?" Tailgunner Joe said. He was sounding like Nick when I had first told him about it.

"We're after *Reds*," Tailgunner Joe said, "not *chinks*. So, Jake, if those are the fucking conditions, I can meet those."

Then he thrust out his forefinger and said, "One, I don't tell anybody that she gave us the list." He then thrust out his middle finger next to his forefinger. "And two, I won't tell anybody that she fucks Koreans."

He took a hefty swig of the second drink. "What a sick broad," he said, "screwing fucking chinks."

He drained the remains of his second drink.

"I gotta get back to the Waldorf," Tailgunner Joe said. "I knew I could trust you, Jake, I knew you wouldn't let me down. This list will be the knockout blow to the Reds, you just mark my words."

Tailgunner Joe got up from the booth. "You pay the man, yet?" he asked Nick.

Nick said, "No, not yet."

"Pay him." Nick reached into his briefcase and withdrew an envelope. I didn't open it but it felt like a hefty chunk of cash. Even if the bills were five-dollar bills, it would be a pretty good pile. I didn't think they would be fives.

Tailgunner Joe stuck his big hand in front of my face and I shook it. "You're a good man, Jake. We might have to use you again. Okay with you?"

"Sure," I said, although that was the last I wanted to see of Tailgunner Joe McCarthy. He was a character to have a couple drinks with at Dowling's Oyster Bar. He was a rowdy, raucous man's-man type of a guy, but he had trouble written all over him. That writing was like an indelible tattoo that everybody could see except him. I could drink with him in an Irish bar, but I don't think I would watch him ever again on television. Hopefully, this closed my dealings with Tailgunner Joe McCarthy. Let the world deal with him.

"Bobby," Joe yelled over to the young guy at the bar. "Let's go, let's go, we've got the list and you can jack off to it tonight." Tailgunner Joe laughed hard again. He was about as crude of a guy as you could get, but he was our very own Red Chaser.

Before I left Dowling's, the Phillies had scored a run in the sixth. Then on the walk home, I heard Andy Seminick hit a two-run homer in the bottom half of the eighth. Three-three tie going into the ninth. I stood out on the street in front of my house. I could hear Red Barber's every call from the radios up and down the street flowing out of open windows. In the shadows, I could see some of my neighbors sitting on their front steps. If a neighborhood could collectively hold their breaths, we were doing it.

The Dodgers didn't score in the top of the ninth.

I went over to a neighbor and bummed a cigarette. He lit it with his Zippo. I thanked him and walked back to my house. I sat on the steps. In the bottom half of the inning, Richie Ashburn got a Texas-league single down the left field line.

Then they sacrificed him to second. Carl Erskine was still on the mound. Red Barber told us that Erskine was going to go all the way, win or lose. Manager Charlie Dressen wouldn't bring in relief one of his two aces, Don Newcombe or Preacher Roe. He was saving them for the last two games. Another starter, Ralph Branca, had pitched the day before.

The Dodgers intentionally walked Bill Nicholson. That brought up Puddin' Head Jones. I had finished the cigarette. I felt like going back to my neighbor and bumming another one, but he had gone inside. He probably couldn't take it.

Earlier in the month, Puddin' Head Jones had hit a Grand Slam homer against Clem Labine to win a game. Now he was trying to steal another one from us.

Erskine delivered the pitch. Puddin' Head Jones hit a single to left center. Andy Pafko fielded it. Ashburn raced for the plate. Roy Campanella was a cement wall waiting for him. Ashburn slid well in front of Pafko's throw. Phillies won. Dodgers lost. Giants tied the Dodgers.

I looked down the street. I didn't see anybody on their steps. They had melted into their houses. There was no orange glow from cigarettes. I didn't hear anybody say, "Ya bum ya."

The volume of Red Barber's voice slipped a notch when a nearby radio was turned off. Red's voice dropped again when another radio was turned off. It was getting difficult to hear his words. Another radio must have been turned off because Red sounded so far away. Then there was no Red. The last radio had been turned off.

34

Saturday, September 29, 1951

Now that the Ice Queen business appeared to be in my rear view mirror, you'd have thought that I slept like a baby. Well, this baby was up all night tossing and turning. It was because of one name on the Ice Queen's list that shouldn't have been there. To make sure Tailgunner Joe didn't get that one name, I had removed that entire page from what I had given Joe.

I had to find out why that one name was on the list.

Just before noon, I walked out to my car. I got in and drove over the Long Island Expressway. I was going to Levittown to see my folks. As the crow flies, it wasn't very far, probably just thirty miles or so. I could take the Long Island Expressway for part of the way, but they were still plowing under potato fields to extend it. If that road to nowhere was ever finished, I could take it to Levittown in probably about a half an hour. But, the traffic on Long Island was getting worse than New York City. They couldn't extend the L.I.E fast enough. How in the world could this area take any more cars than what they have right now in 1951? However, they were going to get more cars, a lot of cars, as homes were popping up like pimples thanks to a guy named Bill Levitt.

Levitt built houses as fast as they could deliver the wood and nails. Levitt had bought a big potato farm out in Hempstead and soon replaced potatoes with his version of Cape Cod houses that all had the same floor plan. In the late 1940s, he sold them only to returning veterans. Fifty-eight dollars down. Seventy-nine hundred to own. Levitt even called his houses a city, Levittown. In 1950, he started to build expanded ranch style houses. These weren't restricted to veterans. They cost almost ten grand. Each house was complete with backyard, carpeting, washing machine, an Admiral TV in the living room, the works.

My folks had been thinking for quite awhile of moving out to Long Island. When I got back from Germany and they realized I had the cash for a down payment on the family brownstone in Brooklyn, it was like a greased chute for them to Levittown.

Their house in Levittown was small. It seemed their whole house would fit into the living room in Brooklyn. Nevertheless, my Mom had always wanted a backyard with trees and grass and maybe even a little tomato patch.

My father was retired now. He told me he could still work at a car store out in Long Island. Out there, folks were buying cars like crazy. There was always a need for a guy that could tell a piston from a muffler. He loved that little house out in Levittown because he didn't have to do anything with it, being so new and all.

I pulled into their driveway. I had called ahead to tell my dad that I was coming. I didn't want to drive all the way out here and find out that they had gone to my sister's or something.

Dad greeted me at the door. He had a Schaefers in each hand. He handed one to me as I stepped into the living room. The Irish have that certain touch in welcoming people—hand them a beer. The Irish certainly are beautiful people.

"Your Mom's over at the neighbor lady's," Tommy McHenry said, "pull up a chair. The Yankees are on TV."

My Dad had been a 'Tommy' his whole life. I somehow thought that a Tommy or a Billy or a Bobby should be a little kid or a baseball player, not a retired auto mechanic. When men got big and old it seemed like they would outgrow the 'y' at the end of their first name. 'Big Tom' would be more appropriate: my Dad was about six-two and probably weighed two-sixty, maybe more. His stomach probably weighed more than Hiromi.

"You watching the *Yankees*?" I asked, looking at the TV. The Yankees were playing the Red Sox in a doubleheader at Yankee Stadium.

"Yeah, I can't listen to the Giants game," he said, "I'd be afraid of busting up the house. Then, tonight with the Dodgers, I don't know what I'm gonna do. I can't listen because it'll drive me crazy, but I can't *not* listen because it'll drive me crazy."

The Motorola in the living room wasn't the one that came with the house. He'd got a bigger one.

We watched a half an inning of the Yankees against the Red Sox. The day before, when the Yanks clinched the pennant, Joe DiMaggio had hit a home run. There was talk about him retiring. If Joltin' Joe didn't hit a home run against the Red Sox, that homer yesterday might have been his last in Yankee pinstripes, except for the World Series. That kid, Mickey Mantle, the one that gave a wolf-whistle at Hiromi, would inherit Joe's centerfield.

"So, how's business?" Tommy asked me. He didn't like the private detecting business that I was in, but he was being polite. He thought that a college boy like me should have a job in a real office, maybe in Manhattan. I had never told him about the riches I had come home with from the war. He would have liked the idea of dedicating my life to the Dodgers and beer, but then I would have had to get into that ugly stuff about assassinating Nazis. He probably would have liked that part too, but it's not easy for a son to tell his father that he had killed in cold blood.

"I'm doing a little work for Joe McCarthy," I said.

"The guy on television? The guy that's chasing Commies all over the place?"

"The same," I said, nodding my head.

"How'd you get hooked up with him? He sure is a pistol."

"Nick Salzano set me up with him," I said.

"Nickie, from the neighborhood, the good-looking kid?"

I nodded my head again.

"What they gotcha doing?" he asked.

"They got me lookin' for Commies," I said. "I found some. I found a bunch."

I took a folded sheet of paper out of my shirt pocket. I unfolded it. It was the sheet of paper that I had taken from the Ice Queen's list that had a list of Commies.

"I was able to get this one list of Commies that was twenty-five pages long. Single spaced."

"No shit," my Dad said, getting up. He went to the kitchen to get two more beers. "Hey, you seen your Mom's garden?" he called from the kitchen. "Take a look."

I got up out of my chair and walked to the kitchen. It wasn't much of a walk. I don't know how my parents could live in such a small house after the Brooklyn house. But, lo and behold, out in the backyard it looked like Iowa. There was corn almost as tall as me. There was a burgeoning row of tomatoes. It looked like they would have to bring in a carload of migrant workers next week to pick them all.

My Dad handed me a Schaefers. At least he still drank the beer that supported the Dodgers with that big sign out in centerfield at Ebbets Field.

"There was a surprise name on the list, Dad."

"Yeah? Who?" He said, taking a pretty good slug of beer.

"You."

"Me? What the fuck you talkin' about? *Me?*"

"That's right, you."

"That's a fuckin' joke. Who the fuck do you think you are comin' in here like this and accusing me of being a Commie? My own fuckin' son," he yelled. "My own fuckin' son!" He slammed the bottle of beer down on the counter. The beer popped out of the bottle like it had been champagne. My father was a good two-fisted Irishman, who often used salty language, but he very rarely swore in front of my mother or me.

"You're on the list, Dad," I said calmly. "I yanked this sheet from the list that I gave Joe McCarthy. He hasn't seen your name. You're safe for a while, but let me tell you, you don't want a guy like Joe McCarthy coming after you. He would eat you alive. I want you to tell me about it. Tell me about it, Dad, I can help."

"Jesus fuckin' Christ," he said. He reached into the cabinet by the refrigerator. That was his liquor shelf. He brought out a bottle of Irish whiskey. He opened the refrigerator, took out a tray of ice, cracked out a bunch of ice cubes and dumped them in a glass.

"You want any of this?" he asked.

"Beer's fine," I said.

He poured about three fingers of Irish whiskey in his glass. With his huge hand, three fingers just about equaled the height of the glass so he was drinking whiskey like it was beer.

"Let's sit out on the back porch, in case your mother comes home," he said. "I got a story to tell you." His Irish temper had cooled as quickly as it had erupted when he figured out that I wasn't there to pinch him; I was there to help him.

The back porch was a slab of cement with a small green awning over it.

"Let me see that sheet of paper," he said.

I handed it over to him. I pointed out where his name was. Next to his name was his current address. The Ice Queen had somehow kept up to date. The last column on the right was the name of the Commie organization he was supposed to have affiliated with, the Laborers Progressive Committee.

"At the time, Jake, and you got to appreciate the time," my Dad said, "we *all* went to meetings of the Laborers Progressive Committee. Hell, we were all laborers. I was working the docks then, before I got to fixing cars. That was what, twenty years ago?

We were in the Great Depression, we still had jobs, but nobody had any money. But, the rich weren't hurting. You still could look in the paper and see the rich having their polo matches, the rich attending their parties. The Laborers Progressive Committee was a bunch of union guys bitching and moaning and pissing. There was a fancy talker—I can't remember his name. He could really get us riled up. He said all the right things about how the rich were robbing from us."

"Did he talk about Communism?" I asked.

"I don't think so, but we were all *union* guys," he said, sucking down about two fingers of Irish whiskey. "What do you think a union is anyway? It's got the same principles as Communism. You know, one for all, and all for one and all that shit. So, what he was saying to us wasn't anything different than what the union bosses would say to us. Except with the union, we knew they were lying because the mob always helped themselves *first*. But, what'ya gonna do? You listen and get pissed."

"Did you sign anything?"

"I don't really remember, but who knows, I might have. When I think about it, I'm sure I did. What's wrong with that? Look at our country, Jake, at the time. Until the war, the rich were getting a lot richer and the poor were getting a lot poorer. Is that democracy? Is that the democracy they taught us in school? Of course it isn't! And maybe when I went to those meetings they did use the word Communism. But, this was during the depression. Democracy wasn't working. Capitalism wasn't working, except for the rich guys. It worked plenty good for them. However, if democracy was working for everybody, we wouldn't have been in the Depression. We were just working stiffs, all of us were. We just wanted to be able to provide for our families. We just wanted a fair shake. We didn't care if you called it democracy or socialism or Communism or democrat or republican or shit-in-the-sky. We just wanted to survive. During the Depression, the only people that were surviving were the rich people."

Tommy McHenry knocked back two more fingers of Irish whiskey.

"So, I gotta pay for some meetings I went to twenty some years ago?" my Dad asked.

"No, I'm keeping you out of it," I said, finishing off the beer. I went inside and got another one. I brought out the bottle of Irish whiskey and poured a couple of my fingers into Dad's glass. I sat the bottle down on the cement.

My father laughed, a big hearty Irish barroom laugh. "Your mother will come home and find us shnockered out here in the back. She'll have my hide! Oh, she'll have my hide!"

"I'm keeping you out of it, Dad. McCarthy has been going after people that work in the State Department. I haven't seen him going after working stiffs," I said. "I think you were included on the list for one reason—and one reason only—to send *me* a message."

The Ice Queen just wouldn't let go. She knew that if she hadn't told me to look for a surprise that I probably wouldn't have seen my Dad's name. This was her little way of letting me know that she could get to me. She would even use her archenemy, Joe McCarthy, to make my family miserable. She thought she was going to have the last laugh, and she might. However, I would make it the last laugh she would ever take.

35

Saturday, September 29, 1951

On the drive back to Brooklyn, I didn't turn on the radio. I didn't want to hear anybody talking about the Dodgers. The Dodgers weren't like going to a movie and being entertained for a couple of hours. After the movie, you'd walk into the night air and the memories of most movies would stay mostly in the theatre. With the Dodgers, there was the game, then you'd walk out and that game was imprinted on your mind for a long time. If it was a hugely emotional game like last night, that game might be embedded in your mind until the worms crawled from one ear to the other in your grave.

Instead of thinking about the Dodgers, I thought about the Ice Queen and Korea.

Hiromi had said something really interesting about the Ice Queen this morning. Hiromi sat with me at the breakfast table. Slowly, she was developing the ritual of reading the morning paper. Unlike me who always started with the sports section, she would start with the front page. It was good that somebody in my house knew what was going on in the outside world.

After reading the sports pages, I would glance at the front pages. I had started taking an interest in the Korean War mainly because Korea had been pushed into my radar with the Ice Queen and Chet Morgan and Tailgunner Joe.

Interestingly, there wasn't a story about the Korean War on the front page of either the *Daily News* or the *Brooklyn Eagle*. I had found a story in the *Daily News* on page twelve. The *Eagle's* Korea story was on page seven. This war had been going on for about a year. Americans had been losing their lives for a year. The papers covered it as if it was a civil war in some unknown country in Africa. Asia, Africa, what's the difference? Nobody cared. Both of the stories I read were about two things: One, the peace talks were going nowhere, and two, the Americans suffered another humiliating loss. These two writers from two different papers seemed to think the same thing about the war.

Tailgunner Joe and Nick Salzano were like the newspapers—they sure didn't think the Korea War meant anything important. And they were officially known as the Senate Government Operations Committee and its Subcommittee on Investigations. It was more commonly recognized as the McCarthy Committee. Korea didn't even seem to be an irritant, not even a pimple.

Conversely, Wild Bill, Richard Nixon and Chet Morgan thought the Korean War was really important. Nixon was officially part of the House of Un-American Activities Committee or HUAC—a different group than Tailgunner Joe's—and Wild Bill and Morgan with the CIA—or shadow CIA.

Then there was the Ice Queen. After I had lunch with the Ice Queen at Dempsey's, I had told Hiromi about the conversation. I cleaned up the fucking part, of course, but told her about the Ice Queen's condition about not implicating her with the Koreans, how desperate the Ice Queen had wanted to keep the Korean link below the surface. Hiromi had said, "The lady doth protest too much, methinks."

"What did you just say?"

"The lady doth protest too much, methinks. That's Shakespeare," she had said, smiling that little smarty-pants smile that she occasionally flashed at me.

"When did you read Shakespeare? I don't know one person in this world that had read Shakespeare."

"Internment Camp. We didn't have many books to read, but one of my teachers in the Internment School had Shakespeare. We read it and reread it and read it some more."

I had been amazed, truly amazed. Japanese prisoners reading Shakespeare, now doesn't that take all?

I didn't have the context that Shakespeare had put that in, but it seemed to fit the Ice Queen perfectly. "The lady doth protest too much, methinks." One way of looking at this was that I should care how much she protested. There was, however, an important exception. That exception was linked to Roberta.

Last night, I had opened the envelope from Roberta that Mary O'Halloran had given me. Inside was my stack of 'baseball trading cards,' as Roberta had referred to them. There was also a handwritten note from Roberta.

Roberta wrote: "In case I'm not here when you stop by, I've identified three of your mug shots. The moustache guy I found first. I wrote each guy's name on the back of the card. All three work at the United Nations. Let me see the rest of the picture, not just the head shots. My spinster sister is asking me for them."

I had looked on the back of the first picture. Roberta had written: "Ingmar Swensen, Under-Secretary, Sweden, U.N."

The second card listed a French man. The third listed a guy from Yugoslavia. The United Nations was the link among the three. None of the other pictures had any writing on the back. Knowing Roberta, if she would have had another day, she would have identified each one of those photos.

I asked myself, why did somebody murder Roberta? Was it just a random robbery gone wrong like the cops said it was? No way could I believe that.

Was it because somebody suspected her of doing research for me? If that was the case, that somebody had to be really paranoid, really frightened. Who was that paranoid, who was that frightened? Who knew what she was indeed researching?

The finger had to point to the Ice Queen. She, of course, flatly denied it at lunch at Dempsey's. She had been convincing—very convincing—in her denial. She was a marvelous liar.

These photos were the one thread of a link I had with the murder of Roberta. It wasn't much, which was for sure. If I wanted to find out who had murdered Roberta, I would have to pull that thread a little bit. Would something start to come unraveled? The thread would most likely lead to the Ice Queen, but I didn't think that she was the one that had done the actual killing. By pulling that thread a little, I might be able to find who the Ice Queen had sent to kill Roberta and Wolfemeyer. I was willing to take a *slight* tug on that thread. My first little tug wasn't a tug at all. It was a small step to find out a little bit more than what I knew about the United Nations.

After I got back to Brooklyn, I put the pictures in my pocket and walked over to Gonnella's Candy Store. Dominic was out in front of his store sweeping the sidewalk.

I took the broom from Dominic and started sweeping spots where no dust had settled in years.

We didn't want to talk about the Dodgers. Talking about the Dodgers was like talking about somebody on their deathbed. I'd pray that that person would make it, but the doctors were shaking their heads side to side.

I held Dominic's broom up to my face. "So, Dominic, how many brooms do you go through a year?" I asked.

He shrugged, "Yeah, we might as well talk about brooms. Who knows how many brooms? But, if *you* would sweep in front of *your* house every day, you would sweep away all worries. You'd live to be a hundred. Sweeping is good for the soul."

"What, I've got worries?" I asked.

"Look at your face sometime, Jake, you got worries written like a painted sign on your face."

I *had* looked at my face this morning while shaving. I *did* look worried, in fact. Either that or just tired of this whole mess with the Ice Queen.

"You own that storefront next to your candy store, right?" I asked.

"You know I do. Ever since Emil the shoe repair guy died I got an empty space. So, what'ya askin' for?"

I told him about my idea of an art gallery featuring Hiromi's paintings.

"She's good, very good artist," Dominic said. "In fact, I bought one from her yesterday."

"You did? She didn't tell me about that. Which one?"

"The ocean," Dominic said, "the Pacific Ocean. Very beautiful. I've never seen the Pacific Ocean, probably never will, but I liked how she put the sunset and the colors together." I knew which painting Dominic was talking about. It was one of my favorites. It had been sitting against a wall up in her attic studio. Hiromi had painted it from a photo of the Santa Monica Pier out in Los Angeles.

"I paid her a hundred bucks," Dominic said. "That's a lot of money for a picture, but what'm'I'gonna do? Take it with me? Who woulda ever thought just a few years ago that I would willingly buy a picture from a Jap? No offense—I really mean it, no offense—by that, but the world works in strange ways, don't it? So, I paid and I enjoy; it's upstairs in my room."

Dominic's room was his haven. That's where he read his magazines. That's where he stored his magazines. Knowing that his boys were down in the phone room, I would figure that it would be very difficult to break in and steal Dominic's magazines—not that anyone cared to. Jack Benny, on the radio, would joke about his money vault that had a drawbridge and alligators in a moat, but that was child's play compared to Dominic's sense of security.

"So, how much you rent that storefront to me?" I asked, leaning on Dominic's broom.

"You ready to move in pictures today?" Dominic asked, taking the broom and sweeping over the imaginary dust that I had just swept away.

"No, I'm just in the planning stage right now," I said.

"So, when you're ready, talk to me. I'll be good to you and Hiromi. Don't worry. Sweep your sidewalk like I do mine and your world will be better."

Changing the subject, I asked Dominic, "Say, Dominic, what do you know about the United Nations?" Because of his magazines, Dominic was more informed about current events than anybody I would know. Roberta might have given him a run for his money, but she, of course, had taken her knowledge with her, wherever good souls went. If anybody in the neighborhood wanted to know what was going on in the world—and most of the time we didn't—we'd just ask Dominic. He was our civics teacher.

"What'dya want to know?" Dominic asked back.

"Well, I read we're in this Korean War because of the United Nations."

"That's right," Dominic said. "Here's the deal: North Korea invaded South Korea. This became a big deal because of the new United Nations. They were set up to sorta be the watch dog so that another world war couldn't happen. What if there was a United Nations like there is today when Hitler was gaining power in the 30s? Well, there was a *League of Nations*, but the United States wasn't part of it and the League of Nations wouldn't oppose aggression. They just looked the other way with Hitler and Mussolini and Japan. So, would *today's* United Nations been able to do something when Hitler rolled into Czechoslovakia? Hell, when Hitler did roll up to Czechoslovakia the world just watched. Nobody did nuthin'. That's why we're in Korea. United Nations. We're part of the United Nations. Roosevelt invited them to set up the headquarters in New York City. Truman followed through. So, we're in the U.N. and we aren't just supposed to watch if some country wants to steal some land from another country."

In my pocket were, of course, pictures of at least three representatives of the United Nations who had been boffing the Ice Queen.

"When I read the papers," I said, "it doesn't seem like we're doing too good over there."

"Politicians," Dominic said. "Politicians."

"What do you mean?"

"Why do you think MacArthur quit? Politicians. They wouldn't let him fight the war to win it. Hell, Jake, you read about the 38th Parallel haven't you?"

I nodded.

"That's just a made-up line. Made up by politicians after World War II. The Japanese had controlled Korea during the war, so when we beat the Japs, there was nobody in place to rule Korea. So, the politicians just divided it. It's sorta like the state line between Pennsylvania and New Jersey—try to find that line. Well, try to find the line between North and South Korea. I read where two students at Princeton actually came up with the line. Can you imagine that? The line ain't there except where the politicians say it is."

Dominic picked up his broom and said, "C'mon inside for a cup of coffee. If we keep on sweeping this sidewalk there won't be any cement left to sweep."

I walked into the candy store with Dominic. In the back of the store were a couple of tables where a person could get a soda with their candy.

Mary Ann, Dominic's third daughter, saw us coming and put out two cups on a small round table.

We both dumped a load of cream into our cups and a tablespoon of sugar. A good cup of coffee—loaded with cream and sugar—was the best way to put a jolt into the day.

"You know, Dominic, there isn't much written about this war," I said, taking a small sip of coffee. It was steaming hot; if I would have spilled it on myself, I would probably get third degree burns.

"You're right," Dominic said. "Take a look at the covers of *Time* magazine. If you *just* looked at the covers over a full year, you'd get an *idea* of what this past year was like. In 1944 and 1945, we had generals, we had presidents, we had a lot of military stuff on the covers of *Time*. The war was the centerpiece for most of the covers. I remember just one exception. They put the ventriloquist Edgar Bergen and his dummies, Charlie McCarthy and Mortimer Snerd on the cover. *They* made a cover of *Time* magazine. Everybody else was a general like Eisenhower or MacArthur or Lee or Hodges or even *Canadian* General Crerar. It was a great time to be a general—you got your mug on the cover of *Time Magazine*. This past year, we've had Groucho Marx on the cover, for Christsakes. Ava Gardner made a cover. The president of U.S. Steel made the cover. So did Bert Lahr—the cowardly lion for God's sake. Nothing about Korea on the cover of *Time* except two times: One was when Truman fired MacArthur, the other when they named Ridgeway to replace him. I'm waiting for them to put Kim Il-sung on the cover and that's when I cancel my subscription."

It sounded like Dominic had said 'kimmy sung' which meant nothing to me. He might have been a ballplayer, Bobby Kimelsung, from some minor league team as far as I knew. "Who's he?" I asked.

"What, you don't read *Time*?" Dominic said, as if he was a teacher and was going to flunk me in my civics class.

"Sometimes," I said, hoping that the lie would get me a 'C'.

"Kim is the top guy in North Korea. He's their version of Hitler. But, even *he* isn't mentioned that much. If you don't read *Time* each and every week, you don't know who that guy is. He's never mentioned on the nightly news on television."

Dominic was right; I had never even heard of the guy.

"It's a funny war," Dominic said. "I got a nephew over there. You've met him, my sister's boy, she lives in Queens now. Jimmy Corrao, good kid. He wrote me from Korea and tells me what happened to him. He had been with his outfit for a few months, they'd been in some pretty good firefights, then they go to the rear. After a couple of weeks, they're given a 'top secret' mission. They gotta take off all insignia from their uniforms, take off all identification from their trucks and weapons. They only traveled at night. No lights, no lighting of cigarettes even, real secret."

That didn't sound like a regular army movement to me; it was more like commando stuff.

"He a commando?" I asked Dominic.

"Naw, just a regular army grunt. Anyway, this was real secret stuff—doesn't make any sense to me, but that's what Jimmy wrote. They got to their new position the night before they were supposed to fight. They'd start clobbering the North Koreans at daybreak the next morning. At ten at night, all of a sudden a bunch of searchlights are turned on and American music is blaring over some loud speakers. This ain't from the U.S. This is from the *North Koreans*. Then over the loudspeaker a voice—in pretty good English, Jimmy tells me—calls out a special 'welcome' naming Jimmy's division, the regiments and battalions by number and even the names of all the leaders, by name, Jake, *by name*. When the guy got tired of talking on the loudspeakers, the other side opened with a barrage of mortar and artillery fire. This never made *Time* magazine, or anything else I've read. But, I trust Jimmy—he's just a soldier—he got no reason to lie to me. The question I have is probably the same one Jimmy had—if Jimmy didn't know where they were going because it was so secret, how'd the fuck the enemy know? How did the enemy know their *names* for Chrissakes? That's a helluva good question. I don't see any answers in *Time* magazine."

If *Time* magazine didn't have the answers, I sure couldn't come up with any.

I thanked Dominic for the coffee and the conversation. I told him that I'd talk to him in a few days about renting the empty storefront.

"Don't rent it out in the meantime," I said.

"Fat chance that'll happen," he said, "Christ, it's been vacant for five years. But, you got it if you want it. I'll make you a good deal. I might even *give* it to Hiromi for a while; you, I'll charge a little bit."

As I walked back to my house, I thought that when I left Eastern Europe that war was in the past chapters of my life. I might reminisce about those chapters in the far future—I guess as old men might do—but I never thought that there would be new chapters revolving around war. The Korean War wasn't officially a war. They called it a police action, not a war, but it was a war with our boys getting killed.

The war I didn't understand. I did understand, however, the photos of the three United Nations officials. I would follow that thread. I'd pull it a bit, see if that pointed me to who had killed Roberta.

36

Sunday, September 30, 1951

There were times that I would like to have asked a real private detective what to do in certain situations. A guy that was a homicide cop for twenty years had far better know-how of the ins and outs in tracking down a murderer. I haven't had that type of professional training. Sure, I tracked down Nazi SS after the war—and they were usually murderers—but my type of tracking was a lot different from a homicide cop. A lot of times, those SS bastards found me. Cops didn't have too many experiences where the bad guys came, knocked on their door and said, "Here I am."

The Nazi SS wanted out and they had something to deal—their spy networks in Eastern Europe. To track down more Nazis, I'd just ask a lot of questions to the guys that did come to me. I was sorta fishing for referrals. They knew who was who among their brethren. They knew which Nazi SS was trying to pass as just a regular ex-soldier in the area. To complete the deal and get their ticket to South America, they'd have to tell me. Once I had names and addresses, then I'd go out and do some detecting work. I hadn't had any experience in investigating murders. I just followed people.

In the detecting business, there are some parts of following people that are pretty easy. Those I could do. There are also some that are damned difficult. It takes me a while longer to do than, let's say, a private detective with a deep background as a cop.

For instance, if I'm tailing a husband who's getting something on the side, that's easy. First off, I know where the jerk lives. The address was usually handed to me by the wife's lawyer. I then just tail the guy when he goes to work. I stay on him during the day. Sure, it gets boring, but I don't do this *every* day, day in and day out, like a regular working stiff has to work for a living. This ain't like putting on a steel hat with a little light on it, taking a cable car two miles into the Earth and beating up black rocks for twelve hours.

I do private detecting to break up a day when the Dodgers are out of town or during the winter when there's no baseball at all. So, I guess I do something that other people might consider boring, but for me it was really a way of breaking up a boring day. The main point of difference was that I didn't need the money. If I needed the money, I might consider getting a real job.

I'd follow the wayward husband and sooner or later he would lead me to his honey-pot. Then it was up to me to figure out a way to get the evidence that would make that guy crumble before his wife's lawyer's very eyes. That wasn't a very difficult part either.

The degree of difficulty was ramped up a few notches when I didn't know where the guy lived or worked. Fortunately, the guy that Roberta had identified—Ingmar Swensen—was listed in the telephone book. If the only thing that I had known was where he worked—the United Nations—it would be like saying that the guy worked in St. Louis. The United Nations building seemed that big. The job would then have been a lot more difficult.

So, my job with this Swede was to stake out where he lived just like I had done with the Ice Queen. That's why we started so early on a Sunday morning. I wanted to be able to catch him before he went to visit the zoo or something. After getting a feel for his habits, I didn't know exactly what I was going to do. Somewhere along the way I'd have to confront him and show him the picture. For right now, I was satisfied in just following the guy.

I was glad to be doing something today. The Giants had won their afternoon game yesterday against the Braves. Sal Maglie pitched a five-hit shutout, winning three-zip. I'd heard on the radio that in the second inning that Willie Mays had stolen second. He'd stolen that base off of the Braves ace, Warren Spahn. Spahn was supposed to have the best move to first base, but Mays stole second on him anyway. Then on the next pitch he stole third. He scored on a groundout and that was all that a guy like Maglie would need.

Don Newcombe followed Maglie with a seven-hit shutout against the Phillies, five-nothing. So, coming into the last day of the season, the Giants and Dodgers were tied. They both had records of ninety-five wins and fifty-eight losses.

Both teams had day games today. The Giants were going against the Braves in Boston. Larry Jansen, a twenty-one game winner, was going for the Giants; the Dodgers were sending to the mound Preacher Roe. Preacher had a record of twenty-two wins and only three losses. Roe, however, had a sore arm that was about ready to fall off.

Rafael Ordonez and I were standing in front of a small coffee shop on the corner of 1st Avenue and 46th Street. We had met at my house in the morning. Rafael had brought his latest 'chiquita,' Dolores Espinoza, with him. I didn't mind when Rafael brought a companion. He was so good at tailing people—with or without companions—that I didn't mind. Rafael knew that this was a low-level tail. He shouldn't get close enough where he would be in any danger. Also, Rafael would not be doing anything illegal. This was just a day out in the sun, walking and cabbing around Manhattan.

Dolores, however, was a lot different than any other companion that Rafael had brought with him. There are some people that God should allow *not* to age. I've got a pretty good idea of what I'm gonna look like when I'm fifty or sixty. All I need to do is look at my Dad. I'll probably get the same beer gut and fallen chin that he has. That's okay by me as long as I've got my Brooklyn Dodgers and can still hoist a few beers. Now, Dolores was a different story altogether. If God did allow one person not to age, I would put my vote into God for Dolores. I might even do the old Brooklyn union trick and have a few dead people vote for Dolores to be the one.

She was dressed as if they were going to Coney Island. The small top that she was wearing didn't hide her boobs very well. Her nipples were like thimbles poking through the taut fabric. With the short shorts she was wearing, they were so tight I figured she had to have been born in them. God should preserve her for all of our future generations to appreciate. She was probably only seventeen or eighteen, but, at that age, she knew she was ripe enough to grab a man, like Rafael, and start a family. In five years she might have three little kids. We'd all mourn that her marvelous body was gone, never to return. She was in such a tiny sliver of life right now. Years from now she would probably reflect back on that sliver as the time she could stop the world just crossing the street.

I had asked Rafael, "Are you two going to the beach?" It would be pretty difficult to tail somebody when an army of leches that would fall in behind Dolores, dressed as she was.

Rafael was a bright kid and he knew right away what I was talking about. "Nah, we're working today, man." Then he said to Dolores, "Show the man."

Out of an oversize purse, Dolores brought out a pile of cloth material. She unfolded a fluffy summer dress and pulled it over her head and down her sides. She would now just corral half of an army of leches.

We had driven over to Manhattan in my car, parked it in a spot on 47th. Swensen lived just a block over on 48th between 1st and 2nd Avenues. I walked over to the address that was in the phone book. Rafael and Dolores stayed on the corner of 2nd and 48th.

Swensen lived in an apartment building. It had a doorman. I wasn't sure that Swensen hadn't moved since the telephone book had come out, so I walked up to the doorman.

"I got a message to deliver to Mrs. Marten Swensen" I said. I had taken an envelope from a small pile that I had in the trunk of my car. I had written Mrs. Marten Swensen on the outside of the envelope. I had written down just the street name, not the individual address. There was a blank piece of paper inside the envelope.

"Sure it ain't a Mr. Ingmar Swensen?" he asked. "We got an Ingmar Swensen that lives here."

I looked at the envelope. "Nope, it clearly says Marten Swensen, Marten spelled with an 'e' and an 'n' at the end. Thanks anyway." I walked away, whistling.

I joined Rafael and Dolores at the corner. Rafael wasn't carrying his normal satchel that gave him the appearance of being a messenger boy. Businesses didn't need messenger boys on Sunday. Dolores, however, had her oversize purse. That was probably where she would stuff that dress the minute our little stakeout ended.

I showed them the picture of the guy we were looking for— Ingmar Swensen from Sweden, handlebar moustache and all. Dolores giggled, holding her hand in front of her mouth.

I then walked over to the other end of 48th on 1st. If Swensen left his apartment, we'd be on him no matter which way he headed.

From the corner of 48th and 1st, I had a clear view of the United Nations building. It was shaped like a large book. The spine of this 'book' was stone, the sides of the book all glass. It was probably fifty stories high.

It was so big I thought a huge corporation like General Motors—if they ever decided to move from Detroit—could fit itself inside and still have room leftover for Ford and maybe Chrysler. Swensen worked at the United Nations, but except for what

Dominic had told me, I knew practically nothing else except that they had built its headquarters in Manhattan this past year. That was probably more than a lot of folks in Kansas knew. Dominic had told me that the land for the United Nations was donated by that old robber baron, John D. Rockefeller. Boy, he must have really had a guilty conscience to give up a huge piece of property in Manhattan like that. Or, maybe the Feds made him an offer that he couldn't refuse. There were over a hundred fifty countries that had representatives at the United Nations. If Tailgunner Joe was looking for Commies, this would be the place. Heck, there were representatives from Russia and China. We knew those guys were Red through and through. Thinking like Tailgunner Joe would think, probably half the Americans working there were also Red.

Rafael and Dolores were stationed at 1st and 48th. We hung around our respective corners for a couple of hours. Dolores had come down to my end to say hello one time. Then she walked back to Rafael. Seeing her walk was the highlight of the morning.

I think we were all looking down 48th when Swensen emerged on the sidewalk. He was walking toward me. I stepped down 1st Avenue to a little grocery store. They had fruit in boxes out front. I was feeling the fruit when Swensen came to 1st Avenue and walked toward the United Nations building. I let him walk.

Rafael and Dolores weren't far behind him. I let them take the lead in following the Swede. I then followed them. On the corner of 1st and 43rd, Swensen ducked into a small restaurant. The Swede was probably getting his Sunday morning breakfast. We waited by a magazine shop four doors down.

I was leafing through a magazine and looked up. I saw somebody that I recognized walking down the sidewalk toward me. It was the big guy that jumped me in Washington, D.C. Chet Morgan had told me that his name was Ivan Bogachov. He was the one I could have killed when I slammed the pistol into his temple. He wasn't dead, that was for sure; he wore a cap that could have covered bandages. He didn't see me as he walked toward me. I ducked into the magazine store and let him pass.

"Rafael, see that guy?" I asked pointing to the back of Bogachov as he walked down the sidewalk. "Follow him."

"But, he is not the man with the moustache," Rafael said.

"I know," I said, "follow him anyway. I can't do it, he would recognize me. Tell me where he goes."

"Are you going to wait for Mr. Moustache?" Rafael asked.

"Yeah, I'll hang out around here."

He and Dolores were off like they were on skates.

Finding the Russian was probably more important than finding the Swede. At least I could link the Russian to violence. Bogachov and his pal had attacked me. That same night somebody had murdered Roberta. I didn't consider these isolated incidents. I considered it teamwork. I had run into one team; Roberta, unfortunately, had run into the other.

About twenty seconds later, Rafael and Dolores were back at the newsstand.

"He went into the restaurant," Rafael said, "where Mr. Moustache went."

"Go on in there and buy yourself breakfast," I said. "I'm buying." I handed Rafael a fin. "If the Russian is sitting with Mr. Moustache, see if you can hear what they're talking about."

"Who's the Russian?" Rafael asked.

"The big guy that you were following."

"He's Russian?"

I nodded.

"I didn't like his looks," Dolores said. "He's a scary looking guy."

"Go! Go get some breakfast. Listen in."

Rafael ran out of the newsstand. Dolores followed in a skipping type of run. They were on a mission.

I'm not a big believer in luck. However, there were times in Eastern Europe where I just got plumb lucky. Seeing the

Russian walk down 1st Avenue and go into the same restaurant as the Swede could be just considered dumb luck. But, it wouldn't be considered lucky if they met every day in that restaurant and this was just another day. It would have just been routine.

If I bumped into them at some restaurant way out in New Jersey, that would have been just blind-ass luck. But, Chet Morgan had told me that Bogachov was assigned to the Russian group at the United Nations. The Swede worked at the United Nations. It seemed that if a person hung around flowers long enough that sooner or later bees would show up. I just hadn't been hanging around flowers that much. Until now. I didn't know if it was luck or routine, but I had the two guys that I had wanted to find.

I was back to waiting. At least I was in a newsstand. I looked at some of the sports magazines. One had Carmen Basilio on the cover. He was a young welterweight fighter from upstate New York that was starting to make some noise. He had to be the ugliest man whose image could be captured on film. Give him another thirty fights and he wasn't going to get prettier. Cameras would have to be a lot stronger by then to capture his mug without breaking a lens or two.

I stayed away from the baseball magazines. If I had looked, they all would have predicted a pennant for the Dodgers. One preseason magazine that I remember even touted the Dodgers as maybe being the best team in the *history* of baseball.

Fifteen minutes later, Rafael and Dolores were back at the newsstand. We huddled at the front of the newsstand, keeping our eyes on the front door of the restaurant.

"Could you hear anything?"

"They were speaking a different language, almost whispering, I couldn't understand anything, man."

"The Russian man kept looking over at us," Dolores said. He might have just been cautious as any KGB agent should be or he might have just been wondering why Russia had no women comrades that looked like Dolores. He should have seen her before she put on that cotton dress.

"Then another guy joined them," Rafael said. "He didn't come in from the front door. He came in from the back, by the kitchen, where the waitress would go."

"He looked like the Russian man—rough," Dolores said, "and somebody had broke his nose. It was all bumpy and crooked."

"How big was he?" I asked. I figured it was the guy that wanted me to see Mr. Jones down in DC.

"Smaller than the Russian," Rafael said, "but I got picture."

"You took a picture of them in the coffee shop?" I asked. That would have been too crazy for safety.

"Of course not," Rafael said. "The waitress didn't want us there. I guess she don't like Puerto Ricans. I find that stupid, them being right across the street from U.N. where they've got lots of different peoples. So we left."

"No tip," Dolores said. That was an immediate payback for prejudice.

"Where'd you get the camera?" I asked.

Dolores smiled and held up her large purse. "Raffie was going to take picture of me on the Cyclone at Coney Island. His camera was in my purse."

"We went across the street to take pictures," Rafael said. "I started to take some pictures of Dolores. She very pretty, no? I used long lens and just shot over her shoulder. I got picture of the three men—the Russian, Mr. Moustache and the other Russian— through the front window while they were sitting at the table."

I don't know what good the pictures would do, but we had them. I was sure that the third guy that joined the party was Bogachov's buddy. I'd develop the pictures later on to make sure.

"Those three will be leaving sometime soon," I said. "I'll follow Mr. Moustache. I can't follow the Russians. They know me. So, it's up to you two to follow them. But, Rafael, they're dangerous. If it looks like they're on to you following them, back off. We'll meet back at my house, then you can go out to Coney Island."

I handed him twenty dollars for cabs and subway. That would leave about eighteen bucks for some trinkets for Dolores.

37

Sunday, September 30, 1951

I arrived at my house just minutes before Rafael and Dolores walked up. It was about five in the afternoon.

"I know where the Russians live, man," Rafael said back at my house.

"C'mon inside," I said. The Dodgers game on radio blared in the background. Every house on the block had at least one radio tuned into the Dodger game. When I stepped out onto my porch to greet Rafael and Dolores, I didn't miss a syllable of Red Barber's description of the game. I thought that if I walked to anyplace in Brooklyn that I could hear the game every step of the way from thousands of unseen radios behind open windows.

The Giants had already won their game against the Boston Braves.

The Dodgers game was the seventh inning. The Dodgers had been down six-to-one in the third, but now were behind by only two, eight to six.

"I got pictures," Rafael said, holding the Leica up. I had four radios on in the house. Red Barber's voice followed us and led us as we walked in to the living room. The game had taken over the neighborhood; it had taken over all of Brooklyn. But, I had started today with Rafael and Dolores to track down the Swede and we had pulled in a couple of Russians in the process.

Rafael was a camera freak. Rafael had taken some pictures for me on a previous job. He usually got the shots I wanted. On the same roll were a few candid shots of his latest chiquita. That chiquita had preceded Dolores by two or three chiquitas. The five photos showed his chiquita naked, capturing her from head to toe, including every one of her pubic hairs, if anybody wanted to count. Rafael knew what he was doing with a camera—in his chiquita shots he had the lighting down to the professional level. I had made him a copy of his personal photos. He asked me for five more of each. "For friends," he said. That's what friends were for, I guess.

Hiromi came from out of the kitchen. She said hello to Rafael. I introduced her to Dolores. Hiromi tried not to stare at Dolores. If I could read Hiromi's mind—which I can't read *any* woman's mind—she was probably wondering how any woman could be sculpted as a Greek Goddess like Dolores was. I hadn't seen any Oriental sculpted that way, but I'd never been to the Orient to get a bigger sample size. I'd bet a dollar to donuts, however, that I could spend a month in Japan and not see one Japanese woman waltzing around with a frame like that.

Hiromi, always polite, asked us if we wanted something to eat and drink. They each said yes. She went to the kitchen to fetch some beer and potato chips. Only one batter had gone to the plate before Hiromi returned with a tray of chips and Schaefers.

The Dodgers had a man on in the eighth. Rube Walker hit a pinch-hit two-run double to drive in two runs to tie the game at eight each. Our house erupted in cheers. I could hear the neighbors cheering.

"Tell me about the Russians," I said to Rafael.

"We have *address* for the Russians," Rafael said. "Just a couple of minutes after you left to follow Mr. Moustache, the two Russian guys leave together and walk toward 43rd. We follow them. They kept walking and talking and then took a left on 44th. About halfway down the block they went into one of the apartment buildings. No doorman. I got the address for you, and another picture. I also take a picture of the mailboxes—where they have the names of the people living in the apartment building. Many funny names. I think Russians living in 4G."

Both Mr. Moustache and the Russians lived close to the United Nations building. That made sense. That area was a pretty expensive area, but since they were foreigners, they probably got a special allowance from their countries for rent. If Tailgunner Joe really wanted to corral a whole lot of Commies at the same time, he should surround that neighborhood around the U.N. and do an apartment-to-apartment search to root out the Commies. That, of course, wouldn't be in the spirit of what the United Nations was all about.

Rafael handed me the roll of film. "You develop," he said. "You see names."

I pocketed the film.

"We have to go," Rafael said. "Coney Island." Coney Island could really be wild tonight if the Dodgers won. It would be worse than a cemetery if the Dodgers lost.

The Dodgers were going through pitchers. Dressen was using starting pitchers in relief. That showed you how desperate he was. In this one game, a fan could see every starting pitcher that the Dodgers had. Dressen finally brought in Don Newcombe. How could that big guy still pitch? He had thrown a nine inning shutout against the Phils just *last night*.

After Rafael and Dolores left, Hiromi said, "That Dolores seems like a nice girl."

I agreed.

"She from Puerto Rico?"

I said that I didn't know, but that she was Puerto Rican.

"Do many women from Puerto Rico have...a...do they look like her?"

"You mean her body?" I asked.

She nodded.

I laughed and said, "I've never seen one like that before." I would have just won some donuts. It was too bad I didn't really like donuts. Bagels yes, donuts no.

"Jake, sit down," she said, "I need to ask you something."

I sat down. Hiromi put a cup of green tea in front of me.

"Why, if I may ask, are you tailing that Mr. Moustache and the Russians?" She asked. "I thought your government men were going to do something with the Ice Queen. Why, as you Americans say it, *butt* in?"

That was a good question. I would prefer to say that I was tugging at a thread, but I wasn't sure if she would understand the analogy. Even if she did, it would still look like I was butting in.

"You're right," I said, discarding the thread analogy, "I've washed my hands of the Ice Queen. This is all about Roberta. The police have written off those murders of Roberta and that old detective. I *think* Mr. Moustache and the Russians can at least give me a glimpse of an answer. I don't know for sure, but I think there is a link. The police will not look for the killer of Roberta. It's what they call a closed case. I think I can find *something* that will open the case. If I do find something, I'll hand it over to the cops. If I don't find anything, then, well, I guess I won't find anything."

"That's all?" Hiromi asked.

"That's all," I said. That wasn't quite all, but it was enough. What I didn't tell Hiromi was that I might have to resort to some rough stuff to find that something that would reopen the cases.

"You are so tense about this Mr. Moustache man," Hiromi said, "and the two Russians. I can understand it, I think…"

I interrupted, "Yes, I am tense about those guys. I find out that the cops think that Roberta's murder was just a break-in gone bad. I don't think so. I felt there was a link to the Russians that attacked us. I didn't think that I would find Mr. Moustache this quickly, or that he would be with the two Russians that attacked us, but we did. Now, I know I have to act..."

"Act?"

"I have to find out things quickly," I said. "I think there is a link between Mr. Moustache and the two Russians and Roberta. And, then the Dodgers maybe blowing the pennant, that's got me all wound up. So, am I tense? You better believe that I'm tense. I haven't felt this way since Berlin. I'm gonna spend the next two or three days checking out Mr. Moustache and the two Russians. If I can find something, I'll go to the cops. If I can't, then, like I said, I can't. I'll drop it. But, the next two or three days are Roberta's."

Hiromi refilled my cup of tea. She thought that might calm me down. It didn't touch me.

During the ninth inning, I went down in the basement to develop the roll of film that Rafael had given me. I flicked on the radio. Red Barber's voice filled the darkroom.

Rafael did indeed have a great eye as a photographer. He had captured the Swede and the two Russians to where they were clearly identifiable inside the restaurant. The guy that Dolores said had the bumpy and crooked nose was the very same that I had driven my elbow into in Washington, D.C. I knew that those two Russians weren't the ones that had killed Roberta. They had been busy with Hiromi and me that night. However, I thought that Roberta's killer, or killers, were probably in the same fraternity, maybe even the same fraternity house. I would find out.

There were at least a half-dozen shots of Dolores or at least parts of her. Rafael had aimed the camera at Dolores, but then focused over her shoulder. In some of the shots, there was a blur of Dolores' hair or a blur of her shoulder. In another shot, Rafael had caught Dolores full bloom walking down the street. Two old guys off to the side of the picture had eyeballed Dolores. It looked like they were remembering thoughts about women that they had forgotten decades ago. A drugstore photo department would not have printed two other shots of Dolores. These were shots taken with the United Nations in the background. Dolores had already shed her summer dress. She was smiling and had flipped up her top to expose her breasts. I got to see that she hadn't taped thimbles under the fabric—those were genuine stand-up-and-salute giant nipples sitting on top of two mountains. I, of course, would make copies for Rafael, and maybe his friends.

I walked back upstairs; the Dodger game was in the tenth inning.

The eleventh inning passed with no scoring.

In the top of the twelfth, the Dodgers didn't score. Then the Phillies loaded the bases with just one out.

Their slugger, Del Ennis, was due up. Newcombe then struck him out. Two outs. I could hear the cheers in the neighborhood through the open windows. It sounded like I could hear an army cheering for the Dodgers on the radio.

Eddie Waitkus came up. A lefthander.

"Waitkus hits a low line drive to the right of second base," Red Barber said, practically gasping. "Robinson dives for the ball...HE CAUGHT IT! The Phillies are out on the field arguing that he trapped it...the Dodgers are out of the inning." I then whooped and hollered.

The roar in the neighborhood couldn't have been any greater than if we had won the World Series.

In the top of the thirteenth, the Dodgers couldn't score a run. In the Phillies' half, Newcombe gets the first two batters out, then walks two. He had gone five and two-thirds innings. That was after shutting out the Phillies for nine innings just the day before. His arm right now must have been jello.

Dressen brought in Bud Podbielan. I sat next to the phone. Dressen needed Podbielan to get one out. He did. The neighborhood cheered again.

I said to myself, "How long can this goddamn thing go on?" It was probably the same question that Charlie Dressen and tens of thousands of Dodger fans were asking at that exact moment.

The Phillies couldn't win the game and they couldn't let it go.

With two outs Jackie Robinson hit a fastball into the upper deck in the left field stands for a home run. I stood up and hollered. Hiromi, caught up in the spirit of Dodgerland, twirled in the living room. The neighborhood sounded like a grandstand cheering.

Now it was up to Bud Podbielan, the little twenty-seven-year-old righthander.

Richie Ashburn led off with a single. Puddin' Head Jones sacrificed him to second. Then Podbielan faced Del Ennis. Ennis drew a full count, three ball and two strikes. I almost could feel the neighborhood collectively inhale. Pop up! Gil Hodges takes it and Ennis is out. Two outs. Eddie Waitkus to the plate. Eddie almost ended the game in the twelfth, but Jackie Robinson made the miracle catch. Waitkus flied out to Andy Pafko in left. The Dodgers won!

I cheered with Hiromi. We ran out of the house and shouted to the heavens with our neighbors. This game had been the greatest thrill in my life. This particular game provided meaning to me. This was meaning for a guy that just wanted to go to Dodger games and drink beer. This was what life was all about. Everything else was just noise.

38

Monday, October 1, 1951

I was back at the Swede's apartment on 48ᵗʰ Street at seven in the morning. I felt like shit. I hadn't slept much. If it was possible to be exhausted and hyped up at the same time, that was me after the Dodgers beat the Phillies. The game took fourteen innings. I was like a dishrag, each inning squeezing out more emotions until there was nothing left.

I heard on the radio this morning driving over to Manhattan that the Dodgers got into Penn Station in the wee hours. They had been greeted by a throng of Dodger fans. Winning that last game didn't give us the right to play the Yankees in the World Series. It gave us the right to play the Giants in a three-game playoff series. The newspapers had started calling the Giants the "Miracle Men" and lo and behold, they had pulled off a miracle. The Giants had won twelve of their final thirteen games, their last seven in a row. The Dodgers had only won four of their last ten.

If I was having a difficult time adjusting to daylight, how're the Dodgers doing? They had to go right back at it. The first playoff game was today at one o'clock at Ebbets Field. The second game and possible third game would be at the Polo Grounds. The winner of that playoff would face the Yankees.

I was sitting in my car reading the *Daily News*. I would read a few paragraphs, then let my eyes bob up and give a quick look-see. Then my eyes would fall back on to the exact spot on the page and resume reading a few more paragraphs. My head wouldn't move, but my eyes darted around like Mexican jumping beans.

After about three hours, I saw the Swede come out of his apartment building. He looked like he was just on a leisurely stroll to work. I jumped out of my car.

"Mr. Swensen," I called, "Mr. Swensen?"

He turned and looked at me. I didn't alarm him. While I felt like shit, I had at least showered and shaved this morning making myself look at least semi-legit. I was wearing a dark suit with a tie. The suit was one of my working suits; I'd never use my new Bergdorf suit for a job like this.

The Swede's big moustache made his face look small. He was not a tall man and had a slight layer of blubber on him that must come in handy for those long winter nights in Sweden.

I held out my wallet. It had a phony ID card that identified me as FBI. That would put the fear of God to anybody in the United States. That was one thing that J. Edgar Hoover had done to perfection. Hoover might not think that there was organized crime, he might not think that Oriental Communists were a threat, but he had sure conditioned the American public to fear the FBI when they came knocking. Foreigners like Swensen probably feared the FBI even more than if Lucifer showed up with fire spitting out of his fingers. However, if my phony ID was laid down next to a real FBI ID, mine would look like a comic book version of the legit one. Heck, I had it made at Coney Island at one of those little shops where the tourists could make funny business cards.

The Swede was not a tanned guy, but whatever color he had in his face was drained when he saw my phony FBI identification. His face gave a pretty good impression of a Dracula victim.

"What's this all about?" he asked with a slight accent.

"We need to talk," I said. "You need to identify some things for me." I held up the envelope.

I had to play the tough guy role. This came pretty easy to me when I thought of Roberta.

"Shall we go to your apartment? Or, you can come down to FBI headquarters," I said. Heck, I didn't even know where FBI headquarters in New York was. If he would have asked me, *"where's that,"* I would have just had to answer, *"You don't really want to find out,"* and then hustle him inside his apartment.

"Inside," he said, "let's go inside."

We walked past the doorman. I tried to look the other way so that the doorman couldn't get a good look at my face. I didn't know what was going to happen upstairs, but it was always better to be anonymous.

We took the elevator to the fourth floor. The Swede opened the door with his key. He didn't call out any name so I assumed he lived alone. That assumption was a no-no in my line of work. That's what all the tailing was about—finding as much information about a guy so that I wouldn't be surprised. However, I had thrown caution to the wind. So far I was lucky. There were no surprises for me inside his apartment.

"Now, what is this all about?" he asked. He had regained his composure now that he was on his home turf. Some coloring was coming back to his light complexion. In a few more minutes, Dracula could take another sip.

I took a quick glance around his apartment. It had been a bare bones furnishing job. There was a couch, two chairs, a couple of side tables with lamps and a dinette set with four chairs. There was one door leading, I assumed, to the bedroom and bathroom.

"Come this way," I said, pointing to the door. "I want a tour of the place." I wanted him in front of me, not behind me. He cooperated; after all, I was the FBI. We walked into the bedroom. Nothing there, but a bed, a side table and a dresser. There were two framed pictures on his dresser. I picked up one for a closer look. There was a blond wife and two teenage kids. The wife was quite homely, but I guess on those long winter nights in Sweden a warm body was a warm body.

"That's my family," he said.

"Nice looking family," I said. The wife gave me a little bit of the shivers.

We walked out to the living room and we sat down in the two chairs.

I took the photo of him and the Ice Queen out of my suit coat pocket. I had blown it up in my darkroom so that it was an eight-by-ten in full, writhing black-and-white. To make it fit in my pocket, I had folded it in half; both halves of the photo was incriminating. I unfolded it and handed it to Swensen.

He took the photo and looked at it. I could tell that he had seen it before.

He dropped the photo on the coffee table as if it had maggots on it. "What's this all about?" he asked. The color was totally gone from his face. Dracula couldn't get any more blood out of that one.

I had expected one of two reactions. One of anger. If he had been angered, his face would have boiled to red. Red usually led to action. In that angered state, he might try to rush me. The other reaction he could have had was fear. He had given me the fear look. He was just a working stiff. The fear look was better for me; I could build that fear up in him to so much that I could make him literally piss in his pants.

"Tell me what she wants," I said. I didn't have to give him the Ice Queen's name; he knew who I was talking about.

He didn't know how to answer me. He *wanted* to lie, but he had not prepared for a lie and his fear was suffocating his thinking.

"It was a mistake," he said, "I have a family. You saw the pictures. A lovely family. I have a good job at the United Nations; I am representing my country."

"Look, Swensen, I will *ruin* your family," I said, laying on the tough guy role as hard as I could. Sweet talking wouldn't work with a guy that was frightened. "I will *ruin* what your kids think about you, I will put you in prison here in the good old U.S. of A for the rest of your life. I'll have faggots fucking you in prison until you think your asshole is Grand Central Station. *Tell me what she makes you do.*"

The easy lie for him would have been *money*. But, he was too afraid to think of any answer, even the easy lie. He was thinking about the consequences, not the lic. He was an honest man.

"I can't....I can't tell you," he said, sobbing.

I jumped out of the chair and fired my fist into his jaw. He and the chair he was sitting on went over like a bowling pin. I jumped on him. I didn't like to have to use the rough stuff—particularly on what seemed to be an honest guy, a guy that was caught in the middle of something he shouldn't have been in. But swift brutal violence would ramp up the fear. He wasn't fighting back; he wasn't the type to fight back. I straddled his chest with my knees, my butt on his stomach, my knees pinning his arms. I grabbed him by his ears and slammed his head into the floor.

"I will not kill you," I said, my face about two inches from his. "I *will* hurt you, I will hurt you bad. I will *ruin* your life. I will *ruin* your kids' lives. I'll *rape* your wife until she tells me she loves it. I *promise* you all those things." I said this with such force that it was scaring *me*. I was as out of control as I was with Scheffler in Germany. "*Tell me what she wants. Tell me what she wants!*"

I could feel warmth coming through the seat of my pants. Swensen was pissing in his. I hitched myself up a bit like I was riding a horse, in this case a wet horse.

"Tell me, Swensen, you dumb fuck, and then I'll leave. You'll never see me again. You'll never see the FBI again. *Tell me what the bitch wants!*"

I could smell the piss; he had let go with a full bladder. I should have let him go to the bathroom first.

"Information..." he finally mumbled.

"*What!*" I yelled. I was terrifying myself. "*What information!*"

"My superior...my boss...is on the Security Council of the United Nations," he said, crying. "He works hard, he needs my assistance many times..."

"*What information?*" I yelled, spittle flying from my mouth onto his face. I didn't want a conversation with Swensen. I didn't want him to think. I just wanted him the blurt things out. He was scared beyond belief. Swensen wasn't a seasoned spy, he was a diplomat. I hoped he wouldn't shit in his pants.

"Information about the Korean War," he said, his face streaked with tears. "Strategies...plans that the United Nations troops will use. All the battle plans go through the U.N. Security Council. The Security Council is briefed all the time, almost every day on strategies. After all, we're all involved in this war."

A bunch of light bulbs went off in my head like a thousand Broadway marquees had turned on. That's right—this war wasn't the United *States* war; this was a United *Nations* war. There were twenty-one countries that were in this war providing troops and equipment to fight North Korea. The United States was the lead dog, appointed that by the United Nations, but there were seven countries on the Security Council. Because there were troops from twenty-one different countries, the Security Council had to act as advisor in the U.N.'s effort in Korea. They had to know everything that was going on.

Dominic Gonnella—my local bookmaker and my walking world affairs expert—said that the United Nations pulled the strings on Truman to fire MacArthur. I remembered some of those countries from what Dominic had told me. There were such military stalwarts as Ethiopia and France and New Zealand and Sweden. These countries had a voice in how we fought the war?

"*What type of strategies,*" I asked. My mind was going a mile a minute. I remembered Dominic telling me about his nephew and how the North Koreans knew about their secret mission—right down to the *names* of the commanders of the U.S. troops. That made our secret mission a surprise party hosted by the North Koreans. We ended up like mincemeat at that surprise party.

"Troop deployment, troop movement, equipment, ammunition supplies, things like that," Swensen said. "It is necessary that we review this. It is not *your* war, it is not just *your* troops. There are troops from fifteen different countries."

"Yeah? How many fucking troops does Sweden have in Korea?"

"None," The Swede said. He flinched, probably thinking I was going to belt him. When I didn't, he said, "We are only providing medical supplies and medical personnel. Us, and Denmark and Norway and Italy. Most of the troops are from the United States, England, Canada and Australia."

"Why do you get to review these battle plans?" I asked.

"*I* don't, the Security Council does. In September of last year, look what happened. General MacArthur, on his own, launched an amphibious landing at Inchon two hundred miles behind enemy lines. From there he launched an attack against the North Koreans at Pusan. *That* was not in any plans that had been presented to the United Nations! It had severe effects. It gave the North Koreans no choice but to retreat or they would have been cut in two."

"So? Sounds like a pretty good plan to me."

"MacArthur *ignored* his orders and acted on his own. He advanced north toward the Chinese border at the Yalu River. This *provoked* the Chinese. They are a member of the United Nations, even though they are not on the Security Council. The Chinese then were forced to launch a massive attack against the U.N. forces and South Korea. The Chinese army had 180,000 soldiers with 100,000 in reserve. The Security Council never authorized MacArthur to fight China. That's why we have to review everything. With the United Nations, we just can't allow your generals to become cowboys."

"Tell me about Arabella Van Dyck," I said.

"I was persuaded by Arabella to give my information to the Russians…"

"*Persuaded?* She got your little head to do things for the big head," I said.

"Yes, well, you've seen the picture. She persuaded me to give the information to the Russians. They aren't on the Security Council. They don't believe in this war. They want to stop this war."

Of course, the *Russians*. It was common knowledge—I didn't even have to ask Dominic about it—that the Russians were providing weapons to North Korea, along with the Chinese.

Korea was just a large poker game. The table had a name: Korea. The United States, Russia and China were seated at the poker table. The United Nations was the dealer. The chips were soldiers. We were given South Korea and so many United Nations soldiers; the Russians and Chinese were given the North Koreans and provided as much weapons and assistance that they could. It didn't matter which cards were dealt. The difference was the peanut gallery—the onlookers. Diplomats like Swensen and whoever else on the so-called United Nations Security Council were standing behind the United States. They could see the cards that were dealt. They flashed signals to Russia as to what cards the United States had.

If the Russians were stupid cardplayers, they could win big and early. They wouldn't do that. If they won, let's say, nine hands in a row, the United States would smell a rat. The Russians would just win here and there and when it counted. When you added it all up, it would be a loss for the United States.

If I took the time to find the identity of the guy in each and every picture that was caught between the Ice Queen's legs, they would probably all be diplomats from the United Nations. Some would be on the Security Council. Each would probably be an onlooker at the game of United Nations War Poker. They were wild cards.

With that many eyes in the Security Council looking at the United States hand, the trick for the Russians wasn't a victory. They would eventually get that, even if it was a stalemate. Their victory did not have to be the final outcome of the war. They would measure their victory in how costly it was to the United States. What price would the Americans pay for the lost lives of tens of thousands of soldiers? What price would Americans pay in spending a fool's fortune on a war that shouldn't have been fought? What price would the Americans pay to seriously wound their national 'can do/let's do' psyche? What price would the Americans pay for a long, extended war that the people didn't even give a shit about?

When it was all said and done, the United States would experience a global embarrassment—and a hugely costly one in lives and dollars and psyche. The most powerful nation in the world would take a serious shot to the chin.

The North Koreans were puppets, the South Koreans were puppets, and unfortunately, we were puppets. I may be a lot of things, but the last thing I ever would be was a puppet.

The Swede had shit in his pants. It was starting to stink up the room.

He was a mess. Crying, shaking, stinky.

I made him sit on the floor, sit in his own shit, his back leaning against his livingroom wall.

"Take a look at my face," I told him.

His eyes were looking down at the floor. I slapped him across his face. It brought blood out of his nose. He wailed. Now he was wailing, crying, bleeding, shaking and stinky.

This was a guy that dealt in secrets, but he wasn't trained to hold secrets. The Ice Queen had found that out with her pussy. I had found it out with some rough stuff. I felt like I should kill him. He had given secrets to the Russians that ultimately killed some of our soldiers in Korea. After I had killed three Nazis in Eastern Europe, I hadn't felt any remorse. The only question that I had in those killings was *why* I didn't feel remorse. I had never been able to answer that question. I had justifications for killing, but no real answers. I had killed human beings. I didn't have to kill them. They weren't enemies. The enemy part was over when the war ended. Yes, I could kill this Swedish bastard and not feel it. That was scary to me. I think the Swede felt my fear.

I grabbed his chin and pointed his face toward mine. *"Look at my face!"*

Through bleary eyes he looked at my face.

"I want you to *remember* my face," I said, spittle flying like popped corn. "If you tell anybody about our meeting—the Russians or Arabella Van Dyck or *anybody*—I will find out. Do you believe that?"

His eyes widened.

"Do you believe it!"

He nodded his head quickly.

"If you tell anybody, you will see this face again," I said, "I will ruin you, I will rape your wife, I will rape your kids, I will send you to prison. You will not be able to stop me from doing those things. You're dealing with the fucking FBI here. We can do anything. *Do you understand?"*

He nodded his head vigorously.

I still held his chin in my hand, pointing his face toward me. Blood from his nose dribbled onto my fingers. "What do you understand? Tell me. *Tell me what you understand!"*

"I do not...I do not tell anybody about our meeting..." he stammered.

"Or me!"

"I do not tell anybody about our meeting...or you."

"Stay there," I said. I walked to his bedroom. I took the framed picture of his wife and kids and brought it to the living room. I smashed the frame against the coffee table and ripped out the picture. I held the picture out in front of the Swede.

"I will remember your family," I said. I rubbed the picture against my crotch.

"I do not tell anybody...please...I do not tell anybody."

I had pushed the Swede's fear button as far as I could. It might shut him up for a day or maybe a week. But, eventually, he would either tell somebody or act. His action would probably be a quick exit back home to Sweden. What I needed from the bastard was a few days of silence from him; I didn't want him to warn the Russians that I was going to visit them.

"I'm leaving," I said. "Clean yourself up. Call in sick. Don't go to work. I've got people watching to see if you leave. I've got your phone tapped."

I left the Swede quivering in the corner.

39

Monday, October 1, 1951

I walked down the back steps of the Swede's apartment building. I didn't want to see anybody. I left through the back door. Nobody had seen me leave. It was a little after nine in the morning. In the alley, I took several deep breaths. I didn't feel any better. I still felt like shit. I walked around the block to try to cool myself down. It helped. I walked around another block. Then another. It helped a little more.

I drove back to Brooklyn. My hands were still a little fluttery. I needed a drink bad. Almost as a reflex, I stopped at a bar on Flatbush Avenue, Hugh Casey's Steak and Chop House, a popular watering hole for Dodgers fans. I had forgotten about the first playoff game today. It was going to be played at Ebbets Field in just a few hours and already guys were wandering into Casey's.

I ordered a beer and a shot. I downed the shot and breathed a little better.

I bummed a cigarette from a guy next to me at the bar. He held out a lit match and the cigarette quivered in my lips as I poked out my face to the light. It seemed like it took just two puffs to smoke it down to nothing. I knocked down the beer.

The bar was filling up. There'd be a lot of guys missing work today. It seemed that everybody walking in was carrying a portable radio.

There were a few Giants fans inside Casey's. They pretty much kept to their obnoxious selves. They'd better; somebody could get killed in there.

One Giants fan making a little noise was told to shut up. "This is a free country, pal," the Giants fan had said in response.

"This ain't no free country, shithead," a Brooklyn guy said. "This is Brooklyn."

There were a million more people living in Brooklyn than Manhattan. All of us Dodger fans were all from Brooklyn, most of us born and raised. A lot of those Manhattan people had moved in from someplace else like Illinois or Kentucky or Michigan. They didn't have the fierce loyalty that us Brooklyn guys had. Sure, those Giants fans would *like* to win; we *needed* to win. Big difference.

The guy I had bummed a cigarette from left. I wanted another. I bought a pack of Old Golds at the bar. I didn't really like to smoke, but what was I going to do with the hand that wasn't holding a beer? I bought Old Golds because they meant homers, Dodger homers. Every time a Dodger hit a home run at Ebbets Field, somebody from the press box would slide a carton of Old Golds down the screen behind home plate for that player. Sometimes the player who hit the home run would just run over to the backstop after rounding the bases and pick up his free carton; other times a ballboy would retrieve it for him. Today I hoped those cartons were sailing down the screen like a waterfall. I'd light up an Old Golds every time one of our boys yanked one out of the park.

I sat there thinking what strange twists my life had turned in to lately. My life had become a lot more complicated than just baseball and beer. Just today I had beaten the shit, literally, out of a United Nations official. If that wasn't psychotic then I didn't know the meaning of the word.

I got out of Casey's before it got too packed. I drove home. I could have bought tickets to the game, but I couldn't go to the game. Not today. There was too much going on with my psychotic life.

I sat in front of the TV and watched the game on WOR-TV. Red Barber said that this was the first coast-to-coast broadcast of a baseball game. Hiromi came down from upstairs to watch with me.

There were celebrities in the crowd.

Tailgunner Joe was there. So was General MacArthur. There were movie stars and more politicians.

When Jackie Robinson came to the plate, the place erupted. I could hear the cheering from the TV and from outside in the neighborhood. Jackie had made the catch last night that might go down with the Al Gionfrido catch in the '47 Series. Then he hit a monstrous home run in the fourteenth. I was cheering like a maniac. My neighbors probably heard me. Hiromi looked at me and figured I was drunk, which I might have been, and went back upstairs to her studio.

When Dodger leftfielder Andy Pafko hit a solo home run in the second inning the noise could have been heard in three states.

Bobby Thomson hit a two run homer off of Ralph Branca in the fourth. The Dodgers were down two-to-one.

In the innings after Pafko's homer, we hit into four double-plays.

Then in the eighth, the Giants rightfielder, Monte Irvin, hit a homer off of Branca. We were dead.

The Giants had won the first game three-to-one. We'd have to win tomorrow's game at the Polo Grounds.

I felt worse than Swensen did when I made him shit in his pants.

I went outside and sat alone on the front steps of my brownstone nursing a Schaefers. I sat there for a long time. The neighborhood was quiet. The few people walking the night looked like Dodger fans that couldn't sleep. We would mumble a hello to each other as they walked by.

I thought of Swensen. I thought of what I would have to do tomorrow.

I thought of Roberta.

I thought of Richard Wolfemeyer, the ancient detective that read Mickey Spillane's Mike Hammer books.

I thought of Rafael. He really did have the touch and the vision as a photographer. Could he take that skill and turn it into a legit living? Or was his destiny the streets of Red Hook in Brooklyn? Where would he be in five years? Ten years? Would he look back at his youth and consider it an important launching pad for the rest of his life? Or would he consider his youth as the beginning of a slide downhill?

I thought of Dolores. What would happen to such a pretty girl? Where would she be in five years? Ten years? Would she look back at her youthful beauty as a treasure lost? Or a treasure maintained and matured?

I thought of myself. Where would *I* be in five years? Ten years? Would I be an owner of an art gallery? Would Hiromi still be part of my life?

I thought of the Dodgers. I tried not to think about tomorrow's game at the Polo Grounds. It was probably going to be Sal Maglie going against Clem Labine or Carl Erskine. Maglie was the pitcher that any manager would want to close out a series. Instead of thinking of tomorrow's game, I thought of where would the Dodgers be in five years? Ten years? The Dodgers had been such an important part of my life when I was a kid. The Dodgers were even more important now that I was older and back from Germany. There was no Brooklyn without the Dodgers.

There were so many questions; the answers I would find out as I went. Could I change the answers? Should I ask different questions?

40

Tuesday, October 2, 1951

The Swede was just a diplomat that got sucked in by the Ice Queen. I don't believe that he was a bad guy; I don't believe he intended to be a spy. It's not like he went to spy school in Moscow. He just got caught in one of the oldest traps in the spy business—the honey trap.

Once he learned the consequences of that one roll in the hay with the Ice Queen, would he take it back if he could? Would he cram his penis back into his pants and walk away from the Ice Queen? Sure he would. But, it was too late for that. As long as he had his family to protect, he was property of Moscow.

It was a pretty slick operation that the Russians had going for them. They did their homework on which diplomats were part of the U.N. Security Council and had families with small children. There would be an orchestrated 'chance meeting' between the Ice Queen and the diplomat. Show me the diplomat that could turn her down! There weren't any.

Diplomats were used to getting things for free. A big red pussy? Sure, "I'll take one. How about two?" would be the answer for each one of them. If one of the diplomats turned down the Ice Queen, then the Russians would figure him for a fag. So they'd set him up with some attractive swishy guy.

If I took the time to find out the identities of each one of those pictures that had been in the Ice Queen's safe, I had a pretty good hunch that most of them would be diplomats at the United Nations. The ones that weren't diplomats probably had access to key information someplace else concerning the Korean War.

This, of course, wasn't something that I could walk away from. It was also something that was a lot bigger than me. I would turn everything I had over to Chet Morgan. What he did with the information was his business, the business of the CIA. He could turn it over to where he worked—the CIA—or he could turn it over to his shadow CIA. Either way, our guys would have this critical information. I would get myself out of the picture.

Bogachov and his buddy, however, were a little different. They were *my* business; they made themselves my business by most likely being involved in the murder of Roberta. They were a vital component of the Ice Queen's whole operation, and should be the private reserve of the CIA, but I was going to get to them first.

They didn't kill Roberta, of course. They were jumping me when Roberta was murdered. But, you could bet your life on that they knew who had killed Roberta. Or, I guess they would be betting their own lives. They wouldn't freely tell me, of course. Hell, they wouldn't tell me if I was torturing them. Besides, I wasn't much into pulling out toe nails to get a guy to have a conversation with me. I was going to go beyond torture. Then they would tell me.

I don't believe in vendettas. I don't believe in revenge. I did believe in *balance*. There would have to be a consequence for them murdering a little old lady librarian, a woman that had been like a favorite aunt to me for most of my life. I was going to deliver the consequence.

In the morning, I was up before Hiromi and the birds. I had retrieved three weapons from their individual hiding places in my house.

I inserted a Colt Detective Special into the little holster that I had strapped on to my ankle. This was a snub nose gun that wouldn't be effective from long distance. It wasn't going to be long distance; this was an in-your-face gun for me.

I strapped on a shoulder holster and put in another Colt Detective Special. Each one of these little guns had a capacity of six bullets before reloading.

I then stuffed a Smith & Wesson 39 in the small of my back under my sports jacket. This one had a capacity of eight bullets.

I learned over in Eastern Europe that it was better to have too many bullets than too few. You never knew when you would need *just one more* bullet. It was better to have one more than to be one short. That one bullet could be my life.

One last piece of equipment. I retrieved my other sawed off shotgun from its hiding place. I wouldn't be walking around with this thing, but it would be my bench strength sitting in the trunk of my car waiting to get the call.

I got in my Ford, looked back at my house. I saw Hiromi's light on in her room. She must have just got up. The birds were starting to sing.

Over the Brooklyn Bridge, I drove into the city.

It was more difficult to find a parking space this early in the morning. I drove around the block three times looking. I finally found one about a half a block down from the Russians apartment building.

I left the shotgun in the trunk. It was still early in the morning. I saw just one person walking to work as I walked to the Russians apartment building. I looked at the mailbox. There was an *I. Bogachov* printed on the mailbox for 4G. It was just as Rafael's photo had showed. Ivan Bogachov—that was the name that Chet Morgan had given me. The big Russian that I could have killed. The crooked nose guy must have been B. Karakadymov, also listed at 4G. I didn't know what the 'B' stood for. There was no doorman for this apartment building. The lock to the lobby door was easy to pick. Hiromi would have just laughed at it and it would have opened.

The elevator doors were open. I walked past the elevator and opened the door to the stairs. I could feel my heart pulsate, but I felt calm. I felt like I did in Eastern Europe. Yes, my senses were elevated, but it gave me an edge. The two Russians would most likely be sleeping; their senses were slumbering.

The lettering for the fourth floor appeared in front of me on the stairwell in an instant. I couldn't remember seeing the indicators for the second and third floor, I was so focused. I opened the door and stepped into the hallway. It was quiet. No kids crying, no television blaring. The smells in the hallway were remnants from nights gone by.

I found 4G. There was a small doorbell to the right of the door. I pulled out my Smith & Wesson and held it close to my side. I pressed the doorbell and stepped toward the hinges of the door. The person looking through the peephole wouldn't be able to identify me. I pressed the doorbell again, a long burst.

"Whaaaa?" I heard from the other side of the door.

From Berlin I had learned a few Russian words. In Russian, I said, "Let me in."

He wouldn't recognize the voice even if he was fully awake. Coming out of sleep, he would first recognize the words in his language. The voice would become unimportant. It had to be one of his countrymen.

Even though Bogachov and the other guy, B. Karakadymov, were KGB, they were in America. They knew that no Americans spoke Russian. So, whoever this fool Russian was that got them up too early would pay a price.

The door opened. I didn't wait to find out which Russian opened the door. I lifted my leg and kicked the door square in the middle. It swung back as if a bazooka had hit it. I heard the crunch. I heard the "oof." I jumped in with my Smith & Wesson in front of me.

Bogachov was wearing just his skivvies, holding his nose, blood flowing around his fingers. With the barrel of the gun I hit him on the same temple that I had in DC. I didn't hit him as hard. I took a little off the blow, enough to knock him out, but hopefully not enough to kill him. He fell against the wall, bouncing off it like a billiard ball. I looked down at him; I might have killed him this time. I'd find out later.

The apartment's layout was like a train. The front door opened into the living room. There was a hall that ran down the left side. Down the hall would be the bathroom, the bedrooms and then the kitchen in the back. I ran down to the first door. It was open. The bathroom. Nobody was there.

I jumped to the second door. I was quiet in my movements, but the floor was wood. There was some creaking. The second door was to a bedroom. The bed was large enough for just one person. It was empty. I assumed that this was Bogachov's. I walked quietly to the third door. It was to the second bedroom. There was a single bed. On the nightstand was a bottle of vodka. Lying on the bed, naked, with the covers on the floor was Karakadymov, the "bumpy nose Russian," as Dolores had described him. He was asleep. There was a naked woman next to him. She was sleeping. Her legs were splayed open with one leg draped over Karakadymov. She had the largest mound of pubic hair I had ever seen. I tiptoed over to her side of the bed. I hit her in the temple with the butt of the Smith & Wesson as hard as I could. I hoped it wouldn't kill her. There wasn't even a scream; it was more like a grunt or maybe it was just the solid whack of my gun hitting her head or maybe it was my grunt. She would sleep for a few more hours than she thought she would. When she woke up, she would wonder why she had such a terrific headache. And, where in the world did that ugly bruise come from?

Karakadymov woke up. I held the Smith & Wesson straight out in front of me.

"Get up," I said.

Even coming out of a deep sleep, I could tell that he recognized me.

"What the fuck is going on?" he asked, his English almost perfect.

"Get up," I said. "We're gonna talk."

Karakadymov got up. "Don't put on your clothes," I said. "Put your hands behind your head." He slowly clasped his hands behind his head. He pushed out his jaw, sucked in his gut a little. He wasn't afraid.

I backed up toward the bedroom door. I motioned with my gun to follow. Out in the hallway, keeping the Smith & Wesson zeroed in on his chest, I stepped back toward the kitchen to let him get into the hallway.

"Walk slowly to the living room," I said.

He walked slowly toward the living room. He saw Bogachov lying on the floor. There was a stream of blood pouring from his nose.

"Drag him over to the couch," I said.

Karakadymov dragged his comrade over to the couch, lifting him so his head rested on the back of the couch, his feet on the floor. Karakadymov sat next to him.

"What do you want?" Karakadymov asked. There was no fear showing in him as he sat naked on the couch. There was anger, of course, a smoldering anger that could easily manifest itself to killing me if I allowed it.

"The night that you guys jumped me in Washington, D.C., there was a little old lady that was in Brooklyn. She was a librarian," I said. "I know that one of your Russian comrades killed her. I want to know which one of you Russians did it."

He looked at me blankly. "I don't know what you're talking about," he said. He said it convincingly, but he was *KGB*, these guys were trained to lie with the best of them. I could pull out his toenails and he would still be a convincing liar. If there was a lying contest between him and the Ice Queen, both would win.

"I won't allow you to play stupid with me," I said. "I know it wasn't you and I know it was'nt your sleeping buddy next to you. You tell me who it was, I let you guys live."

"Yes, I admit that we had our difficulties with you in DC," he said, "but that was it. We did what we were instructed, you did what you had to do. That was the end of it. I don't know anything about a little old lady."

"Who instructed you to get me?" I asked.

"Arabella Van Dyck, of course," he said. "You know that."

"Was she the one that ordered the hit on the old lady?"

Karakadymov let his anger boil out. *"There was no hit on an old lady. I know nothing about it!"*

On the chair that I was sitting in was a small throw pillow. I picked it up and wrapped it around the Smith & Wesson. I aimed the gun at Karakadymov. He didn't wince, he didn't recoil. He was one tough son of a bitch, I could tell. I shot him in the kneecap. His knee exploded into pieces. He would never again walk without a limp. The sound of the gun was muffled by the pillow, but inside the room it still sounded like a gunshot. This apartment building was one of the older ones—the types that were built solid instead of the flimsy ones they were putting up nowadays. I hoped that the sound wouldn't carry through the walls.

Karakadymov was on the floor holding his knee. There were bone splinters on the couch. He turned his head toward me. "You fuck," he said, gritting his teeth. If looks could kill, his face would have dropped me dead on the spot.

"Get on the couch," I said, "or I'll take out the other knee."

He crabbed himself up on to the couch. Bogachov's eyes were open. He was starting to focus. He blinked hard, then again and again.

I said to Bogachov, "When you guys jumped me, there was a little old lady killed in Brooklyn. Your buddy here couldn't remember who did it. I shot out his knee. He'll never walk straight again. I'll do the same to you if you don't tell me. Then I'll shoot out your other knee. Then his other knee. You can have races in your wheelchairs."

Bogachov said, "I don't know what you're talking about. We didn't kill any little old lady."

"Who did? Which one of your pals did?"

"Nobody, *nobody* killed a little old lady," Bogachov said.

My hand still wrapped the pillow over the Smith & Wesson. I aimed at Bogachov's knee. He put his hands over his knees as if they would somehow protect them. I shot his left knee. The bullet went through his hand and shattered his knee cap. Karakadymov somehow propelled himself off the couch, lurching toward me. I shot him in the left shoulder and he went down hard. Bogachov reached for something behind the couch. I shot him in the neck. It hit his jugular. Blood spurted out as if he was a fountain.

I sprung up. There had been too many shots. Some of that noise had to make it through the walls. I looked down at Karakadymov. I thought I had shot him in the left shoulder. I wasn't as accurate as I would have liked. My aim had been a little low. There was a bullet hole where his heart was. If I had been on a shooting range, the paper target would have showed dead solid perfect in the heart. An incongruous thought flitted into my brain. I had never found out what the 'B' stood for in B. Karakadymov on the mailbox.

Both Russians were dead. There was blood all over the place. I ran to the second bedroom. The babe with the big muff was still out cold. I felt for a pulse. It was still there. She would live.

I stood there and thought for just a minute. I tried to remember if I had touched anything in the apartment. I hadn't. Except for the throw pillow. It was still in my hand. No fingerprints there. I dropped the pillow on the floor.

I walked to the front door. I put my ear up against it, listening for noise in the hallway. There was none. Yet.

I took out my handkerchief from my back pocket and used it to grip the doorknob. I pulled open the door and closed it quietly behind me. My gun was still in my hand. I put it in the small of my back.

I walked to the door to the stairs and opened it. Nobody was in the stairwell. I went down the stairs two at a time, but as quietly as I could. My heart was racing faster than I was.

Before I opened the door to the ground floor, I tried to catch my breath. I thought I must look like a raging lunatic. Maybe I was.

41

Tuesday, October 2, 1951

I had trouble focusing on the television.

I heard somebody yell behind me. Then somebody else slapped me on the back causing me to spill my beer onto my pants. That was okay, I just picked up the shot of whiskey and downed that. I heard the Giants announcer Russ Hodges better than I could see the TV. Jackie Robinson had just hit a two run homer for the Dodgers in the first inning. The Dodgers were winning and I was hammered in some saloon I didn't know where.

"Man, you in a bad way," Rafael said.

"Where'd you come from?" I asked.

"I been here for an hour," Rafael said.

Time sure flies when I was having fun. Actually, I found out that time just skips around like a bouncing ball when I had just killed two guys and had passed the wobbly drunk stage probably a couple of hours before.

I hadn't gone straight to this saloon after I had knocked off the two Russians. I had driven back to my house. I hadn't realized that I was pretty close to being in shock. The drive was against the grain of traffic, so I got home before I could even think. I arrived home before the neighborhood had really come alive.

Hiromi was in the kitchen drinking her green tea.

I said hello. She turned to me and her mouth opened wide like a yawn, but it wasn't a yawn by any means. It was more like a scream, but with no noise. She quickly put her hand over her mouth.

"What happened to *you!*" she asked. This was one of her questions that was really an exclamation.

"What do you mean?" I asked.

"Go look in mirror."

I walked down the hallway to the foyer mirror. There were a couple of dozen drops of blood that had dried on my face, shirt and pants. I looked like I was a sloppy housepainter that had been painting a ceiling a dark burgundy. I hadn't even noticed the spraying of the blood when I had shot the Russians. It was a good thing that I hadn't seen anybody leaving the apartment or getting to my car.

"Well?" Hiromi said over my shoulder. She said that not as a wife would say, but more out of curiosity. She was so calm. While Hiromi and I had become closer, there was still a separation of privacy.

"I'll explain it later," I said.

I went upstairs and stripped. The clothes and shoes would have to be ditched, that was for sure. I stuffed them in a paper bag. I'd get rid of them later. I jumped in the shower to wash the Russians' blood off of me. I didn't want any evidence that linked me with the Russians. Sure, the two guys that were killed were bad guys—they were KGB agents—but they had been *murdered* in New York City by an ordinary citizen—me. This wasn't the case of a spy killing a spy in Istanbul or Prague or Morocco. This was two so-called diplomats from Russia coldly assassinated by an American citizen.

I felt about as much remorse as I did when I assassinated Scheffler or any of those other SS killers: none. No remorse whatsoever. The lack of remorse reminded me of some thoughts I had after I returned from Europe. Was there a thread running through me that was clearly psychotic? After all, I had just killed two guys in cold blood—it couldn't be any colder than what I had done—and I slugged a defenseless sleeping woman senseless. I wasn't feeling any guilt at all. That wasn't natural. How could that be good?

Maybe it was because I could justify in my mind those murders just as I had done with my Nazi victims. The Nazis that I murdered were going to continue killing in South America. Scheffler had even told me so. We, the United States, were actually helping them to get safely out of Europe. By killing the Nazis, I had done a huge favor for a lot of unknown South Americans—and the world for that matter. I would just never get public credit for doing that favor. If I did get credit, it would be when they fitted a noose around my neck. Sure, I made out financially, but that was an accidental byproduct of what I had done.

Killing the Russians was different. However, if I wanted to take a twisted look at it I could figure that I had done some American soldiers in Korea a favor. I would never know their names, of course, but to me I didn't need to know who they were. I had saved American lives. Because of what the Russians were doing, they were causing American soldiers lives to be lost in Korea. There was no doubt about that.

It's not that those Russians wouldn't be replaced, but my action would have at least temporarily slowed down their spy network. Hopefully, Chet Morgan and his guys could close it down altogether. After I had disposed of any evidence—the clothes and the gun—I'd give him a call and tell him everything I knew about the Ice Queen, the pictures, the extortion on U.N. diplomats, everything. Everything except the murders of the two Russians, of course. He'd find out about that someplace else rather than from me.

When I got out of the shower, I realized I had left my three handguns laying on my bed. I walked over to put them out of view from the open bedroom door. Hiromi walked by, going up to her attic/studio and saw my movement and stopped.

"Oh," she said, looking at me. I had a towel wrapped around my waist. "I've never seen you like this before." I think she blushed. Her eyes drifted off of me to the handguns. I hoped she thought of me as *samurai* and not as a crazed killer.

The moment was awkward, and in the future, we might laugh about it. She and I had shared the same house for a year and this was the first time that she had seen me naked except for the towel. It had been a similar thing for me—I had never seen her legs above her kneecaps. Such a strange relationship.

Later that morning, I had driven over to Red Hook. That was a section of Brooklyn where most of the docks were. Rafael and a lot of transplanted Puerto Ricans lived in Red Hook.

There were sections of the docks where folks could just drive up near the water. The channel was deep. Who knows what was at the bottom? There were stories that the area had been the final resting place of a number of gangsters. You know, sleep with the fishes and all that. I was going to add to the garbage.

I had taken my clothes that I had worn to the Russians and wrapped them around three bricks. I then taped everything together like it was a mummy. Even my shoes were inside that mummy. I hated to throw away those shoes. They weren't new, but they hadn't been resoled yet. But, I had seen blood stains on the soles. Most likely, I left tracks in the apartment and even on the stairs. Those tracks could be matched. I sat on the dock at the water's edge. I would have preferred depositing my little package at night when I was less likely to be seen, but seeing somebody toss something into the East River during the day wasn't very unusual. Anybody watching could tell that my package didn't include a body. It was just too small for a body. I just wanted to get rid of this thing as quickly as possible. When I looked across the bay I saw the Statue of Liberty. The Staten Island Ferry glided by. Passengers were looking at the shore at Red Hook. The ferry made a quick right toward the point of Staten Island, the homestretch.

The passengers were looking ahead. After the ferry turned, I dropped my bag of weighted clothes into the bay.

I watched it disappear into the dark murky waters. I waited ten minutes. It didn't come bubbling back up. Now, I had just one thing to do.

That one thing was to get a hold of Chet Morgan. I had to dump all the stuff I had on the Ice Queen on to Chet Morgan. I wanted it to disappear just like the clothes I had thrown into the bay.

I got back into my car. Getting into the car, I noticed a saloon down the street. I got out of the car and walked to the saloon. A quick boilermaker or two would help take the edge off.

The saloon was open. A few Puerto Ricans were sitting at the bar. They probably worked at the rope factory in Red Hook. The talk at the bar was about the Dodgers. The Giants were not going with Sal Maglie today. They were going with Sheldon Jones. His nickname was "Seldom," a play on his first name and that he had won only five games this season. Giants manager Leo Durocher was playing a huge hunch. Charlie Dressen was going with a hunch too, Clem Labine. Preacher Roe should have started, but his arm was mush. Labine had been in Charlie's dog-house for a month. If there was a tomorrow, it would have to be Maglie against Don Newcombe, ace against ace.

Even before I sat down in that saloon in Red Hook, I ordered a Schaefers and a shot of whiskey. I don't even remember drinking them they went down so fast. I ordered another. I thought about the two Russians that I had killed. It wasn't the killing that bothered me; it was that I didn't care that I had murdered them.

"It's not really *killing*," the cousin of my limousine buddy Allie Bettino had told me months ago, "it's *shortening*." Allie's cousin, Jimmy, was a low-grade button man for the mob. Someday, he might be able to murder somebody that was a big-shot. He brought up his strange philosophy over too many beers at Dowling's Oyster Bar after we all had gone to a Dodgers game.

Jimmy had asked me point blank if I had killed any Krauts during World War II. While I hadn't killed any Germans *during* the war, I didn't clarify that, saying, "Yeah."

"How'd it feel?" he asked.

"Not good," I lied. It didn't feel *bad*, but it didn't feel good. It just didn't feel at all.

"Well, the way I look at it is this," Jimmy had said. "Nobody lives forever, right?"

"Right," I had said.

"So everybody dies. When you kill a guy, he's gonna die anyway. All you did was take a few years away from him. The guys that get whacked usually deserve having a few years taken away from them. But, you never know, maybe a bus woulda killed the guy anyways. So, you're taking fewer years away than you figured, right?"

"Right," I had said. Somewhere Socrates was flinching.

Both of those Russians were in their thirties, so I took about thirty years away from each guy. Them being Russian spies might not be the best recipe for a long life, so I might have taken just twenty years away from each guy. I didn't kill them, according to Jimmy, I just took some years away. Unless they both got hit by a bus. Then I would just be taking away a few less years. Socrates just had a spasmodic lurch.

In the Puerto Rican bar in Red Hook, I had put a twenty on the bar and drank until it was gone. I couldn't have drunk the full twenty. I must have bought some drinks for the house, but I don't remember. When the twenty was gone, I put down another. That I remember. It was about that time when Rafael walked in.

Gil Hodges, Andy Pafko and Rube Walker all hit homers to put the game away for the Dodgers. The Giants played like bums. They had five errors. They also fanned every time in the clutch. In the third inning, when the game was still close, the Giants had the bases loaded. Their hottest hitter was at the plate, Bobby Thomson. One swing of his bat and the Giants would have the lead. Labine struck him out on a 3-2 pitch. I remember one of the Puerto Ricans saying, "He's a bum, da' bum." How quickly our new citizens adapt.

The game was delayed by rain for about an hour, but that didn't delay our drinking.

The Dodgers ended up winning ten to nothing, but I don't remember the end of the game. I was going to drive home. I asked Rafael to help me find my car. He agreed, but the last thing I remember from that night was walking up three flights of steps to his apartment and falling onto his couch.

42

Wednesday, October 3, 1951

The angel's face hovered over me as if I was a fallen statue lying on the ground. The angel tilted her head and looked and then craned her head and looked from a slightly different angle. I looked back, but my head was locked down. If I moved it, I thought it might fall off.

"He's alive," the angel said. "I saw him blink."

I remembered her face. I remembered her body as she had leaned over to look at my face. She was wearing short shorts and a small halter top that pushed her breasts just short of the point of launching.

I couldn't remember her name. She was Rafael's chiquita.

Dolores. That was it. Dolores.

Rafael walked into my sight with a cup of coffee. He reached to hand the cup to me. I pulled myself up slightly; the room started to spin.

"You're gonna miss the Dodger game," he said, still holding the cup of coffee in front of me.

"What?"

"The Dodger game," he said, "it starts in a half-hour."

"What time is it?"

"Twelve thirty, man, you've been sleeping like the dead all morning."

I swung my feet out on to the floor and held on until the room slowed its spin to a manageable level. I couldn't miss the

Dodger game. It was the third and last game of the playoffs. Whoever won played the Yankees in the World Series.

Even though I probably could have pinched a couple of tickets from somebody, I hadn't been planning on actually going to the game. I would get too nervous. And, I wasn't going to watch it in a bar. I was living that lesson from last night. I'd go home and watch the game on my Admiral sixteen incher. Almost as good as being there. During the game, maybe I'd have a little bit of the hair of the dog to take the edge off. Heck, I needed some of that hair right now.

"You gotta beer?" I asked.

"Sure, boss," Rafael said. Dolores got me the beer and was back in a flash. I started to feel some life in me just watching her walk toward me with the beer. She then told Rafael that she had to go to work. I watched her walk to the door, open it and then disappear into the hallway.

Beer in the morning smells just awful. I felt like pinching my nose as I took two healthy slugs from the beer. I took a sip of coffee. I took another slug of beer. I bummed a cigarette off of Rafael. Nicotine, alcohol and caffeine were enough juice to lay a spark in my system. I didn't feel much better, but at least I felt that I could navigate my way home.

"I gotta go, Rafael," I said.

"I'll take you to your car," he said.

"You know where it is?" I asked. I was having trouble remembering where I had left it.

"Yeah, just down the street from the bar. That's why I went in there last night. I saw your car. I told some kids to watch it. It'll be there."

I would have never found my car without Rafael. With him as my guide, I was putting the key into the ignition just ten minutes after I had finished the beer, coffee and a smoke.

I had driven two blocks when the engine started to sputter. The fuel gauge said empty. I didn't know if I had run the gas down to fumes or whether the kids that Rafael told to watch my car decided to siphon out some free gas. The last few days had been a cyclone and one of my top priorities wasn't to watch the fuel gauge.

I left the Ford on the side of the street. I'd take a bus. Or walk. Or hitch a ride. I just wanted to get home and watch the game.

The sky was full of dark rain clouds and it looked like the sky could bust open anytime. Instead of waiting for a bus, I decided to hoof it. It was only a couple of miles to my house. As lousy as I felt, the walk would probably burn off some of that beer that churned inside me like it was boiling. I'd just take Hicks Street straight from Red Hook to close to my doorstep on Middagh Street in Brooklyn Heights.

As I walked, the game had started and I didn't miss a pitch. Portable radios were all over the place. Store owners sat in front of their stores with the radio on. Cars driving by had just one thing on their radios—the Dodgers against the Giants at the Polo Grounds.

Red Barber's voice was carried by a green Chevy, which slowly rolled past me, then his voice was picked up by the red Ford then passed on to a blue Plymouth. The only noise that was constant was Red Barber.

With one out in the top of the first, Sal The Barber Maglie walked Pee Wee Reese. A cheer went up on Hicks Street. Then Maglie walked Duke Snider. A guy on the sidewalk told another guy, "Maglie must be feeling the pressure, he don't walk guys. The bum." Jackie Robinson then hit a single to score Pee Wee. One-nothing Dodgers at the end of the first.

Don Newcombe was on the mound for the Dodgers and he was throwing bullets. At the bottom of the second inning, however, Whitey Lockman of the Giants hit a single. Bobby Thomson was at the plate. Bobby Thomson hit a shot down the left field line. A sure double. The Giants would have runners on second and third. Thomson was barreling head down to second, but Lockman had pulled up at second. They ended up looking at each other like two deer caught in the headlights. Jackie Robinson got Thomson in a run-down. Willie Mays flied out, end of inning. Bobby Thomson was turning into a goat.

The Giants went down with no runs all the way to the seventh inning.

I got to my doorstep. I had sweated through my shirt and most of my slacks. The score was still one-nothing Dodgers. Surprisingly, Nick Salzano was waiting for me on my front stoop.

"Hey," I said, "watcha doin' here?"

"I couldn't go to the Polo Grounds," he said. "If we lost, I'd probably kill a few of those bastards over there. And, I couldn't go to a bar. So, I just came here, sat on your stoop, listening to the game on all of your neighbors' radios."

"Yeah, I know what you mean," I said. In a moment's time, Nick and I were like kids again, living and dying with the Dodgers. "C'mon in. We'll watch it on TV, as long as you promise not to throw a bottle through the picture."

Nick laughed.

I walked up to the front door; it was locked tighter than a drum. Hiromi must be out running an errand or wrapped in her own world of art in the attic-studio. I wondered if she was worried about me. Normally a tenant didn't worry about a landlord, but it seemed like we were skating past that relationship. Well, if she wasn't worried, then she'd be pissed. Probably both. And I was guilty as charged. Then I *would* know for sure that our relationship had changed.

I unlocked the door and asked Nick in. No sign of Hiromi.

I turned on the television. Since the game was at the Polo Grounds, the announcers for the game were the Giants' announcers. We'd have to listen to Russ Hodges, the play-by-play announcer for the Giants. That was like listening to a dentist's drill. I'd like to listen to Red Barber and Vin Scully, but they were on radio. My Admiral television console had a radio, but I couldn't play the radio and the TV at the same time. I didn't have a radio in the living room. We'd have to listen to those bastards. I then went to the kitchen and brought out a couple of Schaefers. I handed one to Nick, who was sitting on the big wing chair. I sat over on the chair by the bookcase, facing him and the front door.

"You've been busy," Nick said in the same tone somebody would say, "How're yuh doing."

"Always busy," I said, "maybe I'll relax a little if the Dodgers knock off the Giants."

Nick reached into his coat pocket and brought out a Colt Police Special. I was, of course, familiar with that type of weapon. I had two of them on my visit to the Russians. "Jake, I don't think you're gonna care who wins the Dodgers game."

43

Wednesday, October 3, 1951

I stared at Nick. What the hell was this? My brain was racing like crazy.

"What the fuck's with you?" I asked, pointing at the gun.

"You big dumb bastard," Nick said. He almost sounded sympathetic. His voice did sound sympathetic, but the Colt Police Special drained any sympathy from the words. "You held out on me, Jake. You shot pictures of those photos in the Ice Queen's safe."

"No I didn't," I said, lying, not knowing where Nick was going with this.

"*Jake, don't lie to me now,*" Nick yelled. "I know you did. You identified Ingmar Swensen from his picture, didn't you?"

In the bottom of the seventh, the Dodgers still held that one run lead. Then the Giants Monte Irvin opened the inning with a double. Here I was, my boyhood buddy holding a gun on me threatening to shoot me and we both amazingly let our attention drift to Russ Hodges' descriptions. We both listened to the Giants announcer as if time suspended. That was okay by me. I needed to collect my thoughts. I didn't care who was holding a gun on me— boyhood buddy or somebody else—that wasn't a good sign. I needed to stall. I needed to find a way to reach around to the bookshelf behind me, remove the books, push the back of the bookshelf and retrieve the gun hidden there. I wasn't going to be able to do that in the blink of an eye. I needed some ruse for Nick to allow me to reach for a book. The game had to be the ruse. Maybe, just *maybe*, I could retrieve the gun before a bullet blew off my head.

Whitey Lockman sacrificed Irvin to third. Bobby Thomson was up again. He hit a high fly to Duke Snider in dead center. Irvin scored easily. Then Newcombe got out of the inning. Score tied at the end of the seventh.

Nick and I looked at each other again. I had had a little bit of time to come up with an answer about the pictures. I figured that lying wouldn't work. I'd just tell Nick the truth. What was he going to do, shoot me?

"So, big fucking deal, I took pictures of the pictures," I said.

"The dumb bitch left those photos in her safes," Nick said. "You were sent in to get the Ice Queen's *list*. The dumb bitch wasn't supposed to have the pictures there. They were supposed to be off her premises, someplace safer. And those drawings of the bomb! Jesus Christ! Commies are one thing, but plans of bombs are another thing. Those were old plans—*ancient* plans—the bitch was just keeping them around as a memento. Anybody that wants to build an Atomic bomb already has the plans, including the North Koreans. But the *list*, the famous list, was left out for you to find. *The fucking list was just sitting there on her desk.* Were you blind? Should it have had a bow on it or something? Are you an idiot or something? Why didn't you just pick up the fucking list?"

That was a good question. How could Hiromi and I not have spotted something just lying on the desk? I figured that the Ice Queen had really screwed up; she hid the list off premise and kept the photos in the safe and then lied to Nick. Nick was right; she was a dumb bitch. But, it looked like I was going to pay for her mistake. The price was a bullet between my eyes.

"Why did you want *me* to find the list?" I asked, stalling.

"Well, Jake, it all started with our operation at the United Nations—which I know you know about."

322

"You're involved with that? How?"

"I *invented* it, Jake, I *invented* it," Nick said. He was talking like he was pulling a practical joke like when we were kids, but we weren't kids anymore and I knew it wasn't any practical joke. He wouldn't be saying "Gotcha" anytime soon. "I've known Arabella since we were teenagers. You think she just learned that she liked to fuck? I used to screw her every week when I was fifteen. My Dad used to screw her mother. Hell, *your* Dad screwed her mother."

"What are you talking about?" I said. I started to get up.

"Sit back, Jake, or I'll use this, I will," he said. This was not the Nick that I knew as a kid; it wasn't the Nick that was like a twin brother to me growing up.

In the top of the eighth, the Dodgers Pee Wee Reese singled off of Maglie. Nick and I stopped to listen and watch the game again. Then Duke Snider singled sending Pee Wee to third. Maglie then did something out of character—he threw a wild pitch. Pee Wee scored. Dodgers up by one. Nick said, "*Yeah!*" Nick was still a fan. Was this the moment I could dive for the gun? I sat there.

"Easy," Nick said. He must have sensed that I was going to do *something*. "Just sit there and watch the fucking game."

"Nick, look at us," I said, "you've got a gun on me and we're watching the Dodger game. Put down the gun, let's crack a couple of beers and we'll talk about the Ice Queen and the Swede and all that shit after the game."

"Shut the fuck up, Jake!" Nick yelled. "I could kill you now, but you at least deserve to find out if the Dodgers beat those fucking Giants."

Maglie intentionally walked Jackie Robinson. Andy Pafko then got a scratch single off of Bobby Thomson's glove at third, scoring Snider. Dodgers up by two runs. Billy Cox then singled past Thomson into left field. Robinson scored. Dodgers up by three runs, leading four to one. Maglie got Rube Walker to end the inning.

How strange was all of this? Sal Maglie was the best clutch pitcher in baseball and he tossed a wild pitch to let in the go-ahead run; third baseman Bobby Thomson let a couple of balls get through that he should have had; my boyhood pal was going to kill me on the last out. Only six more outs and the Dodgers win the pennant. On that last out, I was going to be a dead man.

"I'll explain," Nick said, picking up the conversation like we were kids and had just taken a moment to watch a good looker sashay down the sidewalk, hips swinging like there was a bongo beat. "Sit back and relax, I'll tell you the whole story. Our fathers used to go to the same workers meetings together—specifically the meetings of International Workers Order."

"Yeah, he told me about them. He told me it was the Laborers Progressive Committee, something like that, but it was no big deal, a lot of guys went."

"You're right, on the surface it wasn't a big deal. The Laborers Progressive Committee was the first step. The real organization was International Workers Order. IWO was and is the Communist fraternal organization—it's sorta like a Reds version of Kiwanis. They also have classes for the kids—sorta like catechism for Catholics. This organization isn't just to rant and rave—it's to educate the adults *and* the kids. So, our fathers used to go. There was a rich wannabe Commie from Manhattan who used to come— Victoria Van Dyck. In case you couldn't guess, that was Arabella's mother. Victoria was beautiful like Arabella—maybe even more so, but it was difficult for me to judge an older woman when I was just a kid. Victoria liked to go with the guys after the meetings to have some beers. She'd pair off with one guy after a meeting, fuck him blind, then after the next meeting she'd pair off with another guy and fuck *him* blind. With some guys, she'd screw blind four, five, ten straight weeks and then she'd switch. One thing was consistent: she would screw *somebody* after every meeting she attended. That kept attendance up, wouldn't you think?

"My father was at least a ten-timer. Your father was about the same. The interesting thing was that Victoria started to bring her fifteen-year-old daughter to the meetings and my old man started to bring me. Your old man, however, didn't want you to attend the meetings. I remember my old man pleading with your old man to bring you so that you and I could hang out together. No way! Your old man kept going to the meetings not for what was being said, but to screw Victoria. Not a bad reason, but not a really pure Communist reason was it? When she wouldn't have anything more to do with him, he stopped coming to the meetings. Not a very dedicated Communist; no, not very dedicated at all."

The bottom of the eighth went quickly. The Dodgers Don Newcombe was a horse out on the mound. He struck out Bill Rigney, batting for Wes Westrum. Hank Thompson, batting for Maglie, squibbed one back to the mound for an easy out. Newc struck out Eddie Stanky to end the inning. Three up, three down. The Giants—and I—had three outs left.

"Your dad was just there to screw Victoria," Nick said.

My Dad hadn't filled in the spaces between the lines about his attendance at the meetings. But, what father would tell his son that he went to the meetings so he could pork this beautiful and horny Commie lady?

"Anyways, after Arabella and I started to go to the meetings, we'd hang out on the streets when her mother was boffing somebody in a car. Arabella gave me my first blow job. In an alley. I was just standing there against a brick wall and she pulled my drawers down and sucked me until I thought my teeth were going to be sucked out through my cock. Then the next time she gave me my first piece of ass. Like mother, like daughter, I guess. I was going to tell you about it—about how you could boff this fine thing—but my old man swore me to secrecy because your old man wasn't a true Commie. Think how difficult it was for me not to tell you—my best friend—that I was getting blow jobs? But, you know my old man. He woulda killed me if I breathed a word."

"So, you've been screwing the Ice Queen for a long time," I said. I was still thinking about the bookcase. How could I ever dive for the bookshelf, push open the trap door, grab the Colt and shoot at Nick? I needed something big to happen to do that.

The Giants Alvin Dark led off the bottom of the ninth with a single off of Gil Hodges glove. Nick leaned closer to the television. Don Mueller, the singles hitter, got, what else, a single to right. Russ Hodges told us that the Giants fans that were leaving were coming back to their seats. The next big play I would have to make my move.

We could hear the groans of the fans on the radio as Monte Irvin popped out. One out; two outs to go for the Dodgers. Two outs to go for me. I had to make my move. Left-hand batter Whitey Lockman laced one over third base close to the left field line. Alvin Dark scored easily. Mueller went into third, half-standing half-sliding, indecisive whether he should have turned that third base corner and ran like a maniac to the plate. I dove for the bookshelf. Before my hand reached the wood panel, the panel erupted into splinters from a bullet. I yanked my hand back as if it had touched a blowtorch.

Nick laughed. "You got a gun hidden back there, pal?"

I was on my knees in front of the bookshelf.

"*Get back into that chair,*" Nick said. "We're gonna see the rest of this game!"

Mueller had wrecked his ankle with his indecisive base running. He was on the ground as if *he* had been shot. They were going to take him off on a stretcher.

"More important than the pussy," Nick said, picking up the conversation before that bang-bang play, "I became a dedicated Communist. When I say 'dedicated', I really mean it—Communism is more important to me than anything. I studied history in college, not because I gave a shit about George

Washington or Alexander the Great, but to study why Communism would last the test of time. It's the *only* system that can. Your so-called democracy doesn't have any lasting power, Jake, because it's based on one thing—greed.

"I then studied law. It was there that I met some Russians—not just American Communists, but the real McCoy. That was an important link—me meeting Russian Communists that I could trust. A few years later, I thought of an idea that could change the world. My idea needed my energy, my Russian connections and Arabella to pull it off. It wouldn't be secret meetings with rants and raves from the working stiffs. My plan would be bigger. It would be the beginning of the end of democracy. The idea became crystal clear when FDR embraced the United Nations and wanted it to be based in New York City, our backyard.

"I used Arabella to lure special diplomats that were on the Security Council at the United Nations. My friend Bogdan Karakadymov—who I know you killed yesterday morning—identified for me which diplomat would be susceptible to the Ice Queen and which one would have information that would be useful to us."

"So, with this inside information," I asked, "you thought that Korea could win the war against us, the United States?"

Nick laughed. "There's no way that North Korea could win a war against the United States," Nick said. "But, with our help, we could *extend* the war, we could make it much more costly for the United States, we could make this a ten-year war, we could make it very unpopular here. All this helps Russia in advancing the Communist cause."

I guessed that I should have paid more attention in my civics class in high school. I didn't get what Nick was talking about.

"This is getting a little sickening, Nick, listening to you about your Commie ways," I said. "What do you want from me? Or are you just going shoot me dead right here?"

They had carted Don Mueller off the field on a stretcher. Clint Hartung went in to run for him. Everything was going in slow motion. The Dodgers manager Charlie Dressen walked to the mound like it was a death march. Pee Wee Reese, Jackie Robinson and Rube Walker joined him. They talked to Don Newcombe. It looked like they said five words between them.

"I would like to shoot you right here, right now, and I just might, but I thought we should have this little talk first and at least for old times' sake you should know whether the Dodgers win the pennant or not. I know you've talked to your old commander *Wild Bill* Donovan," Nick said, laying the sarcasm on pretty thick on the Wild Bill part. "Who else have you talked to?"

"Answer me a question first, and then I'll give you your answer, the complete answer," I said. The only hope I had was that there would be a big play. I wouldn't go for the gun in the bookcase. I would go right at Nick like some bull after the matador. The problem with that was that the bull always died.

"Okay, shoot," he said and laughed. "I guess I'm the one that will shoot, but go ahead, ask your question."

"I don't understand Joe McCarthy's part in this fool thing. Is Joe involved in all this? And the list thing, why send me in to get the list from the Ice Queen? You could've just given the list to Joe—you didn't need me. Why was the list important?"

"That's *three* questions, not that I was counting," Nick said, smiling, "but they're all related, so I'll count them as one. I had started to do work for Joe about a year ago. It was the perfect place to be. He was chasing shadows. Actually, he didn't give a fuck what he was chasing as long as he got publicity. However, there was always a chance he would stumble—and I mean stumble, the old drunk—on to something real. Where better to be than on the inside of Tailgunner Joe's operation? But the United Nations operation was the important thing. The North Koreans were fed a lot of information that helped them neutralize the United States. Joe McCarthy was a *diversion*—something that would make a lot of press—but that would produce *nothing*. If I gave him the right names, I knew that Joe would eventually self destruct. The way to end the red scare—the scare about Communism in America—is to debunk, to ridicule, to shame the giant of Communist haters, none other than our Tailgunner Joe."

"Arabella already had the Red reputation so why not use it to our advantage? We put together that list—a lot of media types, some are indeed Communists, some just strongly left, some just schmucks—and we wanted Joe to know that it was acquired illegally. That gave it credibility—somebody *breaking in* and *stealing* the list. Joe would like that. Voila, who comes to my mind but my old buddy from the old neighborhood."

"I knew that you had been a Red Chaser for Wild Bill Donovan, that you were a private dick doing the seamy thing to break up marriages. Jake, you were the absolute *perfect* guy for the job. And Joe loves you to boot! That list was wonderfully created. We had a lot of media folks on that list that would fight back, and had the wherewithal to fight back and win."

"I put your old man's name on the list—that was my 'gotcha.' I saw that you didn't include that page when you handed the list over to us. Anyways, all the time that Joe would be chasing shadows and making a fool of himself in public, we're making out like bandits at the United Nations. Where we screwed up was that stupid bitch Arabella left the pictures in the safe. Dumb bitch. And then you had to—just *had* to try to track down those faces to see who those schmucks were. If you wouldn't have taken that step, my friend, we wouldn't be here having this conversation and old Roberta would be working at the library today."

"*You* killed her?"

Bobby Thomson was at the plate. He was destined to be the goat of the playoffs. He did that bonehead play in the second when he almost ran into the baserunner in front of him and was tagged out. Then he let two grounders get through him in the eighth. He should have had both of them. Now he came to the plate with men on second and third with one out. Dressen decided to take Newcombe out. He waived in Ralph Branca from the bullpen.

As Branca took that long walk in from the left field bullpen, Nick said, "That bum, he lost to the Giants two days ago. He gives up too many homers."

Branca took his warm-up pitches. We watched.

"You asked me about Roberta," Nick said. It was amazing how he could keep a conversation going. "That's an extra question, but I'll answer it. Of course I did," Nick said. "I hired that old detective to follow you…"

"He told me that it was the Ice Queen."

"Well, it was, if you want to get technical about it, but I found the old guy, I orchestrated it. I just wanted to keep a tail on you. When the old guy said you met with Roberta and that you gave her an envelope, I started to smell a rat. Call it paranoia, but paranoia is the best tool to make sure things don't go wrong. So, the night you were in DC—we fucked up here; we thought your meeting was the *next* day, and their job was to kill you *before* you got to Donovan…"

"You ordered those guys not to just rough me up, but to *kill* me?"

Nick shrugged. "Yeah, when I found out that you were going to Washington, D.C., I figured it wasn't to see me or Joe McCarthy. Who else would you be seeing, I thought? Wild Bill Donvan, most likely. I figured that you had found out more than you should have. You had to die, Roberta had to die, Wolfemeyer had to die—we had to close that loop. It was as simple as that. With you dead, I could always 'find' the Ice Queen's List at your house. Joe woulda loved that—you gave up your life in the fight against Communism. He woulda made you a hero on the television."

"The Russians were going to take you out. I was in New York, so I went to see Roberta at her apartment. You weren't the only guy that used to go to the library you know, although you were her favorite, which was for sure. I told her that you told me to pick up the information for you. She didn't believe me. I guess she never liked me. So, I pushed myself in her apartment, tried to talk sense to her, shook her a little bit, but I killed her—by accident, I swear. She was just a brittle bag of bones. I never did find out what that old biddy was doing for you. But then, two days ago, you told me."

"I told you?"

"You roughed up Ingmar Swensen. Did you think he wouldn't tell anybody about it? He described you to a 'tee'. FBI, huh? Where'd you get the badge—the five-and-ten? What a dumb bastard that Swensen is. But, he's just a scared diplomat; what does he know about dime store badges?"

"So why did the Ice Queen then finally give me the list at Dempsey's?"

"Why not?" Nick said. "I thought I might as well follow through with the original plan—you giving the list to Tailgunner Joe. Then I'd have taken care of you."

"You were willing to have me killed without knowing what I knew?"

"Sorry, pal, that's the way this game is played."

Branca was ready to pitch to Thomson. Willie Mays was in the on-deck circle. Branca's first pitch to Thomson was right down the pike—served on a platter—and Thomson took it for a strike. Everybody at the ballpark, and me and Nick watching on TV—even with Nick holding a gun pointed at me—knew that Thomson should have jumped on that pitch. It was a meatball. The next pitch was high and inside. Thomson swung. Thomson connected; I heard the crack of the bat on the ball. I dove at Nick.

The sound of the gun firing was as loud as if the gun had been fired right next to my ear. I, however, didn't topple over. Nick did. The bullet hit him in the left temple, catapulting him further into the living room, face down on the floor.

Hiromi stepped in from the foyer. She held the Colt 45 in both hands. I didn't even know that she had been standing in the foyer. Neither had Nick. She always could walk as quietly as a ghost, even in a house that had creaky wood floors.

44

Wednesday, October 3, 1951

Hiromi bent over and carefully set the gun on the floor. So polite, these Japanese.

Then she ran to my arms. I opened my arms and she jolted into me and I closed my arms and held her tight. I was glad that I had something to hold onto; my hands would have been a quivering mess if I didn't have Hiromi to hold onto.

Somehow cutting into my consciousness was Russ Hodges, the Giants TV announcer, "The Giants win the pennant! The Giants win the pennant! The Giants win the pennant. The Giants win the pennant, the Giants win the pennant! Bobby Thomson hits into the lower deck of the left-field stands! The Giants win the pennant! And they're going crazy! They're going crazy! Oh-ho..."

I tried to blot out everything that Hodges was saying.

Everything had happened so fast. I had not seen Hiromi creep down the stairs. Nor, of course, had Nick. She told me that she had heard the gunshot, that she had crept downstairs, that she had been standing there for a couple of minutes—she had heard Nick talk about how he had become a Communist, how he and the Ice Queen had trapped those poor men that worked at the United Nations. She had never met Nick before, but she knew that he had been a long-time friend of mine; she wondered why Nick was holding a gun on me. She realized that Nick was going to kill his long-time friend. That's when she decided that she had to pull the trigger, she had to kill him. She couldn't warn him and tell him, like in the movies, "Drop the gun." To do that, she would have to trust her voice. She would have to trust herself to hold the gun firm. She would have to trust herself to pull the trigger when he was facing her. She didn't think that she could do that in a face off. But, if she didn't do something, she knew that Nick was going to kill me.

"I didn't think," Hiromi said. "I just pulled the trigger. I couldn't let him kill you."

She snuggled her head close into my neck. Her face was wet from crying. I held her tight and stroked her back with my hands. I held her that way for a long, long time. Hiromi tilted her head up. I put my hand on her chin. I leaned down and kissed her forehead. I then kissed her lips. She kissed back. I then held her hard and firm to my body. I don't know how long we stood there, but eventually we let go of each other. There, on the floor, was the dead body of Nick Salzano. It was like the dead body hadn't been there as we had stood, clutching each other, trying to shore up our nerves. But, it was there. It wasn't going to go away by itself.

I held Hiromi's hand and walked her to the kitchen. I put water in the coffeepot and turned on the burner on the stove. I waited for it to boil, Hiromi's hand in mine, and led her to the dinette table. When the coffeepot boiled, I made two cups of Green Tea and brought them over to the table.

We sat drinking our Green Tea. I don't know what Hiromi was thinking; I was thinking about how to get rid of the body.

Calling the police was out of the question. If I did, it would probably be difficult to prove that Nick was shot in self defense of me. What would the story be: A Jap from an Internment Camp murdering one of Joe McCarthy's most trusted aides? That wouldn't play. Most likely, Hiromi would face a murder charge. There was a huge risk. I wouldn't let us take that risk.

Dominic, I was sure, knew how to dispose of bodies. But, Nick was a neighborhood kid, a neighborhood kid that had done good, working for the famous Joe McCarthy no less. Dominic might have as many questions as the cops. And, if he helped dispose of the body—probably right around the vicinity in Red Hook where I dumped my clothes in the river—that would certainly involve the mob.

I thought of the Nazis that I had killed and buried in Europe. That wouldn't work here. I just couldn't dig a hole in my small backyard and plant Nick there.

I dismissed the thought of me and Hiromi disposing of the body. Right now, she was tiptoeing around the borderline of entering shock. I didn't want her to plunge headfirst past the borderline. She needed to drink her Green Tea and put some space in her mind away from Nick's corpse.

All these options were swirling in my mind as Hiromi and I drank Green Tea. There was one other option. Chet Morgan. He was CIA, he was *shadow* CIA; he knew what to do with dead bodies that needed to disappear. I had planned on calling him anyway after I had sweated the Swede, and tell him the whole story about the Ice Queen, her extortion racket, the United Nations, the Russians, everything. But, things had happened too fast—it was one sequence crammed tightly against the next—until now when time was standing still. Now, of course, I knew even more about the United Nations spy network thanks to Nick, the now dead Nick.

I walked over to the kitchen phone. I retrieved Chet's business card from my wallet. I dialed his private number. The last time I dialed it I was going to have lunch with the Ice Queen, and he wasn't there to take my call and advise me. I got a weird sound from the phone. It wasn't a busy signal coming from Morgan's phone. It was more like a whirling whine. I dialed again. I got the same sound. Could the phone system be overloaded? Yeah, I almost forgot that the Giants beat the Dodgers; the phones were probably jammed to the gills with everybody in Brooklyn calling everybody else crying about Bobby Thomson's home run.

I dialed again. The same sound again. I sat down and drank some Green Tea.

I tried dialing every minute. Finally, after about twenty minutes, Morgan's phone rang twice. Chet Morgan said hello.

"This is Jake," I said.

"Jesus, everything's going nuts," he said. "What's it like out in Brooklyn?"

I only knew two things: Bobby Thomson had killed the Dodgers and Nick was dead on my livingroom floor.

"I need to see you. Right now, at my house."

"What's wrong?" he said. It didn't take a trained CIA agent to tell that things weren't right, that it was more than Bobby Thomson's home run.

"I need to see you."

"Can you talk?" he said. Maybe he thought somebody was holding a gun to my head or something.

"Yes, I can, but I need to see you right now. When can you get here?"

"I'm in the City right now. I can be there in twenty minutes—depending on traffic."

Normally, most people at this time of day would be heading home from a full day at work. Today, I would think a lot of folks were in bars. Giants fans would probably stay in bars, celebrating. Dodger fans would probably stay in bars, crying in their beers. Traffic wouldn't have been bad going over the Brooklyn Bridge on a normal workday. Now it would probably be less.

"I'll be here," I said and hung up.

Twenty minutes later Chet's car pulled up in front of my house. He and Gonski got out of the car. I was waiting for them on the stoop. Two houses down, there was a smashed radio on the sidewalk. There were a few people on the street walking around like those zombies in the b-movies.

Hiromi was inside, sitting at the dinette table, sipping her Green Tea. We had talked in those twenty minutes that it took

Morgan to get here. I was heartened, and a little surprised, at her resiliency. Her tears had dried, the color in her face had returned.

"I don't feel bad about killing your Nick," she had told me. She used the possessive in attaching Nick to me. He really wasn't mine, but we had been friends since kids.

"I am not crying for him," she continued. "I am not crying because I pulled the trigger on the gun. I cried because what *could* have happened if I wouldn't have pulled the trigger on the gun. I would have lost you. That's why my tears came."

I put my hand on hers.

"I won't put you in that position again," I said. "I've been thinking about it for quite awhile. I'm getting out of the private detective business."

Her eyes looked up, right in my eyes. "What would you do?"

Hiromi didn't know that I had enough money to burn half of it and not even miss it while I was doing nothing but living a life of the Brooklyn Dodgers and beer. But, I did, of course, have something in mind, something that would involve both me and her.

"I'll tell you later today," I said, "right after I see Chet Morgan."

I invited Chet Morgan to sit on one of the steps on the stoop. He sat. Gonski grunted a bit as he lowered himself on to another step.

I told Chet everything. I told him how it all started with Tailgunner Joe and Nick Salzano and me over at Dowling's Oyster Bar. He took some notes, but mostly he listened.

I told them about breaking into the Ice Queen's.

I told them about my boarder, Hiromi Kitahara, and how she learned to open locks faster that people could with a key.

I told them about the pictures that the Ice Queen had in her safe. I had the pictures in an envelope at my side and slid the photos out and showed them. Chet didn't say anything; Gonski muttered *shit* when he saw Tailgunner Joe on the Ice Queen.

I told them about Rafael—my associate—and how he followed the Russians. I even told them about Rafael's 'associate,' Dolores.

I told them about Ingmar Swensen. I pulled his picture out of the pile. "That's the Swede," I said, "Ingmar Swensen."

I told them about the Russians, that I had killed Ivan Bogachov and Bogdan Karakadymov. Chet raised his eyebrows. I don't think that he had heard that two KGB agents had been killed. Hell, they had probably already been replaced.

I then started to tell them about Nick.

"Joe McCarthy's guy?" Chet asked.

I nodded.

I then told them how he had been the mastermind of the United Nations spy ring and how he was using that information in the Korean War. I told them about how Nick had been raised essentially as a Communist, and that he had befriended some Reds when he was in law school. I told them that the Ice Queen's mother was a socialite Red. I didn't tell them about my Dad boffing the Ice Queen's mother.

Lastly, I told them that Nick was dead.

I told them that Nick had showed up late this afternoon to kill me. He knew that I knew about the United Nations spy ring because I had sweated the Swede. As Nick and I had sat in my living room, Nick told me that he was the one that had murdered Roberta and the ancient detective Richard Wolfemeyer. I told them why. I also told them Nick had explained to me how it all had come together, and that Russia wanted to turn the Korean War into a long drawn out expensive divisive fiasco for the United States.

I told them that just before Nick was going to pull the trigger that Hiromi, standing in the foyer unseen by Nick and me, pulled the trigger and killed him with one shot.

"Where'd she get the gun?" Gonski asked.

"I've got guns," I said. "I've got plenty of guns in the house."

They nodded; somehow it sounded logical to them that I would have a small arsenal in the house.

"Well, Jake," Chet said, "let's go inside."

As soon as they stepped in to the house, they saw Nick was splayed out on the livingroom floor. They walked over to take a closer look.

"A bullet in the temple," Gonski said. "He woulda been dead before he hit the floor. Good shot."

I took them to the kitchen.

Hiromi was still in the kitchen at the dinette table. I introduced her to the two CIA agents. She bowed. Always polite, these Japanese. She looked so slight, but she didn't look weak. She had regained her composure. I guess that the Internment Camp had been pretty good training in handling tough situations.

We all sat down at the table. I made them some coffee; they weren't Green Tea guys.

When we all had something hot in front of us to drink, Chet asked Hiromi, "You shot that man in the living room?"

"Yes," she said in a clear voice. She was prepared for an interrogation. I wondered if she had had practice with those types of things in the Internment Camp. Yes, she probably did.

"You fired just one shot?" Chet asked.

"Yes."

"Was he going to kill Jake?" Chet asked.

"Yes."

Chet then looked at me. "If it wasn't for Wild Bill's belief in you, we wouldn't be able to do what we're going to do," he said. I guess that was the end of the interrogation of Hiromi. Three questions; three yeses. That was it.

"We'll dispose of the body," Chet said. Then he turned to Gonski and said, "Call Ronnie right now. Have them get a cleanup crew over here right away. When it gets dark, I want to take the body out the back way. Take the carpet—we'd never be able to get the blood out—and have them clean the floor out there like it was brand new. Make the call right now. You can use the livingroom phone."

Gonski walked to the living room. I heard him talking. The phone lines in Brooklyn must be back to normal. I wondered when Brooklyn would be, if ever.

"Jake, I'll want all the pictures and all the negatives from the Ice Queen," Chet said. "I'll want all the pictures and all the negatives that your Puerto Rican 'associate' took—the Russians, the Swede, the Ice Queen the whole works. I want those before I leave the house." I would be glad to give him all that. I might even throw in a couple pictures of Dolores.

"We're going to jump on this right away," Chet said. "I'm sure that Wild Bill will want to talk to you about this personally. So, figure on coming down to Washington, D.C. in the next couple of days or so. Figure on a couple of hours with Bill, that's all it would take. Bring Hiromi with you—you'll have time to sightsee a little. Let her see the White House. Hell, Bill could even get you a tourist pass."

I held Hiromi's hand. She squeezed mine.

"This is where we take over," Chet said. "I want you, Jake, in case you haven't figured it out, to walk away from all this. You're out of it completely, right?"

Hiromi squeezed my hand again.

"Right," I said.

"Okay. Now you can do two things for me tonight," Chet said.

"Sure, what?"

"Get me all those pictures and negs, every one of them."

"No problem." I said, getting up from the table.

"And, right after that," Chet said, "go take this lovely little lady out for a nice dinner someplace."

I looked at him.

"I don't want you around the house when we take Nick out the back door," Chet said. "You're finished with this case—now and forever—so let us do our work. You, you take Hiromi out for dinner, come back around ten or so. You'll have a new rug on your livingroom floor—it might not be your taste—but you can buy something different later on. You come back into your house at ten, Jake, we won't be here, and none of this stuff happened. Understand?"

I nodded.

Hiromi went upstairs to get refreshed and changed. I went downstairs and got the negatives. I put them in the envelope with the pictures. I looked at the pictures of Dolores. I dropped them into the envelope.

Within fifteen minutes Hiromi and I were walking out the front door. We weren't dressed to the nines like we were when we went to the Stork Club.

Neither one of us looked toward the living room. We were going on a date. Since this wasn't really job related like the dinner at the Stork Club this might be considered our first date. We didn't look very happy, but, hell, *nobody* in Brooklyn looked happy. Having dinner in some diner would be like having dinner in a morgue.

I clasped her hand in mine. "Let's go," I said, and we stepped out into a Brooklyn night.

Epilogue

Thursday, August 21, 1952

The next day Charlie had driven Hiromi and me out to Idlewild Airport.

We got on the Stratocruiser flight that would take us to San Francisco. First class, of course. I had told Hiromi that she could take just one suitcase and plenty of painting supplies. We'd buy everything else we needed.

It was a long flight to San Francisco. Then we had to wait around the San Francisco airport for another hour. We were tired when we got back on the plane. This time it was an eight-hour flight to Honolulu.

We spent two weeks on Waikiki Beach. I actually got a sun tan. This Irish-German skin of mine accepted the sun, with liberal amounts of suntan lotion, to produce a tan that wouldn't embarrass a surfer. Hiromi, always the modest one, surprisingly bought a swim suit that I could crumple up and make it disappear into my fist. It left just the slightest part of her body white—just a slim line over her breasts that barely covered her nipples and a slim line around her more private parts below—the rest was a golden tan. It was a great contrast, the slim lines of white on a body of tan. I know—I had seen it in its entirety.

Hiromi had done no painting in Honolulu. She hadn't even unpacked her brushes and paint. We lounged around the pool. We made attempts at surfing—Hiromi must have been more athletic than me because she could ride a small wave for about thirty feet before plunging. We had exotic dinners. We made love most every afternoon. And most nights.

We took a boat over to Kahalui, Maui. Maui was far different than Honolulu. There were still a lot of American jeeps and equipment leftover by the Navy after World War II. We rented one of those jeeps and drove over to a small town, Lahaina, on the western side of Maui. The road was winding and sometimes scary in parts as it edged around cliffs. It took us four hours to reach Lahaina. However, they were building a new road that would link Kahalui to Lahaina. In fact, they were blasting out a tunnel that would make the drive a lot easier. That would be finished sometime later this year.

Lahaina had been an old whaling town. It wasn't difficult to visualize what it had looked like fifty years before. The town now was exactly the same. The old pictures showed the storefronts and the bars the same as they did as we walked down the sidewalk. We stayed at the Pioneer Inn, an old hotel that if we listened carefully we could hear the echoes of the ghosts of old whalers shouting drunken epitaphs to a time gone by.

In Lahaina, Hiromi started to paint again. She'd set up across from the Pioneer Inn under this old banyan tree that had probably been there since time began. I walked around the small town while Hiromi was painting.

On one of my little sojourns through Lahaina, I found a string of five buildings that was for sale. Each building was a two-story job with a store on the first floor and living quarters on the second. It was on the ocean side of the street at the north end of town. I inquired about the property. It was twenty-five thousand dollars. I had that. Hell, that was far less than what I had taken off of the Nazi Scheffler years ago. Twenty-five grand was a fortune; folks in Lahaina didn't think that anybody would be foolish enough to spend that type of money for what amounted to five shacks. I wrote a check for two-grand to buy it. It would take me about a week to get the rest of the money wired to me. I then became a landlord again—this time in Lahaina, Hawaii. And, I had the same boarder, Hiromi.

I was the new landlord to the shops and bars. I met the folks and told them that business would go on as usual. I didn't raise the rent and I signed leases if they wanted. The upstairs in three of the buildings had been used for storage. That's where we made some changes. We moved all the stuff out of there. One of the units we made into a big studio that overlooked the ocean. Another we made as a living room and dining room. The last one we made as a large bedroom and bathroom. The units were separate, but instead of knocking holes in the wall to make doorways, we built a large deck overhanging the waters below. That large deck became a delightful extension of our living quarters and served as our hallway going from unit to unit.

After six months, just after the start of the baseball season, we flew back to Brooklyn. We didn't rent out our living quarters in Lahaina. We'd be coming back.

I stopped by to see Dominic Gonnella. "You look like an Italian," he said, referring to my tan.

I saw that he still had the vacant storefront.

He saw me looking at it. "You want to rent it now?" he asked.

I nodded.

"For Hiromi's paintings?"

I nodded again.

"Fifty bucks a month."

That was cheap.

"Plus one painting every year," he said, smiling.

"Deal."

We sold one of Hiromi's paintings the first day we opened up. Then we sold another a week later. The Maui paintings became a magnet, so I raised the price on those to where nobody would buy one.

She had adopted a one name signature—Hiromi. One day, if a person had a '*Hiromi*,' we hoped that they would consider it something special. I felt the same way. I, of course, had the real McCoy, or in this case, the real, live Hiromi.

We were making a small profit off of the studio, and I didn't have to reach into my stash after I had paid Dominic the first month's rent in advance. A couple of socialites from Manhattan came over to our little gallery in Brooklyn and one of them snapped up one of the Maui paintings at an outrageously high price. That lady must have been using stolen money. But, then that shouldn't bother me.

Wild Bill Donovan had actually stopped by the art gallery one day. He had told me that he had been in New York on business. At least that's what he had told me. I got the impression that the business was me. Wild Bill was always recruiting.

"We could use you as a contract employee for special assignments," he had said.

I didn't ask him who I would contract with—the CIA or the shadow CIA.

It didn't make much difference to me. "General Donovan, I appreciate you thinking about me, but I run an art gallery now."

I thought I heard him say, "Good cover," but he might have just mumbled something about one of the paintings. He ended up buying one; he wouldn't let me present it to him as a gift.

I had gone to a few Dodgers games during the summer. They were in first place again. My passion for the Dodgers would never die. Sure, they got beat by Bobby Thomson's home run, but we'd win the pennant this year; I just knew it.

I even saw the owner of the Dodgers, Walter O'Malley, at one of the games I attended. I had done some private detecting work for him at one time—checking to see if one of his bit players was a big gambler. He had an usher fetch me and deliver me to his office.

The smoke in the office was as thick as the smoke in Dowling's Oyster Bar. There was a domed stadium model on a table in his office. I guessed the rumors had been true. O'Malley wanted to build a domed baseball stadium in Brooklyn.

"I'm having trouble with Bob Moses," he said. Moses was the politician that was so-called 'master builder' of New York City and Long Island.

I didn't say anything.

"I'm willing to build that domed stadium," O'Malley said, pointing to the model. "It'll cost me eight million bucks. Buckminster Fuller is the architect. But, I can't get Bob Moses to put the land in eminent domain. God, he wants me to build my dome out in Flushing Meadows. That's not Brooklyn! That's Queens! If the Dodgers ever have to move out of Brooklyn, don't blame me," he said, "blame Bob Moses."

I didn't like to even hear that. There should be *no* possibility of the Dodgers moving out of Brooklyn, Bob Moses or not.

He'd asked me if I would do some 'background check' on Bob Moses. Although he didn't say it, he wanted dirt, he wanted some leverage. I declined. I told him I ran an art gallery.

He said, "Oh." That ended the conversation. I went back to my seat, and had a beer.

Tailgunner Joe had not been faring very well. He'd gone after Edward R. Murrow of CBS television. Unlike the state department guys and movie script writers, Murrow could fight back. And did he! CBS allowed him to fire all barrels at Tailgunner Joe. He had Tailgunner Joe on the run.

Tailgunner Joe looked awful on television. He'd aged in just a year; he sweated like a pig, and I could tell the drinking was getting to him.

The other Red hater, the guy that actually put Reds away, Richard M. Nixon, was Dwight Eisenhower's running mate as vice president of the United States, five o'clock shadow and all. War hero Ike would be tough to beat. Maybe Wild Bill was right, maybe Nixon would one day be President of the United States. I doubted it, but stranger things have happened.

Chet Morgan called me on the phone. "Heard you were back," he said. "How about a coffee?"

We had coffee just down the street from the studio on a day the Dodgers weren't playing, Thursday, August 21, 1952.

He told me that his shadow CIA was now using the United Nations spy network. They used it to give bogus information to the Russians. The information wasn't completely bogus—if it was all bogus, the Russians would clearly smell a rat. He said that there was a lot of accurate stuff intertwined with the bullshit, but there was enough bogus to throw the North Koreans off and give the United States the edge. The war was starting to turn in the right direction for us. Because of that, the peace talks were starting to discuss real issues. He felt that the war would end in a stalemate of sorts within a year. It wouldn't drag on as Nick and the Russians had planned and hoped.

"We'll essentially call it a great victory and leave," Chet said. "The 38th parallel will survive another day."

He also told me that he thought the United Nations was a great idea as an organization, with some exceptions. For instance, it was great for the United Nations to focus on world hunger. It was not great, however, as a multinational consensus on how to fight a war. When the current crop of diplomats went home—the ones that Nick and the Ice Queen had controlled, and now controlled by the shadow CIA—who would pull the strings on the new crop?

"What our fear is," Chet said, "is future wars will be manufactured in some third-world nation. Us on one side providing military strength—mainly our soldiers and weapons—along with our U.N. countries who don't provide shit. The Russians would be on the other side providing military equipment. You might as well throw the Red Chinese alongside the Russians.

Through the United Nations we would, of course, fight the war *politically*. When it's political, we have to share information and strategies with our allies, but we're talking about *dozens* of countries we have to share this with. With a situation like that, we could fight a war in some god-forsaken land for *decades*. What will that type of war do to our country? It wouldn't be a Hitler we're fighting. It would be just some goddamned land that nobody had heard of before, and the only people that would really give a shit about that land would be the farmers that are living there, and they don't count."

The waitress had come over and refilled our coffee. We sat for a minute just relaxing.

"The Ice Queen, by the way, has turned out to be a jewel for us," Chet said.

I raised my eyebrows, "Really?"

"We needed her to help us in the transition between the Russians," Chet said. "We, of course, turned her upside down and inside out. We've got a really tight leash on her, really tight. If we had blown her out of the water, we wouldn't have been able to operate her network. After all, the two Russian KGB guys were dead—thanks to you. Nick was dead—again thanks to you. But, the Russians inserted two new guys into their lineup. The Ice Queen had to play the part that everything was okay. She shoulda won an Oscar. She continued to manipulate guys like Swensen like a puppeteer. To keep her happy, I've even got a young guy that goes over and services her—a big stud of a guy who would scare a mare. We've got all the bases covered. At least for a while. But, like I said, one day those diplomats—one by one—will go home. Then we've lost our network."

I walked back to the house. Hiromi would be in the attic-studio. She could have her studio anyplace she wanted, but the attic-studio was it. We had added a couple of dormer windows to provide better ventilation, but it was still an attic. It was her favorite studio this side of Lahaina, Maui. Back at the gallery next to Dominic's candy store there was a sign on the door that said, *Gone to the Dodger game, come back tomorrow.* I wasn't going to the Dodger game, I was just going home.

As I walked home, I thought of what Chet Morgan had told me, how he was operating the Ice Queen's network.

Once again—I'm sure that this time was the last time—the Red Chaser, me, had delivered a Commie network to Wild Bill Donovan.

Putting the story together

To provide credibility to the story, I needed a lot of details of people, places and the times.

Here's a list of the books that I read to give me some of those details. I didn't know which fact I would need, of course. You don't know what you need until you need it. So, I just read and read and then read some more. I just immersed myself with Joe McCarthy, Wild Bill Donovan, Brooklyn, New York, the 1950s, the Dodgers and the Korean War. Interestingly, the facts and anecdotes that I needed just popped up when I needed them.

There are some details that aren't in these books. For instance, I have not read of any plot where the United Nations leaked military secrets to North Korea, China or Russia. To me, it seemed plausible, but I can't defend it with known facts. There were reports, however, that the North Koreans knew of our surprise raids early in the war.

Odessa—the ratline—has, of course, been documented plenty of times. I first read about it in Frederick Forsythe's fine novel *The Odessa File*. But, the concept that the United States supported the ratline came from the series on The History Channel *Dead Men's Secrets, Hunting Nazi Fugitives*. It was from that series where I learned that Wild Bill Donovan did, indeed, have his men track down Waffen SS officers for their Eastern Europe spy networks. Not based on fact, I concocted how Jake made his illicit fortune.

The Internet, of course, was a terrific resource. It was particularly good where I could instantly call up the play-by-play sequence of the Dodgers during their historic pennant race in 1951.

The books below are my primary references in writing *Red Chaser*.

Joe McCarthy & Wild Bill Donovan

The Life and Times of Joe McCarthy by Thomas Reeves
Shooting Star by Tom Wicker (Joe McCarthy)
The Last Hero by Anthony Cave Brown (Wild Bill Donovan)

Brooklyn, New York City, the 1950s and the Dodgers

Old Brooklyn Heights by Clay Lancaster
Summer in the City by Vic Ziegel (NYC & Brooklyn 1947-57)
Brooklyn Then and Now by Marcia Reiss
A House on the Heights by Truman Capote
The Greatest Ballpark Ever by Bob McGee (Ebbets Field)
The Home Run Heard 'Round the World by Ray Robinson
Brooklyn's Dodgers by Carl E. Prince
The Era 1947-1956 by Roger Kahn
The American Dream, the 1950s by Richard Stolley
The Stork Club by Ralph Blumenthal
The Fifties by David Halberstam
The Power Broker by Robert Caro (Robert Moses)
Puppetmaster by Richard Hack (J. Edgar Hoover)

The Korean War

The Coldest Winter (about the Korean War) by David Halberstam
The Forgotten War by Clay Blair (Korean War)
As Seen on TV, The Visual Culture of Everyday Life in the 1950s by Karal Ann Marling

Japanese Internment Camps

And Justice For All by John Tateishi
Tule Lake by E.T. Miyakawa
Prisoners Without Trial by Roger Daniels

World War II

The History Channel video, *Dead Men's Secrets, Hunting Nazi Fugitives*

The History Channel video, *America's Secret War*

The History Channel video, *The Last Days of World War II*

The History Channel video, *The Odessa File*

     In 1955, The Brooklyn Dodgers did win the pennant and beat the New York Yankees in the World Series. However, in 1958, the Dodgers moved to Los Angeles. At the time, columnist Pete Hamill wrote that the three most evil men of the 20th century were "Hitler, Stalin, and Walter O'Malley," the Dodgers owner. Not a soul in Brooklyn would disagree.

     That move, however, allowed me the opportunity for Jake to follow the Dodgers to L.A. under a special assignment by Walter O'Malley and his controversial new ballpark in Chavez Ravine.

     Look for Jake McHenry's new adventure in 2011. If you want an email alert to know when it is coming out, send an email to findjon@msn.com. I'll let you know.

Dedication

There's one person, more than any other, whom I dedicate this book to. And, I think you know that person on a first name basis.

At first, I thought of my family, of course. My wife of over 40 years, Lisa, certainly deserves the dedication for all the cheering she has had to do. My daughter Monica is a terrific writer in her own right. Son Erik is the head coach of the Miami Heat, who is really outrageous in his dedication to winning. So, I dedicate this book to them, but they do take a secondary position. I think, however, they'll applaud the top person that this book is dedicated to.

Then there's Ed Stackler, who did some heavy duty editing. He put an axe in my hand and gave me some pretty strong directions as to where to whack. (Unfortunately, one of my favorite segments was when Jake and Hiromi went back to Tule Lake, California, to visit the remains of a Japanese Internment Camp. But, alas, it just didn't fit, and after a couple of chops it was gone.)

My first edition had a ton of typos. Yes, embarrassing to me and tiresome for readers. One of my early readers, Debbie Bigelow, is a proofreader. She attacked *Red Chaser* with a proofreader's zeal. I think she fixed every one of them. If you do find a typo, it's not Debbie's fault; I probably inadvertently changed her correction.

My mind runs to some of the first readers. Two of the readers, Steve Pettise and Darrell Rutter, were reading chapters before I finished the manuscript. Sorry, they had to wait on a couple of latter chapters as the action played out. Then there were some first readers from Goodreads.com. Jim MacLachlan was terrific with his thoughts and ideas. Additionally, there's Keith, Wendy Golenbock, Marvin, Marcia, Angela, Gary and Stormhawk who were nice enough to put up favorable reviews on Goodreads and Amazon.

When I run through these names, there's one other name that needs to be on the top. But, first let me ask you to do one writing assignment. This one is easy. Just print your name on the line below.

I dedicate this book to _____. After all, you've taken the time to read to this very last page. I thank you for picking up *Red Chaser*, getting caught up in the story and getting to this last page. So, including all those folks mentioned above, I dedicate this book to you. Thank you.

About the author

I spent most of my adult life running pro sports teams, first NBA teams and then a group of seven minor league baseball teams.

With each job, there was a tremendous amount of travel. With all those miles I read and I wrote, and when I got tired sitting of reading and writing I would read and write some more. My fifth book, *Marketing Outrageously*, became a Wall Street Journal best-seller.

And then, Amazon Kindle came out. I loved it. Someplace along the line, I vowed never to read a book that wasn't on Kindle. (That vow didn't last, but most of the books I read are on Kindle.) Kindle also got me thinking about my own writing.

I wrote *Red Chaser*, my first novel. I put it up on Kindle. It sold reasonably well, which inspired me to write a second novel, *Do-Overs, a* time travel romp that readers tell me is a fun read.

Happy reading!

Jon Spoelstra
Portland, OR
findjon@msn.com

P.S. Lastly, if you enjoyed *Red Chaser*, I sure would appreciate you if you could submit a review on Amazon.com.

Made in the USA
Middletown, DE
26 January 2021